PRAISE FOR DEADLY DECLARATIONS

Landis Wade has given us a page turner, a novel rooted in history and mystery and imagination. This is a crackling good book.

–**Frye Gaillard,** American historian, and author of *A Hard Rain: America in the 1960s*

~

Deadly Declarations is what you'd get if *National Treasure* and *The Firm* had a book baby. Part historical mystery, part courtroom drama, part Scooby gang romp, 100 percent whip-smart, engaging, and deliciously un-put-downable. Two thumbs up!

–**Tracy Clark,** multi-nominated Anthony, Shamus, and Lefty Award finalist and winner of the 2020 Sue Grafton Memorial Award for the *Cass Raines Chicago Mystery* Series

~

Landis Wade combines the precision of a lawyer with a natural storyteller in this historical thriller. A page turner brimming with North Carolina history – and fun!

–**Scott Syfert**, author of *Eminent Charlotteans* and *The First American Declaration of Independence?*

Landis Wade has taken the Meck Dec controversy and catapulted it into a sizzling combination of historical mystery, courtroom drama, and warm, burgeoning friendships in a retirement community built in the shadow of Hezekiah Alexander's old rock house.

I tried to stop reading *Deadly Declarations*. I simply couldn't put it down.

–**Dannye Romine Powell,** author of *In the Sunroom with Raymond Carver* and *Parting the Curtains: Interviews with Southern Writers*

Scholars and statesmen have argued for two centuries about the authenticity of the Mecklenburg Declaration of Independence. But it took a certain retired-trial-lawyer-turned-novelist to bring this controversy so fully and dangerously to life! Landis Wade is a master of the light-hearted legal thriller.

Deadly Declarations features plenty of drama to make the heart thump with suspense, balanced by loveable characters and outrageous humor. And, if you're not careful, you might just get a history lesson. There's so much life in these pages! You'll be turning them so fast, you might just break the sound barrier.

–**George Hovis**, author of *The Skin Artist*

Deadly Declarations is a little bit like putting Thomas Jefferson on Paul Revere's horse with North Carolina cornbread in the saddle bag. What a recipe: Mix a North Carolina, Mecklenburg County 1775 mystery with Thomas Jefferson and constitutional history; then throw in a present day retirement home and its quirky characters. You end up with a feast of good reading.

Landis Wade has mixed it all together with a writerly touch that will have you licking your chops. Delicious, funny, suspenseful.

–**Clyde Edgerton**, author of *Walking Across Egypt* and *Raney*

Tackling a 250-year-old mystery proves deadly, but the crew at the Independence Retirement Community are far from retired—or retiring. Humor, a good puzzle, a peek inside some artful legal maneuvering, engaging characters—all the absolutely perfect ingredients for a mystery.

If I knew Craig Travail, Yeager, and Harriet really lived at the Indie, I'd move there. Such good fun. More, please!

–**Cathy Pickens**, author of *Charlotte True Crime Stories* and the *Southern Fried Mystery* series

Deadly Declarations is a hugely entertaining cozy mystery featuring, at its heart, an intriguing historical conspiracy. From its charming southern setting to its memorable mystery-solving trio, this novel will have you staying up way past your bedtime. You'll find yourself chuckling at the characters' antics and clutching the pages tighter as they head into danger.

In Landis Wade's capable hands, what starts off as a challenge to a perplexing will becomes a heart-pounding race to discover the truth.

–**Heather Bell Adams**, author of *Maranatha Road* and *The Good Luck Stone*

Deadly Declarations is a work of fiction, but you'd never know it, so well does Landis Wade meld history with the present. He draws on decades of legal experience and natural story-telling ability to combine a significant piece of North Carolina history, insights into living in a unique retirement community, and government corruption at the highest level.

You'll fall in love with his quirky characters, southern folk who guard their secrets well. The plot bursts with danger, complications, and intrigue right until the last page. A terrific page turner—you won't be able to put it down. May this be the first of many.

–**Webb Hubbell**, former U. S. Associate Attorney General and author of the award-winning *When Men Betray* and *The Eighteenth Green*.

For Gus and Lori

COPYRIGHT

DEADLY DECLARATIONS

AN INDIE RETIREMENT MYSTERY

LANDIS WADE

Huzzah!

Landis Wade

"We must hang together, or most assuredly we shall all hang separately."

-Benjamin Franklin, at the signing of the Declaration of Independence in 1776

AUTHOR'S NOTE

The Mecklenburg Declaration of Independence has been an enigma for close to two hundred fifty years. According to oral history, the Meck Dec was signed in the turbulent wake of British hostilities at Lexington and Concord, when prominent Mecklenburg County citizens and militia leaders met in the North Carolina backwoods of Charlotte, the town George Washington called a "trifling place." There, at a log courthouse, they debated their future allegiance to King George, and with their passions high and their principles firm, they declared their independence on May 20, 1775, from the most powerful nation in the world, assuming all risks attendant to their lives and property earned by such a treasonable act.

Historians have treated the Meck Dec with disdain, running the gamut from contempt to indifference. Many called it fake. Others borrowed the words of Thomas Jefferson and called it "spurious." Unlike Jefferson's Declaration of Independence signed one year later, there is no surviving Meck Dec document. And yet, locals continue to celebrate the day and the date May 20, 1775, remains on the North Carolina state flag and on the Mecklenburg County seal. Were the North Carolinians first in freedom, as one North Carolina state license plate says? Or was the Meck Dec nothing more than a fabrication to gain favor in the nation's revolutionary history?

There is no dispute that a meeting was held at the log courthouse in Charlotte on May 20, 1775, and that a tavern owner named Captain Jack rode his horse five hundred miles to deliver documents from that meeting to the Continental Congress in Philadelphia. And there is no doubt that controversies followed. Burned documents. Missing documents. Stolen documents. Falsified documents. And, yet, curiously, virtually identical phrases appeared in the Meck Dec and the Declaration of Independence, raising the question: If the Meck Dec did exist, who copied from whom?

PART I

AT DEATH'S DOORSTEP

CHAPTER 1

CONCEALMENT

June 22, 1819,
John Adams's Letter to Thomas Jefferson

Dear Sir:

May I enclose to you one of the greatest curiosities and one of the deepest mysteries that ever occurred to me? It is in the Essex Register of June 5, 1819. It is entitled the Mecklenburg Declaration of Independence.

How is it possible that this paper should have been concealed from me to this day?

Had it been communicated to me in the time of it, I know, if you do not know, that it would have been printed in every Whig newspaper upon the continent. You know, that if I had possessed it, I would have made the hall of Congress echo and reecho with it fifteen months before your Declaration of Independence. What a poor, malicious, short-sighted, crapulous mass is Tom Paine's Common Sense, in comparison with this paper.

I am and always shall be affectionately and respectfully yours,
J. Adams

CHAPTER 2

WAKING UP DEAD

Yeager Alexander's motto for retirement living was, "Ain't dead, yet," but when he heard a siren and saw an ambulance, lights flashing, heading for one of the residential buildings at the Independence Retirement Community, he said aloud, "Waking up dead is rarely a good thing." The red and white swirling lights came into view as he finished his pre-dawn walk. This was not the first time he'd seen this vehicle at the Indie. He was sure it wouldn't be the last.

Yeager stood on the crushed gravel path that fronted his cottage and bordered Lost Cove Lake, the smaller of the two Indie lakes. He liked to get up early and walk the land. Around the community center. Past the five-story residence buildings. Between the cottages that fronted Freedom Lake. And across the property line to admire the Hezekiah Alexander Rock House, the jewel of the Queen City History Museum. The house was built in 1774 and had stone siding with strange carvings (if you knew where to look, and Yeager did). It had been home to one of the signers of Mecklenburg County's controversial and long-vanished declaration of independence from Britain, signed on May 20, 1775.

Yeager's best friend, Matthew Collins, was taking him on a road trip in a few hours that had something to do with the Mecklenburg

Declaration of Independence. The ninety-six-year-old Collins was known to everyone as the professor because of his love of history. The professor did not believe the Meck Dec had ever existed, but he'd promised Yeager a surprise on their outing, one he said Yeager would like.

What Yeager didn't like was the ambulance being parked in front of the professor's building. He walked the fifty yards up the hill and stopped in the shadows, not twenty feet away from a woman dressed in a medic uniform who was talking on a radio. The early morning air was cool and smelled of pine and rain. Clouds gathered. The quiet before the coming storm allowed the seriousness in her voice to carry on the freshening breeze.

"He's dead. Collecting the body now."

Yeager followed the paramedic into the building and onto the elevator for a ride to the third floor. He let her step out first, held the door until she was out of sight, and slid into the elevator lobby. He peeked around the corner of the narrow hallway and saw her enter room 312, the residence of his best friend. Yeager felt unsteady, like the floor had pitched. He squeezed his eyes shut and reached out to the wall for balance. He bit his lip to suppress the tears he felt coming, but it didn't do much good. He thought of Lori, the professor's granddaughter. She would be heartbroken too.

Minutes later, the paramedic and her partner came out the door of 312, rolling a stretcher that held a covered body.

A woman in a pink silk nightgown and robe walked beside the stretcher. She had her right hand resting on the body's chest. Yeager knew who the woman was, and it was a shock to see her there. He leaned back against the faded green wall. He had nowhere to hide.

The woman's eyes widened when she saw him. "What are you doing here?"

"I saw the ambulance."

Sue Ellen Parker turned away and watched the paramedics load the professor on the elevator.

"Anything I can do?" Yeager said.

She stepped past Yeager onto the elevator and turned around.

"People will talk. You should keep your mouth shut." And then for emphasis, as the doors closed, she said, "For once."

Yeager was alone in the quiet of the dim hallway. He wiped his eyes and ran the fingers on his right hand through his thick, tangled beard like a comb. What would people talk about, and what did she want him to keep quiet about?

The professor hadn't mentioned any spend-the-night parties with Sue Ellen, and Yeager hadn't heard any rumors about them. But rumors grew faster than weeds at the Indie and were harder to kill. Still, Yeager didn't believe cohabitation was the issue. He owed it to the professor to find out what secret Sue Ellen really wanted to keep. Yeager took out his key, the one the professor had given him, and let himself in the professor's place.

Yeager wasn't sure what he was looking for, but since the motivation for his unauthorized inspection was the sight of Sue Ellen Parker coming from the professor's unit in the early morning and in her night clothes at that, he started in the master bedroom. The double bed was not the answer. Covers and sheets were pulled back on one side only. The bedside table held a clock, a lamp, and a pill bottle turned on its side, with the cap on the floor and pills spilled on the table and the floor. Yeager inspected the bottle. It was the professor's prescription medication for insomnia.

Yeager opened the closet and found it full of men's slacks, shirts, and sport coats. No woman's clothes in sight. The bathroom was next. Just one toothbrush and cup next to the sink. No blow dryer. Nothing under the sink but a man's Dopp kit and extra shaving lotion.

After his brief search, Yeager surmised the professor bedded down without Sue Ellen Parker at his side. It didn't mean she'd never slept with him. Anything was possible when it came to old-people sex at the Indie, but other than a few pillows and a blanket strewn on the sofa in the great room—the only clue she or somebody else might have spent the night there—Yeager found no other evidence to explain her presence.

Raindrops streaked the large window in the great room. Normally, Yeager liked early morning rain, but this was no mist. Droplets pelted against the pane as limbs on trees swayed. He saw lightning streak and heard thunder boom. It sounded like God was angry. As she should be.

Yeager reached over to the side table and picked up *Trout* magazine. The professor had dog-eared the page with the latest in rod and reel technology. The pictures reminded Yeager of the conversation he'd had with the professor by Freedom Lake three weeks ago, the last time they fished together.

"My fly rod," the professor said, "may not be as efficient as your .22, but it gives the fish a fighting chance." Yeager smiled at the memory.

The professor was a man who never threw away books, even when they were torn and worn. Where there wasn't enough space on the professor's shelves, books spilled onto the floor or were stacked in corners. The one concession he'd made to what seemed at first glance like disorder was how he grouped his books by topic.

The section Yeager liked the best held the Revolutionary War books. Out of habit, he glanced toward his favorite section and was surprised to see empty shelves. Those books were missing, even the books about the Mecklenburg Declaration of Independence.

Yeager was one of the few people who could ask the professor questions about the Meck Dec without the professor getting riled up. Yeager's mother told him there were no stupid questions, so he kept asking them, stupid question after stupid question after stupid question. It made the professor laugh. "Chuck Yeager Alexander, you think you're related to Hezekiah," the professor would say. "You want the story to be true."

The professor was right. Yeager did want to believe that local patriots had declared independence from Britain over one year before they got around to it in Philadelphia. He loved the idea, thanks to his mother who had been a high school social studies teacher. Yeager was an only child, because, she'd said, "After you, I didn't have the energy to raise another devil." She was the reason he fell in love with history and the reason he came to the Indie when he was fifty-five years old, to look after her. When she died of cancer, he stayed on and became the youngest resident, despite the hiccup with the business office when they checked his credit. Once they confirmed his mother left him the cottage, the rest of her teacher's pension, and a nice life insurance payout, they reluctantly accepted the likes of a man who never would have lived at the Indie were it not for his mother. That was twenty years ago, the same time he struck up his friendship with the professor and the same time he learned about the Meck Dec.

The professor had been adamant the Meck Dec never existed. "It's a fairy tale, nothing more."

But a week ago, in a strange twist, things changed. "Yeager, you can't tell anyone what I am about to tell you. I'm working on a sequel to *An American Hoax*."

An American Hoax was the professor's bestselling book that debunked the Meck Dec story once and for all. Why did the professor need to write a sequel? What more could he say? It seemed like overkill to say it twice. But Yeager had kept his thoughts to himself when the professor told him about the sequel. Something was different and serious about the professor's behavior that day.

Over the next five days, the professor ordered his meals sent to his room. Every time Yeager checked on him, he was hard at work on his laptop. He said he needed to finish the book before it was too late. He didn't explain the urgency.

Yesterday, Yeager stopped by at lunchtime and the professor was wearing the same clothes from the day before. He hadn't slept, and he'd acted nervous, like he'd had too much coffee. Yeager encouraged him to take a break.

"I can't."

"Why not?"

The professor's nervous energy must have provided a spark. His face lit up. "I found something. Something that changes everything."

Yeager wondered what that meant. Would the professor's sequel reveal the Meck Dec was not a hoax after all? And if so, what had the professor found?

He asked the professor to explain, but the only answer he got was, "Wait until tomorrow. Meet me at eight in the morning. Pack an overnight bag."

Now the professor was dead.

Yeager swept the great room, looking for the professor's laptop. Like the Revolutionary War books, it was nowhere to be found. He approached the open rolltop desk, touched the papers on the desk, and pushed them around. The pile was mostly bills, medical records, and letters from insurance companies. The laptop was not under them.

As he nosed in the pile, he accidentally knocked a piece of paper to the floor. When he picked it up, he saw four words at the top: "Last Will and Testament." It was dated the previous day, within twenty-four hours of the professor's death.

Why did the professor have a will that fit on one sheet of paper? He could afford the most expensive law firm in the city to give away his assets.

Curiosity trumped respect for his friend's privacy as Yeager examined the document under the small lamp on the professor's desk. All the words appeared to be written in the professor's hand. They said:

"I, Matthew Collins, being of sound mind and body, do hereby revoke all prior wills, disinherit my only heir, my grandchild Lori Collins, and bequeath my entire estate to Sue Ellen Parker."

Yeager would have laughed aloud if someone had told him this story in a bar. But here he was, staring nonsense in the face.

The professor said nothing to Yeager about making a new will or anything that would cause him to change the old one. Yeager knew how much the professor loved Lori, and as best Yeager could tell, the professor never loved Sue Ellen Parker. Why would he cut Lori from his will and give his fifty-million-dollar fortune to Sue Ellen? The missing books and laptop bothered Yeager too. They were important to the professor.

Yeager found it hard to accept the professor had fallen in with the likes of Sue Ellen Parker. He was a courageous man who made a pile of money in the magazine business and—a veteran himself—used it to start a foundation for veterans. That was long before finding his passion—or his obsession—as the amateur historian turned famous author who liked to keep to himself.

Sue Ellen Parker was the opposite of reclusive. She was the self-appointed captain of the Indie ship and queen of the biting quip, a snob without an empathetic bone in her body. And while the professor was opinionated about things that truly mattered—like getting history right—she was opinionated about things that didn't matter—like the flower arrangements in the lobby, the color for the carpet renovation, and the uniform style worn by the staff. She gave no quarter to residents who dared disagree with her decorating, renovation, and style judgments and was not a pleasant person to be around, period.

Yeager faced too many questions to tackle them alone. There Sue Ellen was in her pink silk robe, warning him to stay out of—what? The reason she was with the professor when he died? The reason the professor gave her his entire fortune? The reason the professor's history books, laptop, and manuscript on the Meck Deck sequel were missing?

Yeager needed to speak with Harriet Keaton, the smartest and most practical woman he knew. Next to the professor, she was the only resident who treated Yeager like he mattered. She was also the only resident who could take on Sue Ellen Parker.

But Harriet Keaton wasn't a lawyer. They would need a lawyer to know if the will was valid. That gave him an idea.

Yeager's sources among the Indie staff told him the vacant cottage next to him was about to be occupied by a lawyer named Craig Travail. Yeager decided he'd make a good first impression on the man and then secure his help.

CHAPTER 3

TAKE THIS JOB

Craig Travail ripped the envelope open, then gripped the court's ruling in one hand while he used the other to flick a soiled tobacco leaf from the page. It was from the superior court judge's office, and it smelled like chewing tobacco. Chief Judge Roscoe "Chaw" Brady must have sealed it himself. The county had a no smoking policy in public buildings, but Judge Brady found a loophole that led to his nickname and the installation of the gold-plated spittoon under his courtroom bench. Lawyers could measure their impact based on the spittoon's use. The judge spit when he didn't care for your argument, and Judge Chaw Brady spit often during Travail's argument in this case, the biggest case Travail had argued in ten years.

Travail scanned the document, dropped it on his desk, and took a deep breath. He'd lost again. And this time, the dollar amount the firm's client had to pay was staggering.

Rain beat against the ceiling-high window of Travail's skyscraper office like someone tap dancing on his head, and the fog blocked his city view and his next step. It was as if he was short on fuel and flying on instruments when his office phone rang. The extension number on the phone's digital screen belonged to an unfriendly navigator.

"We need to talk." The phone slammed on the other end. The law firm's principal had called Travail to his office.

Travail had an acute feeling his career waging conflict was about to find a resolution at age sixty-five. The management committee of the Am Law 100 law firm, where he'd worked for forty years and been a partner for thirty-three, demanded victories and profits and saw nothing of value in a well-fought contest that came up short, not even when the lawyer did it while dealing with the emotional burden of a family tragedy.

It wasn't so much the law's demands that brought him to this point; it was the natural order of things, where priorities, desires, and competence got sorted out with age.

Why did he continue to practice law? And what was the purpose? These were questions he'd asked himself often during the last two years. And yet he'd kept at it, every day, like a dutiful paper boy, up and at it every morning and never missing his route. He just kept showing up, tackling old and new cases, and filling out his time sheets, because he didn't know what else to do with his life.

It was a problem for trial lawyers his age, and he knew it. They didn't know when to let go, when to let something other than the legal profession define them. They achieved Super Lawyer and Best Lawyer status and thought it gave them special powers. It didn't. It only blinded them to the reality they should do something else with their lives. A lawyer-turned-artist friend explained it best over a pitcher of beer. "Lawyers need to transition to their Act 3 before they turn sixty-five. After that, it's like practicing law at the Hotel California. They can check out, but they can never leave."

No matter how well Travail tried to compartmentalize his personal loss from his work life and how effectively he'd used his courtroom skills, he'd come up short in his last three cases, come in second to be exact, and second was no good for a trial lawyer where first and second places are the only two options. Travail's brain told him he was not a bad trial lawyer, that facts were facts and even the best lawyers lose cases. Yet he knew a losing streak was like a trial lawyer's poison.

Clients didn't want to bet on you. And in his case, the firm's managing partner would not allow one more loss.

Did Travail care? Yes, and no. He cared about doing a good job for his clients. He didn't care one lick about pleasing Robert Elkin, the firm's managing partner, who was known by all who worked for him as the biggest jerk of all the jerks who'd held the position.

Travail measured his breath, something he'd learned to do to manage his stress and anxiety. Sometimes the tactic worked, but today, the in-and-out breathing exercise was an irritant, a reminder he was still alive and someone he loved wasn't. He stepped from his office and walked with a regular stride down the east corridor, where the law firm's commercial litigators breathed but barely lived. No one appeared in the hallway to give him encouragement. Solid wood doors with brass handles were shut, with lawyers huddled behind them, typing, dictating, or talking on their phones. Unsociable is what the billable hour had made the uptown lawyer. Not like the old days.

Travail walked past the elevator and into the stairwell, where he climbed four flights to the forty-fifth floor of the America Bank office tower. When he emerged, he was within view of Elkin's corner office, the one the firm leader used when he worked in Charlotte. He could hear the man yelling through the door. He counted to ten before he knocked and entered.

Charlotte was a New South city where staid law firm traditions had given way to more casual operations. It was why the Charlotte lawyers in the firm called Elkin—behind his back, that is—by a nickname that drew inspiration from Walt Disney's Cruella de Vil. Three clever associates who preferred to remain anonymous coined the nickname based on Elkin's attitude that tradition was important, and Virginia had more of it than North Carolina. He issued most law firm edicts from the Charlottesville office, the city of his birth and education. When he tried to turn the more casual Charlotte into Charlottesville, coat and tie only, solemnly Southern, and everything else old Virginy, he became Robert de Vil.

Elkin and the other two management committee members were waiting for Travail. One, a thin rail of a man named Birdsong who rarely spoke to Travail, reached behind him and closed the door. The other man was Dunkler. He was a bit on the heavy side and always had a dour look on his face.

"Have a seat." Elkin's words came out as a demand.

"I'll stand, thanks."

Elkin came around from behind his expansive mahogany desk with the inlaid gold border and walked to within a Dictaphone's length of Travail's nose, close enough for Travail to smell his breath. He expelled breath that had a caramel flavor with a briny, salt-water touch, the aroma of a pungent cigar with a liquid chaser, most likely, whiskey with an *e*, as Elkin liked to remind the less informed. Elkin's choice of Jefferson's Ocean Aged at Sea Straight Bourbon Whiskey was more about the name on the side of the bottle than it was about drinking whiskey aged in a ship's bow after it traveled the seven seas.

It was ironic, Travail thought, that Thomas Jefferson—who Elkin idolized—didn't like distilled spirits and Elkin lapped them up. Elkin breathed his next question on Travail's face.

"What the hell is this?" Elkin tapped him twice on the shoulder with the rolled paper.

"You know what it is."

"Damn it, Craig, what the hell is wrong with you? Another loss, and for our firm's biggest client."

Travail knew how he wanted to respond. He wanted to say this was no surprise, that "I warned you and I advised the client to settle, but you stepped in and convinced the client it could win." He also wanted to say Elkin's approach was typical of corporate lawyers who knew nothing about litigation, making unrealistic promises and leaving the heavy lifting to the trial lawyers. But Travail kept quiet and let Elkin vent. The man had built up a lot of steam.

While Elkin babbled, Travail glanced at Thomas Jefferson's bust on the pedestal in Elkin's shadow and thought of the speeches Elkin made to the law firm every quarter when he invoked the words and deeds of the former president. He did it to inspire the partners to generate more bucks for the bang. Thomas Jefferson doubled the country's size with a pen's stroke, Elkin would say time and again, "and we can double the firm's size too, if only you think strategically and work hard, as did Jefferson."

Amidst Elkin's droning voice, Travail wondered if Elkin really was related to the former president, as he liked to claim. Travail doubted it, but he never figured it was worth the trouble to call him on it, nor was it time to pick that fight now.

Birdsong and Dunkler stood still like well-behaved mannequins in a department store window. They added nothing of value to the conversation. Elkin fired at Travail again. "What? No excuses?"

Travail remained silent, which triggered another outburst from Elkin. "You should have retired after the accident."

When Elkin spoke, there was no appendage of "God rest her soul" nor any sympathetic words for Rachael, the wife Travail had grieved for the past two years. They'd married the month before he took the job, and he never thought her life would end before he stopped practicing law. Law was a career, one Travail thought he loved, but that turned out not to be true. Rachael had been his true love and law his true regret. Regret for spending too much time at the office and not enough time with her.

Elkin's insensitivity shook Travail. He'd prepared himself to stand silently while the man blew through his anger. But because of his caustic and uncaring mention of Rachael, as if she were to blame for the case Elkin torpedoed, he felt anger boil deep inside his gut. Until now, it was an emotion he had controlled in Robert Elkin's presence.

Elkin scowled at Travail. "Do you know what kind of hit it will be to our bottom line if we lose this client?"

The bottom line was Robert Elkin's clarion call of progress. To Elkin, law practice was more about collections and billings and prospecting and sales than it was about the flare and excitement of pretending to be the fictional English barrister, Rumpole of the Bailey. That symbol of change—from noble profession to stark business enterprise—now stood less than one foot away making noise with his mouth and disrespecting Travail's loss of Rachael.

Elkin was four inches taller and bellowed from a frame that had Travail by a good thirty pounds, but Travail was not intimidated. In his younger days, he'd been an undersized but scrappy outside linebacker on his high school football team. That fifty-year-old memory about how to make a solid tackle came into focus as Travail eyed Elkin's silk tie, his frame's center.

The slow building heat in his stomach reached the boiling point. He was not a violent man, but he was human. He needed to stand up for his wife, if he did nothing else right today.

Travail bent his knees, dropped his arms to his sides, and sprang forward like he'd done under the Friday night lights on the gridiron.

"What the—?" Elkin couldn't finish before Travail planted his head in Elkin's chest, wrapped his arms around the managing partner's buttocks, lifted him two feet off the ground, and drove him over the most expensive desk in the law firm. Papers and pens flew in all directions. They toppled the pedestal that held the former commander-in-chief's bust. Thomas Jefferson fell headfirst, glancing off Travail's shoulder and headbutting Elkin. They landed in a stack of Bar Quarterlies.

Birdsong and Dunkler shrieked and dove onto the pile to rescue Elkin. They grabbed Travail by the collar and pulled at him while Elkin, eyes wild with fury, pounced on the former president's head like it was a fumbled pigskin in a Virginia football game. Elkin shouted curses, grabbed at the desk, and pulled himself up with Jefferson's bust cradled in his left arm.

Travail was stunned by the aftermath of his adrenaline surge, but he had perfect vision. De Vil's designer shirt was torn, his hair disheveled, and blood trickled down his brow to the top of his nose.

"You're fired."

"No need. I quit." Travail spoke in a calm voice as he dusted himself off.

"Even better. When you quit, you forfeit your year-end profit share. Your pay ends today."

That was fine. It was a small price to pay to be away from Elkin and those like him. Travail turned his back on the threesome and walked out the door. Elkin yelled at him.

"Insurance ends today too. From now on, you pay for your own therapy. Lot of good it did you."

Travail returned to his office, where he wasted no time packing a few personal files and family pictures in a paperboard box. He slipped his personal laptop in the leather satchel Rachael gave him for his sixtieth birthday. That was the night she pitched the idea of the trip she wanted them to take to visit national parks in an RV. She wanted to go that summer, but he negotiated to wait until he was sixty-three, figuring he'd be closer to retirement and better able to take two months off. Her accident happened two days before they were scheduled to leave. He cancelled the trip, buried Rachael, and went back to work, because he didn't know what else to do.

Travail shook his head as he looked around the work prison he'd built for himself the last two years. He picked up his stuff and walked to the cubicle closest to his office, where he found Angela, his long-time assistant, sadness etched on her face. News traveled fast through the firm's grapevine.

Travail stumbled through an apology, which she said wasn't necessary. He apologized anyway for leaving her at a job with Elkin in charge. With misty eyes, she smiled a dutiful smile as she dusted some of the grime from Elkin's floor off his shoulders.

"What can I do to help?"

"Please send everything else that belongs to me to the house."

"The new address?"

The reminder made him stop and consider how he had compounded one transition—the end of his law career—with another, his move from the place he and Rachael had called home. Only Angela, his two grown children, and his therapist knew he'd bought a small cottage at the Independence Retirement Community.

"I'm not retiring," he'd told Angela. "I just need less space." The statement was half true. He needed less space, but his therapist and adult children had urged him to move out of the shadow of loss and into the light.

"Yes." He shrugged. "Send everything to the new address."

"Did you hear Professor Collins died this morning? It was on the radio."

He hadn't heard. It was not a shock though. Professor Collins had to be in his mid-nineties. But the news made him think about his prior representation of the professor, and he could hear the professor's voice in his head like it was yesterday. "Of course I did my own work."

Fifteen years earlier, he'd handled a defamation case for the professor. A newspaper ran a story saying the professor committed plagiarism in *An American Hoax*. Travail had taken the case at the urging of Elkin, who for some reason, loved the professor's book. The jury came back with a ten-million-dollar verdict for the professor.

"Strange coincidence, the professor died the same day you move to the Indie," Angela said.

Not so strange. One dies. Another takes his place. Circle of life. But it caused Travail to reflect. The professor had been indignant when he'd shown Travail around his Indie condo. "Do you think this is the library of a man lazy enough to copy work from other people?"

The shelves in the professor's great room were more cluttered than Travail's garage, but with papers and books, not lawn and sports equipment. The mess helped Travail prove to the jury the professor had done the hard work of researching and writing the book himself, a man obsessed with his topic.

"You don't think his death had anything to do with the Meck Dec, do you?" Angela had always enjoyed a good mystery. It was why she was such an excellent assistant, always asking "what if" when Travail was stumped on a case. Her eyes sparkled when she asked the question and her grin was wide, as if she were trying to create a distraction to take his mind off his last day at the law firm.

Professor Collins had made enemies at the chamber of commerce and the May 20th Society by denying the Meck Dec was real, but the friction's source was couched in local tourism and historical debate, hardly enough to warrant foul play. His detractors didn't like the fervor of his ultimate conclusion in *An American Hoax*, which the professor insisted was fact, not opinion. He also became the go-to guy every May 20 for a soundbite for media outlets in any cities jealous of Charlotte's growth and economic success. "Is there any truth to the story," they would ask, "that the first declaration of independence from Great Britain was signed in Charlotte on May 20, 1775?" The professor, clutching his *New York Times* bestselling book, would put on a show, saying "absolutely not" every time, with a great deal of passion and enthusiasm.

"I'm sure it was old age," Travail said. "He was ninety-something. As for the Meck Dec, it is just an interesting bit of disputed local history, and as far as I'm concerned, rather insignificant history in the twenty-first century."

"Still, I have to wonder." Angela opened the satchel on his shoulder and stuffed "something you might need" inside.

Travail hugged her tight. "Thanks for everything you've done for me."

Five minutes later, he departed the elevator into the parking deck and walked away from the law firm where he'd devoted his entire legal career. He was now convinced there was no higher purpose to helping big companies win legal battles. And yet, he felt a touch of sadness. Law practice was all he knew how to do to make a living. It was all he knew how to do, period. It was his identity. Who was he now?

The motor in his aging sedan came to life as he had a feeling he was about to be buried alive among people with nothing to do. He was convinced they would turn him into a do-nothing clone. And it was only 11:00 am.

When he left the parking lot, the storm had passed, but the pavement was wet. He glanced at the sunlit Carolina blue sky, but it didn't feel sunny or bright. He lowered both front windows and touched the radio to try to turn off the noise. Instead, he accidentally changed the channel. A disc jockey on a country music station thanked God it was Friday and introduced an old favorite by Johnny Paycheck, "Take This Job and Shove It." As the song's refrain filled the air, he couldn't help himself. He let slip a half-hearted smile and hummed along. The country music gods had a sense of humor.

A fresh breeze blew through the front windows as Travail turned left onto Third Street, crossed Tryon, and sped through one green city

19

stoplight after another. He nodded at the courthouse, passed under the I-277 loop, and cut over to Independence Boulevard, his pathway to the Indie. On the way, he would pick up his four-legged best friend from the old house and let Blue ride shotgun to the new one.

At the song's finale, Travail spoke a question to the radio. "Was it worth it, Johnny?"

The musician didn't answer. It was no matter. Travail figured it wouldn't be long before the Indie answered the question for him.

CHAPTER 4

SPURIOUS

Monticello, July 9, 1819
Thomas Jefferson's Letter to John Adams

Dear Sir,

I am in debt to you for your letters.

*What has attracted my peculiar notice, is the paper from Mecklen-
burg County, of North Carolina, published in the Essex Register, which
you were so kind to enclose in your last letter of June the 22nd. And you
seem to think it genuine. I believe it spurious.*

*I must not be understood as suggesting any doubtfulness in the
State of North Carolina. No state was more fixed or forward. Nor do I
affirm, positively, that this paper is a fabrication: because the proof of
a negative can only be presumptive. But I shall believe it such until
positive and solemn proof of its authenticity shall be produced. And if
the name of McKnitt be real, and not a part of the fabrication, it needs
a vindication by the production of such proof. For the present, I must
remain an unbeliever in the apocryphal gospel.*

I am and always shall be affectionately and respectfully yours,
TH. Jefferson

CHAPTER 5

SHOOTING FISH

Craig Travail felt no connection to the Indie. He knew he should give it more than five hours, but the move unplugged him. From the city. From his friends. From life as he knew it. He and Blue took a walk that ended with some sit-and-think time on a stone bench by the far end of Freedom Lake, at least five hundred yards through the woods from his new home. The bench was a suitable spot to feel sorry for himself before God and her many creations.

Travail was at the Indie because his two children encouraged him to give up the Carmel Road house. They pitched the values of a retirement community. Less house to maintain. Prepared meals. Laundry service. Things to do. He might even meet some new friends. And wonderful health care, if something unexpected happened. "Do it, Dad. It will be your gift to us." He knew he was too young for a retirement community, but he conceded the house was too big for him.

At the same time, he jockeyed good-naturedly with his children. "I don't want my life to become one game of checkers after another."

They laughed but were not dissuaded. "You need a fresh start. One move. Not two."

When Travail gave his children the green light to look for his new home, he imposed three requirements. "It can't smell like rubbing alcohol, number one, and number two, they have to let me bring Blue. And three, I'd like a small place of my own where I can breathe fresh air, not some condo on a hall with the old people."

His children went to work and came up with the perfect spot, or so they said. "Dad, it's called the Indie. You can live in a cottage beside a lake. You'll love it."

When signing the papers, Travail learned that the residents—he imagined them as the Walking Dead—called the community the Indie because they were an independent bunch who enjoyed living next to the home of one of the alleged signers of the Mecklenburg Declaration of Independence. As he sat and gazed across the lake at the oak, pine, and poplar trees the developers hadn't found time to destroy, he felt about as independent as a man in solitary confinement and decided to keep it that way. Why bother to make friends? The residents in a retirement community were there to die, not live, with one-third up to their shinbones in their graves and the other two-thirds too preoccupied with their next meal to see the reaper creeping up. Exhibit A for his argument was the "Welcome Home" sign at the community's entrance. He'd heard that message preached one too many times on a Baptist Sunday growing up.

His children had been right about the cottage though. The craftsman style suited him. He liked the brown wood siding with almond-colored posts and trim. Two bedrooms. Two baths. A den with a stone fireplace. And a kitchen. Everything he needed, along with his choice of two resting places outside. The front porch swing offered a view of the community's tree-lined gravel road and the forest beyond, a mix of pines, hardwoods, and bike trails. Easy for exploring. At least the deer and raccoons thought so. But because they were drawn to water, he and Blue liked the view from the back more, where they could rock on the deck or screened-in porch and peer across the shaded backyard, down the slope to the small lake with its resident waterfowl and walking trail.

Travail reached down and patted Blue's head. The twelve-year-old black and tan coonhound was happy to be with him no matter where they lived.

"You'll like retirement, Blue. All you ever do is eat and sleep." Blue stood up and wagged his tail.

Seconds later, Blue growled. Travail heard movement before he heard the voice.

"Did you see that fish rise?"

Travail looked up to see a .22 rifle pointed over his shoulder toward the lake's center. He peered from the nose of the rifle to the center of the lake and saw the ripple. Before he could turn back and answer the voice, the gun went off.

"What the—" Travail flinched.

A fish floated to the surface.

Bang. Another shot. Another fish floated.

"Here, hold this rifle," a man said.

Somewhat confused, Travail held the .22 while the man dropped on his rump and began to undress. He pulled off his leather cowboy boots, unbuckled his Levi's, and slid them and his boxers off. When he stood up, he was wearing nothing but his red-checked flannel shirt, which he quickly unbuttoned and cast aside.

"Don't you think the water will be cold?"

"It'll feel good." The naked man dove off the bank and splatted hard on his belly. Waves welled up in all directions.

A few minutes later, the naked man climbed from the lake with a trout in each hand. On the bank, Blue barked as a welcoming party of one, tail wagging. The shinier fish still had some life in it.

"Other one's dead." The naked man dropped his catch on the bank. Blue poked his nose at the fish.

Water dripped from the man's body and beard. He shook himself, grabbed his tangle of hair with both hands, and wrung the water out. He pulled on his boxers and jeans and slid into his boots. His shirt was the last thing he put on, but he didn't button it. By this time, Blue had nudged one fish a good five feet from the other. The man grinned at Travail.

"Thanks for the assist." He reached for his rifle. "Name's Yeager Alexander. I go by Yeager."

Travail handed the rifle back to Yeager and introduced himself. "Craig Travail. And my dog, who is about to eat your fish, is Blue."

"I'm happy to share. You're the lawyer, right?"

Travail drew back.

"Peaches told me."

Peaches was the activities director who'd bombarded Travail with invitations when he arrived at noon. Stretching class on Monday. Line dancing Tuesday. Bus ride to the Uptown Museum on Wednesday, lunch provided. Book club on Thursday in the library. "It doesn't matter if you haven't read the book," she'd said. "Nobody ever reads them all the way through." Saturday is the best, she'd said. "Croquet in the morning, and The Yacht Club meets at the lake for the regatta in the afternoon. Miniature remote-control boats, but you'll get the hang of it."

Travail had politely declined every invitation. "Did Peaches give out my address too?"

Yeager laughed. "Unnecessary. The women knew it was cottage 24 before your movers unloaded your first box. Did you know women in retirement communities outnumber men five to one? You better check your Viagra supply."

Travail didn't laugh at the joke. He wasn't here looking for sex, and he didn't need a Viagra supply.

"Here comes one of our women now. Be on your toes, Craig Travail."

Yeager moved fast to button his shirt, but only made it halfway up before the woman's voice carried through the late afternoon air. He pushed Blue away, grabbed the two fish, and stuffed them halfway down the front of his pants, hidden by his untucked shirttail. Blue stood next to him, nudging Yeager's belt line with his nose.

"Chuck Yeager Alexander." The woman yelled the name from the lake's edge. "Are you shooting fish again?" She moved at a brisk pace from fifty yards off.

Yeager slid the rifle behind his back. "Brace yourself, Craig Travail. You're about to meet Harriet Josephine Keaton."

Travail stood and looked around for a place to hide. No luck. He had done nothing wrong, but with Yeager at his side, he felt guilty of something. Yeager looked like he was enjoying himself.

Travail could tell by the way she walked, she was a confident woman. She had a purposeful stride. Travail guessed she was about four or five years older than his sixty-five years. The energy in her voice extended to her thick, red, curly locks, which fell from her head in waves and landed somewhere near her shoulders.

Travail whispered to Yeager as they waited. "Your parents named you Chuck Yeager?"

"Man broke the sound barrier in 1947, the day I was born. Mom said I was louder than he was."

Travail looked up to see Harriet Keaton standing three paces away with her arms crossed. "Are you two getting your stories straight?"

"Good afternoon, Harriet." Yeager didn't seem fazed by his accuser's brusque tone.

Harriet wore a blue V-neck sweater over a white blouse tucked into brown denim jeans. She looked at Travail in a way that invited him to introduce himself.

"I'm Craig Travail."

Yeager put his wet hand on Travail's shoulder. "My new neighbor." This was more intimacy than Travail wanted from a man who swims with the fishes.

"My condolences for having to live next door to our version of Little Big Man."

Travail racked his brain for where he'd heard the name, Little Big Man.

"She's just joshing you, Craig Travail."

Now he remembered. *Little Big Man* was a movie in which Dustin Hoffman played 121-year-old Jack Crabb, a man with a remarkable but hard-to-believe life story set in the Great American West. Crabb comically stumbled from one occupation to the next.

"Do you see the resemblance?" Harriet extended her right arm and turned her forefinger in a motion as if circling Yeager's body.

"What am I looking for?"

"A man with crazy ideas who can't stay focused on one long enough to finish a job."

Harriet Keaton didn't wait on Travail to solve her riddle but turned back to Yeager and the matter at hand.

"Unlike some timid souls who live here, I don't care if you play with your guns, even if it is against the law." Harriet looked down at the bulge around Yeager's waist and at Blue pawing at his shirt. "I do care about the wildlife."

Yeager deflected. "We need to talk about the professor. Did you get my text about Sue Ellen?"

"I did, but don't change the subject."

Yeager stayed off topic. "There's something strange about the professor's death."

"What's strange is you hunting without a fishing license."

Yeager grabbed at his waist as his shirt flapped and a trout slid below his belt. He took to dancing like a man hopping on hot coals. He kept it up until his gyrating ejected two lake trout from his right pants leg. Blue pounced on the fish.

Travail looked to Harriet for her reaction and was surprised when a grin formed on her face. She and Yeager burst out laughing, and Travail forgot, at least for the moment, that he was sorely depressed.

When Harriet caught her breath, she addressed Yeager. "You are nothing but trouble."

"Trouble is, as trouble does."

That sounded right to Travail. He could see a bit of Forrest Gump in Yeager.

"And you're wet and smell like the lake. You need to take a shower and come to the homeowners' meeting tonight. I need your vote."

"For what?"

"Sue Ellen Parker is up to no good again."

"I know. That's why we need to talk about the professor."

"After the meeting."

Travail felt invisible until Harriet turned to him. "You might as well come too. We can use the help of a lawyer around Sue Ellen." With that, Harriet Keaton walked away at the same pace she arrived, heading for somewhere fast.

Yeager took the gun's butt and slammed it into the squirming fish. Blue howled. "We'll be there," he hollered to Harriet. He grabbed Travail by the collar and pulled him along.

"Come on, Craig Travail, let's go cook us up some dinner."

CHAPTER 6

BIRDS OF A FEATHER

Harriet arrived and took a seat in the back of the Indie fellowship hall, which doubled as the site of the monthly homeowners' association meeting. She readied herself for another spat with Sue Ellen Parker.

A few minutes later, the rear door opened and Sue Ellen entered like a queen, her head held high. She acknowledged her subjects with a wave and a tight smile. She patted one resident on the arm. "Hello, dear." She greeted another and then another, as she made her way down the center aisle between the metal folding chairs, much the way a president might enter congress for the State of the Union address.

"Goodness," Harriet muttered. Now everyone was standing.

Sue Ellen liked to be both the center of attention and in charge, which were two of the many things that bothered Harriet about Sue Ellen when she'd first met her in high school. Sue Ellen was student body president. Harriet was environmental club president. Sue Ellen was student liaison to the booster club. Harriet played the lead role in the school plays. Both were top of their high school class. Sue Ellen got a full-ride scholarship to Columbia University and Harriet a full-ride scholarship to UNC-Chapel Hill. Both were hardworking and passionate about their different interests. It was always a competition between them.

Sue Ellen eventually made her way to the front and took her appointed place, next to the board chair, so she could ride shotgun over the meeting. The chair, Becky Trainer, and the other board members, nodded at Sue Ellen from behind their card table facing the assembly. Sue Ellen said with a half-smile, "Hello, Becky," which was Becky's cue to start the meeting.

Becky was a thin woman whose bouffant hairstyle was a 1950s throwback. She looked like a Number 2 Pencil, as Yeager called her, with an oversized brown eraser clipped to the top. Despite Becky's reticence, Sue Ellen had nominated her for the position and sealed her election with a rousing speech.

Becky looked at her notes and then at the crowd. "Good evening."

Everyone but Harriet responded with a warm greeting. The fix was in, and Harriet didn't like it.

"We have much to cover." Becky looked at Sue Ellen. "First, let's take a moment to pray silently for the soul of fellow resident Matthew Collins."

Everyone bowed their heads for thirty seconds. Harriet kept her eyes on Sue Ellen, who bowed her head but didn't close her eyes. As if sensing she were being watched, Sue Ellen lifted her chin and looked to the back of the room, and there was a moment when the two women, so much alike and so different, stared at one another. Sue Ellen didn't appear to be mourning the professor's death.

Becky next mentioned the agenda item that brought Harriet to the meeting. She nodded at Sue Ellen, who stood and faced the attendees. "Thank you, Becky. We have—"

The side door swung open and slammed against the wall. Everyone turned to see Yeager in the doorway with a smile on his face. "Sorry, folks. Don't know my own strength. Carry on, Sue Ellen. I see you have folks spellbound as usual."

Sue Ellen stiffened at Yeager's sarcasm.

"Come on, Craig Travail." Yeager was loud enough for everyone to hear. "They won't bite. Except maybe Sue Ellen."

Becky Trainer stood up with an ashen tint to her face. "Mr. Alexander. Please. Sue Ellen has the floor. Would you and your friend kindly take a seat?"

Harriet was glad to see the two men. They were an odd twosome, but they were here for her, as she had asked.

"Does everyone know Craig Travail?" Yeager asked. "Fresh man on campus. Single too."

Travail ducked his head and slumped into the nearest seat. He wore khaki pants, a blue button-down shirt, and a soft brown sport coat that blended with his light hazel eyes. His hair had a touch of grey in the black waves that brushed his ears. He had a well-shaped nose that accented his strong, clean-shaven face. Harriet knew he would be a hit with the women.

Becky's posture changed. More friendly, now. "It's nice to have you with us, Mr. Travail. Welcome to the Indie."

Travail mumbled his thanks.

"May I continue?" Sue Ellen said to Becky.

"By all means."

"As I was saying, we have a problem. A serious problem."

As Sue Ellen spoke, her face bunched up in alarm, like she had to pee, and the toilet paper roll was empty. "If we don't prohibit bird feeders on the property, the birds will cover our porches with... Well, I can't bring myself to say it."

"Bird shit," Yeager added. His voice carried.

Becky Trainer was on her feet. "Mr. Alexander. Watch your language."

Yeager laughed and elbowed Travail.

"This is serious," Sue Ellen said. "The condominium porches have become a mess because the cottage residents feed the birds."

This was Sue Ellen's version of class warfare. She was a condo resident, not a cottage resident. Fifth floor, at that, where she could look down on her kingdom, from her six-by-four-foot balcony.

Harriet stood from her back row seat and addressed Sue Ellen. "Just say it."

"What is the problem now, Harriet?"

"It's not the cottage residents you're complaining about. It's me."

"This is not personal."

Harriet pushed her hair from her face and walked down the center aisle. She stopped halfway, set her eyes on Sue Ellen Parker, and put her hands on her hips. "You know darn well this is personal. It's been that way all our lives. If I'm for something, you're against it. But this one should be obvious. I'm the only cottage owner that has bird feeders."

"It's not you I'm complaining about. Just your feeders."

"So you think me feeding the birds is to blame for bird poop on your porch?"

"Of course."

"Are you telling everyone that until I got here, birds didn't exist at the Indie? Not in the trees? Not near the garden? That this was a no-fly zone?"

"You've attracted more. It has to stop." Sue Ellen turned to Becky and said, "Call the question. I move we prohibit bird feeders at the Indie."

Becky looked around the room. "Does anyone second Sue Ellen Parker's motion?" Several people spoke at the same time. "Second."

Harriet had an idea. "Before you vote, I'd like you to hear from my lawyer." She pointed to where Yeager and Travail sat.

"Yeager is not a lawyer," Sue Ellen said.

"Not Yeager. Him."

"Mr. Travail is your lawyer?"

"Yes. And a very good one." Harriet had done her research. Craig Travail had been a well-respected trial lawyer, primarily handling complex litigation for well-funded corporations, but he sometimes represented individuals who found themselves as underdogs against moneyed opposition. Like the time he prevented a large municipality from shutting down a woman's farm.

Becky tried to take control. "This is not a legal proceeding, Harriet."

"Are you going to deny Mr. Travail the right to speak?"

Yeager pushed Travail to his feet. Becky looked their way. "Do you want to say something, Mr. Travail?"

"Sure he does." Harriet tried to coax him in. "Tell them about the Jefferson Farms case."

Travail stiffened, and he looked at the door. He kept his comments brief.

"Yadkin County built an office building next to my client's farm. It then filed a nuisance lawsuit to shut down the farm."

Harriet pressed him. "What kind of nuisance was it?"

"The county said the farm smelled bad and interfered with the use of the office building."

"How did it smell?" Harriet smiled.

"Like the smell of what cows leave on the ground."

A few residents snickered. Sue Ellen frowned. Harriet now had everyone's attention.

"Did you win your case, Mr. Travail?"

"Yes."

"Why?"

"The cows were there first."

Harriet threw up her arms and looked around the room. "Kind of like the birds were here before Sue Ellen Parker."

Yeager laughed, along with the cottage owners. Even a few condo owners smiled.

Sue Ellen stared at Becky Trainer. "Can we vote now?"

Harriet wasn't ready to give up. "Has everyone forgotten the history of this place, the reason we call our home the Indie, and the spirit that brought us here?"

Becky Trainer banged her gavel on the table, but it had no effect as heads turned to look at Harriet.

"The house next door stands for something. A great patriot lived there. He was a man who stood against tyranny and for freedom from unjust laws." She knew she was laying it on thick, but she continued anyway. "What do you think Hezekiah Alexander would have done if King George told him he couldn't have a bird feeder?"

People laughed again, even the condo owners.

"Don't tread on me and my birds, Sue Ellen Parker." Harriet pointed at her nemesis.

More laughter.

But that was all Harriet accomplished, a brief bit of humor, as everyone turned their attention back to Becky Trainer and voted with a show of hands. Because the condo owners outnumbered the cottage owners two to one, Sue Ellen had the votes she needed to starve the birds.

"The motion carries," Becky said. "All feeders must be removed by month's end." She looked directly at Harriet, but Harriet refused to acknowledge Becky's directive. She walked to the exit, turned, and stomped her feet. Everyone turned to look at her.

"You can outlaw bird feeders all day long, Sue Ellen Parker, but no bird within five miles of this place will resist the opportunity to crap on your porch." Harriet walked out of the room with her head held high.

Yeager slapped Travail on the back and shouted for all to hear, "Huzzah!"

CHAPTER 7

THE PROFESSOR'S NEW BOOK

Preface to *An American Truth*
by Matthew Collins

In light of circumstances that must be made plain to even the most serious of skeptics—as I once was—by the discoveries to be revealed in this book, it was incumbent upon me to write this sequel to reconcile my conclusions in *An American Hoax*.

In 1831, the North Carolina governor, acting in concert with the North Carolina General Assembly, completed a report in defense of the April 30, 1819, publication in the *Essex Register* of what was referred to at the time as a "Declaration of Independence." The declaration was made on May 20, 1775, in Mecklenburg County, North Carolina. The delegation that drew it was chaired by Abraham Alexander, and it was attested by John McKnitt Alexander, secretary, with twenty-six delegates present. Because the original declaration and copies either burned in an 1800 fire or were lost to time, the *Essex Register* set off a controversy as to the Meck Dec's authenticity among states, regions, and well-respected American patriots.

John Adams, successor to the presidency of George Washington, and a Massachusetts delegate to the Continental Congress, upon learning of the 1819 publication in the *Essex Register*, thought it genuine; whereas, Thomas Jefferson, successor to the presidency of John Adams, and drafter of the American Declaration of Independence in 1776, did not. Rather, he thought it "spurious," a fact quoted in the preamble to the 1831 report.

Jefferson's callous retort motivated the state of North Carolina to publish the 1831 report to defend the honor of the North Carolina patriots who stood for and witnessed a declaration of independence on May 20, 1775, in the backcountry of North Carolina.

In *An American Hoax,* I, like many historians before me who disputed the validity of the Meck Dec, gave little or no credit to the sworn statements of eyewitnesses whose accounts appeared in the 1831 report, calling the witnesses either biased or confused or both. The 1831 report accepted the witnesses' accounts without question, showing that North Carolina had much invested in the emotional fabric that is patriot pride and it wanted the story to be true. No longer could Virginia or Massachusetts take all the credit. North Carolina was important too. The 1831 report made a case for the validity of the Meck Dec, and I disputed it. I was not the first to do so, but I did so with (in hindsight) too much vigor.

Convincing hardened skeptics boils down to producing a document —which I intend to do—proving that independence was born in Mecklenburg County. I look forward to revealing the true story of what happened on May 20, 1775, and just as important, the conspiracy involving the official Dispatch 34 that kept the truth a secret for so long.

CHAPTER 8

SITCOM ORIENTATION

Travail awoke at 5:30 a.m. and made a cup of coffee. He was on edge from the previous day's introduction to the Indie and hadn't slept well. He needed something to do, so he emptied his satchel, the sixtieth birthday gift from Rachael and the one Angela had stuffed papers into the day he quit the firm. The papers she'd provided were not the complete file of the professor's case, but they brought back memories of the trial fifteen years earlier.

He flipped through papers he recognized until he saw a document he had given little thought to at the time. It was a copy of the letter approving the professor's grant application to fund the research and writing for his book, *An American Hoax*. The funding organization was called The Jefferson Experience. He used his phone to Google the organization. When he found the web page, he clicked on the board of directors link. A name jumped out at him. Robert Elkin. That was interesting. A fact he'd never known.

Before Travail could dig deeper, he heard rat-a-tat-tat on his back door and a loud voice. "You home in there, Craig Travail?"

Travail sighed. He thought about ignoring his neighbor, but so far, that strategy hadn't proved successful. He stepped to the door and opened it.

"You ready to go?" Yeager pushed his way in.

The sun was showing itself. "Go where?"

"To a stakeout."

Before Travail could say no thanks, Yeager had him by the arm and out the door. "Time for you to learn something about the residents."

Travail pulled back. He had no interest in spying on other residents, if that's what Yeager had in mind, but Yeager was strong.

"Oh no you don't. Ya gotta eat." He guided Travail up the gravel path to the community center. He pushed him through the back door at the basement level and up a flight of circular steps that emptied in the first-floor lobby. "Let's sit over there, between the food and the booze." Yeager gestured toward two leather chairs separated by a fake tree with plastic green leaves.

Travail was confused but remained quiet. He'd know soon enough.

After they settled in their seats, Yeager looked at his watch. Travail checked his own. It was 6:55 a.m.

"Anytime now," Yeager said. "The first shift is about to arrive."

The lobby was a hexagon. To Travail's immediate left was a wall with double glass doors that opened to the main dining room. The wall to his immediate right had a similar design with a door that opened to the well-stocked bar. The wall at ten o'clock became a wide hallway that led to the business offices and the main entrance. That was where Travail had signed in and had the unfortunate opportunity to meet Peaches, the activities director. The wall at two o'clock opened to a long hallway Travail had traveled when he was trying to escape Peaches. It led to the chapel, the library, the game room, the swimming pool, the salon, and the work-out facilities. Straight ahead at twelve o'clock were a bank of two elevators.

"Very few take the steps," Yeager said. "You can't miss them from here."

Before Travail could comment about how noticeable they would be on Yeager's version of a stakeout, one set of elevator doors opened. A man in a sweatshirt got out first.

"Here comes Fifth of Jack," Yeager said. "Too early to head for the bar, even for him."

"You give them nicknames?"

"Best way to remember them."

Another man followed close behind. He wore a blue blazer and had a woman in a floral dress at his side. "Mr. and Mrs. Thurston Howell the Third."

"You must be really bored."

Yeager laughed and elbowed Travail. "Here come the Skipper and Gilligan." A big-boned fellow with thick sailor arms and a thin man with a mop of hair followed the millionaire and his wife into the dining room. "The Skipper calls his roommate 'little buddy.' They're gay, but nobody cares."

Travail didn't care who was or wasn't gay. He stood to leave, but Yeager grabbed his arm and pulled him back in his seat. "Wait. There's more."

When one set of elevator doors closed, the other set opened. An elderly attendant pushed an old woman in a wheelchair into the lobby. "That's Tommy Do-Little. He's driving Ms. Daisy."

"Do-Little?"

"Yep. As little as he can. Been here since the place opened. Keeps getting annual raises while doing less and less each year. He's thinking about writing a how-to book."

And so it went for the next thirty minutes. Yeager introduced Travail to all the residents, Bert and Ernie, Laverne and Shirley, Archie and Edith, Deputy Fife, Gomer Pyle, and an assorted group of contestants from *The Dating Game*.

"Oh, and here comes President Bill Clinton." Yeager pointed to a handsome elderly man with grey hair, who had a woman twenty years his junior on his left arm. The president nodded to Yeager as he passed.

"Let me guess."

"Yep. He's never had sex with 'that woman.' Or that one over there. Or that one right there either. That's his story, and he's sticking to it."

Yeager wasn't totally stuck in the '60s and '70s sitcom era. He liked to put names to residents who looked like recent politicians too. He had a match for George W, Obama, The Donald, and Uncle Joe. He even dallied in pop culture, naming characters on TV shows Travail had never watched. Travail was surprised Yeager had watched *The Bachelor*.

Two women left the elevator bank next, and Yeager nudged Travail. "Here come Sue Ellen Parker and her sidekick, Becky Trainer."

Travail recognized the women from the homeowners' meeting. They turned their heads and looked down on Yeager and Travail when they passed. Travail avoided eye contact and leaned into Yeager. "Are we done here?"

A feminine voice with an edge to it responded. "That's a good question." Harriet Keaton stood to their right with her arms folded across her chest.

"I was just about to tell Craig Travail the news about Sue Ellen," Yeager said.

"Not here," Harriet said. "Follow me."

Yeager was on his feet. "Come on."

Travail was perplexed but followed Harriet and Yeager to a table in the bar's corner. They had the place to themselves.

Harriet eyed Yeager. "Okay. Tell him."

"Sue Ellen Parker just inherited fifty million dollars."

"Good for her." It was a large sum, but Travail wasn't interested in the story.

"You don't understand."

"Obviously." Travail was losing patience. He'd had all he could take of Yeager in less than one twenty-four-hour cycle.

Yeager and Harriet looked at each other like there was something more that needed to be said. Harriet said it. "Have you ever contested a will in court?"

Travail grumbled. "Is this because of your bird feeder fight?"

Harriet flinched. But not Yeager. "The bird feeders are not a problem anymore, Craig Travail. Harriet ordered beehives."

"What?"

Yeager slapped Travail on the shoulder. "Sue Ellen won't have the votes to get rid of the birds *and* the bees. Get it, Craig Travail?"

Harriet gave Yeager the same look she had on her face when she caught him shooting fish. Then she stared at Travail. "This is more serious than the birds or the bees."

Travail was sure of that. "Contesting a will is no simple matter, nor is it something to do out of spite."

Harriet huffed and spoke to Yeager. "I told you this would be a waste of time." She walked away angry. It was the same way she'd left the homeowners' meeting.

"She doesn't handle rejection well, does she?"

"You know what your problem is Craig Travail? You're a retired lawyer who still thinks like a big-shot lawyer." Yeager pressed ahead before Travail could respond. "Harriet's a good person. She cares about Lori."

"Who's Lori?"

"Matthew Collins's granddaughter."

"I didn't know he had any grandchildren."

"Lori is *the* granddaughter—his only heir—who got cut out of his will."

"How do you know that?"

Yeager reached into his pocket and pulled out one sheet of paper. He dropped it on the table. Travail didn't touch it. He sensed it was a document that shouldn't be in Yeager's possession, and he didn't want his fingerprints on it. Yeager grabbed it back and read the words on the page aloud. He emphasized the part about how Sue Ellen Parker was the sole recipient of the professor's fortune.

"Where did you get that?"

"The professor's condo."

Travail got up. "I can't be a part of this."

"Why not? You got something better to do?"

"I mean, I can't be an accessory to a criminal act, which is what you did when you took that document from his condo."

"Should I put it back?"

Travail wondered if Yeager's toolbox had always been missing the important tools and then he remembered Yeager's afternoon fish hunt and swim. Of course it had. "Yes. You should put it back."

41

"But what about Lori?"

"What about her?"

"She needs a lawyer."

"As you said, I'm retired."

"You'd rather sulk by the lake—'cause I know that's what you were doing—than help right a wrong?"

Travail didn't appreciate criticism from a man he hardly knew, and he didn't care to get involved in a domestic dispute. "Why do you and Harriet care so much about Matthew Collins's granddaughter?"

"After her grandmother died, Lori was always the professor's 'plus one,' and after my mother died from cancer and Harriet took me under her wing, I was Harriet's. The four of us did things together. Movies. Picnics. Hikes. Lectures. Museums. Funerals. Hell, we even went to the beach together one Fourth of July, but Harriet insisted on the boys being on one floor and the girls being on another. She didn't want me near her bathroom."

That sounded reasonable given Yeager's consistently scruffy appearance. "You were friends then?"

"More than that, really. I was more the great-uncle who told tall tales and made Lori laugh. Harriet was like the mother Lori no longer had. She was the female ear that a young woman needed. They became very close."

That explained why Yeager and Harriet were pushing Travail to help Lori, but it didn't explain why Matthew Collins would disinherit his granddaughter. Maybe they'd had a falling out. "I can refer her to someone who handles these cases."

Yeager ran his right hand through his beard as a relaxed smile crossed his face. "The professor sometimes called me Captain Jack."

"What?"

"He said it was because I could deliver."

"I don't understand."

Yeager slapped Travail on the back. "Yes, sir, Craig Travail. You're going to like Lori."

CHAPTER 9

ELKIN'S STRATEGY CHANGES

The phone rang in the forty-fifth floor corner office of the America Bank office tower and Robert Elkin let his assistant pick up the call. It would have been easy to do it himself, and since he knew who was calling, it would have been more efficient, but Elkin enjoyed having others wait on him. It gave him more control, and control was Elkin's game.

The gold-plated clock on his mahogany desk said it was 8:45 a.m., and his south-facing view revealed lines of vehicles no bigger than black dots inching their way into the center city, a reminder that Charlotte traffic was getting worse by the day. When his assistant stuck her head in the door and announced it was Congressman Butterworth, he said, "Be sure the congressman's assistant puts him on the line first."

He smiled at the idea of manipulating the most powerful man in the US Congress, a fellow Virginian who could be a real ass. After a few minutes, his phone rang. He waited until it rang three more times. He lifted the receiver from the cradle. "Walter."

"I don't like to be kept waiting, Robert."

"Walter, it's good to hear your voice." Elkin held the phone to his ear with his right hand and extended his left arm to allow the cuff on his silk dress shirt to extend from under his jacket sleeve. He did not remove his suit jacket in the office even with no appointments. He liked the powerful feel of well-tailored clothes.

"You were supposed to call me two days ago."

"Could you hold a moment, Walter?" Elkin placed the phone down and looked out the window. In the distance, he saw the shiny oval roof of the old Charlotte Coliseum. As a child, it looked like a humongous flying saucer. When the structure was built, it was the largest indoor sports venue in the state. He had fond memories of his mother taking him to the circus there in the 1960s, after his father exiled them from their home in Charlottesville. It was fun and exciting, but the once-a-year outing to see the Greatest Show on Earth was all his mother could afford. They were too poor to see basketball and hockey games like the other kids. He'd promised himself when he grew up, he'd never miss out again. He now had courtside seats to Hornets' basketball games, fifty-yard-line seats for Panthers' football games, and first-row seats in the Grand Tier Circle at the Blumenthal for plays, musicals, and concerts. Lesser venues like the old Charlotte Coliseum were remnants of his past. They reminded him of his uncaring, overbearing father. The only people he despised more than his father were politicians. He picked up the phone again.

"Sorry, Walter, I had something important to do."

"Robert, I don't know what kind of game you're playing—"

"Nonsense, Walter. We play for the same team on the same field and with the same rules." He wondered which of the two issues Butterworth would bring up first, the one that mattered to Butterworth or the one that mattered to the board.

Butterworth pretended to care about the bigger picture. "Did Matthew Collins back down?"

Elkin thought of his recent conversation with the professor, the professor's timely demise, his phone call with Sue Ellen Parker, and how everything was coming together nicely. "Our strategy has changed."

"Dammit, Robert, I'm in charge, not you. I say whether the strategy changes."

Elkin enjoyed this part of being the fixer, having the ability to put people like Walter Butterworth in their place. "You forget who gets you re-elected every two years, Congressman. And you forget the director appointed me, not you, to take care of the problem of the professor's manuscript. Your job is funding. You are not in charge of operations. You can offer your opinion, like how to proceed against Lori Collins, but I make the call. If you don't like what I decide, you can hire a second-rate law firm to represent you."

Elkin let the silence linger for ten seconds before he shared the news that solved the problem with Matthew Collins. "The professor is dead."

There was a pause. "I won't ask how that happened." Butterworth didn't sound disappointed. This was the politicians' code talking. Don't learn what you may have to deny later. Elkin chose not to explain.

"What about the professor's research?"

"In good hands." Elkin explained the professor left all his assets to a woman named Sue Ellen Parker. "She is on our side, Walter. She just hired me to represent her."

"So it's over? The director can finally relax?"

Elkin was sure the director of The Jefferson Experience would not relax, not anymore. The organization that began as The Jefferson Venture in 1837 had changed its name and reinvented itself in the early 1900s. It then clicked along as a well-run foundation promoting the accomplishments of the third president of the United States, until the director's paranoia led him to decree that they needed to protect Jefferson's reputation no matter the financial cost. The director's latest focus was the Meck Dec.

The congressman was impatient. "Do you believe the rumor circulating among the board that Thomas Jefferson plagiarized from the Mecklenburg Declaration of Independence?"

"Thomas Jefferson was a scholar and a gentleman. He didn't need to—wouldn't—use the words of others." But as he said it, Elkin thought about the claim against Jefferson's character that Jefferson fathered children with Sally Hemmings, one of his slaves. When the controversy heated up in the 1990s, the director forced the board to fund the work of several historians who pushed back at the claim, but the Ken Burns documentary in 1997, the DNA test in 1998, and the Monticello Foundation's 2001 study turned public opinion against Jefferson.

When Monticello opened its Sally Hemmings exhibit in 2018, the director called it a cowardly act and an unproven stain and vowed nothing like that could ever happen again. The director tasked Elkin with ensuring the Meck Dec did not become another problem for Jefferson's reputation, saying belief in the Meck Dec created "a slippery slope." If tangible evidence of the Meck Dec ever surfaced, people might talk about the similarity between the language in it and in the Declaration of Independence. That kind of talk led to damaged reputations.

Elkin worried about the director's declining mental state, born out of an unnatural belief that a knock on Jefferson was a knock on the director himself, because Jefferson's blood coursed through his veins and was, and must remain, pure.

Butterworth interrupted Elkin's thoughts. "You need to reassure the director before things get out of hand."

Elkin had appeased the director's worries in the past with assurances and action. He didn't do it out of loyalty. He did it because of the one thing he loved more than protecting Jefferson's reputation: the money. "I will speak with the director."

"What about the other board members?"

"I will speak with them too. Like you and me, they want things to go smoothly and know what's at stake." It was true. All the board members traced their lineage to Thomas Jefferson and were proud that The Jefferson Experience funded educational programs about Jefferson, gave away scholarships and grants in his name, and contributed money to Monticello. But like Butterworth and Elkin, the board members loved the dark money more and knew the director held the purse strings. "I'm confident the board will approve funding for the lawsuits I have in mind to protect the secret of the Mecklenburg Declaration of Independence and keep the director happy."

"So the secret is safe?"

Butterworth's question took Elkin back to the last conversation he'd had with the professor. He'd visited with him at his condo within twenty-four hours of his death. The man was a physical and emotional wreck.

"You don't look well," Elkin had said.

"I've been working."

"I hope it's not on the sequel."

"How do you know about that?"

Elkin had been surprised at how naïve the professor was to the danger of opposing The Jefferson Experience. The conversation veered into treacherous waters when the professor said he intended to publish the sequel, "the truth," as he'd called it.

"You obviously didn't read the fine print of your contract for *An American Hoax*. You agreed not to publish anything contrary to your findings in the book."

The professor protested, but Elkin interrupted him. "How's your granddaughter? Is she still running your nonprofit?"

"Keep her out of this."

"That's up to you. If you try to undo what you accomplished with *An American Hoax*, there will be consequences, to you and your granddaughter." Elkin spoke with conviction as he foreshadowed those consequences. "The government is moving forward to strip the nonprofit of its tax-exempt status and I've been asked to file a libel lawsuit against Lori for her articles about esteemed Congressman Walter Butterworth. If you do your part, I can stop both the investigation and the lawsuit. But only if you do your part."

The professor was pale and sweaty when he gave up. "You need to promise to keep Lori and the nonprofit out of this."

"Only if you abandon the sequel and ensure she doesn't learn the secret."

The professor promised. "I won't tell Lori what I learned about the Meck Dec, and I'll make sure my research papers and manuscript don't fall into her hands."

Butterworth's question still hung in the air. Was the secret safe?

"Very likely," Elkin said.

"What do you mean?"

Elkin wasn't sure how the professor had stumbled onto the truth about the Meck Dec. The evidence was well-protected, and the knowledge circle was tight. He would have sworn only the director and the board knew about the key historical document that unlocked the truth, but nothing was guaranteed when it came to keeping secrets. When Elkin left the professor that day, he was confident the professor would do his part, if only to protect his granddaughter.

In his call this morning with Sue Ellen Parker, he learned how the professor did it. Disinheriting his granddaughter seemed like overkill, but as long as the one-page will stood up in court, Lori Collins would never see his work papers and would not learn the secret.

Elkin smiled as he thought about the last words he'd said to the professor. He had dug into his pants pocket and took out a package from the local drugstore. "I almost forgot. This was on your doorstep. I think it's a prescription delivery. The way you look, take whatever it is and go to bed early."

Butterworth didn't wait for Elkin to answer his question. Instead, he turned to the other reason for his call. "Did you send the granddaughter the demand letter?"

"I did. Four weeks ago."

"Did you call and threaten her as I insisted?"

"Threat is not a friendly word, Walter, but let's just say she got the message. Any further articles about you will lead to a lawsuit that will bankrupt her and her nonprofit."

The congressman didn't appear appeased. "But the articles she wrote are still online. My opponent will use them against me in the next election."

"Is there something you're not telling the board about her allegations?"

Butterworth hesitated, which was abnormal. He usually had a comeback, whether or not it was true. Elkin had his suspicion the man was a thief.

"I want you to sue that woman."

Elkin couldn't understand how a man who had become a high-ranking congressional committee chairman could be so stupid. "If you

48

sue her, you draw attention to her stories, and people will wonder whether they are true. And with Matthew Collins's death and new will, her income source has been cut off."

Butterworth exploded. "But her nonprofit is flush with cash."

"That's where you come in. Press your contacts to ramp up the government investigation targeting the nonprofit. When the nonprofit loses its tax-exempt status, it will lose all financial support, and its credibility will be shot."

There was a long pause before Butterworth spoke again. Elkin heard what sounded like pencil on paper. "Her grandfather was loaded. She may challenge the will."

"If she does, we'll file the libel lawsuit and pile on."

"And if she wins the will contest—"

Elkin cut him off. "She won't win. I'll make sure of that."

Butterworth grumbled but didn't press the matter further. He returned to the subject of the Meck Dec. "Does she know the secret?"

Elkin used the voice that had soothed many a client over the years. "I am certain she doesn't."

Elkin ended the call and thought about the retirement community where Sue Ellen Parker, his new fifty-million-dollar client, lived. He rang Angela, Craig Travail's former assistant, to ask her about Travail's new home. He smiled at her response. He'd make it a point to run into Travail and remind him how much nobody missed him at the law firm.

CHAPTER 10

TWO DECLARATIONS TOO MUCH ALIKE

Notes In Matthew Collins's Work Papers

1. The Meck Dec reads, "Great Britain, is an enemy to…the **inalienable rights of man**." By comparison, the Declaration of Independence reads, "…that they are endowed by their creator with **certain inalienable rights.**"
2. The Meck Dec reads, **"…do hereby dissolve the political bands** which have connected us to the mother country & **hereby absolve ourselves from all allegiance to the British Crown**." By comparison, the Declaration of Independence reads, "…that they **are absolved from all Allegiance to the British Crown**, and that **all political connection** between them and the State of Great Britain, is and ought to be totally dissolved."
3. The Meck Dec reads, "…do hereby declare ourselves a free and independent people – **are & of right ought to be, a sovereign and self-governing association.**" By comparison, the Declaration of Independence reads, "… That **these United Colonies are, and of Right ought to be Free and Independent States.**"

4. The Meck Dec reads, "We solemnly **pledge to each other our mutual co-operation, our lives, our fortunes & our most sacred honor."** By comparison, the Declaration of Independence reads, "**We mutually pledge to each other our Lives, our Fortunes and our sacred Honor."**

CHAPTER 11

FUNERAL SURPRISE

From his front porch swing, Travail heard the motor before he saw the BMW roadster sprint past his cottage, kicking up gravel and dust in its wake. He'd seen that car one too many times, and its presence caused his pulse to pick up a few beats.

He turned the corner of a page to mark his spot in the latest John Grisham legal thriller, set it on the swing, and walked to the road, where he watched Robert Elkin's sportscar pull into the parking area next to the Indie chapel. It was ironic; he'd been reading legal cases one day and legal thrillers the next, and neither satisfied him. And now Elkin was on the property.

The professor's memorial service was set for 11:00 a.m., and although the time had arrived for Travail to leave if he was going to pay his respects, he had not committed to Yeager's invitation. It had been years since he represented the professor and he felt no personal connection. He also worried Yeager might continue to push him to represent the professor's granddaughter.

Seeing Robert Elkin's vehicle so soon after his forced exit from the law firm brought bad memories to the surface. Ten years earlier, when the shift in the firm's management was underway, the scuttlebutt had been that Travail would be tapped as the new managing partner. No partners openly admitted why Elkin was elected instead, but Travail had a partner friend who shared the nominating committee's thoughts. "It was all about his connections." Which was another way of saying it was all about the money.

Elkin had a knack for bringing in big clients and lining lawyers' pockets. The client who won him the managing partner position was Viribus, LLC, a government contractor intent on supplying the US military with cyber widgets to fight the war against terrorists. Elkin negotiated a substantial success fee with Viribus, put a team together, and used his connections in Washington to land the government contract for the company. As a result, the US pumped millions of dollars into Viribus every month, and Elkin and the law firm got fatter by the day.

Realizing Elkin was headed to the professor's service but not knowing why set Travail's antennae to high alert. He reached into his pocket, pulled out his phone, and texted Yeager. "Save me a seat."

Travail put on his tie as he walked to the chapel. He heard piano music before he entered. He stepped inside, looked around for Yeager, felt a tug on his jacket, and heard a hoarse whisper. "Down here, Craig Travail." Yeager slid over on the back row, and Travail took a seat next to the man he'd spent most of the last few days trying to avoid.

The chapel had a small dais in front and ten rows of pews on each side of a center aisle. Travail's rough calculations put the crowd at about twenty-eight people, not enough to fill the space. He guessed most were Indie residents, and he assumed one of the two women seated on the front left pew was the professor's granddaughter, Lori Collins. Sue Ellen Parker and Robert Elkin occupied the front right pew. Travail's mind raced. Why was Elkin with Sue Ellen Parker at the professor's funeral?

Travail whispered to Yeager. "Does the granddaughter know about the will?"

"Not yet. Harriet is having her over for lunch after the service so we can tell her. You're invited."

The music stopped, and a man in a coat and tie took center stage. "Welcome to this service to remember the life of Matthew Collins.

Please join me in singing the hymn printed in your bulletin, 'Amazing Grace.'"

After the hymn, the congregation read the Twenty-Third Psalm. A generic homily followed by the pretend minister who sounded like he'd never met Matthew Collins but loved him dearly. The service ended with the audience singing "How Great Thou Art."

Travail and Yeager left the church first and waited for Harriet, who joined them and repeated Yeager's invitation to lunch. "I'd like you to meet Lori."

Before Travail could answer, a voice carried from the chapel steps. "Craig. Craig. Is that you?" Robert Elkin whispered something to Sue Ellen Parker, let go of her left elbow and walked in their direction.

"So this is where you ended up." Elkin smiled at Travail. More of a smirk, really. "Not quite the uptown life, is it, Craig? But I suppose they have arts and crafts to keep you busy." Elkin looked at Yeager and Harriet. "Are these your new playmates?" He eyed them like they were statues needing to be removed from public property.

Travail was still trying to process why Elkin was at the service with Sue Ellen Parker when Yeager introduced himself.

"Name's Chuck Yeager Alexander." He stuck out his hand, but Elkin ignored it and turned his attention to Harriet.

"And you are?"

"Harriet Keaton."

Elkin bowed. "Ah, yes. I thought I recognized you. I believe I sued your family's construction company, and the jury awarded my client 1.2 million dollars."

"Which was overturned on appeal."

"But that was followed by a nice settlement."

Harriet's voice sharpened. "What brings you to the Indie, Mr. Elkin?" It was a good question and better that Harriet asked it than Travail.

"I represent Sue Ellen Parker, the beneficiary of Matthew Collins's estate."

"I don't remember Ms. Parker being a client," Travail said.

"She's a new client. Heard about my reputation."

Yeager added his salty retort. "Must take one to know one."

Elkin's eyes narrowed. "Do you know who I am?"

Yeager made a show of rubbing his beard and pondering the question. "Can't say that I do, but there is a doctor at the memory center who can tell you who you are."

Travail couldn't help but laugh, and Harriet joined him. Elkin's face reddened. "Hilarious, Mr. Alexander. I'd be careful with the sarcasm. I might just sue you one day."

Yeager slapped his thigh. "Guess you know who you are, after all, and a lawyer at that." He patted Travail on the back. "Can you represent me, Craig Travail?"

Elkin turned his bullying on Travail. "Is this your new life, Craig? Representing the likes of Rip Van Winkle."

Travail felt movement from Yeager and wondered what a man who shoots fish would do to a smart-mouthed lawyer. He put his arm out to hold Yeager in place. It was time to move on from Robert Elkin. "Your client is waiting on you."

Elkin looked at Sue Ellen Parker standing beside his BMW. "Enjoy your life on the farm, Craig. And don't forget to take your meds." Ten paces later, he turned around, as if he had forgotten something. "Let me be clear about one thing. If you ever make the mistake of taking a case against me and my law firm," with the emphasis on the word "my," "I will crush you. Don't forget. I manage thirty offices in the most powerful law firm in the country, and your little law practice here, if that is what you are cultivating, is nothing but a country store on a road to nowhere."

Travail, Yeager, and Harriet watched Robert Elkin and Sue Ellen Parker drive off in the two-seater with the top down.

"Well," Harriet said, "that was entertaining. You coming, Craig?"

Travail didn't answer. As he watched the BMW leave his sight, he realized Elkin was right. He had no law practice, and he lived on a retirement farm in the woods. Worse, his neighbor was a man who could only remember people's names if they resembled sitcom characters.

"Well?"

Elkin's condescending tone vibrated in his head. Maybe it wouldn't hurt to meet Lori. It didn't mean he'd have to take her case. He'd just meet her, show his respect.

"Sure. Thank you."

Yeager smiled at Harriet as he slapped Travail on the back. "I told you he was with us."

CHAPTER 12

WHERE THERE'S A WILL THERE'S A WAY

Harriet walked quickly toward her cottage, with Yeager and Travail trying to keep pace. When they reached her front porch, Yeager tossed out a question. "So Lori and Tate finally made things legal after seven years living together?"

Harriet bristled at Yeager's ignorance. "Until the US Supreme Court spoke, it wasn't even possible, and for a while after that, Lori and Tate weren't sure they needed the state's blessing."

Yeager threw up his hands in self-defense and said he was happy for them, while Travail remained silent, which caused Harriet to address Travail on the topic of marriage equality. "Craig, what do you think about a woman marrying a woman?"

"It's not something I've thought a lot about."

"Well, you have about five minutes to think about it."

Yeager chuckled. "Craig Travail, it's time you got to know the opposition leader to the *status quo*, ever impatient for the world to change and come to its senses."

As much as Harriet tired of Yeager's quips, he was right this time. "I won't apologize."

Travail was conciliatory. "I try not to be judgmental about how other people live their lives."

"Good for you," Harriet said, as she opened the front door and let them in. "And good luck sticking to that policy living at the Indie."

Lori and Tate arrived five minutes later. Harriet was the first to welcome them into the foyer, with Yeager close behind. Unlike her parents, who had dark brown skin, Lori's skin color was lighter, closer to that of her mixed-race grandfather. Lori and the professor were a lot alike in other ways too. Intelligent, quiet, stubborn. Harriet felt a tightness in her chest. It was going to be hard on Lori to learn that her last remaining blood relative had turned on her.

Yeager stepped forward. "Hello, Lori Darlin'." He gave Lori a warm hug and lowered his voice. "I miss your grandfather every day. He was a great friend. And he loved you very much."

Lori's eyes were wet when they broke their embrace. "He loved how you made him laugh." Her smile was tender.

"That's it," Yeager said, pointing Harriet to Lori's smile. "You should try that, Harriet."

"I'll smile when you find something worthwhile to do with your life."

"Ha. I will tell you this, Mrs. I'm-going-to-file-a-bird feeder-class-action-lawsuit, I have worthwhile projects."

"Name one."

Both Lori and Tate were laughing now. Tate reached out her hand to Yeager. "Good to see you again, Yeager."

"Naw, I need a hug." He pulled her in tight.

In the living room, Lori took notice of Harriet's latest assortment of potted plants, adding, "It feels like only yesterday you helped me with my middle school horticulture paper," to which Yeager said, "I can't tell if I am inside or out."

Tate leaned forward and smelled the cut flowers on the mantle. "I love these scents."

Again, Yeager beat Harriet with a reply. "Her food smells are better. I can tell when she's cooking pork chops from across the lake."

Harriet finally got her chance. "I always cook two porkchops, so I can put one extra on the back deck to feed a hairy, two-legged beast who roams the woods at night foraging for free meals."

"She's talking about me," Yeager said.

Harriet poked Yeager in the shoulder with her right forefinger. "They know who I'm talking about." Lori and Tate laughed.

Amidst the laughter, Harriet realized she had not introduced Travail, and he hadn't spoken up. He was probably being respectful, but it could be shyness. She played hostess against his reticence. "This is Craig Travail. He's a new resident. He's also a lawyer. He represented the professor fifteen years ago. I asked him to lunch in case you have any questions about the professor's estate."

"I remember your name. My grandfather had good things to say about you. Nice to meet you." Lori extended her hand.

Travail nodded, shook hands, and offered a polite, "Same here."

"But as far as the estate goes, I haven't looked at my grandfather's will in years and didn't bring a copy of it with me. There should be plenty of time for that later."

Harriet signaled with her eyes for Yeager and Travail to stay quiet for the moment, then said, "Let's eat. We're having pimento cheese sandwiches, a cold bean salad, chips, deviled eggs, and sweet tea."

The men waited for the women to serve themselves first. Yeager nudged Travail to go next. "I'll bat cleanup."

After Travail filled his plate, Yeager went to work on what was left. He piled a heap of bean salad in the center, surrounded it with three full-size pimento cheese sandwiches, four deviled eggs, and covered it all in chips. When he set his plate down, Lori smiled again.

"Really, Yeager," Harriet said, "show some respect. Even pigs don't eat like that."

"Pigs are not as healthy as me."

Lori and Tate laughed.

"I'm sorry," Harriet said to Lori.

"No, no, it's okay. This is the first time I've laughed since I heard the news about my grandfather. It feels good." She looked at Yeager. "Eat what makes you happy."

"I told you she was a smart one, Harriet."

"I've always known Lori to be intelligent. Would you like a shovel?"

Yeager smiled with a mouth too full to speak, and Harriet changed the subject. "Tell us about the wedding."

Lori took Tate's hand. "I was a wreck, but Tate pulled it off. She's the organizer. And it was beautiful. Just what we wanted."

Yeager spoke with half a mouth full. "Did the professor give you away?"

Harriet huffed. "Women are not property you can give away."

Tate placed her arm around Lori's shoulder as Lori dabbed her mouth with her napkin. "He couldn't make it to Austin."

Yeager chewed slowly. "But—"

Harriet kicked Yeager under the table and pressed for wedding details. Lori's smile returned. "Austin was beautiful. We had a sunset wedding, with tiki torches to light the occasion on the bank of the river."

Harriet followed up with questions about their honeymoon and their new home, and Lori and Tate answered. Travail didn't take part in the conversation that Harriet kept alive. Of course, he was a stranger among old friends, but Harriet sensed it was his nature too. He tended to observe and absorb before he talked.

"Get this," Yeager said as he elbowed Travail. "Lori runs a charity the professor started called We Salute You. Tell Craig Travail about it, Lori."

"We educate the public about issues affecting veterans. We also provide veterans with temporary housing, medical help, and job training. Did you serve in the military, Mr. Travail?"

"No. I was too young to go to Vietnam and too old to fight anywhere else." There was a hint of embarrassment in his voice.

Yeager reached over Travail for another sandwich. "Lori's charity also shines a big ole spotlight on politicians, Craig Travail, the ones who don't do enough to support veterans, and they fight for the underdogs too, taking up for all the gays and transgenders who serve in the military." Yeager stuffed a deviled egg in his mouth before adding his postscript. "I'm against discrimination too, like what people can wear and what they can't. Take the Indie's dining room dress code, for example, it's—"

"Seriously?" Harriet cut Yeager off.

Lori smiled at Yeager and addressed Travail again. "The nonprofit was the professor's idea. Dad ran it until he and Mom died. My grandfather kept it going until I finished graduate school and could take over."

"Do you enjoy the work?"

Travail's question surprised Harriet, but she was curious about the answer. She'd never thought to ask Lori why she took over the nonprofit and whether she liked the work.

"I enjoy helping others." Lori paused and tilted her head to the side. "Honestly, I took the job to honor my father and grandfather. This was their passion. My passion is writing."

"A talent she gets from the professor," Harriet added.

Yeager asked another question between bites. "Besides taking down pork belly politicians with your powerful pen, what are you writing?" He held a pimento cheese sandwich in one hand and a spoonful of beans in the other.

"Mostly grant applications, emails, newsletters, and articles in various publications to highlight the rights and needs of veterans."

Tate leaned toward Lori. "Don't be modest. Tell them about your novel."

"It's too early."

"Not true," Tate said. "A respected publisher gave Lori a book contract a few weeks after we got married."

"That's great," Yeager said. "I bet the professor was excited."

"He was, but—" Lori looked down at her hands.

Harriet stared at Yeager and shook her head "no." It was obvious Lori didn't want to talk about it. But Yeager plowed ahead, anyway. "But what?"

Lori lowered her voice. "He wasn't himself."

"Why, darlin'? What's the book about?"

"It's a historical romance set in Charlotte in 1775."

"1775." Yeager popped another deviled egg in his mouth. "He should've ate that up."

"That's what I thought. I told him I was writing the book to honor

61

his work in that time period. It was the last conversation we had, the afternoon before he died. He told me not to write it. He insisted. It wasn't like him."

Harriet placed her hand on Lori's. "Did you notice any other strange behavior before the professor died?"

"Just that he seemed extremely stressed."

"How so?" Harriet glanced toward Travail. Was he taking this in? Was he thinking like a lawyer?

"It was the way he talked to me on the phone. He seemed anxious about something."

Harriet caught Yeager's eye and nodded at him. It was time to tell Lori about the will. He pushed his empty plate to the side and addressed Lori. "Did the professor ever talk with you about his will?"

"About ten years ago, he made a will leaving everything to the foundation and me. He was very generous, except when it came to the government. He didn't want the government to get one cent. Said the government was too incompetent to spend it the right way."

"Right-o, there."

Harriet grunted at Yeager. "What do you know about paying taxes?"

"I know about not paying them. And that's what we're talking about."

Harriet gave Travail the eye, prompting him to get engaged. He cleared his throat and addressed Lori. "Did your grandfather tell you how he planned to avoid paying the estate tax to the government?"

"He did. He said he was going to leave me the full amount that was exempt from estate tax law and give the rest to the nonprofit as a tax-free gift.

"That would work."

"See there," Yeager said. "Quality legal advice from Craig Travail, Esquire in Residence at the Indie." Yeager slid closer to Lori and looked in her eyes. "Did the professor say what to do with his condo after his death?"

"Yes. He said I was too young to live here with a bunch of old..." She stopped herself.

Yeager laughed. "It's okay. Craig Travail doesn't want to live here either." Travail shifted in his chair but didn't comment.

Lori continued. "He said I should sell the condo and invest the money. Which reminds me. I met a lawyer at the memorial service who seems to have an interest."

Harriet didn't like the sound of that. "Who?"

Lori reached in her handbag and pulled out an unopened envelope. "He offered his condolences and handed me this letter. I assumed he represents an interested client."

Yeager's eyes narrowed. "Did this lawyer drive off in a sports car?"

"He did."

Lori tore the envelope open, slipped the letter out and unfolded it. After reading the letter, she looked puzzled. She handed the letter to Tate, who read it quickly. Her face tightened, and she snapped. "This is ridiculous. Robert Elkin, whoever he is, says he will make sure the authorities prosecute Lori to the fullest extent of the law if she removes anything from the condo."

Yeager pulled the napkin from under his chin, swiped his mouth with it, and said, "Maybe I can explain." The tension in the room went up a notch.

"Darlin', I hate to tell you this, but the morning the professor passed away, I had just finished my early morning patrol of the grounds when I saw the ambulance. The lights attracted my attention. It was about to rain, so—"

Harriet cut Yeager off. "Sometime, today."

"Okay. Okay." He gave Lori his full attention. "I found a hand-written will in the professor's condo the morning he died. It cut you out of his earlier will and left everything to Sue Ellen Parker."

Lori sat up, her brow raised. "He left everything to Sue Ellen Parker, the woman you told me tries to run everything at the Indie?"

"I'm not a lawyer," Yeager said, "but it looks that way."

Everyone waited for Lori to speak. She leaned toward Tate. "I thought he loved me. And you too. And the two of us, together."

Tate hugged Lori. "He did."

"That's true," Yeager said. "He definitely loved you both. Told me so, often."

"Then why?"

"That's the mystery," Yeager said.

Lori looked like she might cry. Harriet stood. "We'll give you a moment. The men and I will clear the table."

Harriet, Yeager, and Travail grabbed plates and platters and made their way to the kitchen. "This is a shame," Harriet said. "We need to help her." She looked at Travail. "Will you represent her?"

Yeager answered for Travail. "Course he will, won't you Craig Travail?"

When they returned to the dining room, Lori wiped her eyes. "Thanks, Yeager, for being honest with me. And to all of you, for being here. I know this wasn't easy information to share." She turned her attention to Travail. "I guess I do have a legal question for you, after all. Is the handwritten will legal?"

"Assuming it is in the professor's handwriting, then yes, it's likely legal."

Tate jumped in, eager for a fight. "Does Lori have to accept this?"

"There are certain grounds for challenging a will, like lack of testamentary capacity and duress, but a will contest is a hard case to win, and Sue Ellen Parker has hired an excellent law firm."

"Craig Travail will represent you," Yeager said. "He can beat that guy Elkin and his fancy law firm."

Travail had a wait-a-minute look on his face, but Harriet pretended not to see it. "Don't worry about the cost," she said. "I will chip in whatever is needed."

Lori turned to Harriet. "Thanks Harriet. That's very kind, but not necessary." She focused on Travail. "I don't know why my grandfather did this, and it hurts to think about the why, but I get the impression you don't think I can win, if I do fight it."

"I can't predict how it will turn out. It will be hard on you emotionally, either way."

"She's tough," Tate said.

"I see that, but I know the lawyer on the other side. He will attack Lori's character and twist the facts to make Lori look greedy."

Everyone deferred to Lori. After a long thirty seconds, she spoke.

"What bothers me most is, my grandfather and I talked many times about how I should spend the money. He wanted me to help veterans. If the will is valid, it contradicts what he wanted me to do with the money and a lot of veterans will be hurt."

Tate drove Lori's point home. "The professor provided over half the funding for We Salute You and was very supportive of the cause. This whole thing smells like crap."

Yeager and Harriet seconded her emotion before Travail added a legal point of interest. "By giving everything to Sue Ellen Parker, someone who is not his wife, and by giving nothing to the nonprofit, the government is going to get a large estate-tax payday."

"That makes no sense either, not the way he felt about the government," Yeager said.

"Maybe he had a good reason for the will," Lori said.

Tate bit her lip. "I can't think of one."

"Me neither," Harriet said.

Yeager made it three for three. "I never would have believed it if I hadn't seen it."

"That leaves you, Mr. Travail." Tate pressed again. "What do you believe?"

While Travail stalled with his silence, Yeager looped back to an earlier topic. "When the professor told you not to write your book, did he mention the Meck Dec?"

Harriet heaved a sigh. "Enough with the Meck Dec, Yeager."

"No, it's okay." Lori gazed off. "He said he wanted me to forget about the Meck Dec. He said he was worried about my safety, but he wouldn't explain, just pleaded for me to drop the idea of writing the book."

"Did you know he was working on another book about the Meck Dec?"

Lori's shoulders drew back, and her mouth parted. "What else could he possibly say about the Meck Dec after *An American Hoax*?"

Yeager scratched his beard. "That's what I asked him. He said he'd been wrong before and was writing a sequel to tell the truth. The day before he died, he promised to tell me what he'd learned, but he died before he could."

This was the first Harriet had heard about a sequel. "Are you sure about this, Yeager?"

Yeager said, "Absolutely. The week before the professor died, he holed up in his condo and didn't eat or sleep. He was obsessed with finishing that book."

Tate grabbed Elkin's letter off the table. "Maybe that's why this lawyer demanded Lori not remove anything from the condo. Maybe the demand letter has to do with the manuscript."

Harriet remembered the lack of emotion in Sue Ellen's eyes during the moment of silence for the professor at the homeowners' meeting. She wondered about the connection between that lack of emotion and the lawyer's demand letter. But before she could conjure up any theories, Yeager shared more surprising news. "The morning he died, I looked for the manuscript. It was not in his condo. His laptop and Meck Dec books were missing too."

Harriet was even more confused now. "Why would someone take them?"

Yeager didn't have an answer. Nobody else did either.

The missing materials made Harriet curious about how the professor died. "Lori, what did the medical examiner say about the cause of death?"

"Natural causes. They attributed his death to old age, but not before asking me about his state of mind. They were trying to rule out suicide."

"Suicide?" Yeager gripped the table. "The professor would never commit suicide."

"That's what I told them. They said something about his sleeping pills, but after we talked, they came around to natural causes."

Harriet wasn't sure what to think, but she would not be an alarmist. "That's probably it, particularly if he was anxious."

Lori turned to Yeager. "You knew him better than anyone, and he told you about the new book. What would he want us to do about his laptop, books, and papers?"

Yeager didn't hesitate. "The professor was a fighter. If someone stole them, he'd want us to get them back. If he hid them somewhere, he'd want us to find them."

Harriet didn't know how to find the laptop, books, and papers, but she knew one thing that needed to happen if they did. "If we find them, Lori needs to inherit them."

Tate kept one arm around Lori as she repeated the question Travail hadn't answered. "What do you believe, Mr. Travail? Is it possible Lori can claim her inheritance?"

"I don't know. What I do know is that I don't trust Robert Elkin."

Tate followed up. "Will you represent Lori?"

"I should recommend another lawyer. My knowledge of estate law is based on what I learned in law school forty years ago."

"Lori needs a good lawyer like you, Craig Travail. You can beef up on the law, and everyone here will help you with the facts. Lori can tell you what she knows, and Harriet and I will round up some witnesses for you to interview."

Travail leaned away from Yeager before he righted himself and acquiesced. "Lori, Yeager has made it clear to me that I have very little on my schedule. I will be glad to look into this and give you my thoughts, but I have to be honest. I can't make any promises beyond that."

"Thank you," Lori said. "I appreciate your help."

Yeager was more specific. "You da man, Craig Travail."

CHAPTER 13

OF THE TROOPS FOR THE TROOPS

On his return to his cottage after lunch at Harriet's, Travail could think of at least ten reasons he should resist doing anything other than offering Lori Collins some limited, qualified advice with a referral to an experienced trusts and estates lawyer. For one, in his forty years of trial work, he'd never handled a will contest. Second, he was officially retired from the practice of law. He had no law office. No assistants. No one to type for him. No one to file documents for him at the courthouse. No one to mail his letters. No one to assist him at trial. All he had was a spare room in his home that was host to a card table, a folding metal chair, and a stack of boxes.

When Travail got home, he said hello to Blue and went straight to the spare room, where he started unpacking the boxes Angela had delivered to him at his request. He pulled out a book on trial practice and tossed it aside. Next, he found a book on negotiation practice. He already had those skills. He was looking for something else, and after digging around in several boxes, he found it. In his hand he held a three-ring notebook for the practical skills course he took as a young lawyer, the course that covered a wide variety of topics, including wills and estates. He checked the index for the course materials, flipped to the middle, and sat down against the wall to read. It was like going back to law school. Kind of refreshing, actually.

After an hour, he took a break. He put down his homework and went to the kitchen to make a cup of tea. A few minutes later, he sat in his favorite chair with the morning paper he hadn't had time to read, checked the headlines, and sipped away. After skimming through the political mayhem on the national level and after learning about the latest renovation plans for the Charlotte airport and the successes and failures of the Panthers and Hornets, Travail turned to the comics to get a laugh. Then, like 90 percent of newspaper readers his age, he turned to the obituary pages, expecting to see someone he had known. He saw no misfortune for his friends today, but the page reminded him he needed to read the obituary for Matthew Collins. He picked through the newspapers next to the fireplace and found the paper he wanted.

At the top of the obituary page, staring him in the face, was the contemplative mug of the man who might bring him out of retirement. The name under the photograph caught his attention: "Matthew Lori Collins." That was interesting. Lori was a family name. Probably Matthew's mother's maiden name. Even so, the man wanted to cut his namesake out of his will. The obituary took up half the page. Travail took his time.

Matthew Collins was born February 6, 1924, and died November 11, 2020. Travail paid mental tribute to the long and full life. Matthew enlisted in the navy when he became eighteen, a few months after the Japanese bombed Pearl Harbor. He chose the navy because he grew up in Annapolis, Maryland, home to the US Naval Academy. His light skin as a mixed-race African American allowed him to overcome the navy's prejudice against African Americans and find a place supporting the engineering staff of aircraft carriers. He became a hero when he helped save the USS *Bunker Hill* from sinking after two kamikaze planes struck it, and he met a young nurse, who not only treated his injuries but later became his wife. After the war, he used the GI Bill to complete his education at Johnson C. Smith University, a historically black university, in Charlotte where he earned his degree in the humanities. To help pay the rent, he took a job selling encyclopedias. He took those practical skills and combined them with his education to create a magazine for veterans. He told the *New York Times* forty years later that his goal with *The Heroes*, a multiple award-winning publication, was to tell stories about those who didn't make it back.

The middle third of the obituary discussed how the professor built his magazine media empire, formed We Salute You to help veterans, and became an outspoken critic of the military's strategies in Vietnam, for which the Johnson administration branded him a traitor. He also got in trouble for his op-eds on Iran-Contra and the unverified weapons of mass destruction that led to the second Iraq war. The obituary ended with this:

> Matthew was known to many as the professor. For his third act, he taught history at Central Piedmont Community College, and he wrote history books. His most famous book was the *New York Times* bestseller *An American Hoax*. He received accolades for the work, but also criticism within the Charlotte community. In his later years, Matthew Collins became more focused on his research and made few public appearances, but those who knew him well at the Independence Retirement Community knew he was doing what he enjoyed most, reading and writing. As he liked to say, "I don't need anybody's help to do that."

> When Matthew sold his magazine business for sixty million dollars, he donated ten million dollars to We Salute You to help veterans and was a lifelong supporter with annual donations because, as he said, "we must help those who gave so much to protect us." The foundation continues to operate under the excellent leadership of Lori Collins, his granddaughter.

> A memorial service honoring Matthew Collins will be held at the chapel at the Independent Retirement Community. In lieu of flowers, donations may be made to We Salute You.

Travail laid the paper down. The obituary was a nice tribute to a man Travail felt like he never really knew. By the time he met the professor, he was in his early eighties and into his reclusive years. Travail wasn't sure what caused the professor to withdraw from public life, but based on his own recent experience, he figured the loss of the professor's wife, son, and daughter-in-law had something to do with it. Was that where Travail was headed? A life of solitude and sorrow?

Travail wondered who wrote the obituary. He didn't think Lori was the type to compliment herself in her grandfather's obituary. He was sure Yeager didn't write it. Harriet, maybe? She had said nothing about it. Maybe Sue Ellen wrote the obituary. She did sit in the front row at his service, and she was the beneficiary of his will. If she did write it, the piece showed a warmth others said did not appear on her resume and a connection to the professor that everyone disputed.

A knock at the front door broke Travail's concentration, but before Travail could answer, the handle turned and Yeager burst in, carrying three stacked boxes. "Afternoon, Craig Travail."

"Didn't we just see each other at lunch?"

Yeager stepped forward and set the boxes down.

"Come on counselor. We're partners now."

"Partners?"

"Absolutely. You run the legal side. I handle investigations and security."

"You never told me you were an investigator."

"You never asked."

"Were you?"

"Kinda, sorta."

Travail felt himself lose patience. "Why do you think I need security?"

"My gut."

Travail looked at Yeager's waistline. It certainly had plenty of storage capacity. But security? "This is a civil case."

"You never know what fifty million dollars will cause people to do."

The front door opened again. Harriet Keaton stood there, holding two more boxes.

"What's with all the boxes?"

"Hello to you too, Craig. Where's your office?"

"I don't have an office."

Travail followed as Harriet passed his bedroom and found her way to the spare room. When they walked in, Harriet set her boxes down and put her hands on her hips. "I thought so."

"You thought what?"

"This is no way to run a law practice."

"I don't have a law practice."

"Where's all the lawyer stuff?" Yeager asked.

"I'm still unpacking."

"I can see that," Harriet said. "We're here to help."

"Look, I don't mean to sound ungrateful, but I need to do this on my own."

Yeager spoke to Harriet. "He doesn't think I can help either."

Harriet launched into an explanation of her qualifications in a tone that made Travail take a step back. By the time she finished, he'd learned enough about her not to ask questions. She had served on and chaired the boards of four local nonprofits and managed the office and books of the construction firm she and her husband ran that employed over two hundred people. The company was highly successful, but because of the "ineptitude of men," as Harriet put it, the company got into legal trouble. When the company was about to fold, she stepped in to deal successfully with the lawyers and the lawsuits. Her husband had passed away, and it became her business to protect. When she finished summing up her credentials, she sought no praise or feedback. "A simple thank you for our help would be sufficient."

Travail thanked her but said he didn't need help because he wasn't setting up a law office. All he was going to do was talk with Lori and give her some free legal advice.

"You're going to need us," Yeager said, as if he were reading Travail's mind.

Harriet agreed. "If this were some run-of-the-mill case you were handling for a rich client at six hundred fifty dollars an hour, I'd let you tackle it yourself and have fun watching you try to make your own copies, organize yourself, and get to court with everything you needed. But this is about Lori. I can't let you make a fool of yourself."

"That's kind of you." He wondered if Harriet detected his sarcasm. She gave him a sharp glance but turned back to her work. He said nothing more. He figured he'd be better off having Harriet's help than arguing with her about it. But Yeager? He looked at his rough-hewn neighbor with trepidation at the idea of having him constantly at his side.

Harriet must have sensed his concern. "Yeager's the real deal," she said. "Eccentric, but you'll be glad to have his help."

"Thank you, Harriet." Yeager gave a little bow.

"Tell him your title," Harriet said.

"Military Occupational Specialist 31B."

"In English."

"I was an MP in the army for a few years. Served at home and abroad."

"Tell him the motto."

"Of the troops, for the troops."

"We're in the same troop," Harriet said to Travail. "Besides, we're bored with retirement. You can't have all the fun."

"But an MP is like a police officer. I don't need a police officer."

Travail waited for the comeback, but all he got was Harriet barking directions to Yeager and then to him. He decided to follow his new office manager's instructions.

PART II

THE INVESTIGATION

CHAPTER 14

GOSSIP IS THE KEY

Yeager and Harriet had a game plan for the morning. While Travail met with Lori, they would do some digging of their own.

Yeager's first stop was the Indie's business office. He waved his way past the receptionist, who could not stop him because she was on a call. The door to the bookkeeper's office was open a crack. He nudged it open further and stuck his head in.

"Hello, Jenny," Yeager crooned. Jenny Montgomery was a tall woman, at six feet four, with an even taller opinion of herself. She ran a tight set of books.

"A bit early for paying your bill, aren't you? Thirty days late is more your style."

"Not here on business. At least not my business."

"Have a seat and make it quick."

After Yeager explained what he needed, she said, "Have you lost what few brain cells you had in your head?" She was not, under any circumstances, going to show him Matthew Collins's payment records and contracts with the Indie.

"I'm helping Lori."

"Helping her do what?"

"I see you haven't heard." Yeager pulled his chair close and lowered his voice. He told her about the will and how he, Harriet, and Craig Travail were going to help Lori challenge it.

"I don't believe it. Matthew would never do that to Lori."

Yeager knew Jenny had met Lori when Matthew moved in, and whenever Lori had questions or concerns about her grandfather, she called Jenny for help or consolation. Jenny liked her.

Jenny leaned back in her chair. "Even if I could give you access to the records—which I can't by law—what exactly is it you think you will find that will help Lori?"

"I'm just searching for the truth. Something that might explain why a man who loved his granddaughter as much as the professor did would give all his life's possessions to Sue Ellen Parker instead."

Jenny walked to a file cabinet, opened a drawer, and found the file. She took her seat and dropped the file on her desk. Before opening it, she made things clear. "I can't let you see this."

Yeager sensed an opening. "If you can't let me see it, look yourself."

"And what am I looking for?"

"Anything unusual."

Yeager watched Jenny thumb through the file. "Hmm," she said.

"Hmm what?"

"This is odd. Hold on." Jenny pulled a sticky note from the file and carried it with her as she left the room. Yeager stuck his head near the door and listened to her conversation with the receptionist.

"When did Matthew call about this?" he heard Jenny say to the receptionist. He couldn't hear what the receptionist said, but Jenny's voice was loud. "Why didn't you tell me?"

When Jenny returned to the room, Yeager sensed that the "unusual" he had been looking for had surfaced.

"Well?"

Jenny stuck the note in Yeager's palm. It read, "Matthew Collins called and asked about the policy on subleasing his unit. He plans to move in with Sue Ellen Parker."

Yeager pulled on his beard as he looked at the sticky note. "When did he call?"

"The day before he died."

~

Meanwhile, Harriet visited the Indie gossip queen. Carrie Roberts answered her door in her bathrobe with a big "hello there" and "come on in." Carrie was eighty-eight, still mobile and with her mental faculties fully intact, but she got a slow start every day. More of a night person. Best time to gather information, she once told Harriet.

Carrie was the kind of resident who voiced her opinions freely, Facebook and Twitter style, although she didn't know how to use either, and she liked to know everyone's business. Yeager once said to Harriet that if Carrie wanted to go into the blackmail business, she'd make a fortune, but then lose it all because she couldn't keep her mouth shut after getting paid. Harriet knew Carrie Roberts was a good place to start her investigation.

"Can I offer you some coffee?"

"That would be nice."

"Come in the kitchen and have a seat while I fix you up."

Carrie poured the coffee and handed Harriet her cup before she sat down at the kitchen table with her. "So to what do I owe the pleasure of this visit?"

Harriet decided the straightforward method might yield the best results. "Information about some residents."

"Well, well. Harriet Keaton. Never took you for a gossip."

Before Harriet could respond, she heard loud scratching and barking at the back door.

Carrie yelled, "Hold your horses, Sport," and leaned over far enough to turn the knob to let the seventy-five-pound golden retriever into the room. Sport looked first to Carrie for some love and then made straight for Harriet. He jumped and landed both front paws in her lap.

"Don't mind him," Carrie said. "Just shake his hand, and he'll be your new best friend."

Harriet wasn't looking for a new best friend, but she shook one paw and used her knee to slide Sport to her side where she placed her free hand on his head to keep him down.

"I'm not a gossip," Harriet said. "I'm doing some research on an important matter." Sport must have understood. He licked her elbow.

Carrie laughed. "At the Indie, there's no difference between gossip and research."

Harriet knew this was true but chose not to admit it.

"It wouldn't have to do with that new man on campus, the lawyer, would it? I've seen you hanging around with him. Are you sweet on him, Harriet?"

"Heavens, no." Harriet drew in a deep breath, pulled her hand from Sport's head, and placed it in her lap. "I am helping him with a case, however."

"I see." Carrie's smile raised her cheeks to a prominent level.

"Honestly, Carrie, you think everyone's sleeping with everyone around here."

Sport nudged Harriet's knee again with his nose, and Carrie yelled, "Come, Sport." She got up, pulled out a few bacon pieces from the refrigerator, and tossed them on the floor. Sport left Harriet and pounced on the bacon. He stayed busy licking a square foot of bacon-scented linoleum.

"You see the books on those shelves?" Carrie pointed to her den. "All romance novels. Can't get enough." She told Harriet how she just finished one, about two men and a woman. She eyed Harriet with a sparkle in her eye and a grin on her face. "Yeager's on this little case too, isn't he?"

"Oh, come on." Harriet flushed. "I don't have enough time or interest for one man in my bed, much less two. And it certainly wouldn't be Yeager. Maybe if he was the last male standing and the species needed a boost. But even then, I'd have to think hard about it."

"Some say three's a crowd, but not the author of that book I just finished."

Harriet realized her decision to visit Carrie Roberts had offered Carrie an idea for her lunchtime press release about how Harriet was having a tryst with Craig and Yeager. If that was the ridiculous rumor to come from this meeting, she would darn well get the information she came to collect.

"Say what you will about me, Carrie, but do me a favor in return, please."

"At your service, dear."

"I would like to know everything you can tell me about Matthew Collins and Sue Ellen Parker."

Carrie lifted her nose and sniffed. And then Harriet smelled the smoke.

"Dammit," Carrie said. "I knew I forgot something. Gossiping and cooking don't go well together."

Carrie jumped up from her seat and pulled a tin of blackened biscuits from the oven. She waved a dish towel at the smoke, but the smoke alarm went off anyway, which caused Sport to bark. The barking and beeping continued long enough for the maintenance truck to arrive and silence them both. Eddie Ledbetter, the Indie's steady handyman, knew Sport and Sport him, so when Eddie walked in the door, Sport shifted his attention to Eddie's loving head rub. Thirty seconds later, Eddie had the smoke alarm on silent.

"You're a hero, Eddie," Carrie said. "Cup of coffee?"

"You make a good cup, Ms. Roberts, and it is cold out. If it's not too much trouble?"

"Not at all. Harriet and I were just about to solve a domestic problem. You can join us."

Harriet's face reddened. So much for her effort to be discreet with the investigation.

Carrie scraped the black off the biscuits and put them on a platter with some strawberry jelly. She handed Eddie his cup, refilled Harriet's mug, and motioned everyone to the den.

Carrie spoke first. "Eddie, we were just about to talk about Matthew Collins and Sue Ellen Parker. You service their units, don't you?"

Eddie ran his hand through his hair. "What's this about, if you don't mind me asking?"

Carrie pointed to Harriet with her half-eaten biscuit. "Harriet wants to know if they were doing the dirty deed."

"What?" Harriet blushed. "That's not—"

"Now, now, Harriet. You want to know if they were a clandestine couple, don't you?"

Harriet looked at Eddie. "I'm not gossiping, Eddie. There is an important reason for my question."

"I believe you." Eddie's squinted eyes said otherwise.

"Anything you can tell us would be helpful," Carrie said.

"I hate to talk bad about the dead. I liked the professor. I was sad he died."

Harriet put her cup down and leaned forward. "What could you possibly say about the professor that was bad?"

Carrie put her hand up. "If you don't want to talk about it, Eddie, we won't push you."

Harriet smiled to herself. She knew this was Carrie's technique to get someone to do the opposite. Eddie cooperated.

"I saw them together several times during the week the professor died, but never holding hands or kissing or anything like that. It was more like they were doing business together. They were serious." Eddie paused. "The morning before the professor died, I was fixing the thermostat in the professor's unit, and Sue Ellen was there. I heard her question him, like she wasn't happy."

"What did she say?" Harriet asked.

"Something about having second thoughts. She said it was a damn fool idea."

"What did the professor say?"

"He didn't agree. He said it was their best option." Eddie placed his coffee mug down. "I really got to get going. Thank you for the coffee, Ms. Roberts. Good to see you, Ms. Keaton."

When the door shut, Carrie said, "And that's not all."

"You know more?"

"You wouldn't treat me like the Queen of Gossip that I am if I didn't have a little nugget for you, now would you, dear?"

Harriet smiled. "Of course not."

"My sources tell me the professor and Sue Ellen met regularly for the past two months. Sometimes at her place. Sometimes at his."

"Any overnight visits?"

"Not clear, but I'll dig around some more," Carrie said. "Hope that helps."

"It does."

The Queen of Gossip smiled. "Now tell me about you and this lawyer fella."

"Really, Carrie!"

CHAPTER 15

THREE CASES FOR THE PRICE OF ONE

Lori showed up early for her meeting with Craig Travail but parked in front of her grandfather's building by habit. When she realized her mistake, she decided the walk to Travail's cottage would do her good. It might clear her mind. She zipped her fleece-lined coat to the top and pulled on a knit hat and gloves.

The day was bright but cold. An archway led under the building to the lake side. Once through it, she turned and looked up. She'd never paid much attention to the building itself. Tan stucco with white wood trim. Pitched roof with black shingles. Slat blinds in the windows. Her grandfather's great room window was the largest in the building. Someone had closed the blinds and shut the world out. There was nothing inside now but shadows of the past.

Lori picked up the gravel path to Travail's cottage. She'd walked the trail many times with the professor—even she used his nickname— but always in the warm months. With winter hanging on, the tree-lined trail looked the way she felt. Naked. In her mind, she knew her life would go on, just as the leaf canopy would be back with the spring, but in her heart, the leafless sticks of timber were a bleak reminder that someone important was missing from her life.

The professor had always supported Lori. He'd given her shelter as a child, tucked her in at night, and told her stories about faraway places to take her mind off the loss of her parents. He introduced her to fiction and nonfiction books with heroines who fought for their beliefs, and he encouraged her to write her own stories. When she won her first writing contest as a high school senior—a short story told in first person about a young activist who was expelled from high school and shunned by the male population for protesting the administration's refusal to investigate sexual misconduct toward women—he framed the award certificate. And whenever she was home from college—he paid for her college too—and she sulked about the lack of progress for women in a world she said men thought they owned, he reminded her of the heroine in her award-winning high school short story. He said, "Never back down from a righteous fight. Stand your ground, and you won't regret it."

He'd fought such fights many times with his criticism of military policy. Politicians attacked him and called him un-American, but they had short memories and no understanding of what it meant to serve in the military. The professor did, and he told them, no matter the push-back. He didn't run from criticism in the academic world either. He wrote articles about the Jim Crow South. He wrote about the deed restrictions preventing blacks from owning property in exclusive Charlotte neighborhoods like Myers Park, and about the bulldozing of historic black neighborhoods like Brooklyn in the early sixties. The white developers said he stood in the way of progress, the need to rid the city of crime and blight. She loved his retort, how one man's blight was another man's home.

All of these memories made it confounding that the professor cut her out of his will and wanted her to give up on her book. She loved to write. And he knew it. He also knew that a challenge motivated her. When someone told her she couldn't do something, she worked even harder to prove them wrong. If someone took something away from her that was hers, she fought to get it back. The professor knew this about her. Heck, he'd instilled it in her. Is that what was going on with the will? Was the professor telling her to defy him? Was his message coded? He'd pushed her in the past, but he'd always been clear about

85

his intentions. There was nothing clear about the handwritten will and his demands about her book.

Memories of the Meck Dec were in the air as she walked toward Travail's cottage. Her grandfather's interest with the Meck Dec began when he got it into his head that the locals copied the lines for their fictitious Meck Dec from Jefferson's Declaration of Independence and not the other way around. Not that he cared much for Jefferson. He believed Jefferson should have recognized Sally Hemmings, done more than he did for her and their children. He also knew the Declaration of Independence did not mean independence for everyone, and yet, he saw hope in the ideas inherent in the Declaration of Independence. He didn't want these ideas of independence and equality sullied by a plagiarism smudge against Jefferson, so he threw himself into the work that became *An American Hoax.*

Though he received praise nationally, locals with a patriotic bent criticized him for being too close-minded in his conclusions about Charlotte history and too harsh in the way he presented them. He called them Meck Dec fanatics, and said that unlike them, he had not drunk the Meck Dec Kool-Aid. The controversy consumed the last fifteen years of his life.

Lori saw Travail waiting for her on his front porch. He held two cups of coffee with his front door open and Blue by his side, wagging his tail.

"I saw you coming down the trail. You might need this to warm up." He handed her the steaming cup.

Lori thanked him, leaned down, and patted Blue on the head. She followed the dog and his master into the den. She removed her coat, hat, and gloves and settled into one of two club chairs, the only furniture in sight other than the small table between the two chairs and the sofa turned backwards against the front window.

"Sorry about the furniture situation. I haven't gotten around to arranging things." Travail took the other club chair, and Blue settled with his back to the warm blaze in the fireplace.

"How are you doing?" Travail asked.

"Sad and depressed."

"That's understandable."

"And still confused about why he did it."

Travail traded his coffee cup for a legal pad that lay on the table between them. "How close were you and your grandfather?"

Lori looked down at the cup in her hands. "To your question, I thought we were close," with emphasis on the word "thought." She shared examples of how he'd cared for and supported her throughout her life and how it was so different from the actions of the man who wrote the handwritten will.

"How did he make his fortune?"

"Most of his money came from the magazine business. When *An American Hoax* was published, he made decent royalties. And then there was the money from the defamation lawsuit. But you know about that."

"Did he have any enemies?"

This was an odd question. "What would enemies have to do with the will?"

"It relates to whether the professor was under duress to make his will."

"You think one of his enemies may have coerced him to give his money to Sue Ellen Parker?"

"I don't know. I'm just exploring all the possibilities."

Lori set her coffee mug on the table. "As a matter of fact, the professor had many enemies. During the years he ran the magazine and the nonprofit, most of his enemies were military brass and bureaucrats in Washington, DC. Since writing *An American Hoax,* his enemies expanded to include local history nerds. I can't see how him giving his money to Sue Ellen Parker benefits either set of enemies."

Travail made a note. "What about Sue Ellen Parker?"

"What about her?"

"Do you think she was an enemy?"

"I thought they were nothing more than acquaintances living in the same retirement community."

"Did they spend any time together before he died?"

"Not that I know of." She was determined not to cry.

Travail shifted in his seat before his next question. "I hate to ask these next questions, but they focus on the crux of the case."

"You mean why he would cut me out of the will?" Lori sounded harsh, even to herself.

"Yes."

She tried to gain control of her emotions and think logically about the issue. "I've thought about that a lot after our lunch at Harriet's, and I really don't have a clue."

"You said he didn't react well when you mentioned writing a novel set in Charlotte in 1775."

"Do you know much about the Meck Dec, Mr. Travail?"

"Call me Craig."

She smiled. "It is one of the great mysteries in American history, Craig."

Travail set his pad down and picked up his coffee. "It's odd. I've worked in Charlotte my entire adult life and my children attended public schools here. Except for when I represented the professor, I never heard my wife, children, friends, or anyone at work mention the Meck Dec. Harriet said they don't teach it in schools here."

"That's true. The professor would have been furious if they did." Lori pictured in her mind how the professor explained *An American Hoax* to people in the simplest terms. "The crux of the controversy is pretty simple, really. It boils down to a document called the Mecklenburg Resolves."

Travail paused. "It's been awhile, but I remember the Mecklenburg Resolves was important to the professor's conclusion that the Meck Dec was a fabrication."

"It was very important." Lori's grandfather had told the story so many times, she had it memorized.

"In the first quarter of the 1800s, the Meck Dec was a matter of pride for the people of Mecklenburg County and North Carolina, but most everyone else, including Thomas Jefferson, thought the locals were making the whole thing up. The controversy between the Virginians and the North Carolinians grew to a bursting point around 1830. John Adams supported the North Carolina cause in his writings.

Thomas Jefferson fired back. He mocked John McKnitt Alexander and the North Carolina delegates to the Continental Congress and called the Meck Dec 'spurious.' This led to a full-blown investigation, eyewitness testimony, and the release of an 1831 report by the North Carolina governor with the legislature's support."

"And the report said?"

"The Meck Dec existed and it declared independence from England on May 20, 1775. For a few years, the report resolved the dispute in favor of the Meck Dec."

"Until?"

"Until a historian named Peter Force made a discovery in 1838."

"He found the Mecklenburg Resolves?"

"Yes. He discovered four resolutions were published in a Massachusetts paper in July 1775, supposedly written by a committee in Charlotte-Town, Mecklenburg County, on May 31, 1775. Collectively, they became known as the Mecklenburg Resolves, and while they were treasonous against the king's authority, they did not include the single word any good declaration of independence must include. They did not declare 'independence.'"

"That's why the professor and other historians said the Mecklenburg Resolves—which was not a declaration of independence, per se— told the one and only story about what happened in May of 1775?"

"Precisely. Which began the debate that continues to this day. Did one or two documents come out of that meeting? And if there were two, did one declare independence and did the other set up a provisional government with a more detailed set of resolutions?"

Travail asked if she would like some more coffee. Lori declined. A maintenance truck backfired as it rumbled past the cottage.

Lori continued with the Meck Dec story. "The reason it is such a great mystery is nobody has ever proved definitively whether the document—the elusive Mecklenburg Declaration of Independence—did or did not exist. There is plenty of evidence that it did."

"And according to the professor, much evidence that it didn't."

"Exactly."

Travail's mobile phone interrupted the conversation. He eyed the incoming number and, after the fifth ring, said, "Excuse me," and answered.

Lori could hear Yeager's energetic voice. Travail said, "That's interesting," clicked off, and returned his attention to Lori.

"Is he your new paralegal?" She was amused by the thought.

"He thinks he is my investigator and protector. Harriet has assumed every other role."

"What did he find out?"

"He says the professor planned to move in with Sue Ellen Parker."

"Again, news to me." It seemed she didn't know as much about her grandfather as she thought she did. It hurt.

Travail made another note. "Let's get back to the important question."

"Whether the Meck Dec was a real historical document?"

Travail frowned. "No, the reason the professor cut you out of his will. Tell me again about the tension between you and the professor before he died."

"As I told you at lunch, he reacted poorly to my news that I was going to write a novel set in Charlotte in 1775."

Travail's mobile phone rang again. He glanced at the phone, said "I'm sorry," and answered. Travail nodded a few times, said, "Thank you, Harriet," and ended the call. He made another note.

"More news?"

"It seems your grandfather and Sue Ellen were together quite a bit the last few months."

"And it seems you have an attentive staff."

"I don't have a staff or a law practice."

"Does that mean you won't represent me?"

Travail put the phone down on his legal pad, crossed his legs, and leaned back in his chair. "Without a law firm to call home, I'm not that comfortable going to court, and given my recent losing streak, you may not want me to represent you."

"I'm not sure about a lawsuit, anyway. I'm not that big a fan of lawyers. No offense."

"None taken. You have time to make that decision, and it's a good idea to investigate further before you do." He returned to the issue at hand. "You said you and the professor argued."

"Yes. He was dictatorial, so unlike him. When I told him my book would be historical romance and would only touch lightly on the Meck Dec, he forbade me to write the book. I lost my temper and hung up." Lori couldn't help herself as a tear escaped. Travail paused and gave her a moment before he continued.

"Why do you think he cared about you writing a book set in that time period?"

Lori gave a nervous laugh. "If you can solve that mystery, you can probably crack the mystery of the Meck Dec itself."

Travail had a blank face that said he didn't want to tackle either mystery, so Lori reached in her bag and pulled out two books. "These are for you." She handed him *An American Hoax* and one other book about the Meck Dec. "I know it's probably been a while since you read *An American Hoax*, but it could come in handy."

"And this other one?"

"It's a book by a local author laying out the arguments on both sides and making a persuasive case for the Meck Dec."

Travail studied the covers of both books.

Lori softened her tone. "I'm sorry about your wife and your job."

"Thank you."

"How are you doing?"

"Well, let's see." Travail dropped his hand beside the chair and placed it on Blue's head. As he stroked, he lamented. "I am alone in a community where I don't fit in, and I'm considering whether to take on another case I probably can't win. I'd say things are status quo." An awkward silence followed.

Lori decided she should let him off the hook. She gathered her coat, hat, and gloves and walked with Travail and Blue to the front door. "Thanks for seeing me. Walk me to my car?"

Travail told Blue to stay put, shut the door behind them, and walked with her up the path.

"There is one other thing I wanted to tell you. Do you know Congressman Walter Butterworth?" she asked.

Travail said he was familiar with the name but knew little about him, so Lori continued. "He's a Virginia congressman and a congressional committee chairman with considerable power over what contracts they award to defense contractors. These are the same contractors whose political action committees donated ten times more to his last four campaigns than to any other sitting congressman. I took him to task in a series of articles on We Salute You's blog that received national attention. I got a little aggressive, comparing the campaign money to bribes and saying he cared more about lining his pockets from weapon manufacturers than helping veterans."

"What did the professor think about your articles?"

"He loved them, but Butterworth didn't. He hired a lawyer who sent me a demand letter. I didn't pay attention to the lawyer's name until I read the letter again this morning."

She stopped walking and pulled the letter from her bag. She handed it to Travail. He took his time reading it.

"Let me get this straight. One month before the professor died, Robert Elkin sent you a demand letter threatening a libel lawsuit for fifteen million dollars if you continued to write articles about Congressman Butterworth?"

"Yes. But that's not all." She took out another letter and handed it to him. "The same day the demand letter arrived, the IRS sent me this formal notice of investigation into We Salute You's nonprofit status for allegedly being too political for a nonprofit."

Neither spoke for a moment. Lori heard a dog bark. She saw the sun glint off the lake down the hill. She waited for Travail to speak.

"I don't like the fact that Robert Elkin is a common denominator here. He's representing Sue Ellen and the congressman, and most likely, he's involved in the government investigation."

After they resumed their walk, Lori thought back to her investigation into Congressman Butterworth's fundraising activities. One government contractor's name kept popping up. What was it? Vibrant? Veritech? No, now she remembered.

"Have you ever heard the name Viribus?"

"What?"

"Viribus. I suspected there might be some irregularities between the congressman and that company, but before I could dig deeper, I got the letters and the wedding came along, followed by the professor's death."

Travail appeared vexed by her mention of the contractor. "Could you pull your notes on Viribus for me? They might be important."

When they arrived at Lori's car, Travail had one last question. "Can you think of anything else unusual that has occurred in the last three months?"

She laughed. "You mean other than the fact my grandfather cut me out of his will and gave all his money to a woman who is represented by your former boss, the same man who threatened to sue me for libel and who may be connected to the government investigation to shut down We Salute You?" The rhetorical question hung in the air like the clouds above.

Travail didn't reply. He appeared less lawyer-like and more personable in the open air. He asked one last question. "Have you spoken with a lawyer about Elkin's libel letter or the government notice?"

"Other than you, no."

"If Elkin contacts you again, or if you hear something from the government, please let me know."

Lori lightened the mood. "Are you trying to triple your case load, Mr. Travail?"

"As I said, please call me Craig."

CHAPTER 16

THE INDIE WITNESS PARADE

Travail and Blue returned to their cottage from an early morning walk around Lost Cove Lake. They managed to avoid Yeager on the walk, though they got a glimpse of him traipsing through the woods. Travail took a shower and let the hot water beat on his head. As he got out, he heard his phone ring. He grabbed a towel, tied it around his waist, and answered.

"Are you ready?" It was Harriet's purposeful voice.

"Only if you want me to do interviews wet and naked."

"Don't flatter yourself, Craig."

Before he could answer, she clicked off. He tossed the phone on his bed.

Travail poured coffee and made toast before he stepped into the extra bedroom. Harriet, with Yeager's muscle, had turned the room into a working office in less than twenty-four hours, with a desk, two book-shelves, and a desk chair Harriet had in storage. It had belonged to her late husband. They filled the shelves with Travail's law books, cleaned the room, and hung his diplomas.

He didn't care for practicing law out of his house, if that was what he was going to be doing, but the organization comforted him. A neat desktop stared back at him, with pencils and pens in a cup that read "Moot Points." Next to it was a stack of legal pads. His laptop was open in the middle of the desk. Harriet must have sensed his fastidious nature. She also made him feel at home with the five-by-seven picture of Rachael smiling at him on his new desk. Two eight-by-tens on the wall showed trips he'd made with his two children, one with his son on a golf trip to Scotland and one with his daughter on a trip to Italy. These were the only family pictures he displayed in his office at the law firm.

The front door opened, and Travail heard something scraping against the walls in his hallway. He poked his head from his office to see Yeager carrying two wooden captain's chairs. "Harriet had me pick these up. Cushions are in my trunk."

"Don't you ever knock?"

Yeager's response focused on Travail's outfit. "Is this what casual Friday looks like to you?" Yeager laughed at his own joke.

Travail looked down at himself. He wore slacks, a white button down, and a burgundy tie. Seemed right to him.

Yeager positioned the captain's chairs before the desk. "I need your opinion, Craig Travail." He turned and walked back down the hall without explaining.

Travail followed but stopped at the open front door where he saw Yeager pull several items from his trunk, two cushions with one hand and a sign with the other.

He held up the sign and smiled. "Where do you want it? At the front door, or out here close to the street?" The sign read, "Craig Travail, Indie Lawyer."

"I don't need a sign. Especially one like that."

"Got it. Close to the street it is."

Travail heard the humming sound of a distant lawnmower. He looked in the direction of the sound and saw a woman in a motorized wheelchair, instead. She was a hundred yards away and headed toward them at a fast clip, churning up gravel on the path. Yeager waved at her.

"Who is that?"

"Your first interview. Time you assumed the lawyerly position. I'll show NASCAR Nelli to your office."

"NASCAR?"

"Yep. Five-time winner of the Indie's annual Lap the Lakes races, motorized division."

Travail shook his head and returned to his office, where a few minutes later, Yeager pushed his first witness into Travail's new law office. "Didn't want Nelli to bang up your walls, so she let me pilot."

Yeager kicked one captain's chair to the side and rolled Nelli's wheelchair into the empty spot. Her round torso was a tight squeeze for the wheelchair's seat. A Carolina Panthers blanket covered her presumably frail legs. Her round head sprouted short grey hair, with a part in the middle. She pulled a yellow scarf used as a bandana down from in front of her mouth and lifted round plastic goggles from her eyes. She hit a lever on her chair with her left hand that turned her in Travail's direction.

"Name's Nelli." She stuck her right hand out and gave Travail a firm shake.

"Craig Travail."

"I know. Yeager told me all about you."

Travail took his seat behind the desk. "Yeager says you have some information for me."

"Not so quick, esquire," Nelli said. "Yeager said if I give you the information you need, you will help me with my case."

Travail looked at Yeager for an explanation.

"NASCAR Nelli is the victim of an orchestrated plan by Sue Ellen Parker and her followers to strip her of her motorized rights."

"That's the God-awful truth," Nelli said.

Travail doodled on the legal pad in front of him and sighed. NASCAR Nelli had a bias against the beneficiary. She was a questionable witness before sharing a single fact about the case.

"They say she drives too fast on the property," Yeager said. "And that she runs over people."

"That's the conspiracy part," Nelli added. "The old women around here keep stepping in my way, knowing if I knock them on their butts

—which I do from time to time because they are so freaking slow getting out of the way—it will look bad for me."

Travail had a couple of quick thoughts about Nelli's case. Number one, NASCAR Nelli was not a positive nickname for a resident charged with reckless driving. Number two, although there was a defense in the vehicular negligence world known as last clear chance—used by motorists when their victims have the last clear opportunity to avoid injury—an operator complaining that the victims she runs over are known to be too slow to get out of the way is not what the courts had in mind with the doctrine. Sue Ellen and her crew had good grounds to complain.

"They want me moving this wheelchair with my hands. Makes no sense. Just because I'm eighty-five years old doesn't mean I can't run over them with my arms too, which is what I plan to do if they take away my motor."

"Don't worry," Yeager said to Nelli. "Craig Travail can help you out. He's a great lawyer."

Travail thought back to his decision to move into the Indie. A house in the woods. Two lakes. Square meals. Health care. A little exercise. Time to think. He didn't recall NASCAR Nelli being on the list.

"Did you ever see those Tom Cruise movies?" Nelli asked. "*Top Gun* and *Days of Thunder*?" Travail didn't answer. "What about Nicolas Cage in *Gone in 60 Seconds*?"

Travail made a note on his legal pad that said, "Don't let NASCAR Nelli open her mouth in her own defense."

"Will you take my case?" Nelli asked.

"I will talk to management about your...situation," Travail said. "But you have to promise to drive at a safe speed and stop running over old women."

"Even Sue Ellen Parker?"

"Especially her."

"She can do that," Yeager said, smiling at Nelli. "Can't you?"

"Sure. Unless Sue Ellen is just a little careless." Nelli had a glint in her eyes.

With the deal struck, Travail asked Nelli what she knew about the professor and Sue Ellen.

"You want the short or the long version?"

"Let's start with the short version."

"Sue Ellen was after the professor's money."

"Why do you say that?"

"Her Mini-Me has a big mouth."

"Are you talking about Becky Trainer, the homeowners' association chair?"

"That's the one. Overheard her saying how ungrateful the professor was for not taking Sue Ellen up on her offer to be his power of attorney. Said he definitely needed her help."

"Did she say what kind of help the professor needed?"

"Said he was losing touch with reality."

"How so?"

"Forgetfulness, for one. Paranoia, for another. That kind of thing."

"What did you think?"

"Hell, everyone around here is forgetful. I'd be paranoid too, if Sue Ellen was after my money. And this place is not exactly a poster of reality."

Travail didn't think this interview was going to help much. "Anything else?"

Nelli looked insulted by his tone. "Yep. A few days before he died, I was motoring down the hall on the professor's floor looking for someone to scare when I heard them arguing. Naturally, I slowed down so the sound of my motor wouldn't bother them, and when I did, I heard Sue Ellen tell the professor to give her everything he owned."

"What did she say exactly?"

Nelli took the goggles off her head and polished them with her shirt sleeve as she appeared to ponder the question. "She said, 'Fine, give me all your money.'"

"She said 'fine'?"

"Yep, she was fine with it."

Travail didn't think her words sounded so much like a demand as acquiescence. Nelli recalled the professor's response because he was so emphatic. He said, "I can't think of any other way."

"Did you hear anything that would explain his comment?"

"Sue Ellen saw me and shut the door and that was that."

Travail and Yeager thanked Nelli and escorted her out the front door. She positioned her scarf over her mouth, tightened it in the back, and pulled her goggles down over her eyes. She reminded Travail of his promise to end the Sue Ellen conspiracy against her just before she hit full forward on the power box. The chair's front wheels raised up as the back wheels propelled her forward. During her wheelie, she threw her hand in the air, like she was riding a bull. When the four wheels touched ground, she shot up the gravel path and beyond their sight.

"Yeager, you might want to monkey with the governor on Nelli's wheelchair or her driving privileges might end within the week."

Yeager put his hand on Travail's shoulder as he admired the dust cloud. "She won't let me near her motor, Craig Travail, but you have to admit, she's going to be a great witness."

"I don't think you understand the concept of admissible evidence."

"It's simple," Yeager said. "Sue Ellen was trying to get control of the professor's money."

Travail wasn't convinced. His thoughts shifted to Nellie's statements about forgetfulness and paranoia. "Was he in good health?"

"He saw a doctor about something from time to time, but any man ninety-six years old should see a doctor about something."

"Try to find out his doctor's name."

"Will do."

Yeager had another question. "What do you think the professor meant when he said he couldn't think of any other way?"

"It suggests something planned, not something under duress, threat, or disorientation."

"You mean the professor and Sue Ellen cooked this whole thing up?"

"It's possible, but if that's the case, it means he intended to change his will, and that's not good for Lori, nor does it make any sense. It would mean the professor created a plan that would deprive his granddaughter and We Salute You of financial security and give the money to Sue Ellen, resulting in a substantial estate tax payment to a government unwilling to spend it the way the professor wanted it to be spent."

"Maybe Sue Ellen undressed him, as you say."

"The word is 'duress.'"

"You're the lawyer, Craig Travail."

This didn't feel much like lawyering to Travail, but the sooner they got on with this, the sooner he could put this chapter of his life behind him and get back to reading his legal thriller.

"Who's next?"

"Maximiliano Esposito. Everyone calls him the Godfather."

The Godfather looked as if he had come from an important business meeting. He wore black slacks, a crisp white shirt with a red tie, and a well-fitted blue blazer with a soft check pattern. The lapel on his blazer held a white rose.

When he arrived, Yeager gave him a cheek-to-cheek embrace reminiscent of the wedding scene in *The Godfather,* where the guests paid their respects to Vito Corleone in his dark private office.

Maximiliano Esposito extended his hand to Travail. "Please call me Max." He had a deep voice, one that ebbed and flowed with confidence. Travail guessed him to be in his late eighties.

With everyone seated in Travail's office, Travail thanked Esposito for taking the time to speak with them.

"Not at all," Esposito said. "Yeager told me it was important, and it involves the professor. I always liked the professor. Man of his word. Plus, you being a lawyer, you may help me someday."

Travail wondered what favor he'd have to return for the Indie's version of Vito Corleone when the time came. It made Travail a little nervous, but he brushed the feeling aside. Surely no man with mafioso power would live at the Indie.

"Tell Craig Travail why you chose the Indie," Yeager said to Esposito.

"You mean, tell him how an Italian immigrant who spent his business career in New York City ended up in a retirement community in Charlotte, North Carolina?"

Travail's brain jumped to the theory Esposito was in witness protection. If so, the feds chose well, because nobody would ever find Esposito here. It was like being on a remote planet in a distant solar system.

"Let's just say a friend of a friend recommended the place." Esposito straightened the knot of his tie.

Travail left it at that. If Maximiliano Esposito wanted to tell him more, he would do it in his own time.

Esposito got right to the point. "This case involves illegal activity. I can smell it." He put his right forefinger to his nose.

Travail couldn't help but be intrigued by the comment and the gesture. "How long did you know the professor?"

"Twenty years. We were two of the original residents, had a lot in common, and did favors for one another. He helped me out when…" Esposito's voice trailed off, and he smiled. "Let's just say the professor always placed family first."

"Apparently not this time." Travail was focused on the handwritten will.

"Like I said." Esposito opened his hands as if the answer were criminally self-evident.

Yeager picked up the trail. "So you think someone committed a crime?"

"I think the crime is ongoing." Esposito crossed his legs and adjusted the white rose in his lapel, before he added the clincher. "If the professor wrote the will, it meant the professor had a good reason for giving his money to Sue Ellen Parker. He was not a man to be intimidated."

Travail was stumped. If Esposito was right, they were back to the fact the professor planned the handwritten will. That didn't help them prove, either logically or legally, any of the potential claims for overturning the will. And it didn't explain how a crime had been committed. "What about his recent state of mind?"

Esposito contradicted what Nelli had heard from Sue Ellen's minion. "His memory was fine, he wasn't crazy, and he certainly wouldn't let Sue Ellen Parker tell him what to do."

Travail ticked off in his brain the various ways he could challenge the will, and how Esposito, with the certainty of a man who knew where all the bodies were buried, had torpedoed them. If the professor wasn't incompetent, if he didn't sign the will under threat or duress, if he made the will with his signature, and if he meant to do what he did, there was no way to contest the will.

"I sense I am not helping your case."

"That's okay. We're looking for the truth. We appreciate your help. But—"

Esposito laughed. "You want to know about the ongoing crime."

"It would help."

Esposito pointed to Yeager. "He's your man. He'll find your culprit and the motive."

That wasn't comforting to Travail, nor was Esposito's next question.

"Did you know Yeager did some undercover work for my construction companies? He was quite effective. Caught the bastard who was stealing from us."

Travail looked at Yeager, who seemed to smile, although it was difficult to tell behind his free-range beard.

Esposito grinned. "Yeager can do the same here."

"Are you suggesting the culprit may not be Sue Ellen Parker?"

"Too early to tell." As Esposito stood to leave, he promised to keep Yeager and Travail informed of what he learned.

When the front door shut, Travail looked at Yeager. "Have you really worked for him?"

Yeager shrugged. "Once or twice."

Great. Yeager had worked on both sides of the law. "Who's next?"

At noon, Travail thanked their sixth witness for her time, escorted her to the front door, and met Harriet coming up the driveway carrying a brown paper bag and a pitcher of liquid.

"Hope you're hungry. I brought you and Yeager BLT sandwiches, chips, and sweet tea, plus pound cake for dessert."

Before Travail could say thanks, Yeager was at his side. The man had a sixth sense for food. "You're a peach, Harriet." Yeager helped her with the bag and the pitcher. "Let's eat."

During lunch, Harriet pressed for details about their morning. "Did you learn anything helpful?"

"Sure did." Yeager was a mouthful of exuberance.

Travail tamped down the Head of Security's enthusiasm. "Most of the witnesses have an ax to grind against Sue Ellen."

"Tell me something I don't know, like are you any closer to understanding why the professor changed his will?"

Yeager said "yes" at the same time Travail said "no." Travail shook his head in frustration.

"I'll tell you what we have—I mean, what I have. I have a reckless driving case, a slip and fall action, a medical insurance claim, a no-contest divorce, and the case of a spurned spouse who wants to file an alienation of affection claim. That, plus whatever the Godfather has in store for me."

"I meant about the case." Harriet deflected Travail's sarcasm. "We knew the residents would be reluctant to talk with you unless we gave them something in return."

Travail's throat tightened. "You should not have offered my legal services."

The rebuke caused everyone to retreat into their own thoughts, and for Travail, his were second, third, and fourth thoughts about getting involved in Lori's case. Besides his lack of expertise in handling will cases, he worried his involvement would cause Elkin to bring everything at the firm's disposal to bear against Lori, as much for spite against Travail as for the case against her. He also worried about his own motivation. Lawyers were supposed to avoid personal vendettas and attacks, lest they pose a risk to their client's interest. How much of his involvement so far had to do with his grudge against Elkin?

Harriet looked at her watch. "Your next witness will be here in five minutes, so eat up."

Travail's shoulders sagged. "Do they need me to handle a real estate closing?"

"He's a handwriting expert. Honestly, didn't you learn anything in law school about how to prepare for a case?"

Lafontaine Creech was not just a handwriting expert, he was the back-to-back two-person team champion in the annual Indie croquet tournament. He showed up carrying a satchel with the initials "IICO" on them, which Travail learned stood for the Indie Indoor Croquet Organization, of which Lafontaine Creech was commissioner. He was silver-haired and dressed in white slacks and a white collared shirt. The only hint of color came from his red cheeks. "Man, it's cold out there today. Good thing Indie croquet is an indoor sport. I only have thirty minutes before we knock the ole ball through the wickets. Let's get to it."

Harriet smiled from her place in the corner. Yeager had gone to run an unknown errand, so Harriet had stuck around to take notes.

"Thank you for coming, Mr. Creech. I understand you have an opinion about the handwriting on Matthew Collins's recent will?"

Creech had a self-important air about him. He opened his satchel, pulled out a number of papers, and laid them on Travail's desk. One of them was a copy of the handwritten will. Travail didn't ask where he got it. Yeager must have made the copy before he returned the original to the professor's condo. The other documents were letters that began "Dear Lori."

"Where did you get the letters?"

Creech looked at Harriet, who answered the question. "Lori saved them."

Creech cleared his throat. "I reviewed fifty letters written by the professor to his granddaughter and compared the writing on them to the writing in the will."

"And?"

"I have no doubt in my mind Matthew Collins wrote the will."

Travail thanked the man so he could run off to play croquet and turned his attention to Harriet. "That didn't help."

"I wonder about lawyers, sometimes."

"What do you mean?"

"The glass being half empty and all."

"That's how we're trained, to spot the problems."

"You're also trained, I presume, to eliminate issues. You just eliminated one."

Travail laughed. "Okay, sure. We don't have to call a handwriting expert at trial."

"And," Harriet said, "we can focus our time on other issues."

"Like what, the Meck Dec? Yeager tried to bring it up several times this morning with the witnesses and I had to shut him down."

"Yeager is a passionate man. He can get fixated."

"You think?"

"It might be a good idea to let him have his project. Maybe he'll find something in his Meck Dec treasure hunt to explain why the professor did what he did."

Travail shrugged. It couldn't hurt to have Yeager occupied on something that scholars and amateur sleuths hadn't solved in over two centuries. At least it would keep him busy.

Harriet stood. "I think it's time I poked around for a few days to see what other people know."

"It can't hurt. I'll go with you."

"No offense, Craig, but most people don't care for lawyers." She picked up Travail's briefcase, stuffed some papers in it, and said goodbye. "I'll be in touch."

As Harriet left his home office, Yeager entered. He was out of breath. The flurry of activity made Travail uneasy.

"I just made an appointment for you for a very personal orientation session with Peaches. You have five minutes to get there."

Travail leaned back in his chair and looked at the ceiling. "Why would you do that?"

"She's sweet on you, Craig Travail. Don't you know the rule? Honey is better than money when it comes to investigating. You'll see."

Travail reluctantly allowed Peaches to welcome him into her twelve-by-twelve office with bright blue walls and a smile that said, "this is going to be fun." Block letters painted black took up the wall behind her desk: "More than a Retirement Community." The other walls displayed posters illustrating life at the Indie. In one, an elderly couple leaned close with their heads touching, wineglasses in hand. It looked like the same bar where Harriet and Yeager sprang the news on him about the professor's will, and the scene exuded sexuality, which Travail supposed was the point. It metaphorically said, "We're not dying here, we're living, and that means having sex too." In another poster, aged men and women dressed in swimsuits bumped elbows and shoulders and laughed in a shimmering pool.

"That's our water exercise class. You do have a set of swim trunks, don't you?" Peaches winked her I'd-like-to-see-you-in-your-swim-trunks wink and pointed to a chair in front of her desk. Travail sat. She took the other chair, pulled it close, and rested one elbow on an arm of the chair as she tilted forward. Her maneuver and her deep V-cut blouse suggested she wasn't shy about showing some cleavage. Travail tried not to look. He checked out another wall, instead, showing more evidence of the youthful vigor of a retirement community.

One poster showed a smiling couple riding their bikes along the bike path around Freedom Lake. In another, men and women exercised in the fitness center, and another showed a group on the basketball court, which Peaches said they could also set up for pickleball. Travail was confused by another poster. A thin muscled man in a tank top had his legs spread, one in front of the other, with his knees bent as his body leaned forward. His arms were in front of him at a 90-

degree angle, with his palms up, as if they were trying to stop the wind.

"That's our tai chi instructor," Peaches said. "You should take the class. It's great for balance."

During his thirty-minute "special orientation," as Peaches called it, Travail learned Peaches was a resident too, she was single, and she was about his age. These were facts she volunteered with a curtsy of a smile. She was lying about her age though. He tried to be polite.

After she'd run Travail through the brochures and shown him a short video, Peaches brushed up against Travail with her chest as she guided him out the door for a tour. He needed to breathe, but her scent made it difficult. Identifying smells had never been Travail's strong suit. He couldn't sniff flowers or wines and remember what was what. And with perfume, he was lost. But whatever perfume Peaches wore had a kick.

The tour helped Travail better orient the locations for all physical activities at the Indie. "We even have massage therapists," Peaches said with a nudge. "Most people wear nothing underneath the sheet." She giggled.

If Peaches knew who didn't wear what under the sheet, she might know something about Sue Ellen and the professor. He led her into the reason Yeager had set up the tour.

"Did you know Matthew Collins?"

"Everybody knew the professor. Such a nice man." Peaches had a devilish twist in her smile. "You're putting me on the hot seat for Lori's case against Sue Ellen, aren't you?"

"I'm not sure there will be a case, and if there is, I'm not sure I will be involved. I'm just curious. Is that okay?"

"Honey, you can put me on any seat you want. Let's step into the library where we can be more comfortable." Peaches sat and patted the sofa next to her.

In the next fifteen minutes, Travail learned the professor and Sue Ellen were "off and on, hot and cold." For a long time, Peaches had seen no signs that they were playing house together, but in the last few months, she'd had second thoughts about that. She'd seen them eating together in the main dining room, having breakfast together in the deli, and spending time "right here, on this couch, just like you and me."

Peaches had a hard time staying on topic. Somehow, she got off on a tangent as to how the condo owners and the cottage owners have different mindsets about aging. "You cottage owners think you're too young and vigorous to be in the condo buildings, whether you're sixty-five or eighty-five, and the condo owners think they're above you, for some reason. And yet, all that judgment hasn't prevented the cottage owners from hooking up with the condo owners, and vice versa."

Peaches moved closer. "Did you hear about the skinny-dipping party at the indoor pool a few nights ago?"

He slid away and changed the subject. "Anything else you can tell me about the professor and Sue Ellen?"

"No." But her next words made the entire afternoon affair worthwhile. "Did you know the professor's lawyer was hanging around the Indie the week the professor died?"

"Robert Elkin?"

"That's the one."

Travail hoped Peaches would continue. She didn't disappoint him.

"Robert—he told me to call him Robert—visited the professor three times during the last week of his life, and he was here for the last time the day before the professor died. I don't know why he visited, other than him being the professor's lawyer, but he was thrilled on his last visit."

"How so, if you don't mind me asking?"

Peaches blushed for the first time. "We kinda got to know each other during that week, and I could tell he sorta liked me. On his last visit, before he went up to see the professor, we got to talking about the professor's writing. I told him that in the last three months, the professor was always in his books. He never had time for our classes or field trips."

Travail waited to see if there was anything more. And there was.

"I told him the professor was working on another book."

"How did he react?"

"I hope I did nothing wrong, Craig. Can I call you Craig?" She smiled.

Of course she could. He needed the answer to the question.

"I found out, by accident of course, when I overheard a conversation between the professor and Yeager Alexander. He told Yeager he was working on a sequel to his book. It was so exciting to have a best-selling author working on another book. That's what I told Robert and he hugged me. It was the last time I saw him."

"You told no one about this?"

"Nobody ever asked, and when the professor died, it didn't seem very newsy to talk about a sequel to a book that would never be finished."

She had a good point. He thanked her for the tour.

The fact that Elkin found out the professor was at work on the sequel to *An American Hoax* and met with him about it the day before he died led to dueling opinions by Yeager and Harriet that night.

"It's the smokin' gun," Yeager said. "The Meck Dec is tied to the will and the professor's death."

Harriet didn't agree. "That is ridiculous. Next, you'll be saying Elkin killed him." Ridiculous or not, Robert Elkin was everywhere in this case.

CHAPTER 17

ANONYMOUS LETTER

Mailed to the Professor Three Months Before His Death and Kept With his Papers

Dear Professor Collins:

My late husband and I read your book, An American Hoax. *We were not fans, but please, hear me out. What I have to say, or rather, what I am prepared to show you, will change history.*

I write to let you know I possess documentary proof that the Mecklenburg Declaration of Independence was real. I have the proof because I solved the mystery of Dispatch 34.

Unfortunately, it is only a matter of time before those who hid the proof from the world discover it is missing. I am sure they will stop at nothing to recover it and prevent the truth from coming out.

I call on you because you spent the last fifteen years of your life insisting the Meck Dec was a fabrication. Should a person such as yourself, a bestselling author with such conviction on the subject, change his mind and write the next chapter of this important story, it could awaken the historical community to the truth. A truth that needs to be told.

It is too risky to put the proof in the mail to you, and it is unwise to share it electronically, and since I have no way of knowing what you think of this letter, I will not reveal my name or residence address at this time. Please respond to this letter to let me know if you are interested in speaking with me. You may write to me at P.O. Box 2424, Charlottesville, Virginia, 22903. Please include your phone number. I will call you to discuss my findings, explain why and how my husband and his family were involved, and arrange for you to come see the evidence.

I apologize for the secrecy, but it can't be helped. I urge you to be careful and not to mention our correspondence or future conversations to anyone until after you disclose the secret to the world.

Historically and with gratitude,

Your anonymous servant

CHAPTER 18

MONEY TALKS

Harriet stopped by the cleaning manager's office early the next morning to make her complaint. Hilly Span, the manager who Yeager called Spic and Span, was using her Clorox-scented fingers to roll a cigarette when Harriet stuck her head in the door. Harriet bumped into a bucket holding an upside-down mop, and the mop hit her in the face. She pushed the rope strands aside so she could be seen and heard.

Hilly grumbled. "What brings you here?"

"A scheduling issue."

Hilly grabbed a clipboard from her desk and ran her finger down the page. "What? You don't like Wednesdays from one to three?" She tossed the clipboard back on the desk toward Harriet.

"I'd like the cleaning crew to get an earlier start. Any chance you can switch me up?"

"We have a system."

"Systems can change." Harriet picked up the clipboard and scanned it. "How about you switch me with whatever special time you've allotted to your favorite, Sue Ellen Parker?" Harriet found Sue Ellen's unit on the schedule. "Yes, Tuesdays at nine-thirty will work perfectly for me." She glanced to the right of the schedule for the names of the housekeepers.

"You want to make a change, take it up with the HOA. The board approved the schedule."

Harriet had what she needed and set the schedule down. "No harm in asking. Take care, Hilly."

Harriet's next stop was the staff break room. She left notes in the mail slots for the two housekeepers whose names she'd seen on the list. On the way down the hall, she ran into Mini-Me Parker, NASCAR Nelli's nickname for Becky Trainer, the woman who had presided over the bird feeder caper. "Morning, Becky."

"Hello, Harriet. What brings you to the community center? Selling honey from your beehives?"

Harriet wanted to say she was selling truth, justice, and the American way, but she was sure Becky would buy none of it, even on discount. "I had a few questions for you."

"If it's about the professor and Sue Ellen, I already told your Meck Dec-worshiping-side-kick I don't have time for such nonsense."

"You think it's nonsense to find out why the professor disinherited his granddaughter?"

"No, I think it's nonsense you want to persecute Sue Ellen Parker. She's a good person."

Harriet had a laundry list of opposing positions on that score, but it would do no good to quarrel with Becky. She needed information. "Were the professor and Sue Ellen close?"

"Sue Ellen's lawyer says I shouldn't talk to anyone, including you. I'm a witness."

Harriet noodled on Becky's comment while she walked back to her cottage. What did Becky Trainer witness? Had Sue Ellen confided in her? Was she that kind of witness? Or had she witnessed an event, and if so, what event?

One hour later, Harriet was at work on her to-do list for the case when one of the housekeepers she'd left a note for showed up at her cottage, looking uncertain why she had been summoned.

"Come in, Marsha. Can I offer you something to drink?"

Marsha wore her work clothes, black slacks and grey top with the Indie logo. "No, ma'am. Thank you."

Harriet guided Marsha to her kitchen table and asked her to sit. "I completely forgot to contribute to the staff Christmas bonus fund." She smiled as she pulled four twenties from her purse, folded them together, and held them in her right hand as she talked. Marsha's eyes were on the tip money.

"I know you heard about Matthew Collins. Such a terrible thing. And I know how close he and Sue Ellen Parker were. You clean her unit, don't you?"

"Yes, ma'am."

"How long have you been with us at the Indie, Marsha?"

"Eight years."

"I thought so. Very loyal." Harriet reached in her purse and pulled out another twenty-dollar bill she added to the stack in her right hand. "I don't mean to pry, Marsha, but I'm worried about Sue Ellen. Have you noticed anything unusual in the last month? Anything at all?"

Marsha looked at the tip money again.

"It's okay. You won't get in any trouble." Harriet placed the money in Marsha's hand.

"The afternoon before the professor died, I went to Ms. Sue Ellen's unit to finish some cleaning I hadn't gotten to earlier that week and I heard her on the phone. She said everything was 'secure.'"

Harriet coaxed her. "Anything else?"

"I found boxes in her closet when I opened the doors to vacuum. I tried to move them, but they were heavy."

Sensing her discomfort, Harriet reached in her purse and pulled out another twenty-dollar bill. She placed it in Marsha's hand. "For your trouble." Marsha thanked her, and Harriet asked one last question. "Do you know what was in the boxes?"

"I only looked by accident to move them."

"Of course." Harriet smiled to herself. At the Indie, the best gossip was always secured by accident.

"The boxes held books and papers. And a computer."

Harriet thanked Marsha, who left through the side door as Gloria, another Indie housekeeper, rang the doorbell at the front. Another fistful of twenties and Harriet was in business. Gloria liked to listen in on the owners' conversations while she cleaned their units and, unlike Marsha, she wasn't shy about sharing what she'd learned. A few days before the professor died, she'd been in Sue Ellen's unit when the professor was there.

"I was polishing Sue Ellen's silver, out of sight from where she and the professor talked. They tried to keep their words to a whisper, but I have excellent hearing."

"Did they sound like two people in love?"

"Not exactly."

"What do you mean?"

"It started when Sue Ellen said, 'You want me to inherit your entire fortune?' That surprised me."

Nothing surprised Harriet any longer. "How did the professor respond?

"He said, 'Yes, and if Lori hires a lawyer to fight it, you need to fight back, fight to keep it.' The professor pleaded with Sue Ellen, and when she finally agreed, he gave her a lawyer's name to call who he said would be glad to take the case."

Harriet asked the lawyer's name, even though she suspected she knew.

"Eckert, or Edmond. I can't recall, exactly."

"That's okay. How did Sue Ellen respond?"

"She was concerned about his granddaughter. She said, 'It will devastate Lori.'"

That information didn't fit Harriet's profile of Sue Ellen Parker, the selfish woman intent on keeping money and property that belonged to Lori. "How did the professor respond?"

"He said, 'It can't be helped.' I remember exactly. It was strange."

"Do you remember anything else?"

"The professor said, 'Do you trust me?' and she said she did but asked him to drop what he was working on. She didn't say what she wanted him to drop."

Harriet had her suspicion about what Sue Ellen wanted him to drop. She asked how the professor responded to Sue Ellen's request.

"He said he would not give up what he was working on and told

Sue Ellen not to worry. The last thing I heard him say was, 'As long as you follow the plan, everything will be fine.'"

Harriet thanked Gloria and made another late donation to the Christmas fund. After Gloria left, she called Travail. He didn't pick up, so she left him a message about what she'd learned.

CHAPTER 19

SUE ELLEN AND TRAVAIL SPEAK FOR THEMSELVES

To start his day, Travail visited the new wing in the community center Peaches had shown him. The room was empty of people but included every conceivable torture device known to rip one's abs or kill one in the process. Travail had no illusions he would develop bulging biceps or a six-pack. He was hoping to breathe easier when he ran with Blue and to live a little longer, if that's what he decided to do. But really, he needed some time away from Yeager and Harriet and some mindless activity. He programmed the machine for a brisk walk. Sixty minutes should do it.

As he walked in place, Travail thought about the reports he'd received from Yeager and Harriet since the day he'd met with Lori. Their findings were helpful but confusing. From the business office, they'd learned the professor intended to move in with Sue Ellen, but from words flying around on the community gossip vine, the picture of their relationship was confusing, one of tension and conflict on the one hand, and togetherness on the other. And Peaches's revelation about Elkin's interest in the professor's new book was curious. Travail didn't know what to make of all the information.

Travail finished his turn on the treadmill and found and laid a mat on the floor to do some stretches. He paid little attention to the local news playing on the TV in the gym's corner until he saw a reporter standing beside the Welcome Home sign at the Indie's entrance with words at the bottom of the screen that said "Breaking News." He found the remote control on a shelf near him and fumbled with it. He heard the reporter mention Matthew Collins, author of *An American Hoax.* "Our sources tell us Matthew Collins left his fortune to a woman named Sue Ellen Parker and cut his granddaughter, his only relative, out of his will. Neither woman would comment for this story, but the lawyer for Ms. Parker, Robert Elkin, said that there is no question the will is valid. This is a story we plan to follow very closely. For now, I'm Amanda Rogers, Channel 24 News."

Travail muted the sound on the TV and lifted a few weights. Dead weights. A good place to start, given what he'd gotten himself into. He grabbed some barbells and did a few curls.

"You think you're something, don't you?"

Travail turned to see Sue Ellen Parker standing a few feet away. Surprised, he mumbled a "good morning."

"No, it isn't. Yeager says you're going to contest Matthew's will."

"He's getting ahead of himself. But I am looking into it, which means I can't speak with you because you're represented by an attorney."

"You don't have to speak. Just listen." Sue Ellen told Travail what a low-life lawyer he was for sticking his enormous nose—Travail didn't think that was necessary—into Matthew's business. She asked him why he thought he could question Matthew's decision about what to do with his money but didn't wait for his answer. "You're nothing more than a money-grubbing parasite lawyer looking to get rich off others' backs." And finally, "It's un-Christian of you."

Travail kept in mind the ethics rules by keeping his mouth shut, and Sue Ellen must have taken his silence as an admission of guilt. "I thought so," she said, lifting her chin as she slammed the glass door and strutted down the hall.

Travail could imagine the prattle at the dinner tables that night about the lawyer in Cottage 24 trying to make a buck at Sue Ellen's expense. It was time he made a decision about whether to represent

Lori in court, and despite the disappointment it would cause his friends, he knew which way he was leaning. He sent a text to the team to invite them to dinner at his place. Harriet responded immediately and said she'd bring the food. Yeager texted that he'd bring the beer. Before he put his phone in his pocket, Travail listened to a voicemail message from Harriet about what she'd learned from the cleaning crew. Interesting. Now they knew the location of the professor's books and laptop. The fact they were hidden in Sue Ellen's closet had to be important, but he didn't know why.

Travail took the afternoon to focus on the Meck Dec's connection or lack thereof to the professor's will. If he backed away from representing Lori as he knew he should, he wanted to be able to offer his assessment to her or the lawyer she hired.

With Blue resting by his side on the back porch, Travail used his time to flip through *An American Hoax* and the other book about the Meck Dec that Lori had given him. After skimming through both books and doing some research on the internet, Travail realized there was no way to prove beyond a reasonable doubt that the Meck Dec ever existed. Even the local author agreed, and he was a believer in the Meck Dec. This raised two questions. Why would the professor change his mind about the Meck Dec without any new evidence? And could his abrupt and illogical about-face be used against him to challenge the will?

Travail's mind wandered to the reasons he was uncomfortable taking Lori's case. For one, the residents were taking sides, and the last thing he wanted was to find himself at the center of attention. He moved to the Indie to be alone. Taking Lori's case would put him in the middle, not unlike Harriet's and Sue Ellen's fight over the bird feeders. One side would be led by Sue Ellen Parker and her Number 2 Pencil, Becky Trainer, and the other side would be led by Harriet Keaton and her number one worry about what Chuck Yeager Alexander might do to screw things up.

Travail also worried that his dislike for Elkin clouded his judgement. He tried to make himself think of Elkin's involvement as a series of coincidences. Robert Elkin was on the board of the company that funded the professor's first book, *An American Hoax*. Coincidence. Robert Elkin represented Sue Ellen Parker in the will case. Coincidence. Robert Elkin represented Congressman Butterworth in the threatened libel case. Coincidence. And yet, there was a point when coincidence became more than happenstance.

The reason for—but not the explanation as to why—Elkin represented Sue Ellen Parker was revealed this morning when Harriet spoke with one of the members of the cleaning crew. It had nothing to do with Elkin's reputation, as he liked to claim, and everything to do with the fact the professor told Sue Ellen to hire Elkin. That explained why Sue Ellen and Elkin got together, but shed no light on why the professor wanted Elkin involved. It was odd though. If the professor wanted to ensure the will would stand up to any challenge, he could have asked Elkin to have a lawyer in the firm's estates department prepare a typed will that met all the legal formalities, with proper witnesses. It was as if the professor intended to set something in motion and wanted Elkin to be a part of it. Travail didn't know why.

This led to the question of why Elkin was involved in the other two matters. The threatened libel case was the simplest to conjecture about. The government relations team at Travail's law firm had done work for Butterworth's last three campaigns, but as far as Travail knew, Elkin had never been involved. If he was, he certainly kept it quiet from his partners. Even so, the prior relationship explained Elkin's involvement in the libel matter and logically led to Elkin advising on the nonprofit tax proceeding. It was clear his involvement had nothing to do with legal expertise. Elkin was not a trial lawyer, and the idea of him consulting on tax matters relating to nonprofits was laughable.

The simplest explanation for both matters was the congressman was an important client who didn't like Lori and her magazine calling him to account for overspending on cyber toys and underspending on the health and safety of veterans. He wanted to put a stop to it by either bankrupting her with a libel suit or crippling her nonprofit's fundraising efforts, or both. The strategy had Elkin's fingerprints all over it.

Two questions bothered Travail about the meeting Elkin had with the professor within twenty-four hours of the professor's death, as reported by Peaches. The first and most obvious question was what they talked about. The other: Did the conversation cause the professor to change his will?

What's more, Travail knew Elkin wouldn't dirty his hands on legal work if he didn't have something personal to gain beyond the legal fees. What would that something be? It had to be peculiarly unique. Only two things were peculiar and unique to the professor and his granddaughter, and both were intellectual property. One was *An American Hoax*. The other was hidden in Sue Ellen's closet. Why would Elkin care about either?

Travail texted Harriet. "Can you come thirty minutes early? I'd like to discuss something with you, alone." She texted a thumbs up emoji to his request.

While he tidied up the den, Travail thought about his decision. He'd tell Harriet and Yeager his decision first. He owed them that courtesy. Then he'd call Lori.

Harriet showed up at 5:30 with dinner. Travail put it in the oven to warm and offered Harriet a glass of red wine. "Thank you, yes. But you'd better start talking. Yeager will be here in twenty minutes."

They settled in the den, placing their wine glasses and the bottle on the coffee table between them. Travail had placed the file he intended to share with Harriet on top of the table.

"Is that for me?"

"It is. I thought you should know one of the reasons I shouldn't represent Lori."

"You've made up your mind?"

"I think so."

Harriet sighed. "You're not very convincing."

Travail looked away. He had made up his mind, hadn't he? Saying no was the right thing to do, and the file in front of him held one of the reasons.

Harriet picked up the file. "What's in here?"

"Have you ever heard of a company called Viribus?"

"Nope."

"Viribus, LLC, is a billion-dollar government contractor that supplies the military with every possible cyber-widget needed to support US war efforts against terrorists."

"They must have a nice bottom line."

"They do. The government pumps millions of dollars into Viribus every month to further the fight against cyber-terrorism, and Elkin and the law firm get rich too."

Harriet placed the file back on the coffee table and picked up her wine glass. "What do Elkin and his law firm have to do with Viribus and what does any of this have to do with you not wanting to represent Lori?"

"I became obsessed with Viribus—a word that means force, power, strength—when the firm chose Elkin instead of me as managing part-ner. Elkin had landed Viribus as a client; it got him the votes he needed. I kept a file on Viribus. That file." He pointed at the file on the table. "I was sure Elkin was up to no good with this client, but my efforts never amounted to anything."

"Would they have elected you managing partner otherwise?"

"Many partners say yes, but you never know."

"It's good to admit you're human, but that doesn't sound like much of a reason to bail on Lori when she needs you."

Travail picked up the file and held it tight. "I can't be objective because of this."

"Nobody else likes Elkin either."

"It's more than that. It has to do with my judgment being clouded. The day Elkin showed up for the memorial service, the first thing I thought about was Viribus and how it was the reason I got stuck in this retirement community without a job."

Harriet interrupted Travail with a lecturing tone. "Spare me the speech about the lawyer who doesn't know what to do with his life after he retires and wants everyone to feel sorry for his inability to be creative." She took a long swallow, finished what was in her glass, and poured a refill. "Continue. But remember, Yeager will be here in five minutes."

Travail paused and considered how to explain himself. "I've become more fixated on Viribus since the day I interviewed Lori. She told me that she'd had a concern about irregularities involving Viribus and Congressman Butterworth, but she hadn't had time to investigate. It has nothing to do with the congressman's libel case, because she never wrote about the Viribus connection. But I've been acting like Yeager, daydreaming about a conspiracy involving Elkin and the congressman."

Harriet set her wine glass on the table, picked up the file, and flipped through it. "What if you're right?"

Travail shook his head. "Harriet, if you take this detour too, it won't help Lori any more than Yeager's focus on the Meck Dec. She needs a lawyer who is focused on what matters. Viribus has nothing to do with the professor's death, the will, or the libel case, but I can't get it out of my mind, and as I said, it has affected my judgment."

The silence that trailed Travail's response was interrupted by several hard raps on the back door, followed by Blue's repeated barks, and Yeager shouting, "Little help in there, Craig Travail."

Travail and Harriet stood. She touched him on the arm. "Let me focus on Viribus. You focus on Lori."

Travail grumbled at her refusal to accept his decision to quit. He left Harriet and went to the kitchen, where he found Yeager with his shoulder pressed against the back door and his arms full. Travail turned the knob and let him in, only to be presented with four six packs of what Yeager called "the finest beer in town." He pulled a bottle from one six-pack to explain, and the mood in the room became lighter. "Captain Jack Pilsner. Brewed locally. As they say on the label, 'Enjoy the unmistakable taste of freedom in every fresh, delicious swig.'"

A few minutes later, Harriet had the macaroni and cheese, green beans, glazed ham, and baked apples on the table. With everyone settled and Yeager full throttle into the food, the conversation was sparse. Harriet asked Travail to pass the apples. He did, and asked Harriet to pass the green beans. Most of the oxygen in the room was taken up by Blue panting and looking for a handout and Yeager scraping food off his plate and into his mouth. Travail picked at his food with his head down.

Travail felt a pain in his shoulder and looked up to see that Yeager had stabbed him with his fork. "Come on, Craig Travail. Harriet's food ain't that bad."

Harriet dabbed at her mouth with her napkin. "You should tell him, Craig."

"Tell me what?"

Travail set his knife and fork down but avoided eye contact with Yeager as he spoke. "I think it would be best if we got Lori another lawyer to represent her."

Yeager's comeback was sarcastic. "You want me to get Peaches to sign you up for cross-stitch class? You'll have plenty of time if you quit on Lori."

Travail's head began to ache, and his breathing became short. It was a moment that had been building since the day he tackled Elkin, quit the firm, and found himself alone at the Indie. He'd busied himself with Lori's case to take his mind off his plight, but everything he'd done—the home office, the interviews, and the research—had been a placeholder. He had avoided his therapist. He hadn't told anyone how he felt. And the feelings had been intense. He was trapped. Isolated. Unsure of his purpose in life. Unsure what to do next. He figured quitting would help. But it only made him feel worse. Lightheaded. Dizzy. Then the room went dark.

"Craig?" It was Harriet's voice. When his eyes focused, he saw her bending over him and felt a damp cloth being pressed to his forehead. He was on his back under the dinner table. He had fainted. How embarrassing. He tried to sit up.

"Hold on, Craig Travail. Let me help." Yeager grabbed him under his arms and pulled him to his feet. He placed a Captain Jack in Travail's hand. "Hair of the dog."

Yeager helped Travail to the den, where he took a seat on the couch. Harriet handed him a glass of water and took the beer away. "You've been carrying a lot on you since you moved here. How do you feel?"

Travail drank the water. "Better. Thanks. Now, where were we?"

"Well, Craig Travail, as I recall, you had just told us how much you were looking forward to representing Lori in court. Like you, Lori is a fighter. Never one to give up."

Travail smiled as he looked from Yeager to Harriet. "That's what I was talking about, how much I was looking forward to going to court for Lori?"

Harriet smiled back. "Yeager's right about one thing. Lori had many reasons to quit in her life. Her parents died in an automobile accident when she was six years old. The professor and his wife took her in and cared for her. Then, when she was twelve, her grandmother died."

Yeager took a swig from another Captain Jack. "It was a hard time for the professor too. He didn't know how to raise a child, and everyone in his family was dead except Lori."

Harriet finished the story. "Lori and the professor took care of each other. What you see is a woman grieving, not someone who is weak. You will be proud to represent her."

Travail could see what they were trying to do. When the doorbell rang, he used it as an excuse to stand up. When he was steady on his feet, he excused himself and picked up a package left on the stoop. While he was at it, he checked his mailbox, where he found a letter from the North Carolina State Bar. He stood in the hallway and opened the package first. In it was a thank-you note from Lori and a book about what to do with oneself in retirement. She had inscribed it: "This book says nothing about filing lawsuits from a cottage by the lake. I have decided to fight the will but understand if you don't take my case. If you don't take it, check out the craft lessons in chapter four."

Travail loved a client with a sense of humor.

The letter from the state bar was not funny at all, but Travail laughed anyway. Wasn't it enough for Elkin that he quit the law firm?

From the hallway, Travail could hear Harriet tell Yeager, "I know what you're thinking,"

"What am I thinking?"

"You think representing Lori will be good for him."

Travail couldn't hear Yeager's response, but he heard Harriet's next comment. "Don't you see? He's struggling."

Travail edged closer to hear Yeager's response.

"Kind of like I was after Mom died."

"That was different."

"You didn't think so. You checked in on me, gave me things to do, introduced me to the professor and the Godfather and made sure I didn't get thrown out for disorderly conduct."

Harriet apparently didn't like being lectured to by Yeager. "Yeah and look where that got me. Now you think the Meck Dec is real, and it's tied to the professor's death and Lori's case."

"It is real, and it is tied to the professor's death and her case."

Travail re-entered the den. "What are y'all fighting about?"

"The Meck Dec," Harriet said.

"She doesn't want me to bring it up anymore."

Travail looked at Harriet. "You're not a believer?"

"I'm agnostic. I know the professor told Yeager he changed his mind, but why would he change his will over something that happened, or didn't happen, in 1775?"

"You both have good points. You can take them up with a lawyer who has a law license." Travail handed the state bar letter to Harriet. "Since you're my office manager, please file this in the folder marked 'Office Closing.'"

Harriet read the letter and softened her tone. "Why is Elkin trying to take away your law license?"

Yeager grabbed the letter from her hand and read it. "This is crap."

Travail walked to the closest window. He placed one finger on the pane and followed a raindrop on the glass as it moved left, right, and then down as it picked up speed.

"You're right, Harriet. I have been struggling. I suppose it's because I'm really sad. I lost my wife, my job, and now I could lose my law license."

"If you're tired of practicing law, why do you care about your law license?"

"What?"

"Simple question. Why do you care?"

"You sound like my therapist."

"Harriet's got a good question, Craig Travail."

Travail could see images of his law school acceptance letter, his classmates, and his professors. Law school was hard, but he did the work, and he made it through with Rachael's support, and she and his parents were at his graduation and helped celebrate when he passed the bar. He remembered taking his law license to get it framed. "You're an awfully young lawyer," the man behind the counter said. He was. And then he grew into a mid-career lawyer, and then into a wiser lawyer, and he did good work, none of which he could have done without his law license. "I suppose it means more than the job."

Yeager, for once, kept his mouth shut as Harriet asked Travail to "hold that thought." She grabbed a beer from the refrigerator and tossed it to Yeager. She refilled Travail's glass with ice and water and handed it to him with the admonition to "drink it all," and she picked up the wine bottle and refilled her glass. She leaned back and waited for Travail to say more. He talked while Harriet and Yeager listened.

"It was a hard time for me after Rachael died. My grief turned to depression, and it was difficult to focus on work. On a mandatory referral by the law firm, I connected with a therapist through a state bar program that helps lawyers in distress. I wasn't taking drugs or drinking too much alcohol. I was just really, really sad. A mental case. I was and still am. I admit it."

Harriet and Yeager continued to listen. They offered no judgment.

"After three months of therapy and part-time work, they cleared me to return to work full time, but I was not myself. Robert Elkin knew it. He told me if I screwed up, he would see me disbarred, and then he waited for an opportunity to do just that."

Yeager asked the direct question Harriet must have been thinking too. "Can they really take away your law license?"

"They can if they find I'm not mentally fit to be a lawyer."

Yeager leaned forward with a relaxed posture. "It seems to me, Craig Travail, that a man has to be a little bit crazy to be a lawyer in the first place. I doubt we can get you cured in time."

Harriet and Travail stared at Yeager. When he snickered, they all broke up laughing. The mere act, the physical experience of laughter itself, was a well-timed release. He hadn't laughed this hard since before Rachael died. Everyone had to wipe their eyes.

Travail's mobile phone rang. "Excuse me," he said.

He intended to silence his phone until he saw the digital display reveal the caller to be Robert Elkin. On more than one occasion in the last few weeks, Elkin had left Travail voicemails where he spewed words meant to intimidate. "I'm going to crush your client, Craig, and if you get involved, I will crush you too."

He put the call on speaker so Harriet and Yeager could hear, and said, "Hello."

"Craig, this is Robert Elkin. Did you get the letter from the state bar?"

"I did."

"I told you not to mess with me." Elkin clicked off.

Travail lifted his arms above his waist with his hands open. "Well?"

"He's a first-class schmuck-a-roo, Craig Travail."

"I prefer the term bully," Harriet said. "The only way to deal with a bully is to–"

"I know. I know." Travail drank his entire glass of water as Harriet had instructed. "The only way to deal with a bully is to stand up to them."

Yeager sat up on his chair's edge. "Does that mean you're thinking what I think you're thinking, Craig Travail?" The sun always shone on Yeager's parade.

Travail turned toward the window as he heard thunder. The rain picked up and beat against the pane. "You know we don't have much of a case in the will contest."

Neither Harriet nor Yeager reacted. Their silence told Travail it didn't matter to them what kind of case Lori had. They were going to fight for Lori no matter the odds. It caused him to ask himself the question. If they were going to stand with Lori, why shouldn't he? After all, as Yeager often reminded him, "What else do you have to do, Craig Travail?"

Harriet smiled. "Penny for your thoughts?"

Travail turned to Yeager. "Did you say your beer has the 'unmistakable taste of freedom in every fresh, delicious swig.'"

Yeager hustled to the refrigerator and came back with an ice-cold Captain Jack. He placed the beer in Travail's hand.

"Thanks, Yeager. You ever play baseball?"

"Yes-sir-reee."

Travail pressed the cool bottle against his forehead and then, with a wink and a nod to his friends, he took a long swallow. "I'm thinking that if this is going to be my last case, I might as well go down swinging."

Yeager picked up his beer. "A toast to Craig Travail, a freedom-loving lawyer prepared to go down swinging."

Harriet raised her glass too. "To the best lawyer ever to open a law office at the Indie."

Travail tapped drinks with his accomplices and laughed at his predicament. He was the only lawyer ever to open a law office at the Indie.

CHAPTER 20

YEAGER BREAKS IN ON SUE ELLEN

Yeager's teenage stint as a locksmith's apprentice came in handy after Harriet told him about the boxes Marsha had seen in Sue Ellen's bedroom closet. He picked the next day's cocktail hour to pick the lock.

He found two boxes in the closet. One contained books only. The other contained books, a few papers, and a laptop. Yeager recognized the books and papers. They were his favorites to glance through and borrow when he visited the professor. They included stories about the Founding Fathers, the shot heard around the world, the Battle of Kings Mountain, the Southern Campaign in the Revolutionary War, early Charlotte, and best of all, books and papers devoted to the controversy surrounding the Mecklenburg Declaration of Independence. To his delight, in the bottom of the second box, he found the first fifty printed pages of *An American Truth*. Delight led to discouragement when he realized the book was incomplete. Either the professor hadn't finished the book, or he hadn't printed out the entire manuscript. He saw a folder that said "research." It was empty except for an anonymous handwritten letter dated three months before the professor's death.

Remembering the trouble he'd gotten into with Travail for taking original documents, Yeager took out his smart phone and snapped a picture of the letter. He laid the fifty pages on the floor and photographed each one before putting everything back in the boxes. He was about to look at the computer when he heard voices in the hall. He quickly retraced his steps to make sure all was as it should be and left by the front door. Once in the hall, he heard Sue Ellen's voice coming nearer. He was standing at her front door when she came around the corner.

"What are you doing, Yeager?"

"Knocking."

"Why are you knocking on my door?"

"Didn't want to walk in on you, Becky, and the boys playing strip poker. Plus, what if you were on a losing streak?"

"I should report you to security."

"Don't you want to know why I came to see you?"

Sue Ellen said she was in a hurry to meet her friends for dinner, but she admitted, "Yes, I would like to know what brought Chuck Yeager Alexander to my door."

"I'd like to know why the professor left you everything. He never said much about you."

"Maybe you didn't know him as well as you thought you did."

Yeager waited for more, but it never came. Sue Ellen stepped in the door and tried to close it behind her, but Yeager put his hand against it. They eyed each other through the open crack. He had one last question, and it was a good one. "Where did you hide the Mecklenburg Declaration of Independence?"

Sue Ellen's answer was a door slammed in Yeager's face. No doubt, she meant her response as an affront, but Yeager took it as the spark heard round the Indie.

Yeager hurried to his cottage to grab a collared shirt for dinner. Then he ran to the dining room and found his team at the table where they'd planned to meet. He gave a big hello slap on the back to Craig Travail and hugged Harriet. His exuberance left them waiting for an explanation. When he sat, he saw that Sue Ellen Parker had beat him back and was holding court in the corner at the Bull Table, a nickname Yeager had given the table for all the stories told around it. When Sue

Ellen's mouth moved, ten eyes at the table turned their attention on Yeager.

"Well?" Harriet said.

Yeager winked at the server. "Just a glass with ice, partner." He pulled out two mini-bottles and set them on the table. Harriet grunted at his lack of tact as she held her wine glass aloft, one no doubt purchased from the Indie. "Still saving pennies on your bar tab, I see."

"Harriet, it's a crime what they charge for mixed drinks, and speaking of crimes, I have one to report." He paused before delivering the news. "Someone killed the professor, and I know why."

"Killed?" Harriet placed her wineglass down and stared at Yeager.

"Yep. Dangerous stuff, righting history." Yeager pulled on his beard and spelled the word out loud: "r-i-g-h-t-i-n-g."

The server showed up with the ice in a glass, and Yeager poured both mini-bottles on the ice, raised his glass, and said, "To righting a wrong," before he took a big swig.

Harriet turned to Travail. "He's lost his mind."

Travail sipped his beer. "He lost that before I met him."

Yeager knew it would take some convincing, so he took his time. "Based on Harriet's intel, I just finished casing Sue Ellen's condo."

"Don't bring me into this, Yeager. I didn't tell you to break into her condo."

Travail asked them both to keep their voices down and reprimanded Yeager. "You should not have gone into Sue Ellen's condo."

"Really? I shouldn't have confirmed that Sue Ellen has the professor's computer, books, and files in her closet?"

"Tell me you didn't take these items from Sue Ellen's condo." Travail's tone was serious.

"Okay, I won't tell you that, Craig Travail. But I will tell you this. I took pictures."

Harriet reached over and patted Yeager's hand. "Outstanding work, Yeager. I take back what I said about you losing your mind."

Travail listened while Yeager answered Harriet's questions about the pictures. "I have a picture of an anonymous letter to the professor about the Meck Dec and pictures of the first fifty pages of the sequel too."

"Just the first fifty pages?"

"Yes. But I'm sure there's more on the computer. When Craig Travail wins the case, Lori gets the computer. In the meantime, we can write to the person who sent the anonymous letter to find out the answer to the mystery. The address is in the letter." He found the picture of the letter on his phone and handed the phone to Harriet.

Harriet squinted at the screen. "The writer says they have documentary proof of the Meck Dec because they solved the mystery of Dispatch 34. Do you know what that means?"

"Nope. But the writer can tell us. And I plan to study up on it before we hear back."

As Harriet continued to read, her interest turned to frustration. She handed the phone back to Yeager with a frown. "Your photo didn't capture the last few sentences of the letter with the writer's address. You need to work on your photography skills."

"I can go back and take a better picture."

Harriet and Travail both said, "No."

"But it could help us solve the murder."

Harriet put her hand up. "What evidence do you have someone killed the professor?"

"He doesn't have any evidence," Travail said.

Yeager wasn't dissuaded. "What about the autopsy?"

Travail gave Yeager the bad news. "The medical examiner did not have to do an autopsy unless she deemed it advisable and in the public interest. There was no reason to question the death of a ninety-six-year-old man who died in his sleep. Plus, it saved the county twenty-eight hundred dollars."

Yeager countered with a theory. "What if someone poisoned him?"

"There's no way to prove it. They didn't test for any toxins in his system and his body was cremated."

"Neither of you get it. I may not be able to prove how the professor died, but I know he died because he was trying to tell the truth about the Meck Dec."

Harriet intervened, again. "Keep your voice down."

"Listen, Yeager," Travail said, "I know you miss your friend, but you have to be careful with what you say. The question we need to address is why the professor gave his entire estate to Sue Ellen."

"That's what I'm trying to find out."

"Good," Travail said. "Because we need to think about issues like fraud, undue influence, and lack of testamentary capacity. Those are the issues in a will contest case."

Yeager pulled another mini-bottle from his pocket, poured it in his water glass, and dumped the swill from his earlier drink on top. "Explain that capacity thing again."

"It means," Harriet said, "we have to show the jury the professor was crazy, like you."

Good ole Harriet. What were friends for? "I'm crazy about you too, Harriet. Cheers." He downed his mixture in two gulps.

Travail grabbed a pen, made a few notes on a napkin, and admired them. "I have an idea. What if we could convince the jury that the Meck Dec is tied to the professor's will?"

"Now you're talking, Craig Travail."

Harriet sat up straight. "I don't understand."

Travail placed the napkin in his shirt pocket. "The professor was obsessed with the Meck Dec, right?"

"So?" Harriet pointed at Yeager. "He is too."

"Exactly. And you just called Yeager 'crazy,' like the professor. What if the professor's obsession with the Meck Dec is his incapacity?"

Yeager didn't like where this was headed. "Wait a minute."

"Think about it, Yeager," Travail said. "The professor wrote a best-selling book that concluded the Meck Dec was a farce, but before he died, he flipped and became a believer."

"But the Meck Dec was real."

"Stay with me."

Harriet agreed. "Stay with him, Yeager. This is about helping Lori, not proving the Meck Dec was real."

Travail began his argument to his jury of two. "Historians have found no tangible document known as the Mecklenburg Declaration of Independence. The Matthew Collins who was in control of his mental faculties knew this to be true and told this truth in his *New York Times* bestselling book, *An American Hoax*. He'd been right and of sound mind and body when he did. He had good relations with his granddaughter. He supported her and the nonprofit he founded. But! A few months before he died, everything changed."

Yeager grumbled.

Harriet told Yeager, "Keep listening."

"Ask yourselves this question. Why would Matthew Collins cut Lori Collins out of his will? Perhaps he feared she might continue the lie he'd promoted in *An American Hoax* with her upcoming novel. He told her not to write it, demanded she cease. When she refused, he became upset and unbalanced, because he had come to believe in the unbelievable and the conspiracies that surround such beliefs. His psychosis with the Meck Dec caused him to be confused. He left his entire estate to an unrelated woman who took advantage of his confusion in order to inherit his vast fortune."

Harriet clapped her hands. "That's amazing. It might work."

Yeager was about to push back on this idea when NASCAR Nelli wheeled by and clipped Becky Trainer's chair at Sue Ellen's table. The collision sent Becky forward onto the table, where she sought purchase with her arms spread wide. She fell face first into the table full of plates, silverware, and glasses. The equilibrium shifted, and Becky's weight pulled the table backwards. Heads collided amid cries of disgust with NASCAR Nelli, but she buzzed from the dining room, her yellow scarf flying behind her like she was Snoopy fleeing the Red Baron.

Travail, Harriet, and Yeager lent their help to the women and, after everyone was upright, they took their leave. When they were outside, Yeager said, "I don't like your plan."

"Look," Travail said. "You know the professor's conclusions in *An American Hoax* better than anyone. You also know what he was doing at the end of his life. You can help Lori win this case."

"But I don't believe he was crazy. I think he was on to something."

Harriet put her hand on Yeager's shoulder. "This is the best way. Besides, you don't have any evidence the Meck Dec was real."

Yeager rubbed his beard. "I'll make you a deal."

Harriet and Travail looked at each other and back at Yeager.

"I will go along with this plan, but if I find evidence the Meck Dec was real, you have to help me do something about it."

Travail spoke first. "That's fair." Harriet agreed.

"Fine and dandy, Craig Travail. You and Harriet win the will case for Lori, and I'll work on getting proof of what really happened on May 20, 1775."

CHAPTER 21

THE PROFESSOR'S LAST LETTER

November 11, 2020

Dear Sue Ellen,

You sleep as I write this letter, which I shall place among my important papers. I hope you never need open it, but if you do and if I pass on before my work on An American Truth *is complete, please remember what I asked you to do and think kindly on my request.*

Some will say I was on a fool's errand and will argue it makes no difference what happened in Charlotte in May of 1775. They may encourage you to destroy my work, and you may agree with the sentiment. You will know what is best to do at the time.

I have taken appropriate measures to show my gratitude for what I have left you to do, though I realize you have asked nothing from me in return except my company.

I trust you will make the best decisions.

Yours with love, gratitude, and appreciation,

Matthew

PART III

THE MECK DEC ON TRIAL

CHAPTER 22

ELKIN AND SUE ELLEN PLAN TO WIN

Sue Ellen Parker was on a mission and today's lunch with Robert Elkin was part of it. She needed to provide him with assurances, and he needed to be prepared to play his part too.

They met at the Uptown Queen City Club and lunched in Elkin's private room, at a table set for two, with a white linen tablecloth, stainless flatware, and a personal server. The view wasn't bad either. Was this what Elkin did on most days, lunch like a king and look down on the masses below? Maybe she should use her newfound money to rent her own private room at the Uptown Queen City Club. She knew what the professor would think about such luxury, but she didn't care now.

On Elkin's recommendation, they both ordered the corn and crab chowder as a starter. Sue Ellen ordered the Mediterranean salad for her entrée. Elkin picked the seared salmon. Sue Ellen passed on the Manhattan ordered by Elkin.

"White wine, please."

The server got a hand signal from Elkin, bowed to him, and in a few minutes, returned to uncork and pour a Napa Valley Chardonnay into Sue Ellen's glass.

Elkin raised his mixed drink to Sue Ellen. "To life at the Indie."

Please, she thought. "I have a better toast. To the professor."

Elkin clinked his glass with hers. "To the professor." He took a big swallow. "By the way, how is life at the Indie?"

"As unpleasant and boring as always."

"Why not move? You have the money."

Sue Ellen didn't feel the need to explain herself to this man. She'd done more in her seventy years on this earth than he would accomplish in 370 years. He was like most men who gained power: presumptive, pushy, and eventually, he'd be pilloried. His demise might come sooner than he thought.

The server presented their plates, first to Sue Ellen and then to Elkin. He stepped back and bowed to Elkin, again. This was way too much bowing down to Elkin. It was not something Sue Ellen would be doing.

They ate in silence for a few minutes before Sue Ellen touched her mouth with her napkin, sipped her wine, and spoke to Elkin as he chewed his food. "Are you ready to proceed?"

"Absolutely. We file the professor's will for probate tomorrow."

Sue Ellen watched closely for the answer to her next question. "And when Lori's lawyer challenges the will?"

"We break her and her lawyer too." Elkin's voice was firm and confident, but it had a hint of something else too. Was it vengeance? Spite? Perhaps she could use it to her advantage.

"Could you make the trial last at least one week? I'd like them to feel it, to make a point after ridiculing and attacking me for doing nothing more than carrying out the professor's wishes."

Elkin beamed. "I like your spirit. We'll drag it out and make Lori and her has-been lawyer pay a price for trying to take money that rightfully belongs to you."

"I like the sound of that. I'm tired of their meddling."

"As soon as they file the challenge to the professor's will, I will file a multi-million-dollar libel lawsuit against Lori for her scandalous articles about Congressman Walter Butterworth. And we have the IRS on standby to revoke the nonprofit status of We Salute You when we give the word. The legal dominoes will fall, one after the other. We will schedule the hearings back-to-back. The first week, we win the will case. The second week, we win the libel case. The third week, we destroy the nonprofit."

Sue Ellen Parker liked Elkin's plan. By winning the will case, she'd have what she needed, and she could do what needed to be done. The remaining legal matters were of no consequence to her.

Elkin asked her if she was ready for the best part. "We're going to take away Craig Travail's law license. I've arranged that hearing immediately after the libel lawsuit."

"You really don't like Mr. Travail very much, do you?"

Elkin walked to his private locker, pulled out a bottle of Jefferson's whiskey, offered some to Sue Ellen, and after she refused, filled his glass to the halfway mark. He swirled the dark liquid, stuck his nose on the edge of the glass, and inhaled, then tasted the alcohol. "Craig Travail is a relic. He thinks being a lawyer has nothing to do with making money. It was bad for the law firm when others wanted to follow him."

Sue Ellen laughed. "You're jealous the lawyers in your firm like him more than you, aren't you?"

Elkin's eyes narrowed. It was the first time she'd seen a hint of the anger she'd heard others talk about.

"The last person I'd be jealous of is Craig Travail. He's a loser."

Sue Ellen checked her watch. It was a good time to goad Elkin, put him in his place. "Are you sure you can keep your emotions in check? There are other law firms who'd love to handle this case."

Elkin's head jerked. He walked to the window and settled there with his back to Sue Ellen. His shoulders heaved from his deep breaths as he examined the streets below. Was she about to experience the explosive personality she'd heard about, or would he hold it in for such an important client as herself? He tilted his glass up to his mouth and emptied the contents. When he turned to face her, he had composed himself. "Your case is in good hands."

"That's good. I look forward to putting the will contest behind me, after you inflict the appropriate amount of pain, of course."

"Of course."

Sue Ellen reached for the bag at her side. "Thank you for your hospitality. The food and drink were delicious."

Elkin said, "It was my pleasure," before his tone turned nonchalant. "I have one last topic to discuss, if you have a minute longer."

Sue Ellen stayed in her seat. This wasn't about Elkin's fee. He had no reason to worry about that with her fortune. No, the thing he feared was the publication of the professor's sequel. She wasn't sure why he was so concerned, but the topic had come up in every meeting she'd had with Elkin since the professor died. At the funeral, he wanted to know the location of the professor's books and papers. "In a safe place," she'd said. He asked about the laptop. "Not to worry," she'd said. It was obvious he didn't trust her because he kept asking, and now he was asking again, in a subtle way. She would put his mind at ease by showing him how little she cared about the Meck Dec.

"Don't worry, Robert. The books are in the landfill. I shredded his papers. I wiped the hard drive on the laptop. You got what you wanted. As long as you hold up your end of the bargain, I'll get what I want."

CHAPTER 23

FROM CAVEAT TO MONUMENTS

Travail called Lori to let her know that a friend in the clerk's office informed him that Elkin had submitted the will to probate this morning. It was sooner than necessary, but Travail kept that thought to himself.

"What do we do next?"

"If you're ready, we file a caveat with the clerk." There was plenty of time to act, but Travail wanted Elkin to know they were ready to proceed.

"A caveat?"

"Like 'caveat emptor,' which means 'buyer beware.' The word 'caveat' conveys caution. Beware the invalid will, whether by failure to follow the formal requirements, incapacity, duress, undue influence, fraud, or some other bad or illegal act." Travail made the explanation more simple. "It's the name given to the proceeding to challenge the validity of a will. When we file the caveat case, the clerk will transfer the case to superior court. A jury will decide the case."

"Will I have to testify?"

"Yes."

Lori was quiet.

"I will help you get ready," he said.

"It's not that. I just keep asking myself why he wrote the will."

Travail had been thinking more about that too. They had their Meck Dec strategy, but another idea had come to life in his mind. Maybe the professor indeed had his wits about him and wanted Lori to challenge the will. Maybe he'd been backed in a corner and cooked up the new will to prevent someone other than Sue Ellen from getting their hands on his work papers and computer. That would make Sue Ellen a friendly accomplice. But just as quickly as those thoughts entered Travail's head, he remembered what Harriet had learned from the housekeeper who'd overheard the professor tell Sue Ellen to fight back if Lori challenged the will. He even told her to hire Elkin. That made her sound like an accomplice, but not one friendly to Lori. Yeager had offered his theories, most of which were tied to the Meck Dec, but Yeager also had questions about the Apollo moon landing, Area 51, and the assassination of President Kennedy.

"Are you ready for me to file the caveat?" If she had a sudden change of heart, Travail was sure Yeager would find some other project for him, like hunting down Big Foot or UFOs or cruising in search of the Loch Ness Monster.

"I trust you. File the case."

Travail remembered what Yeager's truck looked like from the outside and was sure the inside was no better. "Well-loved" is how Peaches put it, although he wasn't sure how the Indie activities director knew what the inside of Yeager's truck looked like. Anyway, the plan for the day made sense. With Yeager driving, Travail wouldn't have to park in the courthouse deck, and he could get in, file his caveat, and get out without too much fanfare. Having Harriet with him was a good idea too. As his trial assistant, it would be helpful for her to learn her way around the courthouse. The explanation of her role, however, took some convincing.

"You don't trust me to be a witness?"

Travail tried to be diplomatic. "You and Sue Ellen have a history, that's all."

"Is it because I'm not afraid to stand up to Sue Ellen?"

"The legal term is 'bias.'"

"Well, if that's true, 99 percent of the Indie residents can't testify, because Sue Ellen drives them nuts too."

"I'm not saying you're wrong, but it might be better to avoid questions about how you thought every bird in the county looked forward to crapping on her porch."

She said she could see his point—until Travail asked her opinion about calling Yeager as a witness.

"What? You rule me out but want to use Yeager?"

"Would you rather be the one to testify about the Meck Dec?"

She shook her head no, but Travail couldn't tell if she was answering his question or turning against him. He admitted it was a risk to call Yeager. "But we need him to explain the professor was working on the sequel to *An American Hoax*."

"What if he tries to sell the Meck Dec story?"

"Both he and the professor will look crazy. And that's the point."

Travail mentioned another plus to Yeager being a witness. "He can't sit with us at counsel table."

That point sold Harriet. Other than his testimony, Yeager would stay on the fringes doing whatever stuff he does, Yeager-style, and they would do the hard work, convincing the jury that anyone who believed in the Meck Dec was touched in the head.

A horn sounded. Travail looked out the window. "Our driver awaits."

Harriet pushed him out the front door toward a world Travail thought he had abandoned when he quit the law firm. Yeager stuck his head out the window of the truck's cab. "Big day, Craig Travail."

Travail had been at this intersection many times in his life, at the corner across from the entrance to the Mecklenburg County Courthouse. Yeager hit his flashers. "Your Uber driver has completed the first half of his mission."

As Travail and Harriet got out of the truck, Yeager provided a historical sound bite about life in the 1700s. "Charlotte and Mecklenburg County were named in honor of German Princess Sophia Charlotte, who became queen consort to King George III. She was from Mecklenburg-Strelitz, a small area in Germany. And the best part is she was mixed race, like the professor."

Harriet peered in the open window. "Congratulations. I see you've been keeping up with your studies."

"All part of the service. I'll pull back around in thirty minutes."

Travail and Harriet stood on the sidewalk opposite the nine-story justice building made of white concrete walls and glass windows. The ten-foot-tall doors stared at them from under a three-story entranceway supported by several wide pillars. It was an area out of the sun and rain, where Travail had comforted clients, negotiated with attorneys, and bid hellos and farewells before and after hearings and trials. The words carved on one wall read: "THE VOICE OF JUSTICE: obey the voice of justice; Hesiod, Works and Days, ca 700 BCE." On the other wall: "TRIAL BY JURY: the legal judgment of his peers, Magna Charta, Article XXXIX, 1215." Whenever Travail entered the courthouse, he wanted to be that voice of justice, and whenever he walked out, he dealt with the emotional aftermath.

Harriett shook her head. "So this is what my county taxes pay for? It's a little much."

Travail's eyes were focused on the engraving of the Mecklenburg County seal above the covered patio.

"What are you looking at?"

He pointed. "There are four images in the county seal that tell the story of Mecklenburg. The top right features a hornet's nest hanging from a tree, with hornets flying around it, an emblem of how the locals fought and stung the British during their brief Charlotte encampment in the Revolutionary War."

Harriet looked at her watch.

"The bottom right features an image of skyscrapers, reflective of the city's growth in the twentieth century to become a city of commerce in the New South. The bottom left displays a farm and silo, representing where the county started and where the developers hadn't yet arrived, the rural area, with its good dirt, green landscape, and abundant trees."

Harriet didn't seem impressed. "Shouldn't we get going?"

Travail pointed to the image in the top left of the seal, where the morning sun sparkled and danced on a colonial-era quill and parchment. Harriett's gaze followed his gesture, and her mouth fell open. "Well, I'll be. Look at the date on top of the seal."

"Yep. May 20, 1775. Meck Dec Day."

"It's right out here in front of God and everybody. How do you expect to stand up in court and call a man crazy for believing in something that's scrawled across the face of the courthouse?"

"That's a good question."

They crossed the street, walked through the entrance, past the metal detectors, and up to the second floor, where they filed the lawsuit with the clerk. Travail led Harriet down a high-ceilinged hallway to catch the elevator, where, on the wall, a plaque was mounted: "In Commemoration of the Mecklenburg Declaration of Independence, May 20, 1775, And the Twenty-Seven Signers, Erected by the North Carolina Society of Colonial Dames of America, 1912."

Harriet touched the plaque. "The Meck Dec is everywhere."

They got off the elevator on the sixth floor and slipped into the back of a courtroom where a jury trial was in progress. As was typical when the courtroom doors opened, the judge and clerk looked up to see who entered. Travail knew this judge, and the judge knew him. The judge nodded and smiled as they took a seat in the back pew.

Crystal Marks, one of Travail's former partners and still a friend, was grilling a witness about the inconsistency between a statement he'd made in his deposition and a statement he'd just made in court. A series of objections and speeches followed, and when they finished, the judge looked at the clock and informed the jury they were going to take their mid-morning break. After the bailiff escorted the jury to the jury room, the judge rose and said, "Mr. Travail, please join me in chambers. Your assistant is welcome."

The comment rustled Harriet. "What makes him think I'm your assistant? Because I'm a woman? I could be your law partner."

"But you're not."

She huffed. "He doesn't know that."

The lawyer who'd been attacking the credibility of the witness turned around. Travail approached her with Harriet by his side. "I see you haven't lost your touch, Crystal. How's the big law firm?"

"Eighty to a hundred hours a week never felt better."

Travail introduced Harriet to Crystal Marks. He explained to Crystal that Harriet was helping him with a case.

"Is it the case our Supreme Leader said you might file after what he called your forced exit from the law firm? Not that I believe the forced part."

Travail always liked Crystal's toughness and her unwillingness to be cowed by Robert Elkin. "What did he say?"

"He told me to be ready. He might need my help."

Travail knew Elkin was serious when he enlisted Crystal. It meant his job would be that much tougher. She was younger than Travail but a smart and effective trial lawyer. He'd been her mentor, and they'd tried cases together until she no longer needed him. When he quit the firm, she was the best trial lawyer left in the Charlotte office.

The bailiff led Travail and Harriet into the back hallway and pointed toward the third office on the right. The door swung wide when they arrived, and the smiling face of another Travail protégé waited with his robe half zipped in front.

"Craig. It's good to see you. You look well." Judge Emilio Hernandez had the affable demeanor Travail remembered. Like Crystal Marks, he'd done well in the law firm under Travail's guidance, so well the local bar pushed him to run for judge, and he won two six-year terms. The judge's effusive spirit brightened Travail's mood, but before Travail could tell him so, Hernandez introduced himself to Harriet, leaving off the judge in front of his name, a gesture Harriet later admitted changed her initial impression of him.

Hernandez had a way of cutting to the core. It made him a good judge. Some called him a quick study, and today was no exception. Within five minutes, Hernandez had the lay of the land in what was left of Craig Travail's career. He even figured out what was in his brief-case. "It seems you've picked a case with a powerfully determined adversary."

~

A police cruiser sat behind Yeager's truck in front of the courthouse when Travail and Harriet left the building. They hustled across the street and up to the truck to see what trouble Yeager had gotten himself into, only to hear the officer laugh and wish Yeager a good day, by name.

"What was that about?" Harriet had taken the front seat of the four-door truck.

"He didn't like me circling the block, which led to a conversation about lawyers, which led to a few lawyer jokes, which led to a discussion about how we despise being kept waiting by lawyers and things like that."

Travail slid into the back seat. "So you like telling lawyer jokes?"

"Craig Travail, if I'd'a been stopped by a Democrat, I'd'a told Republican jokes and vice a versa." He stepped on the gas and within five minutes, Yeager found street parking across from the minor league baseball park, near what he called "my favorite uptown restaurant." The side of the small brick building had a painted sign, "Green's Lunch Famous Since 1926" and a mural of a smiling hot dog in a bun.

"Charlotte's Best Hot Dogs," Yeager barked. "Says so right there on the window."

Travail had lunched at Green's many times. The rules were simple. Stand in line. Tell the man or woman behind the counter what dogs and toppings you wanted on your steamed buns. Pick your drink and side. By the time you were at the cash register, the assembly line had your order ready. From there, you could take a seat at a small booth or at one of the round stools in front of the big window.

151

At Yeager's suggestion, Travail ordered two dogs with coleslaw and homemade chili. The combination of warm meaty spice and cool chopped cabbage with the right amount of mayo was a tasty accent. Harriet ordered a dog with mayo and mustard, and Yeager, being Yeager, ordered three dogs with the works.

While Travail had his mouth full, Yeager asked Harriet for the skinny on the courthouse visit.

"Elkin has a trial team lined up. He's ready for a fight."

"Love fights. I was runner-up in the Golden Gloves when I was sixteen."

"I meant a legal fight. Stay focused."

"Fight's a fight."

With their stomachs full, the trio left the diner into a chilly, bright afternoon. Yeager led them away from where he'd parked. "I'd like to show you something."

They turned onto the sidewalk along Trade Street and walked about fifty feet. Yeager pointed at a three-by-three-foot granite monument. The plaque read: "This tablet marks the site of the home of Captain James Jack, Revolutionary Patriot." It called him the "bearer" of "the Mecklenburg Declaration of Independence to the Continental Congress in Philadelphia, 1775."

Harriet was not surprised but was reflective. "We're going to have to put the whole dang city on trial for believing in the Meck Dec."

Travail read the inscription. "I never noticed this marker."

Yeager laughed. "You don't notice much, Craig Travail. It's time I gave you a historical tour of your own city. Let's do the Liberty Walk."

Before Travail or Harriet could object, Yeager led the way toward South Tryon Street, where he stopped at Historical Marker Number 1. "This marks the spot of the beginning of the Battle of Charlotte, fought in the fall of 1780 when the British invaded North Carolina. It was part of the Southern campaign that ended with the British surrender at Yorktown, where we kicked their red-coated butts all the way back to England."

Yeager pointed out other markers as they walked up the street, including Marker Number 3, which noted that Tryon Street had been part of an eight-hundred-mile Indian trading path from the Cherokee Nation in the south to the Iroquois in the north. Travail had walked this "path" many times to and from uptown office buildings to fight and argue cases for his clients, but he had paid no attention to the markers. He was always too focused on the mundane in front of him and unaware of all the history in his side mirrors.

Yeager darted into a small visitor's center and picked up a brochure with a walking map. He used it to continue the tour. The Battle of Charlotte reemerged at Marker Number 6, site of the British encampment from September 26 to October 12, 1780. "We're standing at the southern part of the encampment used by Tarleton's cavalry, the Loyalist militia, and camp followers. It ran all the way to the square." Yeager pointed to where four British cannons were located, and while mildly interested, Travail looked at his watch and wondered where Yeager would point next and how long it would take. They had work to do.

Yeager's forefinger aimed at Marker Number 7, the location of the battle itself. He looked at the brochure while he talked about patriots firing volleys at the British from below the log courthouse, causing the British cavalry to retreat. Yeager turned to Harriet and pointed to the guide. She pronounced the word "harangue" for him, as in "Cornwallis harangued the troops."

"Which meant," Yeager guessed, "he was really pissed."

Yeager wrapped the story near the corner of Trade and Tryon Streets, saying the British won the day, but the patriots stung them. "That's how Charlotte became the Hornet's Nest." He patted a stone monument next to him, Marker Number 8, which commemorated, "according to local legend," the signing of the Mecklenburg Declaration of Independence in 1775.

Yeager led them to his truck, saying he had one last stop on today's tour. He headed south out of the city, made a few turns, and pulled into a parking lot next to the greenway.

Travail and Harriet followed Yeager twenty yards from the parking lot to a statue of a man on horseback in the middle of a pool of water. The horse appeared to be in full gallop, with hooves grazing the top of the water. The man astride wore a tricorn hat, hands gripped to the reins, his feet firmly in the stirrups. He leaned forward, as if he were being chased or he had to be somewhere fast.

"I give you Captain Jack." Yeager swung his arm wide and bowed.

Harriet admired the statue. "The craftsmanship is spectacular, of the horse and the man."

Travail agreed. "The sculptor did fine work."

Yeager pointed at the rider "You know what they called him?"

Travail did know. He assumed this was the reason Yeager had brought him to this spot, to get him excited about Yeager's Meck Dec quest, the one Yeager said they were on whether or not they liked it. He waited for the punchline.

Yeager's face lit up with a wide smile. "The Paul Revere of the South."

The next morning, a runner from Elkin's office delivered a copy of Congressman Butterworth's libel lawsuit to Travail's door. It was the reward for Travail filing the caveat case. Robert Elkin, Esquire, was listed as lead attorney on the congressman's libel complaint, atop the names of two associates who Travail was sure did the drafting, since Elkin likely remembered very little from law school. Included was a scheduling order that showed Elkin had convinced the trial court administrator to fast track both lawsuits and schedule them back-to-back three months after their filing.

Elkin also tried to stack the deck with the judges, or so he thought. The order listed Judge Hernandez for the will caveat case, but Travail knew they'd get a fair trial with Hernandez.

The judge on the libel case was a completely different story. Travail was 0 for 3 in Judge Roscoe "Chaw" Brady's court, and Elkin knew Travail's batting average. It looked like Elkin's plan was to wear Travail's one-lawyer team out in the will contest and then pile on in the libel case before Travail could catch his breath. Travail had to admit it was a good strategy.

CHAPTER 24

MAY IT PLEASE THE COURT

Travail opened his eyes at 4:00 a.m., and he couldn't go back to sleep as much as he tried. The alarm was set for 6:00 a.m., but it was the first day of trial. He gave up and got out of bed at five. He shook himself and did a few quick stretches.

He was as ready as he could be, but the case had too many holes to give him any level of confidence. He pulled on some sweatpants, stepped over Blue, who liked to camp out beside his bed, and the two headed to the kitchen. Travail dumped some food in Blue's bowl and poured himself a glass of milk. Blue was happy with the early meal, and while he gobbled it down, Travail decided a jog around Freedom Lake would do him good. He opened the back door and found his way, with Blue close behind.

For the past few days, he'd considered the possibility Sue Ellen had something to do with the professor's death. She was now a very rich woman, and she owned the rights to *An American Hoax* and the manuscript for *An American Truth*. But was her inheritance enough of a motive for murder?

On his third lap around the lake, Travail saw the very woman he'd been thinking about. Sue Ellen Parker wore leggings and a pullover that came to the top of her thighs. They stopped in front of each other near the bench where he first met Yeager and Harriet.

Sue Ellen broke the silence. "Guess you heard about the topless party this weekend. 'Residents gone wild.' That's what Matthew would have said about it." She looked across the lake at condo building 1 and up to the third floor, as if she missed someone.

The friendly banter surprised Travail. He'd heard about the toga party and the hook-ups in the tower from Yeager, who defended it as nothing more than good fun by consenting adults, nothing to get excited about. Travail played along with Sue Ellen. "Did you enjoy the party?"

"Please, Mr. Travail, you know me better than that. Prim. Proper. Reserved. Rule maker, not rule breaker." Her tone was self-deprecating, unlike the Sue Ellen he'd briefly spoken with once before and built up in his mind. And yet, she planned to fight to keep money and property that should belong to Lori. He needed to remember that. Travail wanted to ask her a question, but he held back. Counsel represented her.

"You think me a gold digger, don't you?"

"This is not personal."

"Yes, it is. It's personal to Lori. It was personal to Matthew. And it's personal to me."

"Why do you dislike Lori so much?"

Two ducks paddled toward the lake's edge a few yards off the bank, and Blue ran to the water, hunched over until his feet and head fell in. The sky lightened, and Travail could see the lines on Sue Ellen's face. She hadn't put on any make-up. Her hair was pulled back. She watched Blue run back and forth in the water along the bank.

"I'm doing what Matthew wanted."

"That will be for the jury to decide."

"So it seems."

Blue ran back to them with four wet legs and a wet neck and head. Sue Ellen knelt down and patted him. He shook. Water beads landed on Sue Ellen's face, and she laughed. Two things surprised Travail, the fact Sue Ellen liked dogs and she knew how to laugh.

As she rubbed Blue's head, she surprised him with compassion. "I'm sorry you lost your wife. I hope you find happiness. And I'm glad you found friends here, as crazy as one is and as stubborn as the other one is. But I have to say, with all sincerity," as she gave Blue a last pat on the head, "I hope you lose this case," and then she added, "for Lori's sake."

∽

The Mecklenburg County Courthouse loomed as Travail and his team crossed Fourth Street to the entrance where Lori and Tate waited. Lori wore black slacks and a white top, her hair in a curly tumble. Tate had selected a light blue dress.

Harriet's well-tailored grey suit flattered her well-conditioned figure. As she walked, her feet straddled the crosswalk's outer line. She was one part law-abiding citizen, one part rebel. Yeager wore jeans and the sport coat Travail had loaned him. It was tight, like trying to put a size large on a grizzly bear. Yeager walked outside the lines of the crosswalk, as far as he could push it without getting run over.

Travail's sidekicks were Exhibits A and B for his life, proving he no longer hung out with the button-down uptown lawyer society. He took a deep breath to ground himself.

When they entered the courtroom, Crystal Marks directed two associates and two paralegals, and Elkin was in a sidebar with Sue Ellen. Crystal took a break from monitoring her team and stepped over to say hello to Travail.

Travail returned the greeting and added, "Sorry if I don't wish you good luck. In all fairness, you're not the kind of lawyer who needs it." They did a fist bump like boxers about to engage but parted with friendly nods.

The bailiff announced Judge Hernandez would like to see the lawyers in chambers, and Elkin was the first to enter Hernandez's office. Crystal Marks held her hand to the side, gesturing for the rest of their legal team to enter. She offered for Travail to go next, but Travail deferred to her. He followed with Harriet by his side.

"Your honor, I hope it's okay if I bring my assistant, Harriet Keaton."

"It's only fair. You're outnumbered four lawyers to one." He said this would be quick. He wanted to know if the lawyers would accept a verdict of less than twelve jurors if any jurors got sick during the trial, and he wanted to know how long the trial would last.

The answer to the first question was yes from all parties, and Marks and Travail agreed that the trial would take three days. Elkin amended the projection, saying, "It will take much longer." Judge Hernandez gave him the look judges give to lawyers when they're being more tactical than practical. "How many witnesses, Mr. Elkin?"

"Your honor, first off, it's good to see you again and we're happy they have assigned you to this case. I may cross-examine two or three witnesses, but operational control of our case, including the number of witnesses we use, will be in the capable hands of Crystal Marks."

Travail stifled a smirk. What the hell was "operational control"? Elkin sounded like an air-traffic controller. But in a way, it made sense. That was the way he ran his law firm, telling partners, associates, and staff when, where, and how to move and how to act and where and how they could and would land if they didn't follow his orders.

Crystal Marks eased into the conversation. She said the estate's case was simple. They would put on two quick witnesses to show the will met all the legal formalities for a holographic will and then, "as your honor knows, the burden of proof shifts to Lori Collins to prove the will is invalid." Marks said they might have two or three rebuttal witnesses. "Sue Ellen Parker will be our last witness to testify."

Judge Hernandez turned his attention to Travail. "What theories do you plan to try out on my jury, and how many witnesses do you have?"

Travail didn't want to give too much away, but he also didn't want to be one of those evasive lawyers who talked and said nothing when answering a judge's question. "It's the usual theories, your honor: lack of testamentary capacity, undue influence, and duress. We will have three or four witnesses. Lori Collins will be our last witness."

"Sounds like you're trying to hit a pheasant with a shotgun at one hundred yards."

Elkin laughed and agreed with the judge. "He's not that good a shot."

Judge Hernandez ignored Elkin. "What about settlement?"

The lawyers said nothing, and Hernandez shrugged. "I see. All or nothing, huh?" He said it as he rose from his seat, not waiting for an answer to the question. "Best get to it."

On the way back to the courtroom, Harriet asked Travail about pheasant-hunting. "I assume it's hard to hit a pheasant at one hundred yards with a shotgun." Travail said the judge's analogy was a perfect way to think about their case. It truly was a long shot.

Harriet said, "Bet Yeager could do it."

The parties spent the rest of the morning and into the afternoon picking the jury. It took longer than usual, with too much whispering by Elkin to Crystal Marks and a lot more discretionary challenges than necessary. Travail could see the frustration on Marks's face every time Elkin pushed her to punt on a potential juror and keep the process moving. It was as if Elkin wanted to drag things out. Around two-thirty, Judge Hernandez had had enough. He called counsel to the bench and told them to get on with it, speaking directly to Elkin.

At four o'clock, the court impaneled the jury, ten-minute opening statements followed, and Crystal Marks called the estate's first witness. She was a well-qualified handwriting expert who'd testified in over two hundred trials. She confirmed for the jury that, in her professional opinion, the handwritten will was written and signed by Matthew Collins.

Crystal Marks drove the point home. "Any doubt?"

"None at all."

Travail didn't challenge the witness. Their own handwriting expert, who also was a croquet expert, had confirmed in no uncertain terms the professor wrote and signed the document.

For its next witness, the estate called an Indie housekeeper. She testified about another element necessary to meet the formalities of a handwritten will. She'd cleaned the professor's unit for the last ten years.

"Can you tell us if there was a particular area in the unit he didn't allow you to clean?"

The woman was nervous. Besides a career in cleaning, she'd kept her nose clean and had never been to court. She spoke in a soft voice. "The professor's rolltop desk."

Crystal Marks's voice was reassuring. "Thank you. Now, can you tell us why?"

"It's where he kept his important papers."

"He told you that?"

"Yes, ma'am."

"Did it look like a place where someone would keep their important papers?"

For the first time, the witness loosened up. "Not at all. It looked like somebody emptied a wastebasket on top." A few jurors smiled.

"Would it surprise you to know he left a handwritten will on top of his rolltop desk?"

"No. Except for his books, he stacked everything important to him on that desk and never pulled the top closed."

Travail sensed the jury liked the witness. He thanked her for her time without asking her questions.

Hernandez addressed Crystal Marks. "Anything else for the estate on the validity of the handwritten will?" He was intent on keeping the case moving at a good pace.

"Yes, sir. One more thing."

Marks next offered the handwritten will into evidence as Exhibit 1. Travail did not object. He knew the testimony of the handwriting expert was enough to admit it, and an objection would do more damage than good in front of the jury.

Marks asked the court for permission to read the contents of the will to the jury. "As your honor knows, the last element of proof of the validity of a handwritten will is that the deceased intended the document to be his last will and testament. The law allows such intent to be determined from the writing itself."

Travail had studied the law in depth before the trial and knew Marks was correct. He said, "Of course, I have no objection, your honor." It was his way of saying, in front of the jury, he was not afraid of the words on the page, though in truth, they had bothered him from the first day he said he'd take the case.

Travail glanced at Lori as Crystal Marks read the will in open court. Lori had her head down, but he could tell she was listening, and the words must have hurt. She flinched when Crystal Marks read the words "do hereby revoke all prior wills" and "disinherit my only heir, my grandchild Lori Collins."

As raw as the words were, they stated, unequivocally, what Matthew Collins intended. The handwritten will would stand up in court unless Travail could convince the jury the professor was pushed, threatened, or touched in the head. Simple as that.

Judge Hernandez looked at the clock on the wall and instructed the bailiff to adjourn court until the next day. "Mr. Travail, we'll start with your case in the morning."

CHAPTER 25

COLORFUL TESTIMONY

When Travail and crew arrived at the courthouse for day two, a local news cameraman and reporter met them near the entrance. "Mr. Travail, Amanda Rogers, Channel 24 News, can you tell us why Matthew Collins cut your client out of his will? What went wrong with their relationship?"

Travail motioned Yeager, Harriet, Lori, and Tate to go on ahead. He didn't want them to be caught saying anything on camera, especially Yeager. When they were through the door, he answered the question. "Nothing went wrong with the relationship. Matthew Collins devoted himself to Lori Collins and she to him. They loved each other."

"That doesn't explain his will."

Travail smiled his best camera-ready smile. "You must be a talented reporter to realize there are problems with the will."

Amanda Rogers was a seasoned reporter. "What are the problems?"

"That's what we're going to show in court. Thank you. I don't want to be late."

Fifteen minutes later, Travail's first witness settled onto the witness chair, took the oath, and smiled his way around the courtroom. Travail got a better look at the man than the first time he saw him. He had grey hair with a receding hairline and large dimples that poked out of his happy-go-friendly face. He wore a teal golf shirt with an open collar. It revealed his enormous chest and accented his strong biceps. Travail had yet to give Yeager the credit he deserved for pinning nicknames on the residents. The witness could have passed for the twin brother of Alan Hale Jr., the actor who took his passengers on a three-hour cruise that landed them on Gilligan's Island. He'd have to be careful not to call him the Skipper.

"Good morning, Mr. Blaine."

"Morning to you, sir." He said it with a smile.

"I understand you were friends with the professor." Travail paused when he realized he was questioning a man called the Skipper about a man the residents affectionately referred to as the professor. The Indie truly was an uncharted desert isle. He gathered himself. "Can you tell us about your friendship?"

"Certainly."

The Skipper said he'd known the professor for many years and really missed him. They were two of the original residents and fell into a pattern of having breakfast together every morning. They helped each other out too. The professor shared his books with the Skipper, and the Skipper helped him with projects, like building his bookshelves. "And we both served in the Navy. We had that in common."

"Did he talk much about his family?"

"Not his wife, son, or daughter-in-law. Those losses were too hard for him. He never stopped talking about Lori though. He loved her."

"Even up to the day he died?"

The Skipper pressed his lips together, and the smiling face turned serious. "I know why we're here. The will he wrote was not like him."

"How so?"

"I visited the professor one afternoon, and it looked like he'd been crying. He asked me for a favor." The Skipper shook his head. "It makes me sad to think about it."

"Take your time."

"He said, 'If I can't tell her, please tell Lori I love her, and I really wanted to be at her wedding. Please tell her I'm sorry.'" The Skipper looked from the jury to Lori and then back to Travail. "I hate this is how I have to tell Lori her grandfather really loved her, but I, of all people, know he meant it."

Travail peeked at the jury. The back row had leaned forward to hear what the Skipper had to say.

"The professor was worried Lori might think his decision to skip the wedding had to do with the fact she was marrying a woman. It didn't." The Skipper looked at the jury and said, "Unless your gaydar is broken, you figured out I'm gay." He laughed as he said, "The professor made a toast to the 'groom and groom' at my rehearsal dinner, and after he met Tate, he told me he loved her and said she was a good match for Lori."

"Did you see Matthew Collins close to his death?"

"I saw him two days before he died. The conversation occurred by Freedom Lake."

That made Travail think about conversations he'd had by that lake: the first meeting with Yeager and Harriet that set him on the path to this courtroom and his meeting the previous morning with Sue Ellen Parker, where he saw a different side of the woman.

"How did he seem to you?"

"Agitated. He was worried about something."

"Did he talk about Lori?"

"Again, he said he loved her."

"Two days before he died."

"Yes, sir."

That was all Travail had for the Skipper. Travail suspected Crystal Marks would be efficient.

"Mr. Blaine. I'm sorry for the loss of your friend."

"Thank you."

"You were in the courtroom yesterday when the handwritten will, Exhibit 1, was read into evidence, correct?"

"I was."

"Did Matthew Collins ever mention the handwritten will to you, or say anyone pressured him to create the will?"

The Skipper paused. "No, ma'am."

"Did he tell you someone had threatened him?"

"No."

"You said he wasn't acting like his normal self. I believe you used the word 'agitated' and said he was 'worried about something.' Did he say what he was agitated or worried about?"

"No."

"So he didn't mention the handwritten will as the reason?"

"No, ma'am."

Travail could have objected to the question as "asked and answered." But that was a stupid objection reserved for young lawyers who'd never been to court or old lawyers whose legal acumen never matured. In front of a jury, it simply woke them up. It made them think, "Oh, what just happened? Guess I'd better pay attention to what the witness just said."

"Did Matthew Collins appear forgetful that day, two days before he died?"

"I don't think so."

"Was he able to carry on the conversation normally, just as he had done in the many years you'd known him?"

"I guess so."

"Nothing unusual."

"No, ma'am." The examination depleted the Skipper's spirit.

"Thank you, Mr. Blaine, for your honesty." And with that, the testimony of the man who'd shipwrecked a hapless group of tourists on a desert isle was over.

Travail called their next witness, the one Harriet said would, at the very least, keep the jury entertained.

NASCAR Nelli made an unforgettable entrance in her leather pants and jacket. With deft control of her motorized wheelchair, she dodged tables and boxes and spun at forty-five degrees near the witness box, coming to a stop below the judge's bench, close enough for the jury to see the pale circles around her eyes, made by the sun's inability to pierce her goggles. She took the oath, and before Travail could ask a question, she introduced herself to the jury. "Nelli Nimble, but everyone calls me NASCAR Nelli. I'm ready to tell the whole truth about Sue Ellen Parker." Judge Hernandez turned in his chair to conceal the grin on his face from the jury.

Travail tried to keep the preliminaries brief, but they soon got out of control. Nelli covered her background as a newspaper editor, which she said was why she was so "interested in the truth." She discussed the accident that put her in her wheelchair, but with the wave of a hand, she said, "It never slowed me down."

"And you live at the Indie?"

"I do. The residents continue to make me laugh, like the time a medicinal supply of marijuana unleashed itself on our stranded activity bus and every law-and-order conservative on the bus thoroughly enjoyed the experience. They ended up forming a coalition to lobby for the legalization of small supplies of weed."

When the jury stopped laughing, she did an encore with a story she volunteered about the time Jerry Sidesaddle came to the Indie's Sunday buffet dressed in nothing but a bow tie.

"You want to talk crazy," she said. "Invite Jerry to the party." More laughter.

NASCAR Nelli was as loose with her words as she was her driving. Travail redirected her to focus on Sue Ellen Parker. Without being asked, she said she overheard Becky Trainer ask Sue Ellen if she'd gotten the professor's power of attorney. "She was after his money."

"Hearsay," Elkin shouted. "Motion to strike."

Travail stood. "Your honor, we have no objection to Mr. Elkin's motion to strike the hearsay statement that Sue Ellen Parker wanted the professor's power of attorney, giving her control of his money." The jury got the point, and Elkin frowned at his Pyrrhic victory.

"Ms. Nimble, did you hear Sue Ellen Parker say anything about the professor's money?" Since Sue Ellen was an interested party, what she had said was fair game.

"I heard Sue Ellen and the professor argue about money a few days before he died."

"I see." Travail took her through the conversation she'd heard, and just as she'd told him in his makeshift office at his Indie cottage, she told the jury what Sue Ellen Parker said to the professor.

"She said, 'Fine, give me all your money.'"

Travail suspected some jurors might wonder about the word "fine," just as he had, as if she were reluctant to accept what he wanted to give, and others wouldn't hear anything but "give me all your money." It was a good place to stop.

Crystal Marks didn't quiz Nelli about the conversation she'd heard between the professor and Sue Ellen. Nelli had proven to be skilled at going off script and any re-telling might only make matters worse for Sue Ellen Parker. Instead, Marks asked about her "run-ins" with Sue Ellen and her friends, or as Marks put it, your "run-overs." She wanted to know about their written complaints against her.

"Mr. Travail said he'd fix those for me."

"I see. Mr. Travail agreed to represent you in the reckless endangerment charges against you if you testified?"

"Course he did."

Travail had just paid the price for calling a witness like NASCAR Nelli. He never said he would represent her, only that he'd talk to management so he could find out what she needed to do to avoid losing her privileges. She'd made it into something much more and put a dent in her credibility and a dent in his too. It revealed her to be a witness biased against Sue Ellen and him to be a lawyer who enticed witnesses to testify for something in return.

Crystal Marks said she had nothing more for the witness, and Judge Hernandez called for the morning recess. Over the break, Travail and Harriet looked at their witness list. She pointed to a name on the list, and Travail nodded. It was time to explain what the professor intended to do with his money before he created the handwritten will. He looked behind him to find their man.

~

The Godfather, Maximiliano Esposito, strode down the aisle like a man accustomed to being recognized in a crowd. Maybe even feared. He wore a finely tailored suit. A white rose adorned the lapel on the soft blue jacket. He presented a tanned and clean-shaven face, with the aged lines that come from an experienced life. A scar was apparent on his left cheek, something Travail hadn't noticed before. Esposito pressed his lips into a smile as he bowed to the judge and jury and set his hat to the side as he took the witness chair.

The Godfather's answers to Travail's questions exuded confidence. He told the jury he'd moved from New York City to the New South city to retire, and added, "to get away from it all," what he described as a career working in the cement business. Travail had seen a documentary on Netflix a few nights earlier about how the government took down the heads of the five crime families in New York in the mid-eighties because they extorted money from cement contractors and gained large-dollar contracts for a group called The Concrete Club. Travail wondered what part Esposito played in the concrete drama and how he avoided getting caught, but those were not the questions he intended to ask.

"How well did you know Matthew Collins?"

"Knew him well." The Godfather explained they met when they moved to the Indie twenty years earlier and found they had much in common, such as their interest in books, writing, travel, and history. They ate together often, did favors for one another, and kept up with each other's family. "Like me, Matthew Collins placed family first."

"Did he ever seek your advice on financial matters?"

Esposito smiled. "He did. Neither of us cared for the government, particularly the IRS."

"What kind of advice did he seek?"

"It had to do with his will."

Travail needed to lay a foundation. "What experience did you have that could help?"

"I've had a lot of experience putting things over on the government."

There were murmurings in the audience and a question from Judge Hernandez. "What exactly do you mean, Mr. Esposito?"

The Godfather laughed. "Some might call it stealing, but I assure you, judge, it was all legal."

"Meaning?" Judge Hernandez didn't let Esposito off the hook.

"Meaning I had experience doing what every red-blooded American citizen loves to do, find legal ways to avoid paying taxes to the government." He emphasized the word "legal."

Travail inserted himself back into the conversation. "What did this have to do with Matthew Collins's will?"

"Matthew, like me, had come into a bit of money. He and I discussed ways to avoid paying the estate tax upon our deaths. I shared with him what my lawyer told me." The Godfather turned to the jury. "It was really very simple. There was an estate tax exclusion of eleven million dollars. He could give that amount away to anyone he wanted and not pay estate tax on it."

"And did he tell you what he planned to do?"

"No. He showed me." The Godfather explained he was a witness to an earlier type-written will. "He earmarked eleven million dollars for Lori, his granddaughter."

"What about the rest of his fortune?"

"Again, very simple." The Godfather explained to the jury that gifts to qualifying charities avoid the estate tax. "On the will I witnessed, he gave the rest of his estate to We Salute You, the nonprofit he founded and Lori runs."

Travail needed to make sure the jury understood the mindset of Matthew Collins. "How important was it to Matthew Collins to avoid paying the estate tax?"

"He hated the government more than I do. His bias had to do with how politicians treat veterans."

Travail acted incredulous. "If that's true, how do you explain the handwritten will?"

The Godfather rubbed the scar on his cheek. "That is a mystery. By giving all his money to Sue Ellen Parker, the estate tax charitable exemption doesn't apply, and the government is going to get a big tax payday, assuming Sue Ellen wins this case. The Matthew Collins I knew would never want the government to get paid like that."

Travail thanked the Godfather and turned the witness over to Crystal Marks, who didn't hesitate. "Mr. Esposito, I'm sorry for the loss of your friend."

The Godfather tilted his head forward but said nothing.

"When was the last time you spoke with Matthew Collins?"

"Hmmm. It was a few days before he died."

"Did he say anything about his handwritten will?"

"No, he didn't."

"Fair to say, he didn't confide in you about it?"

"Suppose not."

"Is it also fair to say you don't know why he changed his will?"

"That's fair."

Crystal Marks changed course. "Can you speak to the character of the man?"

"Hard worker. A bit obsessed with his research projects, if that's what you're after."

Crystal Marks smiled. "No, that's not what I was after, but since you mentioned his work ethic, would you say he was a man others could push around?"

"I would not."

"So he could stand up for himself?"

"To use your words, no one pushed Matthew Collins around."

"And if someone had tried to push Matthew Collins around, say to get him to change his will against his wishes, would the Matthew Collins you knew have allowed that to happen?"

Travail thought about whether to object to the question on grounds of speculation. But even if the judge sustained it, the jury would get the point. Travail stayed quiet to see how the Godfather handled the question. He suspected the answer would not be helpful to Lori.

"Counselor, to be quite honest, Matthew Collins must have changed his will for a very specific reason. I don't know what that reason was, but the Matthew Collins I knew would not have allowed someone to push him to do something he didn't want to do."

One of Marks's associates handed her a document. She looked at it and laid it down in front of her. "Just a few more questions."

"By all means." The Godfather adjusted his lapel and smiled.

"Are you married?"

"Sort of. We've been separated for twenty years. She didn't want to move away from the big city."

"Do you know about the estate tax marital deduction?"

"I do. It's another way to avoid the estate tax. You can give all your money to your spouse and avoid payment of the estate tax to the IRS." He smiled. "But in my case, I'd rather the IRS get my money, so I changed my will to remove her from it." The jury and others in the courtroom laughed.

Crystal Marks picked up the document she'd laid in front of her and examined it again. "If Matthew Collins had given all his money to his wife, he could stiff the IRS, true?"

"That's true. But he didn't have a wife."

Travail called Carrie Roberts as the first witness after lunch, and the jurors didn't nod off with Carrie holding court. She quickly established her ability to see and hear pretty much everything that went on at the Indie, which she volunteered was because of her years of experience and well-deserved reputation as "a gossip." She knew who was having sex with whom, who wanted to have sex with whom, and who preferred bridge to sex, which she said reminded her of a story. Travail cut her off with a relevant question.

"Can you tell us about the relationship between Matthew Collins and Sue Ellen Parker?"

"What relationship?"

"The kind that would cause him to give her fifty million dollars?"

"I've lived at the Indie as long as Sue Ellen. I've never seen or heard about them engaging in any public displays of affection."

Elkin objected to what she'd "heard about from others," and Judge Hernandez sustained the objection. Carrie told the judge she was sorry if she'd done something wrong, but "just so you know, everybody at the Indie tells me what's going on, so if I didn't hear about it, it didn't happen."

Elkin objected again, and Carrie looked confused. Or maybe she was a talented actress. The judge shook his head and denied the objection. Elkin pouted.

Carrie Roberts continued. "The professor and Sue Ellen spent many hours together in the two months before the professor died. They were always serious. Businesslike."

"Did you hear a conversation between Matthew Collins and Sue Ellen Parker a few days before he died?"

"I did."

"Please tell the jury what you heard Sue Ellen say."

"They were talking on the dock at Freedom Lake as I walked by, minding my own business." Travail knew nobody in the courtroom believed Carrie Roberts minded her own business.

"Anyway, they were arguing about something. I couldn't hear what they said until Sue Ellen shouted at him."

"What did she shout?"

Carrie turned to the jury. "She shouted, 'You're crazy.'"

Travail let that piece of evidence sink in with the jury before turning Carrie over to Sue Ellen's team for questioning. When Elkin told the judge he'd be handling cross-examination, Travail glanced at Crystal Marks. She had a pained expression on her face.

Elkin stumbled with his cross-examination and let his emotions get to him. When he argued with Carrie, it gave her the chance to share with the jury how "opportunistic" and "selfish" and "domineering" a woman Sue Ellen was—opinions Travail would never have been able to introduce on direct examination. Crystal Marks frequently tugged on Elkin's coat sleeve and whispered in his ear. She probably told him enough was enough.

Next up was Tommy Do-Little, who Yeager said got his nickname from doing as little as possible. He was a longtime health center employee assigned to help residents who had short-term cognitive impairments. He sat with them and fetched things for them and pushed them around in wheelchairs. All the residents liked Tommy. Residents opened up to him, told him their problems, and he comforted them by paying attention and listening to them.

Travail asked Tommy Do-Little about a conversation he witnessed between Sue Ellen Parker and Becky Trainer a few days before the professor died. Elkin objected and Judge Hernandez intervened, instructing Tommy not to say what he heard Ms. Trainer say. "Limit your answer to what Ms. Parker said."

"She said the professor wasn't thinking straight."

"Anything else?" Travail asked.

"She was going to have to take control of his assets."

Tommy Do-Little's testimony didn't last long, but as judges say when they instruct juries, it's not the quantity of the evidence that counts, but the quality, and Elkin could not damage the quality. The most he could do was show that Tommy Do-Little was written up several times for sleeping on the job, a fact Tommy admitted but then added, "I wasn't sleeping when I heard Sue Ellen say she was gonna take the professor's assets."

Marks interrupted Elkin as he was about to ask his next question and told the court that was all the questions they had, which led to a minor verbal scuffle between Elkin and Marks. Travail heard Marks say Elkin could handle the rest of the trial himself if he wanted, and Elkin backed down.

Peaches, the Indie's activities director, was Travail's next witness. She was glad to see Travail, and judging by her wide smile when she took the stand, she was happy to be there.

"Do you know Robert Elkin?"

"Objection." Elkin was on his feet.

Judge Hernandez seemed surprised. "On what grounds?"

"Her knowing me is not relevant."

The judge took less than a second to overrule the objection and told Peaches to answer the question.

Peaches said she knew Robert Elkin. "He was much nicer when he visited me at the Indie than he is now. He asked me all about the professor."

Elkin scowled.

Travail followed up. "Was he interested in anything in particular?"

"The fact the professor was writing another book."

Elkin made a silly objection about the attorney-client privilege, but the judge rebuffed it. "Your conversation with this witness is not privileged."

"What did you tell him?"

"I told him the professor was writing a sequel to *An American Hoax*. He was so happy he hugged me before he went up to visit with the professor."

Travail asked her the date when this occurred. She said it was the day before the professor died.

Travail picked up his copy of Exhibit 1 and addressed the court. "The witness has confirmed Robert Elkin visited Matthew Collins the same day Matthew Collins signed the handwritten will. That's all we have for this witness."

Before Elkin could question Peaches, Marks informed the court they had no questions for the witness. The afternoon break followed.

During the break, Travail walked over and handed Elkin a piece of paper. Elkin looked at it, balled it up, and cursed. "We'll see about this."

Travail announced Robert Elkin as his next witness, and Elkin threw a fit. He swung his hands in the air and shouted "preposterous" several times.

Travail remained calm. "I served him with a subpoena, your honor."

Marks put a hand on Elkin to calm him. "Your honor, may we approach?" Hernandez waved Marks and Travail to come to the bench. Marks handed the judge a motion to quash subpoena. Travail was impressed. Her assistants had worked fast.

Judge Hernandez excused the jury and took up the matter outside their presence.

"Mr. Travail, as you know, absent unusual circumstances, it is inappropriate for counsel to call opposing counsel as a witness. It leads to distractions and creates animosity among bar members. Please explain your reason for wanting to call Mr. Elkin as a witness."

"He was one of the last people to see Matthew Collins alive."

Judge Hernandez held up a thick document. "Mr. Elkin says he was legal counsel for Matthew Collins and anything they discussed was privileged. Do you have any evidence to the contrary?"

Of course Travail didn't have any evidence to the contrary, and he was sure Elkin had lied in his declaration that accompanied the motion to quash. "We'd like to ask him questions about their conversation related to the Meck Dec sequel. Surely, those are not privileged."

Elkin countered. "He hired me to advise him on the sequel too."

"Your honor, I find that hard to believe, given the fact Mr. Elkin found out about the sequel from the Indie's activities director."

"He hired me when I met with him that day."

That was a lie too, but without any evidence to the contrary, the judge quashed the subpoena. The ruling was a setback, but not an entire loss. It revealed Elkin would lie twice to avoid telling what he knew about his visit with the professor that day.

With the jury back in their place, Travail called Chuck Yeager Alexander to testify. Yeager must have taken a brush, or a broom, to his beard, but it still had a wild look to it. He wore a tie, but the knot could have been tied by a second-grader. At least his blue jeans were clean, and his boots didn't have lake mud on them. Yeager patted Travail on the back on his way to the witness stand and whispered, "Don't worry about a thing, Craig Travail."

Travail took a deep breath before launching his first question.

"Tell the jury about your friendship with Matthew Collins."

"The professor was my best friend."

Yeager then went into great detail about their friendship, how long they had known each other, what they liked to do together, and how they supported and confided in one another.

"Tell us about his character."

"He was a war hero. Started a nonprofit to help veterans. Made a lot of money and gave it to the nonprofit. Loved his country, but not politicians." A few jurors nodded their heads.

"Did he love his granddaughter?"

"A hundred and twenty-five percent."

"How often did you hear the professor talk about his granddaughter?"

"Every day."

"And were his words about Lori positive?"

"I never heard him say a negative thing." Yeager sat up in his chair and made eye contact with the jurors. "He loved Lori with all his heart and all his soul."

"What about Sue Ellen Parker?"

"What about her?" Yeager said it like Travail had asked about the temperature in Moscow. "It's no secret Sue Ellen and I don't get along, but I don't have to throw stones at her because I knew the professor. There's no way the professor cared for Sue Ellen Parker more than he cared for Lori."

"Did the professor speak of Sue Ellen Parker often?"

"Nope. Most of the time, she made us shake our heads." Yeager offered a story about the time Sue Ellen insisted they ban a book from the Indie library. "It had something to do with a lady's lover. Lady Chatterbox, or something like that."

"You mean, *Lady Chatterley's Lover?*"

"That's the book. It had too much sex and too many four-letter words to suit Sue Ellen, although if that were true, she never should have moved into the Indie." The jurors laughed. "I thought about checking it out just because Sue Ellen didn't want me to, but there was too long a waiting list."

Travail saw the jurors had warmed up to Yeager, so he had Yeager explain what he thought about the handwritten will when he found it.

"I was shocked. That wasn't the act of the man I'd known for the past twenty years."

"Had his demeanor changed in the months leading up to his death?"

"Was he meaner?"

"No. Demeanor?

"Say again, Craig Travail."

"Did his outward behavior change?"

"Are you talking about his obsession?"

Elkin objected. "This witness is not a doctor."

Before the judge could rule, Yeager agreed, but added, "I have eyes."

Judge Hernandez overruled the objection and told Yeager he could tell the jury what he observed.

"The professor was obsessed with the Mecklenburg Declaration of Independence."

As a frontal counter-measure, Travail made his next question appear to challenge Yeager. "Wasn't it natural for the professor as an author to be obsessed with his subject?"

Elkin couldn't help himself. He objected to Yeager not being an expert in literary matters, a comment that caused Yeager to laugh and admit, "That's your best objection so far."

Judge Hernandez took control and tapped his gavel lightly on his bench to quell the laughter in the courtroom. "Mr. Alexander, you're not being asked to testify as an expert in literary matters. Just tell us what you observed."

"The professor has always been obsessed with the topic of the Meck Dec. His obsession with his new book, *An American Truth*, was very different."

Travail needed the jury to understand the gravity of the professor's recent obsession. "How so?"

"While he worked on his new book, the professor wasn't sleeping well, wasn't eating like he should, and was holing himself up in his condo writing as if his life depended on it. I'd never seen him so exhausted as he was the last week of his life."

"Did he appear to be thinking straight to you?"

Elkin objected to Yeager testifying about what the professor had been thinking. Travail withdrew the question and asked another instead. "Tell us what the professor told you about his work on the sequel?"

177

Elkin was on an objection spree. "Objection. Dead man's statute."

Before Travail could respond and the judge could rule, Yeager piped up. "He weren't dead when he said it." This caused the bailiffs, clerk, jurors, and spectators to laugh. Judge Hernandez restored order and called the lawyers to the bench. He placed his hand over the microphone and asked Travail to respond to the objection.

"Mr. Alexander is not a beneficiary of the will, and his testimony is not about the professor's intentions with respect to the making of the will. The dead man's statute does not apply to the question or the answer."

Judge Hernandez agreed. The lawyers went back to their places, and Travail asked his question.

"Mr. Alexander, did Matthew Collins tell you something different about the Meck Dec before he died than he'd told you before?"

"He did. He said he'd come around to believing the Meck Dec was real. It was totally opposite of everything he'd believed for fifteen years."

"Did this concern you?"

"Absolutely. After he changed his mind about the Meck Dec, he was happy and excited one day and depressed and paranoid the next. He was an emotional wreck that last week before he died. I was worried he wasn't thinking straight." Yeager stared first at Sue Ellen and then at Elkin. "He was, what's the word? Vulnerable."

Travail let the point hang in the air. "That's all we have for Mr. Alexander, your honor."

Another whispering match between Robert Elkin and Crystal Marks followed before Marks rose to inform the court they didn't have any questions for the witness. "We reserve the right to call him at a later time, although based on the strength of our witness testimony, it probably won't be necessary."

CHAPTER 26

THE MECK DEC ON TRIAL

Travail had forgotten how tiring it was to handle a trial. Exciting, sure. But exhausting too. During the day, trial lawyers had to appear calm, even when they felt the stress of not knowing how their witnesses would do or what surprises would be thrown at them. The trial day was long, with morning prep and evening prep and client hand-holding throughout.

Day three of the trial started like days one and two. Travail was up early for a stretch and jog with Blue. He showered and dressed, reviewed outlines, ate a small breakfast, and met Harriet and Yeager at Yeager's cottage for the ride to the courthouse. After Yeager's testimony the day before, he asked if he could take the morning off to do some poking around after he dropped them off. "I'd rather not be in court when you trash the Meck Dec, Craig Travail." Travail said that was fine but to stay close to his phone.

Amanda Rogers waited at the courthouse entrance, apparently having received a tip as to what Travail had planned. "Mr. Travail, is it true you intend to prove the Meck Dec is a hoax?"

Travail smiled at the camera. "We don't have to prove what everyone knows to be reality." He thanked her and guided Harriet through the front door while Amanda Rogers shouted additional questions at him.

"Why do you need an expert if your position is so obvious? Do you really think Matthew Collins was incompetent because he changed his mind about the Meck Dec?"

Travail didn't answer her. He'd be providing answers for those questions soon enough.

When court opened and before the jury was seated, Robert Elkin addressed the judge with a motion *in limine*, objecting to testimony by Travail's expert witness about the Meck Dec. Apparently, Travail had touched a sensitive spot with Elkin, who argued this would be a waste of the court's time. This from the man who had wanted to drag things out on the first day of trial.

The judge turned and addressed Travail. "What about it, Mr. Travail? I'm a history fan, but I'm not sure how this history lesson relates to this case."

"Your honor, if you had allowed me to call Mr. Elkin as a witness, the jury would have learned about the professor's state of mind the day before he died, the same day he wrote and signed the handwritten will. His work on the sequel and his belief in the Meck Dec relate to his state of mind."

Judge Hernandez agreed and denied Elkin's motion.

With the jury seated, Travail announced his next witness. He heard the courtroom door open and turned to see reporter Amanda Rogers enter the courtroom with her notepad at the ready. Dr. Lester Partin, Travail's expert witness, stood from the back row to let Amanda take his spot before he walked up to testify.

"Please introduce yourself to the jury and explain how you came to know Matthew Collins," Travail said.

"My name is Lester Partin. I have a doctorate in history. I was a professor at Davidson College for forty years, specializing in European history. In my retirement, I took an interest in the Mecklenburg Declaration of Independence. I became friends with Matthew Collins after we met at one of his book signings for *An American Hoax*. We met often to discuss history, and the conversation always got around to the Meck Dec."

Dr. Partin was of medium height, with a thin build and narrow but smiling face, topped with receding grey hair, combed meticulously. He wore wire-rimmed glasses. When he spoke, he did so with a bit of a grin, as if he was happy to have a conversation with you. His voice was soft, so soft, the jurors had to lean forward to tune in, which they did with interest. Listening to him was like auditing a class with a talented story-teller. Travail sensed the jury liked Dr. Partin. He asked his expert an open-ended question that allowed him to start his lesson.

"Could you set the historical stage for us?"

"Glad to. The year 1775 was a volatile period in American history. Charlotte was a small settlement in a large area known as Mecklenburg County. A few years earlier, in 1773, colonists posing as Mohawk Indians boarded ships owned by the East India Company in Boston Harbor and dumped three hundred chests of tea worth over ninety thousand pounds sterling into the water, an act that infuriated the English Parliament. We know it today as the Boston Tea Party. It grew out of anger at taxation without representation. And then, one month before the May 20 meeting, on April 19, 1775, British troops marched on the small town of Lexington, Massachusetts, where they fired their muskets and killed several colonial militiamen. A few miles down the road, at a small bridge in Concord, farmers fired back, killing redcoats. We know their act as 'the shot heard round the world.'

"These events painted the backdrop against which Colonel Thomas Polk, commander of the local militia, called for a meeting of all the militia leaders of Mecklenburg County. Each militia sent two representatives to the meeting held in the Mecklenburg County Courthouse. It was nothing like where we sit today. It was only a log cabin on stilts. But the meeting was treasonous, the penalty for which was death."

"Did they sign a document?"

"They did. There is no debate about that."

Dr. Partin explained to the jury the crux of the issue, the difference between the Mecklenburg Declaration of Independence, for which there was no surviving document, and the Mecklenburg Resolves, which survived the meeting but did not include the word "independence." He discussed the timeline, starting with the fire that supposedly destroyed the Meck Dec in 1800, and continuing with the *Essex Register* article that sparked the dispute between Adams and Jefferson, the conclusions in the 1831 report that favored the Meck Dec, and the discovery of the Mecklenburg Resolves in 1838 that turned historians against the Meck Dec.

"I take it you agree with Matthew Collins's conclusion in *An American Hoax*."

"I wouldn't be so blunt as to describe the Meck Dec as a hoax, but I can see how Collins came to use that title. The Meck Dec never existed."

It was time to make the connection from Dr. Partin's testimony to the professor's handwritten will. "How do you explain the fact Matthew Collins changed his mind about its existence?"

"The Matthew Collins I knew would not do that."

"Why not?"

"Nothing has changed. It's not as if he found a copy of the Meck Dec."

Travail thanked Dr. Partin, and Judge Hernandez looked at the clock. "We'll take up cross-examination after the morning break."

Travail watched the jurors as they filed out, hoping to see the light of understanding on their faces. Would they follow his argument that the professor's misguided obsession with the Meck Dec led him to act irrationally with the will? Or, did the jurors believe in the Meck Dec before they arrived and no history lesson could change their mind? He couldn't tell by watching them. He also wasn't sure what Yeager was up to, and it worried him.

Yeager went to his computer and googled "Dispatch 34." It returned search results for dispatch buildings, courier services, and publications unrelated to the Meck Dec. He added "Meck Dec" to the search term and he saw a link to an online posting by Charlotte-Mecklenburg Library, but when he clicked on the link, his computer shut down. He fiddled with the plug and tried to reboot. No success. Fine, he'd go to the Charlotte-Mecklenburg Library's uptown branch and use one of their free computers.

He fired the engine up on Hoss, the name he'd given his truck in honor of the character played by Dan Blocker on *Bonanza*. The truck was to other vehicles what Hoss Cartwright was to the bad guys, large and menacing. When he pulled onto Independence Boulevard for the ride uptown, a black SUV appeared in his rearview mirror. Yeager was in no hurry, and apparently, the SUV wasn't either. When Yeager took the exit onto one of the side streets in the uptown area, the SUV followed. When he pulled into the Seventh Street parking deck and pulled his ticket, the SUV didn't follow him inside. He parked, grabbed his knapsack, and forgot about his follower.

The stairwell dumped him out on Sixth Street, a block and a half from the library. It was cool out, but a nice cloudless day, allowing the sounds of the city to travel. He heard car traffic, the sound of someone unloading a truck on a nearby dock, and bells and creaks of the closing crossing arms for the approaching Charlotte light-rail train. He walked to the corner and stopped at College Street to wait for the stoplight to change. When it did, he stepped into the crosswalk.

Yeager's mother often said he had eyes in the back of his head. She exaggerated, but she wasn't entirely wrong. He had exceptional peripheral vision, which he attributed to something he'd read in *National Geographic* about man's early evolutional development, eyes cut in the head in such a way to detect snakes about to strike. His primal eyesight detected something in motion, something poisonous, and he stopped and turned. The black SUV came straight at him. Yeager heard someone scream. He twisted and dove backwards onto the sidewalk.

The SUV swerved after him, but banged the crosswalk pole, bounced back into its lane and sped away. When Yeager got to his feet, the SUV was gone.

He was unhurt, but his knapsack hadn't been so lucky. The SUV's tires had crushed the bag and the phone inside. He brushed himself off and headed to the library to learn more about Dispatch 34. Next, he'd get a new phone.

~

Word had gotten out about the fifty-million-dollar will contest with ties to the Meck Dec, bringing more spectators to the courtroom gallery after the morning break. Amanda Rogers was in her same spot. The bailiff brought the jury in, and Crystal Marks got right to work on Dr. Partin.

"Is there any question among historians that Captain Jack went on a five-hundred-mile ride from Charlotte to Philadelphia in late May or early June 1775?"

"None. The only question is: What did he carry in his saddlebags?"

Crystal Marks agreed that was a good point. With the judge's permission, she had an assistant place a large map on an easel facing the jury. She asked Dr. Partin to come down and use the map to describe the route Captain Jack took. When he stepped down, Judge Hernandez and the bailiffs moved around so they could see. People in the courtroom moved too.

Travail knew jurors loved visuals. Crystal Marks and Dr. Partin were going to bring the famous ride of Captain Jack to life.

"Before you talk about the route, Dr. Partin, I'd like you to talk about Captain Jack, the person he was."

Dr. Partin laughed. "He was a tavern owner. Rough and tumble kind of guy. Brave. Eager to help. A backwoods patriot who fought in the Revolutionary War and lived to tell about it."

The description made Travail think of Yeager.

"And the conditions of the ride?"

"Rainy. Rough. And perilous. If the British caught him, they would hang him, whether he was carrying the Meck Dec, the Mecklenburg Resolves, or both.

"He rode to the town of Salisbury, North Carolina, first, where they were holding court." Dr. Partin used the pointer Crystal Marks had given him to identify that stop on the fourteen-to-twenty-day route identified on the map by a dotted line. "One of the public officials asked Captain Jack to read what he was carrying to the court, and when he did, two prominent lawyers in the courtroom declared it treasonous and sought to have Captain Jack detained. According to one witness, Captain Jack drew his pistols and threatened to kill the first man who would interrupt him, and he rode on, stopping next in Salem, North Carolina."

"Speaking of that next stop, are you aware of documents discovered in 1904 written by a Moravian merchant named Traugott Bagge that bear on the question before us today?"

Dr. Partin nodded his head. "Traugott Bagge wrote what we call a historical sketch in German. It covered various events going on in the colonies, including Captain Jack's ride through Salem, and it offers circumstantial evidence in favor of the Meck Dec story."

"How so?"

"It said Mecklenburg County had declared itself 'Frey u. Independent.'"

"Frey meaning 'free' in German?"

"Yes."

"Why would he use the English word 'independent' if the other words were in German?"

"We can't know for sure. We assume he wanted to convey the word exactly as he saw it."

Travail glanced at the jury. By their attention to the evidence, Crystal Marks had landed a blow against his argument that the Meck Dec wasn't real. The document Captain Jack carried through Salem, as witnessed and interpreted by Traugott Bagge, declared independence. Would the jury think someone crazy for believing in the Meck Dec with this kind of evidence?

Dr. Partin returned to the map and continued to recount the long and daring ride of Captain Jack. "He passed through Roanoke,

Virginia, and then Staunton, northwest of Charlottesville. From there, he rode through Winchester, York, and Lancaster, before arriving here in Philadelphia." He pointed to the home of liberty, the place where the Continental Congress declared independence one year later.

"Who did he meet with and what happened?"

Dr. Partin said this is where the story got interesting. Captain Jack met with Richard Caswell and William Hooper, two North Carolina delegates to congress, and he gave them what he'd carried five hundred miles to deliver.

"How did they react?"

Dr. Partin described their response as "tepid." "One witness who testified before the 1831 commission remembered Captain Jack coming back with the advice 'to be a little more patient until congress should take the measures it thought best.' Another prominent witness, John Davidson, who was from the same militia company as John McKnitt Alexander and was a signer of the document in question, said the delegates told Captain Jack 'they highly esteemed the patriotism of the citizens of Mecklenburg, but they thought the measure premature.'"

Crystal Marks latched onto the word "premature." She asked Dr. Partin if this was a word often used by historians to describe the reaction in Philadelphia to what Captain Jack delivered.

"It was. You have to remember that even though the British had killed American colonists in Lexington and Concord and begun the siege of Boston, the delegates weren't in agreement as to what they should do next. On July 5, 1775, in one last effort at compromise, the Continental Congress submitted what's known as the Olive Branch Petition, where they pledged loyalty to the king but decried the actions of parliament. They weren't ready for what was in Captain Jack's saddlebag."

"What do you mean?"

"They weren't cowards, but they had concerns."

"About a document that might spark a revolution too soon?"

"That's what some believed."

"What did Richard Caswell and William Hooper say about Captain Jack's visit?"

Dr. Partin smiled. "They never wrote about it. No reference to Captain Jack's visit appeared in their papers or letters."

Crystal Marks looked puzzled. "Are you saying they concealed it, including from the Continental Congress?"

"Good possibility. Or—" Dr. Partin had a devilish grin on his face. "They could have shared what Captain Jack delivered to them with a few leading delegates, perhaps those responsible for drafting important documents, like Thomas Jefferson and John Dickinson, both of whom had a part in drafting the Olive Branch Petition."

"Dr. Partin, you're aware Thomas Jefferson denied ever seeing the Meck Dec?"

"I am." The grin never left his face.

Dr. Partin appeared to be having fun. As a historian, he didn't believe in the Meck Dec, but he seemed to enjoy the Meck Dec story. Travail looked over his shoulder and saw Amanda Rogers scribbling away in her reporter's notebook.

Crystal Marks picked up two documents and held them side by side. "Dr. Partin, does your speculation about Caswell and Hooper showing the document to Thomas Jefferson have anything to do with the similarity between some of the words Thomas Jefferson penned in the Declaration of Independence in 1776 and the words in the Meck Dec of 1775?"

"Objection."

Travail and Harriet looked up from their notes. Judge Hernandez spoke next. "Mr. Elkin, are you objecting to questions by your co-counsel?"

All eyes in the courtroom were on Elkin.

Crystal Marks asked for a moment to confer with Robert Elkin, who looked sullen. For whatever reason, her examination had affected him more than anyone else in the courtroom. Travail made a note on his legal pad and put a question mark beside it. Robert Elkin didn't want anyone to believe the Meck Dec was real, even if it meant it would help his client, Sue Ellen Parker.

Elkin and Marks whispered for a few minutes before Marks addressed the court. "Your honor, we apologize. This was Mr. Elkin's way of letting me know I'd gone on too long with the history lesson. He's right. I got carried away. I will shift to questions related to the deceased's mental capacity."

She faced the witness again. "Dr. Partin, please look at the North Carolina state flag behind you. Does it display any dates?"

Dr. Partin looked at the flag draped alongside the pole that held it. He stood and took the lower part of the flag in his hand and pulled it away from the pole so everyone could see. The flag bore two dates, one above and one below the letters "NC."

Dr. Partin explained that April 12, 1776, the date below NC, was the date of the Halifax Resolves, when North Carolina authorized their delegates to the Continental Congress to sign the Declaration of Independence of 1776. By now, everyone in the courtroom knew the significance of the other date. It was May 20, 1775. Meck Dec Day.

Crystal Marks turned to the question Travail had raised. Should a man be declared incompetent for believing in the Meck Dec?

Marks guided Dr. Partin through a series of leading questions. His answers made a good rebuttal to Travail's Meck Dec theory. Local patriots believed in the Meck Dec. The state legislature believed in it. The Mecklenburg County Commissioners with their county seal believed in it. The May 20th Society believed in it. And even some historians believed in it.

"What about US presidents?"

"Yes. A number of twentieth-century politicians came to Charlotte to celebrate an anniversary of the signing of the Mecklenburg Declaration of Independence. President William Taft, on May 20, 1909. President Woodrow Wilson, on May 20, 1916, for celebrations attended by a hundred thousand people. President Dwight Eisenhower, in 1954, for a rally at Freedom Park with thirty thousand attendees. And Gerald Ford came on May 20, 1975, when over a hundred thousand people gathered at Freedom Park and the headline of *The Charlotte Observer* that day read 'County Declares Independence.'"

Crystal Marks focused her last questions on well-known authors and journalists who'd paid homage to the Meck Dec. Dr. Partin knew the history.

"There was David McCullough, a Pulitzer Prize-winning author, who visited Charlotte in 2007 at the invitation of the May 20th Society. He said in his speech, 'All my instincts, all my experience over the years incline me to believe it is true. And well worth exploring, worth commemorating, and keeping alive.'"

"Any others?"

"Yes. George Will, the writer and political commentator agreed with McCullough in an article he wrote in the *Washington Post*, saying: 'What occurred July 4 in Philadelphia might have been a Declaration of Independence, but the first such occurred on May 20, 1775. Thus did a settlement on the fringe of the British Empire declare war on that empire.'"

"What about Cokie Roberts, the award-winning journalist? Didn't she speak at the dedication of Captain Jack's statue?"

"She did, and she provided the argument we often hear by proponents of the Meck Dec, saying, 'There is not a question in my mind. First of all, there is plenty of evidence, but secondly, when you have folk memory that's *that strong,* it's always right. And often people don't like that, as in Sally Hemmings and Thomas Jefferson. But it turned out to be right ... There is just no question in my mind that this is true.'"

Crystal Marks ended her examination on that note. She didn't have to ask Dr. Partin whether a court should judge a man crazy for believing in the Meck Dec. If all these people believed in it, why couldn't Matthew Collins?

Judge Hernandez asked Travail if he had any re-direct examination. He didn't hesitate and used his most confident voice.

"Dr. Partin, you seem rather knowledgeable about what some novelists and journalists think about the Meck Dec. Why is that?"

"It interests me how people arrive at their conclusions when historical support is lacking. Most often, they base their conclusions on a hunch, and sometimes, they just like the story."

"As a historian, do you have the luxury of basing your conclusions on a hunch, or concluding that something happened because it's a good story?"

His grin appeared again. "Wish I did. It would save a lot of work."

Travail held up several history textbooks and well-known works of nonfiction that looked like they each weighed twenty pounds. "What goes into writing one of these things?"

Dr. Partin explained it involved extensive research, late nights checking and cross-checking primary and secondary documents, putting words on the page, and working with editors, publishers, and fact-checkers, "among other things."

"Is that the kind of process Matthew Collins went through when he wrote *An American Hoax?*"

Dr. Partin nodded and said, "Yes."

"Are you aware of any textbook or other work of nonfiction crafted under that level of academic discipline that took a contrary position to the conclusions in *An American Hoax?*"

"No, sir."

Travail pressed for an explanation.

"History is not religion, Mr. Travail. It's based on fact, not hope or faith or wishful thinking."

"Or delusion?"

"That too."

Travail paused for dramatic effect. "Just to be clear, is it true that when Matthew Collins wrote *An American Hoax*—the *New York Times* bestseller that disputed the validity of the Meck Dec—he employed rigorous academic discipline in his research and writing?"

"Correct."

"He didn't base his conclusions on hope, faith, wishful thinking, or delusion, like he did when he worked on an *American Truth,* did he?"

Marks objected to the question as Dr. Partin said, "No, he didn't." Judge Hernandez sustained the objection, but it didn't matter. Travail had made his point.

During the lunch break, Travail and Harriet tried to reach Yeager by phone, but he didn't answer. They tried texting. Again, no response.

They were having a quick bite in the courthouse cafeteria on the ground floor when Yeager showed up. He'd been to the store to get a new phone. "A Jitterbug, with the big numbers. It's all the rage in retirement. I picked up two extra, in case anyone taps your phones."

He tossed one to Travail and the other to Harriet.

"I can see the small letters just fine." Harriet tossed the phone back to Yeager. "And what's this about our phones being tapped?"

Yeager slid into their booth on Travail's side and pushed Travail up against the wall. He lowered his voice to a whisper and told his friends about his morning encounter with the SUV.

"Did you call the police?" Yeager hadn't, and when Travail suggested he do it, Yeager pushed back. "It won't do any good. The SUV's license plate was covered. And if we make a report, it will only let the criminals know we are scared."

Yeager might not be scared, but that didn't mean Travail couldn't be concerned for his friends. "If you're not going to report it, you need to be careful."

Yeager smiled that big smile of his, only partially visible today in his beard that now looked to be a nest of street debris. "Don't worry about me, Craig Travail." He pushed the Jitterbug phone back to Harriet. "Use only these phones from now on when we talk. I've loaded a bunch of minutes and turned them into burners."

Travail looked at his Jitterbug. Yeager had been watching too many police procedurals.

Harriet's eyes were focused, but not on Travail or Yeager. When her face relaxed slightly, she spoke in a matter-of-fact tone. "After today, it's pretty clear we're doing something right."

Travail misunderstood her. "The case is not going that well."

Yeager patted Travail on the head. "She's not talking about the case."

Travail angled for a little more room in the booth, put down his sandwich, and stared at Harriet. "Not you, too?"

"Admit it, Craig. The Meck Dec has become deadly."

He didn't want to admit it, but after hearing about Yeager's close call with the SUV, he might have to find some time to take a closer look at the Meck Dec. Someone didn't like Yeager poking his nose into that mystery. But for the moment, he had a trial to focus on, and Lori was their next witness after lunch.

CHAPTER 27

LOVE AND MYSTERY

Harriet had spent the previous evening preparing Lori for her testimony. When Travail tried to help, she'd pushed back. "Lawyers think in straight lines and only see a few colors, mostly greys and browns. Emotions matter, Craig, and I intend to make sure Lori knows to be herself and say what she feels." Harriet didn't want Lori to forget the most important part of her story, her love for the professor and his love for her. She didn't want Travail to forget it either. "I need to prep you too."

He'd laughed. "You're going to prep me?" His question had come out with an "are you kidding" quality to it.

"I am. And you need to listen."

She'd handed him a one-page outline for his direct examination of Lori, with the word "LOVE" at the top and the bottom. "The rest is background noise."

"Are you sure you didn't go to law school?"

Harriet scoffed at the idea she'd have wasted three years of her life on law school. "I figured out most of what I needed to know about the law working on this case."

Harriet watched the jurors as Lori took the oath. To a suspicious-minded jury, the professionally dressed Lori—wearing her navy suit with the pencil skirt—might look the well-dressed opportunist after her grandfather's fortune. After all, her grandfather had been specific about disinheriting her. They might think there had to be a reason for his decision and that she had the means to take care of herself. First impressions were dangerous. Lori's testimony would have to be convincing.

Harriet was glad to see Travail follow her script. He spent the first ten minutes on Lori's life from the time her parents died until she took over the nonprofit. The testimony revealed how close she and the professor were during those years, especially after her grandmother died and, as the years went on, how Lori looked out for her grandfather. How often she checked in on him. How she sent him birthday cards. How she saw him through medical procedures. And how she took him to celebrations and funerals.

"Did you expect anything in return?"

Lori drew back. Harriet did too. That was not a question she had thought to ask. Lori's reaction and her answer were unrehearsed.

"I only wanted his love and respect. He was the only family I had until I married."

Travail's tone changed, became harsher, like she was a witness for Sue Ellen's side. "Then what did you do wrong?"

Harriet wouldn't have asked the question this way, but she saw the effect it had on the jury, who appeared curious, and on Lori, who appeared hurt. "Why would you ask that?"

"You must have done something wrong for the professor to cut you out of his will." Travail's voice remained stern.

Lori reached for a tissue from the box on the ledge beside the witness chair. She dabbed at her nose and eyes and put the tissue in her pocket. "I don't know what to say."

"If you did nothing wrong, what happened to change your relationship with your grandfather before his death?"

"He didn't want me to write a novel set in Mecklenburg County in May of 1775."

"Did he say why?"

"He said he thought it would put me in danger."

Harriet glanced around to see how the answer was received. The jury and Elkin perked up at Lori's response, Elkin being the perkiest. Travail ran with the moment, saying the word again, but with skepticism. "Danger?"

"I know. It sounded crazy to me."

Elkin made a speaking objection. "Lori Collins is not a doctor. How could she possibly know if the professor was crazy?"

Once again, Elkin had stumbled, and Travail took advantage. "Your honor, the witness said the professor's statement about her being in danger sounded crazy, not that he was crazy. The jury will decide how crazy the professor was."

Judge Hernandez agreed. Elkin slouched in his chair.

Lori next drew a straight line between her conversation with the professor about her novel and the handwritten will. "When he told me to forget about my novel, I pushed back. I told him I was writing the novel to honor his work on *An American Hoax,* but he said *An American Hoax* shouldn't be honored. He didn't explain himself and I was upset when we ended the call. That call occurred the day before he died. It was the same day he wrote the handwritten will."

Again, Lori touched her eyes with a tissue. She was not acting.

"Were you reluctant to bring this lawsuit?"

"Absolutely."

"Why?"

"I still love my grandfather. Part of me wants to respect his wishes. The other part of me wonders if cutting me out of his will is truly what he intended."

"Why do you say that?"

Lori's voice caught but was firm and convincing. "I'm sure he never stopped loving me."

Her final words created important questions for the jury, like how could a man who still loved his granddaughter cut her out of his will? And what would cause him to do that? State of mind? Duress? Undue influence? Any of those would do.

Elkin jump-started his cross-examination with a snippy "Ms. Collins," but before he could continue, Marks rose to ask the court for a moment to speak with her co-counsel. After a few minutes of whispering, an unhappy-looking Elkin yielded the floor to Marks, whose tone wasn't snippy at all.

Marks cajoled Lori into admitting the financial pressure she was under. She started with a question about the government investigation concerning the nonprofit status of We Salute You. "Losing that status could cripple your organization, correct?"

Lori was forced to agree. "Yes. If potential donors cannot deduct their contributions on their taxes, most of them will be unlikely to contribute."

"And there is the matter of your grandfather's contributions too. How much of the operating costs were covered by his annual donations?"

"Over half."

"If you don't win this case, could We Salute You shut down?"

Lori nodded.

Judge Hernandez said she needed to answer verbally for the record.

"Yes," she said.

Crystal Marks deftly moved the examination to the libel lawsuit. "There is a libel case pending against you that will begin right after this case ends, correct?"

Lori looked lost. Travail rose and said, "Your honor, we stipulate to the timing of the libel lawsuit, which we will vigorously defend."

Marks thanked Travail for the clarification.

"Ms. Collins, your lawyer says you plan to vigorously defend the case in which you are accused of libeling a US congressman, but if you lose and the congressman is awarded the amount of money he is seeking, can you pay that kind of judgment unless you win this case?"

Lori shook her head, prompting a reminder from Judge Hernandez.

"No," she said.

Marks thanked her for her honesty. "Nothing further, your honor."

Harriet was impressed with the way Crystal Marks neutralized Lori's testimony. Travail rested their case and Judge Hernandez excused the jury for an early afternoon break. He called the lawyers and Harriet to his chambers. On her way, Harriet passed Sue Ellen, who didn't speak to her.

They met in the same office where Harriet first met Judge Hernandez. His robe was off and hanging on the back of the door, which he closed behind everyone. "This will be a short meeting. Everyone can stand. Mr. Elkin, do you intend to make a settlement offer?"

Elkin responded with sentences that included the words "frivolous nature of Travail's case" and "the motives of an ungrateful granddaughter," but the judge cut him off. "That wasn't what I asked you."

"My client intends to honor the wishes of Matthew Collins. His granddaughter will receive nothing." Elkin puffed his chest out.

"Assuming you win."

"I have every confidence."

Hernandez addressed Crystal Marks. "How many rebuttal witnesses do you have?"

"Three, your honor, in this order: the professor's doctor, an Indie resident, and Sue Ellen Parker." Elkin added that they'd be quick about it because "we have a libel case next week with Judge Brady. Mr. Travail is 0 for 3 in his last three appearances in that courtroom."

Back in court, Harriet was annoyed by Yeager's misguided enthusiasm about the next witness. He said it was a good sign the professor's internist's last name was Craig. Harriet pointed him to the gallery seats. "Keep your superstitions to yourself."

Crystal Marks wasted little time getting to the point with Dr. Craig. After he introduced himself to the jury, she had him describe for them the results of the professor's annual physical one month before his death. He looked at his records as he spoke.

"All the bloodwork was at normal levels. Prostate was fine. Heart was working a little hard, but that was normal for a man his age. His cognitive abilities also appeared to be intact. He had no trouble conversing."

"Did you ask questions about depression?"

"Yes. It's standard practice."

"And?"

"In my professional opinion, Matthew Collins was not suffering depression or anxiety."

"Not paranoid either?"

"He didn't exhibit the symptoms."

"Dr. Craig, the professor's granddaughter has suggested the professor might have been under some kind of pressure or duress to change his will. Did he say anything to you about that, as his trusted physician of thirty years?"

"He never mentioned it."

Crystal Marks thanked the doctor for his time. Harriet made a note and handed it to Travail. He looked it over and nodded.

"Good afternoon, Dr. Craig."

"Afternoon, sir."

"Dr. Craig, did Matthew Collins mention the book he was working on when you last saw him?"

"He said he was working on a new book, but he didn't say what it was about."

"You said he wasn't depressed or paranoid and didn't express being under any duress." Travail looked again at the note Harriet had handed him. "You didn't mention his energy level."

Dr. Craig looked at his medical records and put his finger on the place in his notes. "I ordered a stress test as a normal precaution given his heart rate. It turned out to be inconclusive."

"Does that mean they ended the test before it was completed because of the exhaustion of the patient?"

Harriet leaned forward to hear the answer she suspected would come from the doctor based on her research. "Yes, that's why they ended the test."

The answer to Travail's next question was less predictable, but it turned out to be worth the risk.

"Did you ask the professor what caused him to be so fatigued?"

"I did. We spent thirty minutes talking about his fatigue. He was spending fourteen hours a day on his new book. I advised him this was unhealthy, and he needed to cut back."

"Did he say he was going to take your advice?"

"No. He said he couldn't slow down because he'd discovered something the world needed to know. He was totally preoccupied with the work."

"I see. Why didn't you put this in your notes?"

Dr. Craig glanced at his notes before offering his excuse. "Being preoccupied with a project is not uncommon among my author patients."

Travail didn't let him off the hook. "Dr. Craig, is the clinical term for the condition one suffers when they are preoccupied with something to the exclusion of everything else called 'obsession'?"

Dr. Craig hesitated. "It is."

"Can that lead to health risks?"

"Yes."

"Confusion?"

"Possibly."

"Paranoia?"

"Maybe."

Travail didn't ask the doctor his professional opinion about whether the professor's obsession with the Meck Dec could have affected his judgment in writing the will. He didn't have to. The jury could figure that out for themselves.

Harriet's watch and the courtroom clock both said it was 4:15. Judge Hernandez pushed Sue Ellen's team to keep the case moving. Marks called Becky Trainer, the Mini-Me Parker and Number 2 Pencil, as their next witness.

Becky appeared to be there primarily as a character witness. She testified about Sue Ellen's academic accomplishments in high school and college and her career leading political campaigns. "Sue Ellen could have run for office herself, and she would have won, but she used her skills as a political operative to help others get elected. She liked working behind the scenes."

Harriet wondered what kind of operative work Sue Ellen had done behind the scenes to get her hands on the professor's money, laptop, books, and work papers.

Becky Trainer also lauded Sue Ellen's nonprofit work, her leadership on various committees at the Indie, and her fundraising campaigns that led to improvements at the Indie. "Nobody ever truly appreciated her for this work."

"Why is that?" Crystal Marks appeared to be trying to humanize Sue Ellen, although Harriet didn't think that was possible.

Becky looked uncomfortable. She glanced at Sue Ellen, who appeared to nod, as if to say it was okay to proceed. "Sue Ellen can come across as uncaring. It's just her exterior."

Harriet could vouch for the "uncaring" nature of Sue Ellen's external personality. She was confident Sue Ellen's interior was a perfect match.

"Were you a witness to something relevant in this case?"

Harriet thought back to Becky telling her, "I am a witness," when she refused to talk with her about the case. The answer to what she witnessed was not what Harriet expected.

"I witnessed the professor sign the will."

Harriet and Travail looked at one another. This was unexpected. They'd assumed the professor was alone when he signed the will. What did this mean? And why bring it up now? Sue Ellen's team didn't need witness testimony to prove the validity of a holographic will.

Crystal Marks asked Becky to set the scene.

"The afternoon before the professor died, I dropped by his place to give a message to Sue Ellen about the upcoming homeowners' meeting. He invited me in and returned to his work while I spoke with Sue Ellen. When I was about to leave, he asked me to watch him sign a document, and then he let me read what he'd signed. It was the handwritten will that gave all his assets to Sue Ellen."

"Did he explain why he asked you to do this?"

"He said he wanted me to know he was doing it because he loved Sue Ellen."

Crystal Marks thanked Becky Trainer and offered Becky for questioning by Travail, but Becky interrupted. "There is one other thing."

Crystal Marks and Robert Elkin looked at each other as if neither one of them knew what Becky Trainer would say. Harriet saw Sue Ellen offer Becky another nod of encouragement.

"When he had me witness the will, he gave me an envelope related to the Meck Dec and said if they called me to testify in a case like this, I could share its contents."

Elkin sprung to his feet. "Objection."

Judge Hernandez told him to sit down and invited Becky to finish. "What was in the envelope?"

"There was a piece of paper with two items on it related to something called Dispatch 34. The reason—"

Elkin interrupted again. "Judge, this testimony is not germane to this case, and we move to strike her testimony."

Yeager yelled at Elkin from the back of the courtroom. "Let her speak."

Harriet tried to get Yeager's attention to hush him, and Travail motioned for Yeager to sit and be quiet. Hernandez banged his gavel. "Bailiff, remove that man from the courtroom."

Harriet watched as Yeager said, "No need, judge, I can't stand another minute of that fleabag of a lawyer subverting the truth." He swung a wide path, shrugged off the bailiff's arm, and exited on the power of his uncontrolled anger.

Judge Hernandez gave a quick lecture to the audience about outbursts. He excused the jury, listened to Elkin's argument, and after a moment of thought, decided the information about Dispatch 34 was unsolicited and Elkin's team had a right to end their direct examination.

With the jury back, Travail tried to keep his cross-examination questions of Becky tight so that Becky would have to answer yes or no, but Becky Trainer was not a yes or no kind of person. To her, the professor was "tired, yes, but very lucid." It was "true, yes, that he loved Lori, but he knew what he was doing when he gave all his money to Sue Ellen Parker." She topped it off by saying, "After all, he loved Sue Ellen."

Travail shifted to ask about Sue Ellen's efforts to get the professor's power of attorney. The court had prohibited NASCAR Nelli from talking about it because it was hearsay, but he could ask Becky about it, because it was her statement. She put the conversation in a light most suitable to Sue Ellen.

"All Sue Ellen ever wanted to do was help the professor. The power of attorney was the professor's idea. He wasn't ill or incapacitated. He just wanted Sue Ellen to have the power of attorney in case he became incapacitated before the book was published."

Becky's last comment confused Harriet. If the power of attorney was meant to give Sue Ellen rights to publish the sequel if the professor became incapacitated, much like the will had done when he died, why was she hiding the manuscript in her closet? Why wasn't she sharing it with the world, like the professor wanted? It was as if she'd turned on the professor.

Travail paused his questioning and directed his attention to Judge Hernandez. "May I have a moment, your honor, to confer with my assistant?" The judge granted Travail's request.

Harriet and Travail whispered about whether to ask Becky about Dispatch 34. Yeager disrupted court to try to get an answer to the question, and the writer of the anonymous letter said Dispatch 34 held proof of the Meck Dec. But if Becky had proof the Meck Dec was real, why hadn't she told Sue Ellen's lawyers what she knew? They could have used it to show the Meck Dec was real and the professor was sane for believing in the Meck Dec. The fact Elkin wanted to hide whatever it was Becky knew about Dispatch 34 was equally confusing. Maybe it meant he had the knowledge already and was afraid to have it become public. Harriet and Travail wanted to know what Becky knew about Dispatch 34, but it was too risky for Lori's case to ask her questions about it.

"Mr. Travail?" Judge Hernandez leaned forward.

"Thank you, your honor. Nothing further, for this witness."

With Becky Trainer's testimony complete, Judge Hernandez called the lawyers to the bench, and Travail motioned to Harriet to come along. It was now 5:45 p.m., and the judge could see the jury was tired. "We'll hear from Sue Ellen Parker in the morning, do closing arguments, and tender the case to the jury tomorrow."

Yeager met Harriet and Travail at the entrance to the parking deck with questions about what happened after he left. He couldn't believe they didn't ask Becky questions about Dispatch 34. Travail explained it wasn't a good idea for a lawyer to ask questions on cross-examination he didn't know the answers to, and Dispatch 34 fell into that category.

Harriet nudged Yeager. "Where's your truck?"

He pointed the way as they walked, but he didn't let up. "Dispatch 34 was a clue."

Harriet laughed. "From the grave, right?"

Two men appeared out of the shadows and blocked their path. They wore black suits and black shirts without ties. A black SUV was parked behind them.

Travail set his briefcase down. "Can we help you?"

"We're here to deliver a message."

Yeager moved toward the black suit nearest him, and the man reached his hand toward the back of his right hip.

"Hold up, Yeager," Travail said. Everyone froze as a ringing sound broke the tension.

"911. What's your emergency?"

Travail held out his new Jitterbug flip phone in his palm for everyone to see. Before Travail could answer the operator, Harriet held up her Jitterbug and took a photo of the two men and pushed a button that gave off a ping sound.

"Hello, this is Craig Travail. I am an officer of the court, here with Harriet Keaton and Yeager Alexander. Two uninvited men are in the courthouse parking deck. They are threatening us. Ms. Keaton has taken and texted their photo to you. They are driving a black

SUV with covered plates. I'm going to let them tell you their intentions."

The men said nothing. Travail held the phone in their direction. "Now's your opportunity, men, to deliver your message. The operator will record what you have to say."

One man tapped the one holding his hip and motioned him to pull back. They turned and headed to the SUV.

"Mr. Travail, are you and your companions okay?"

"We are." Travail provided information to the 911 operator about the size and make of the SUV as it pulled away. He thanked her, flipped the phone shut, and asked Yeager to drive them home.

Harriet had never seen Travail so tense. "That was fast work, Craig."

His face was flushed. "What in the hell is going on here?"

It was a good question, and Harriet didn't have the answer. She looked down at the new phone Yeager had given her. "I will say this though: I need to learn to take better pictures with a Jitterbug. I got an excellent shot of two pairs of shoes."

Yeager laughed and asked who she texted. Harriet didn't know. She'd not plugged any numbers into the phone yet. "For all I know, it went to Craig's girlfriend at Channel 24 News."

Travail's face relaxed into a smile. But then he added that they should take precautions. Yeager said he had some cousins who could watch their backs. It was no surprise he called one Lurch and the other Mad Max. Harriet felt safer already.

CHAPTER 28

SUE ELLEN SPEAKS AND THE JURY DECIDES

Amanda Rogers, Channel 24 News, was at the courthouse entrance to welcome Travail. He didn't want to talk to her, but he saw no way out. He gave his best smile. "Morning, Amanda. Looks like there's nothing else in Charlotte for you to report on."

"There's fifty million reasons to be here, today." She pushed the microphone in Travail's face. "Are you confident your client will win?"

Travail hated the question. Should he preen and predict success for the viewing audience, as some lawyers did? No. It was not his style. Trying a case was about the client, not the lawyer. If any jurors ignored the judge's instructions and watched this clip on TV, he didn't want to be that guy. He played it the way he always played it. "We believe the jurors have paid close attention to the evidence and will come to the right result."

Thirty minutes later, everyone was in place and ready to go, with more spectators on hand than any day during the trial. The Channel 24 News reporter was in her usual spot. Yeager sat with his cousins, Lurch and Mad Max, the twin towers of rough and tumble. Travail had to admit if they needed protection, it was nice to have Yeager's family on their side.

The bailiff did the "oyez, oyez" routine, Judge Hernandez entered, the jurors took their seats, and the final day of the trial was on.

Sue Ellen Parker, the woman believed to have snatched fifty million dollars from a loving granddaughter, was dressed in a stylish wrap-around dress and Neiman Marcus designer shoes. Her hair—a stunning grey that only some women could pull off—was done up in waves sprayed to stay in place. She used her right hand to touch it up in the back, placed her left hand on the bible, and faced the clerk to take the oath. Once she was duly sworn, she took command of her perch in the witness box and surveyed the crowd.

Crystal Marks didn't spend any time on Sue Ellen's virtues or accomplishments. Becky Trainer had done that work. Her first question was the one that had to be on the minds of everyone in the courtroom.

"Ms. Parker, why are you so intent on keeping the fifty-million-dollar fortune bestowed upon you by Matthew Collins?"

"That's a good question," Sue Ellen said. "It's true. I don't need the money." She shifted in her chair, placed her hands in her lap, and looked thoughtfully at the jurors. "I understand you have questions. But I don't think one of them should be whether Matthew cared for Lori more than me. That would be unfair to both of us. Frankly, I have nothing but respect for Lori. She is a fine woman, doing good work, and I believe she and the professor loved one another." Sue Ellen looked at Crystal Marks. "The answer to your question has to do with Matthew's wishes, not mine. The handwritten will is what he wanted."

"Why?"

"Objection."

The jurors looked at Travail. He knew they wouldn't like him blocking the answer to the most important question in the case, the reason Matthew Collins disinherited his grandchild.

"Sustained."

Nor would the jury understand Judge Hernandez's ruling. But the rules didn't allow an interested beneficiary to testify about conversations with the deceased about his intentions. The potential for false testimony was too great, hence, the dead man's statute.

Marks was gracious in the face of the ruling. "Understood, your honor. We can show the jury the professor's reason for writing the will another way."

Travail had the sense Crystal Marks was about to play her best card. He just didn't know what it was.

"Ms. Parker, are you a private person when it comes to your personal life?"

"I am. I don't play on Facebook, Twitter, or any of those other social media channels."

"What about sharing personal matters with people you know?"

"I rarely share information about my private life, except with my closest friends."

"Is that why you didn't share with anyone other than your close friend Becky Trainer the fact you got married before Matthew Collins died?"

Travail felt Harriet grip his forearm as Sue Ellen said, "Yes."

What was happening? Who had Sue Ellen married and why would it matter? Unless. No, it couldn't be.

"Who did you marry, Ms. Parker?"

Travail felt the words before she said them. "Matthew Collins."

The jurors sat up in their seats. They gave Travail's team the look that said, "Game, set, match." The gallery was active too. Travail heard chatter behind him.

Judge Hernandez demanded order. Travail turned to see Amanda Rogers beat a quick exit from the courtroom. She probably needed to file her story, her exclusive, because they had solved the mystery of the handwritten will. The professor gave his fortune to Sue Ellen Parker because she was his wife.

When the judge restored order, Crystal Marks continued. "Did you love Matthew Collins?"

"Very much."

Travail knew Harriet and Yeager would not believe her. They would think Sue Ellen Parker lacked the capacity for love. But Travail wasn't sure about that.

"Would you like to say anything else to the jury?"

Sue Ellen turned in her chair and addressed the twelve people who would decide whether Lori would end up in economic peril. "I never thought I'd marry again. But I fell in love." She looked down, steadied herself, and looked at the jury again. "I hate talking about this, but I owe it to Matthew. He asked me to marry him. I turned him down twice. Eventually, I realized we had more in common than I suspected, and it could work. I was lonely. He was, too. I said yes."

"You didn't pressure him to marry you?"

Sue Ellen stared at Crystal Marks. Her wide brown eyes said, "Heavens, no," but she said nothing aloud, apparently too offended by the question.

"I'm sorry. Please answer the question."

"I did not pressure Matthew to marry me any more than I pressured my first husband to marry me." She remained rigid. "That was not how I was brought up."

Crystal Marks tendered the witness to Travail. He asked Judge Hernandez for a quick recess, which the judge granted.

He gathered in one of the meeting rooms reserved for lawyers with Lori, Tate, Harriet, and Yeager. "Any ideas?" he asked the group. Everyone was trying to process what they'd heard. Lori spoke first.

"I don't understand why my grandfather would get married without telling me."

For once, Yeager was speechless. Tate said it was the perfect example of opposites attracting. Harriet said they needed to make an exception to the rule that you don't ask a question unless you know the answer. "You're going to have to wing it, Craig."

With the courtroom back in session and Sue Ellen looking his way, Travail began.

"How long were you and Matthew Collins married?"

Sue Ellen fixed her gaze on her hands. "Less than twenty-four hours."

That was a good start. Travail let the answer sink in before he continued. Three things had happened in that time frame. The professor and Sue Ellen Parker married. The professor created and signed a handwritten will. The professor died.

He asked who witnessed the ceremony. There were none, except the couple waiting to be married next by the magistrate.

"Did anyone know about your wedding?"

"I told Becky Trainer."

He asked if they spent their wedding night together. They did, at his place. "Matthew wanted to stay up and work on his book. I went on to bed."

That explained Yeager's story about his search of the unit the morning they collected the professor's body. He'd concluded the professor slept alone in his bed. It was Sue Ellen instead.

"Why wasn't Lori invited to the wedding?"

"I encouraged him to invite her, but Matthew said it would be a civil wedding and we'd have a party later. I agreed. We were married in this courthouse, not a church. There were no flowers and brides-maids. We weren't youngsters."

"Especially the professor. He was ninety-six years old."

Sue Ellen paused. "Do you have a question, Mr. Travail?"

"Sure, why were you in a rush to marry a man more than twenty years your senior?"

"I loved him. I don't care if it makes sense to you or anyone else."

"So you don't have a logical explanation in response to my question?"

"No, I don't. When is love ever rational, Mr. Travail?" She empha-sized the word "ever."

Travail knew Sue Ellen would have the jury on her side with that rhetorical question. He tried one last line of questioning.

"What do you know about the professor's work on the Meck Dec?"

"I know he wrote *An American Hoax*, and I know he was working on a sequel."

"Have you preserved his work papers for the sequel?"

"No." Sue Ellen looked at Elkin. "I destroyed them. Tossed the papers and wiped the work from his computer."

Travail was surprised by the heartless act and confused by her motive. "Why would you do that?"

"Two reasons." Sue Ellen Parker touched at her eye with a handkerchief. It didn't look like an act. "I was angry. That sequel killed him."

Her words made sense to Travail. It wasn't Robert Elkin or people in SUVs or some mysterious third party who killed the professor. The book itself had killed the professor.

"And the other reason?"

Sue Ellen pointed to her counsel table. "Robert Elkin wanted me to do it."

Elkin was on his feet. "That's a lie."

Judge Hernandez ordered Elkin to sit down. He told the bailiff to take the jury to the jury room. When they left, he let Elkin have it.

"Mr. Elkin, I don't know why you've abused your own witnesses and lawyers, but if it happens one more time, I will hold you in contempt of court. Do you understand?"

Elkin mumbled an unintelligible response, and Crystal Marks stepped in.

"Your honor, we apologize for his outburst. It was entirely inappropriate. It won't happen again." She stared at Elkin.

Judge Hernandez wouldn't let the issue go. He said he understood why Ms. Marks had introduced evidence that might lead one to believe in the Meck Dec. What he didn't understand was why another lawyer for Ms. Parker wanted to destroy papers to prove the point. "Why is that, Mr. Elkin?"

"I didn't tell her to destroy the documents."

Sue Ellen Parker was still in her place on the witness stand. Judge Hernandez got her attention. "How about it, Ms. Parker? Do you wish to amend your testimony?"

"I did what he wanted. Mr. Elkin is the one who's lying."

Travail watched Judge Hernandez closely. He could tell the judge was angry and wanted to make an example of Elkin, but he must have been thinking about how to avoid a mistrial so close to the end of a long-fought case.

"Here's what we're going to do. There will be no more discussion in this trial of the destruction of manuscripts and computers. The missing documents don't hurt your case, Mr. Travail. You can still argue Matthew Collins was crazy for writing the book. As for you, Mr. Elkin, and you, Ms. Parker, if Lori Collins wins this case, you will pay damages for the destruction of property belonging to the estate. We will hold a separate hearing to determine the value."

Judge Hernandez called the jury back, told them to disregard the evidence about what happened to the professor's work papers and laptop, because "it is irrelevant to your ruling." Travail chose not to ask any more questions.

Crystal Marks did a fine job with her closing argument to the jury. Her style was professional, and she had a mastery of the facts, in particular, the ones that mattered. Travail did the best he could with what he had to work with, though he was never sure about closing arguments. Most jurors made up their minds early in the case. The first evidence they'd heard was the will was validly executed, and that likely made an impression.

Travail had intended to make two arguments. The first had to do with federal estate tax law, the argument being the professor would never give his money to Sue Ellen Parker if it meant the government would benefit from an estate tax. At the start of the case, it was a good argument. That argument became moot once Sue Ellen revealed she'd married the professor and any inheritance by her was exempt from estate tax law.

Travail's second argument—the one he actually gave to the jury— focused on the professor's Meck Dec obsession, which he used to suggest the professor's judgment was so impaired he did not know, could not know, would not know, in the moment of writing his will, what he truly did. Marks countered with the famous ride of Captain Jack and the long list of believers.

After closings, the judge delivered his charge to the jury. The problem with good factual arguments is that the law can sometimes get in the way, and Judge Hernandez's legal instructions to the jury created several obstacles for Lori. Hernandez explained that lack of sufficient mental capacity may not be presumed from the mere fact a person is old, feeble, eccentric, intellectually weak, physically infirm, or "makes what others might consider an unwise, unreasonable, or unjust" disposition of his assets. He told the jury any one of these facts alone does not determine testamentary capacity, but rather, the jury should consider all the facts and circumstances in evidence to decide "whether the deceased understood he was making a will, whether he knew what property he had, whether he understood the effect the act of making a will would have on his property, whether he understood who would naturally be expected to receive his property at his death, and whether he knew to whom he intended to give his property."

When the jury returned after only ninety minutes of deliberation, Judge Hernandez asked the foreperson if the jury had reached a verdict.

"Yes, sir," she said, and handed the verdict sheet to the bailiff, who delivered it to the judge. He looked it over and handed it to the clerk.

"Take the verdict, madam clerk." The judge didn't look at Travail, and the jurors avoided his eyes too. Never the best sign, but not a sure sign either. The clerk asked the twelve jurors to stand as she read the verdict sheet aloud. The courtroom was quiet.

"Issue 1: Was the propounder's Exhibit Number 1 executed according to the law for a valid holographic will?"

The jury answered yes, probably because Travail didn't fight the point in his closing argument. Some trial lawyers fight every issue, but juries see that as unreasonable. Travail took the reasonable route, telling the jury Lori didn't dispute the handwriting, the form, or the terms on the page, only the mind of the man who wrote it. He hoped it would help on Issue 2.

"Issue 2: Did the deceased, Matthew Collins, lack sufficient mental capacity to make and execute a will at the time propounder's Exhibit Number 1 was executed?"

This was the issue Travail and his team had spent much of their time on in the trial. Travail looked at the jury foreperson, but she didn't look back. He held his breath as he waited for the clerk to read the answer. It came quick and the word "no" sounded harsh. Despite their efforts, the jury was unbothered by the professor's obsession with the Meck Dec. Either that, or they had joined the ranks of believers.

Travail heard murmurs in the gallery. Two down. Two to go. This wasn't going well for Lori.

"Issue 3: Was the execution of propounder's Exhibit 1 procured by undue influence?

This issue came down to two questions. Was Sue Ellen the kind of person who would exert undue influence, and if so, did she? As with other issues, the jury was allowed to consider a variety of factors, including the age and physical condition of the deceased, which were points in Lori's favor, and any dependence on or association the deceased had with the alleged wrongdoer, which cut for and against Lori, because while the professor may have been dependent on Sue Ellen during his last days, he sealed the arrangement with a marriage. The judge also had said that "influence gained by kindness and affection, without more, is not undue, even if it induces a person to make an unequal or unjust disposition of his property."

The problem for Lori with Issue 3 was the marriage. That courtroom surprise was too great an obstacle to overcome. Sue Ellen made a convincing case for love in retirement, and the jury bought it. They found for Sue Ellen.

Only one issue remained, and Travail didn't know how to comfort Lori. Thankfully, Harriet had her by the hand.

"Issue 4: Was the execution of propounder's Exhibit 1 procured by duress?"

Unlike undue influence, legal duress involved more than influence over a susceptible person. Judge Hernandez explained to the jury that when a "wrongful act, threat, or coercion" is used to force a person to make a will he would not otherwise have made, duress exists, and the will is invalid.

Travail and his team had long suspected some kind of threat made the professor do what he did. But other than the evidence that Sue Ellen demanded he give her all his money, they couldn't pin specific threats on Sue Ellen Parker. Travail had seen it in the jurors' eyes. She might be perceived as uncaring when she destroyed the professor's work, but she was not seen as the kind of person who threatened him. And even if she had, Marks used one of Travail's most confident witnesses against Lori in her argument. As the Godfather said, "Nobody pushed Matthew Collins around."

When the jury answered the last issue in favor of Sue Ellen, Travail couldn't help but think he and his team had missed their chance, that they'd been looking at the wrong person. Maybe the professor had been threatened by someone other than Sue Ellen.

Judge Hernandez thanked and excused the jury. Travail had lost again. Worse, he'd fooled himself into thinking they had a chance. Had his hatred of Robert Elkin affected his judgment? Probably.

Travail turned to Lori. "I'm sorry."

"You have nothing to apologize about. You did the best you could with what you had to work with."

Travail wasn't sure about that.

Marks walked over and shook Travail's hand. "Remember what you told me when I was young and stupid?"

"What's that?"

"Even the best lawyers lose cases. There is only so much a lawyer can do when the facts and the law are against her."

"Maybe." He didn't like hearing his own advice used as a bandage for his wounded pride.

Marks pulled Travail closer and whispered to him. "There are a lot of things about this case that don't add up, Craig. Elkin and Sue Ellen placed me on a need-to-know basis midway through the trial. When you figure out what really happened, let me know.

"Oh, and by the way," Crystal added. "I've removed myself from the libel lawsuit. Nobody in the firm wants to touch it. Elkin and Butterworth are on their own."

That was positive. Maybe the partners were worried about what might come out in the libel trial. Maybe they were losing confidence in Elkin. Travail's thoughts were interrupted by the man himself.

"I hope you learned your lesson."

Travail ignored Elkin and reached for his briefcase to pack up.

"I'm talking to you."

Yeager burst into the conversation with a protective edge to his voice. "Is he giving you trouble, Craig Travail?" Harriet glared at Elkin too, and the combination led Elkin to smirk.

"Fine," he said to the group. "I'll give the message to all three of you. Tell Lori we will drop the libel case if she runs a public retraction of her libelous articles on Congressman Butterworth and closes down We Salute You."

Travail answered with a dismissive question. "Is that all?"

"Your client is facing a multi-million-dollar verdict." He looked at Yeager and Harriet. "Do you and your highly trained legal team have your malpractice insurance in place?"

Travail gave Elkin the response he deserved. "I never liked you. Thought you were unethical from day one. You've never been a student of the law. You proved that in this trial. I will pass along your offer, but I hope Lori rejects it, so we can face off, just you and me."

"Maybe it won't come to that." Harriet stepped closer so they could hear her. "Especially now that we know the secret about Viribus."

Elkin's left eye twitched at the mention of the government contractor. He glanced at Travail and Yeager, whose poker faces were intact. He then looked around, as if he was gauging who was in earshot. Instead of responding, he walked away.

Travail asked Harriet, "What secret do we know about Viribus?"

Harriet laughed. "None, but it doesn't matter. Robert Elkin thinks we know something."

Yeager said, "Good riddance," under his breath and spoke to Travail like a man who needed an assignment. "What's next boss?"

Travail wasn't sure. Maybe he needed to see his therapist, so he could process the loss, or maybe a priest, so he could confess his sins, but he didn't have time for self-pity. They only had the weekend to get ready for the libel trial on Monday. His thoughts turned to Lori, what was before her and what was behind, and today's loss felt heavier.

Lori waited for Travail in the hallway. "Walk me to my car?"

On the way, she shared how she felt. "This lawsuit has been very stressful. Tate and I haven't been sleeping or eating well. And we're both worried about the next trial. If it's possible, I'd like you to try to resolve everything."

Travail told her that Elkin had made a settlement offer. "But if you take it, you have to make a public retraction and close down We Salute You."

"I don't like the terms, but I am worried about the alternative. I will have to give it serious thought."

When he left Lori at her car, the parking deck closed in on Travail. He'd just lost a huge case for his client and baited her predator to come after her in the second lawsuit. Maybe Lori should settle and start her life over. He couldn't blame her if she did, but settling would leave her with nothing. The nonprofit her grandfather founded would be defunct, she'd be broke, and she'd be without a job and her self-esteem. And as for him, he'd have lost his last case.

As Travail came alongside his car, he wanted to kick the tires because he couldn't kick himself. Whatever made him think he could run a law practice out of a retirement home? Maybe it was for the best that Lori settle and he surrender his law license. He and Blue could retire for good to a slow and uneventful life.

Independence Boulevard was backed up with evening traffic, so Travail took several side streets. The Eagles' "Peaceful Easy Feeling" was playing on the radio, but he didn't feel peaceful, nor did he think the days ahead would be easy.

Travail pulled into his driveway, grabbed the mail, changed into jeans and a sweatshirt, fed Blue, and took him for a walk. He felt adrift as he walked beside Lost Cove Lake. Trees cast shadows on the water, revealing dark spots along the walk. What secrets were hidden below? What secrets had he yet to uncover about Robert Elkin? About Matthew Collins? And why did he have this nagging feeling that Yeager had been right all along about the Meck Dec?

Blue howled at the rising moon. It had been that kind of day.

Back at the cottage, Travail grabbed a beer. Just when he was sure his life couldn't get any more confusing, his phone rang. It was Sue Ellen's personal lawyer.

"Craig, Vance Dagenhart here. Sorry to bother you, but I have some sad news."

Travail set his beer down and held the phone closer to his ear.

"I thought you should know there's been an accident. Sue Ellen Parker is dead."

Travail wasn't sure he'd heard correctly.

"Craig?"

"What happened?"

"Her car ran off the road on the way home from court and struck a telephone pole. She died instantly."

"I'm sorry."

Travail didn't know what else to say. His feelings about Sue Ellen were complicated. She was at once a hard-hearted, unfriendly, domineering individual, and yet, she was a fellow human being, one who loved dogs and who, he'd come to believe, loved Matthew Collins. The first day of the trial, the morning they met by the lake, she'd seemed different. What was it she'd said? Yes, she was only doing this thing with the will because it was what Matthew wanted. But why did he want that? And why was she dead? Did she know a secret? Did she know *the* secret? Travail shook himself when he realized he had started to think like Yeager.

"Craig, I have a letter for you from Sue Ellen. My instructions were to give it to you should anything happen to her."

The words "should anything happen to her" created an uneasy sensation in Travail's stomach.

"And there's one more thing."

Travail couldn't imagine what other surprises the lawyer had in store for him.

"Sue Ellen had a pour-over will."

That meant the will was designed to be like a secret bequest. He wondered why Sue Ellen's lawyer mentioned this.

"I will explain everything when I deliver the letter. Can I come by your place tonight? Say, 9:30? I know it's late, but this is important."

Travail agreed, and the lawyer asked for one more favor. "Could you ask your client and the rest of your team to be there? They will want to hear what I have to say. I have some things for them too."

PART IV

CHASING THE TRUTH

CHAPTER 29

THE ROAD HOME STARTS WITH SUE ELLEN

Travail called the urgent meeting of the team at his cottage but didn't disclose the purpose. Yeager showed up first, followed by Harriet, with Lori and Tate close behind. Travail had put out some beer and wine, but after losing the trial, nobody was in a partying mood, not even Yeager, and he was a man who never turned down a cold beer. Travail didn't tell them the news about Sue Ellen. He only told them they were having a visitor.

"Who's coming?" Harriet asked.

"Vance Dagenhart, Sue Ellen's personal lawyer."

"Why?" The contempt for anything of Sue Ellen Parker's was evident in her voice.

The doorbell spared Travail the need to explain. He welcomed Dagenhart at the door. "I have not told them the reason for your visit."

He showed Dagenhart into the den and introduced him. He said hello to everyone, but the reception was cool. Dagenhart took no offense. He took a letter-sized envelope from his jacket pocket and handed it to Travail. "You should read this."

Yeager had a hard time sitting still, so he didn't. He got up from the sofa and circled it, offering Dagenhart his seat. "Lighten your load, partner," he said, but he and everyone in the room eyed Dagenhart like the enemy. Dagenhart politely smiled and took the empty spot on the sofa next to Harriet.

Travail leaned against the bookcase as he read the letter. He could sense all eyes were on him. When he finished reading, he dropped his hands to his side. The letter dangled in his right hand. "I don't understand."

Vance Dagenhart was not new to Charlotte. He'd been practicing law in the city for over fifty years, but pretension and stuffiness were not in his DNA. He was a man who talked straight to people. That was why he'd earned the reputation as one of the best corporate lawyers in Charlotte. Travail counted on him to explain the unexplainable.

Dagenhart looked around the room at each person present. "As I told Craig earlier tonight, Sue Ellen Parker is dead." Blue barked at something he heard outside, but other than Blue, nobody said a word until Harriet broke the silence.

"What happened?"

"A car accident."

More silence followed, and Travail knew why. Sue Ellen Parker had put Lori through hell, and now she was dead. They had wanted to defeat Sue Ellen, beat her at her game. They didn't want to see her come to any harm, much less this.

"I told Craig that Sue Ellen Parker had a pour-over will, but I didn't provide him with the details of that will." He turned to Lori. "Sue Ellen Parker left everything she owned, including what she received from your grandfather, to you and We Salute You."

"What?" Lori sat up and looked from Dagenhart to Travail and back to Dagenhart. "I don't understand."

Harriet walked over to Travail and reached for the letter before he lost his grip on it. "May I?"

While Harriet read the letter, Yeager played detective. He wanted to know where Sue Ellen's accident happened, time of day, and whether there were any witnesses. The tone of his questions made clear he didn't believe in accidents.

Blue was back and must have been suspicious too, because he raised his head and looked at Dagenhart, who explained he'd received a call from Sue Ellen on her way home from the courthouse. "Elkin had cornered her before she left the building and questioned her about when, where, and how she destroyed the professor's work on the Meck Dec. Sue Ellen was confident she had satisfied him with her answers, but when she called me, she said she was being followed. I told her to call the police, but she had another idea. She hoped to get caught in a public place."

Travail didn't understand why Sue Ellen wanted to get caught, but he didn't interrupt.

"Earlier tonight, I went to the scene of the accident, a rural road, not far from the Indie. I saw a man mowing an adjacent field, approached him, and asked if he had seen the accident. He had. He said a vehicle chased Sue Ellen's car. She lost control and hit a telephone pole."

Yeager asked the question on Travail's mind. "A black SUV?"

Dagenhart's eyebrows lifted. "Yes."

"Anything else?" Yeager was all detective now.

"The passenger in the SUV removed something from Sue Ellen's vehicle. The witness had no idea what that was."

"But you do?"

"Yes. The professor's computer and a copy of his uncompleted manuscript of *An American Truth*."

Travail was confused. "I don't understand. Sue Ellen said in court she destroyed the professor's computer and his manuscript."

"That's what she wanted everyone to believe. Particularly Robert Elkin."

"But that means …?" Travail wondered how many times the professor's work on the Meck Dec could be found and then destroyed, resurface, and then be lost again. He worried the professor's work was lost for good now. He could sense by the quiet in the room everyone shared his thoughts, except Dagenhart, who said, "It was all part of Sue Ellen's ruse."

Travail heard the word "ruse" and his mood brightened. "You mean?"

"Sue Ellen had a plan. She left the laptop and unfinished

manuscript in her back seat the day she testified, believing Elkin would have someone steal them while she was in court. When that didn't happen, and she realized she was being followed, she tried to lead her pursuers to a public place, where they could take them from her."

"Because she had copies?" Travail asked.

"It's one of the reasons I am here, to provide the copies."

"Is the other reason to explain the reason for the pour-over will?"

"Precisely." Dagenhart turned his attention to Lori. "Sue Ellen asked me to draft a will giving everything she'd inherited from the professor to you and We Salute You, but to do it in a way that Robert Elkin and the public could not learn where the money had gone. The pour-over will put everything in a private trust for you and the nonprofit upon Sue Ellen's death, and by law, the recipient of those trust funds remains private."

"Why did she want the will to be a secret?"

"To protect you."

"From what?"

Dagenhart paused and then smiled. "The dangers of the truth."

"Because of this?" Harriet held the letter in her hands.

"Yes," Dagenhart said, "because of that."

If this were a game of jeopardy, Yeager would be the fastest contestant with the buzzer. "What's it say?"

Harriet had a twinkle in her eye. "Chuck Yeager Alexander, you are much smarter than any of us ever thought you were."

Travail shared the solution. "The letter says the Meck Dec is real."

"I knew it. I knew it!" Yeager reached down and patted Blue on the head. "Told ya, boy."

"Excuse me." Lori sounded confused. "I don't understand why my grandfather went to all the trouble and expense to cut me out of his will and put Sue Ellen and me through a public trial if Sue Ellen planned to put me in her will."

"The professor was threatened, but not by Sue Ellen."

Travail could feel the pieces of the puzzle fitting together. "Was it Elkin?"

"And associates."

Dagenhart said the professor came up with a plan to protect Lori and preserve the truth he'd discovered about the Meck Dec. "The plan was simple but harsh. By cutting Lori out of the will, she would not inherit the professor's books, work papers, and laptop, and Elkin would not try to harm her to get them. The professor believed Lori would suspect something was off with his will and would fight the will in court. With his marriage to Sue Ellen, the professor was sure Lori would lose the court case, but that was part of the plan too. He hated to put Lori through it, but if Elkin won the case, and if Sue Ellen was convincing enough, Elkin and his accomplices would believe their secret was safe. Sue Ellen planned to meet secretly with Lori after the trial and give her the books, work papers, and laptop."

Travail considered the price Sue Ellen had paid to carry out the professor's plan. "How was Sue Ellen supposed to play her part?"

"Sue Ellen was supposed to convince Elkin she cared more about the professor's money than the Meck Dec. To do that, she needed to convince not just Elkin but everyone else, too, which meant fighting against Lori in and out of court and making sure Elkin won the lawsuit."

"She played her part well." Harriet said it with a touch of admiration.

Tate shook her head. "It's hard to believe. All this time, Sue Ellen fooled us. She really was a good person."

Dagenhart concurred. "One of the best."

There was more silence, mixed with reverence and perhaps guilt for the way everyone had treated Sue Ellen.

Travail's legal brain spun. Lori had lost the trial but won the lottery. He wouldn't be doing his job as her attorney if he didn't state the obvious. "Lori, you might want to consider keeping your focus on the nonprofit and using the money you inherited to run it as your grandfather wanted. If I can bluff Elkin into a settlement that keeps We Salute You in good graces with the IRS, you can help lots of veterans and nobody else will get hurt because of the Meck Dec."

Yeager grunted. "There you go, again, Craig Travail, thinking like one of them tall-building lawyers, worried about the risk." Yeager opened a Captain Jack beer, swallowed a few gulps, and wiped his beard on his sleeve.

Harriet concurred. "Though it pains me, I have to agree with Yeager."

Lori said she didn't like the idea either. "After what my grandfather went through over the Meck Dec, I don't feel right accepting his money and doing nothing more about the Meck Dec. He clearly wasn't finished with his work."

Tate placed her arm around Lori. She appeared ready to do whatever Lori decided.

"I know you've got a lot to talk about," Dagenhart said, "but before I go, I have some things Sue Ellen wanted me to give to Yeager, Harriet, and Lori."

He excused himself, went to his car, and returned with several items. He handed Yeager a four-foot-by-four-inch box wrapped with twine. "Sue Ellen said to open it early one morning."

He handed Harriet a thick legal-sized envelope. "Sue Ellen said you'd know what to do with this information."

He pulled a key from his pants pocket and handed it to Lori, along with a piece of paper. "This paper has directions to and the combination for a safe deposit box that belongs to this key."

"What's in the box?"

Dagenhart grinned. "Clues."

Yeager's eyes lit up.

"Wait." Travail wasn't sure he'd heard correctly. "Clues? Not answers?"

"The professor had solved the Meck Dec mystery, but he had one thing left to do. You will find a hard-drive copy of the laptop, work papers, and books in the safe deposit box, plus other helpful materials Sue Ellen printed and removed from the computer before Elkin and his associates stole it. It shouldn't take a group as smart as all of you very long to work it out. Plus, Yeager is the professor's backup plan." He didn't explain how.

Harriet smirked. "His backup plan for uncovering a secret that has remained hidden for two hundred fifty years is Chuck Yeager Alexander?"

Yeager was not offended. He parried, instead. "At your colonial service, madam."

Dagenhart had one last gift, which he presented to Travail in the form of a flash drive. "You might want to watch this together."

Travail walked Dagenhart to the door, where Dagenhart wished him well and offered one more piece of news. "I meet with Elkin tomorrow morning to make sure he believes all is well."

Travail rubbed the flash drive between his fingers and invited everyone to crowd into his office, where he plugged the flash drive into his laptop, connected his laptop to his monitor, and turned the monitor around for everyone to see. In the static thumbnail of the video, the professor smiled at them. Sue Ellen sat by his side. Lori gasped as Travail clicked play.

"Hello, Lori. I hope you're doing well, and if you are watching with Tate, I want to say how happy I am for the two of you."

Lori reached over and held Tate's hand at the same time the professor took Sue Ellen's hand in his. Sue Ellen smiled, not unlike the smile Travail had seen when she rubbed her hands through Blue's fur the morning before the first day of the trial. She seemed happy.

"I asked Sue Ellen to help me with this video in case I wasn't able to tell you these things myself. First, I want to say I never stopped loving you, and I hope you know that. Second, I'm sorry I didn't invite you to share in the joy of our marriage." The professor turned to Sue Ellen and gave her a kiss before he turned back to the camera, a kiss-the-bride kind of moment Lori had missed. "I never thought I could love again after your grandmother, but time heals, I suppose, and fate played a perfect hand for me when Sue Ellen came into my life and then again, when she said 'yes.' Please welcome her into your life."

The request came too late though, and Travail could see the effect in Lori's eyes.

"Finally, I'm sorry I saddled you with my Meck Dec obsession. If it is too dangerous to proceed, I want you to drop it. I value your life and your future more than the story about what happened in 1775."

The professor's voice cracked when he said, "I love you." A blank screen and static appeared.

A few seconds later, Sue Ellen's image popped up. The setting was different; she looked tired, and the professor was gone. She addressed her first words to her longtime nemesis.

"Hello, Harriet. I see you moved your bird feeders to the woods behind your cottage and bought some beehives. Good for you." She smiled. "It might surprise you to know that I really do like the birds *and* the bees. But I had to make the world believe that you and I were mortal enemies, no matter how trivial the fight."

Yeager laughed, and Sue Ellen must have sensed he would. "Yeager, I want to say that I had the hardest time deceiving you. It was difficult not to laugh at your ridiculous antics. Being straitlaced and snobbish can be a tough job around a prankster like you."

Sue Ellen said quip-filled hellos to Lori, Tate, and Travail, before turning to a more serious topic. She said if they were watching this video, something had gone wrong. "I don't regret it for one moment though. I loved Matthew and would do anything for him." She said their married life was short, "but it may surprise you to know that we had an affair for two wonderful years, and that includes the sex part too." Sue Ellen chuckled at how she and the professor had deceived everyone. "Not such a good detective after all, are you, Yeager?"

Yeager said, "Touché, Sue Ellen," in return.

Travail realized his skill at reading people had suffered when he moved into the Indie. He had put Sue Ellen in a box and left her there, never grasping her side of the story or how she felt. She'd tried to give him clues, while still playing the part of the evil inheritor. He had missed them all. She was like anyone else. She wanted to love and be loved. He was glad she had found love with the professor.

Sue Ellen ended the video by reinforcing what the professor had said. "I've tried to put you in a position to complete the professor's work, but as he said, if it is too dangerous, please back away. Each of you has too much to live for. For all my offenses to you, I apologize. I wish you each a wonderful life."

When they returned to the den, Harriet was the quietest. Travail asked her if she was okay. "I don't want to talk about it. Let's talk about what's next."

Lori was the first to speak. "I understand the risk of pursuing the Meck Dec."

Travail wasn't sure she did. The risk was severe. Sue Ellen had died because of it. "Maybe we should alert the police."

Yeager shot the idea down. "They will think we're crazy, especially after you bashed the Meck Dec in the trial." Yeager still hadn't gotten over Travail's strategy to prove the professor was mentally unbalanced for believing in the Meck Dec.

Harriet agreed with Yeager. "If the police question Elkin, Elkin will know we know."

Tate concurred. "We don't know who he works with, but we know what they're capable of doing. Maybe it's best if we have a head start without them knowing what we know."

Travail's lawyer brain still spoke caution. He reminded everyone that Lori faced a libel lawsuit on Monday and the government still wanted to revoke We Salute You's nonprofit status. "If both go against Lori, she could pay a big judgment in the libel case, and the government will tax any contributions made to We Salute You, including the money Sue Ellen left to the nonprofit." When Travail finished, everyone waited for Lori to speak. It was her life, and therefore, her decision, after all.

Lori got down on the carpet and patted Blue on the head. "You've got a good nose, fella. Want to help us solve a mystery nobody else has ever been able to solve?"

Blue barked and threw his head back.

Yeager beamed. "That's what I'm talking about."

Harriet caught Travail's eye. "It's time to make a plan, Craig."

Travail nodded as he looked around at his determined group of friends. What was the saying? Success is 1 percent inspiration and 99 percent perspiration. He could see the stains under the arms on Yeager's shirt and smiled to himself as he decided to go all in. Why shouldn't he? He'd given his advice, and his client had made her decision. He'd get another shot at Elkin in the libel case. He'd have a chance to help change history. And above all, this was better than basket weaving or whatever other class Peaches would enroll him in if he wasn't busy.

"We've got two challenges," Travail said. "Neither of them will be easy."

"Let's call them goals." Harriet smiled. "Achievable goals." She was good at reframing, and Yeager gave her an "atta girl" for it.

Harriet was right. He needed to think more like her. He looked from Yeager to Harriet to Tate to Lori, where he held his gaze just a bit longer. She was the one with the most to lose.

"So what's the plan, Craig Travail?" Yeager had one foot out the door.

"Harriet, Lori, and I have a libel trial starting Monday. We will focus on that."

While Travail talked, Harriet busied herself with the papers from the envelope Dagenhart had handed her. She looked up from the papers and smiled at Travail.

"What?" he asked.

"We have the answers we need for the libel trial on Monday. I have some work to do, but I'll be ready."

That sounded promising. Now what to do about Yeager? Perhaps give him an errand to do first. "Yeager, can you go with Lori and Tate in the morning to pick up the materials in the lockbox. Take Lurch and Mad Max along, if you think you need them. Also, take the weekend and compare what you know about the Meck Dec with the clues in the lockbox."

"Won't let you down, Craig Travail."

Lori and Tate grabbed hands. "Let's do this."

"Great. That should take care of everything," Travail said.

"Not everything." Harriet's tone softened from determined to concerned. "There is the issue of your law license."

Travail hadn't given his law license much attention, other than to be glad to be done with it after the recent trial. Now it appeared he needed it a little longer. "Not to worry. The libel trial will be over before they take it."

"Not what I meant." Harriet said they needed a plan to help Travail keep his law license, and her tone had a touch of scolding in it. "You and your law license have kept us in the game. If you hadn't taken Lori's case, the plan created by the professor and implemented by Sue Ellen wouldn't have worked. She wrote you the letter, remember, asking you to continue to help Lori, because she was sure you could be trusted and sure you were up for the task. She said she admired you for what you did. It is the first time I can remember agreeing with Sue Ellen Parker about anything."

Lori and Tate agreed with Harriet, and of course, Yeager was all "Craig Travail" this and "Craig Travail" that.

Travail was taken aback, again. He'd never equated failure with success. He thanked everyone for their concern, and without taking a position on his law license, he shifted the focus back to the work at hand. "Let's do dinner at my place Sunday night to check in on everyone's progress."

"Point of order, Craig," Harriet said. "As much as I like your frozen dinner options, I'll bring homemade spaghetti and meatballs. Yeager can bring the alcohol."

"Tate and I will bring dessert," Lori said.

Harriet got Yeager's attention, pointed at his beer, and held up four fingers on one hand and one on the other. "Let's seal our commitment with a toast."

Yeager grabbed five red Solo cups from the top of the refrigerator and poured a few ounces of Captain Jack in each one. Everyone grabbed a cup, formed a circle, and tapped their cups together in the air.

"To the truth!" Harriet said.

"To the truth!" They said.

Yeager quipped this would forever be "the toast heard round the Indie."

CHAPTER 30

ELKIN TIES UP LOOSE ENDS

Robert Elkin welcomed Vance Dagenhart to his table for breakfast at Mecklenburg Country Club's men's grill. The server placed white napkins in their laps while he described the daily special, which both men ordered, along with coffee. The server poured their coffee and left them alone.

Elkin's first order of business was a practiced display of compassion. "I was very sorry to hear about Sue Ellen. She was a wonderful woman."

"Nice of you to say."

Elkin was curious about the relationship between Sue Ellen Parker and Vance Dagenhart. "You represented her for many years, didn't you?"

"She and her first husband were two of my first clients."

"Well, I'm sorry for your loss." Elkin meant it too. There was no reason for Sue Ellen Parker to die. He'd had things under control and didn't like interference from the top.

Elkin's mobile phone vibrated. Club rules prohibited answering phones in dining rooms and most other areas at the club. He glanced at the number and knew he should take the call. He excused himself and walked out a side door to the patio overlooking the driving range and the eighteenth green.

"You heard the news?" It was Butterworth.

Elkin knew he was talking about Sue Ellen Parker's death.

"I did."

"Why did this happen?" He made it sound like it was Elkin's doing.

"Maybe I should ask you the same question." Elkin was fed up with Walter Butterworth. The only reason he represented the congressman was to protect The Jefferson Experience's relationship with Viribus.

Butterworth was not to be deterred. "You said everything was under control."

"It was. I won the will contest. I did my job."

"Somebody at The Jefferson Experience doesn't think so."

Butterworth was right. Elkin had reported the verdict to the director after the trial, and the director was pleased, but then he started with the questions. Did he search Sue Ellen's car? And her condo? He hadn't done either, because he was sure Sue Ellen had no interest in telling the Meck Dec story. To be sure of that, he had quizzed her again after the trial ended.

The director's tone soured. "You should have been more thorough," he said. And late last night, the director called again with the news. "Sue Ellen lied and died, but thanks to my men, we now have the professor's computer and manuscript."

The director's paranoia, combined with his dementia, had gotten out of control. It had cost Sue Ellen her life.

Butterworth spoke again and called Elkin back to the moment. "Is this finally over? Is the secret safe?"

"Yes. You should focus more on your libel lawsuit than a centuries-old mystery the world cares nothing about." He clicked off and went back to visit with Vance Dagenhart.

"Sorry to keep you waiting."

"Not at all. Everything okay?"

Elkin offered his everything-is-fine face and turned the conversation back to where they were before Butterworth called. "What do the police know about Sue Ellen's death?"

"No leads. It happened on a country road. No cameras in the area."

"What do they think?"

"Single-car accident."

That was comforting. Neither the police nor Sue Ellen's lawyer thought a third party was involved in the crash. Again, Elkin said he was sorry, but he wasn't too sorry. He'd never wanted Sue Ellen to die, but he was so tied up in this Meck Dec mess, his freedom could be at risk because of the director's rash decisions. And if anything went wrong, the director would discard him like a used toothpick, just as he had done years ago.

Elkin steered the conversation in a different direction. "Is there anything my firm can do to help with Sue Ellen's estate?"

Dagenhart politely declined. Elkin knew it would look suspicious if he asked questions about Sue Ellen's will, so he held back. He could check the public record later when the will was probated.

After the two men had eaten their breakfast and had third cups of coffee, Dagenhart left. Elkin called the director to report on his meeting with Dagenhart. The reception he got was not what he expected. The man was furious. "*The Cape Fear Mercury* article is missing."

Elkin held his phone away from his ear as the director shouted at him about the loss of the 1775 newspaper article, the enclosure in Dispatch 34 that held the truth about the Meck Dec.

The director demanded an explanation. "What the hell happened?"

How was Elkin supposed to know? The Jefferson Experience had guarded the contents of Dispatch 34 for over one hundred and fifty years, and nobody outside the board knew its location. The newspaper article should have been destroyed years ago, but the director wouldn't allow it. Now it had come to this, the newspaper article missing from Dispatch 34 and a man who would stop at nothing to protect the secret it held.

The director gave his orders. "Win the libel case, shut down We

Salute You, and take that lawyer's law license. I'll find *The Cape Fear Mercury* article and take care of the people who know its contents." The director ended the call, and Elkin felt as insecure as the little boy who'd moved with his mother to Charlotte so many years ago.

CHAPTER 31

NUMBER 2 PENCIL BAITS THE HOOK

Travail awoke Saturday morning feeling more refreshed than usual. He and Blue completed their morning walk and routine before he went to the pool for a swim, something he hadn't done since before Rachael died. That was her thing, swimming. She'd been a college swimmer and coached the kids' swim teams. He'd always floundered, and she kept at him to keep trying. She said it was good for him. He hated the pool, but she was right. It helped him focus on one thing, staying afloat, and that allowed his mind to rest. He always felt better when he finished and dried off.

After the swim, he went to the weight room, did some stretches, and jumped on an elliptical. He set an easy pace. As he moved his legs and watched his heartbeat on the monitor, he remembered when Sue Ellen Parker confronted him in this very room. She had baited him. "You don't have to speak," she'd said. "Just listen."

She'd told Travail what a low-life lawyer he was for sticking his enormous nose into the professor's business and asked him why he thought he could question the professor's decision about what to do with his money. She answered her own question by telling Travail it was because he was a money-grubbing parasite lawyer looking to get rich off the backs of others. And finally, she threw in the jab about it being "un-Christian" of him. She'd been an excellent actress. She knew what buttons to push. Her nudge, the pleas from Yeager and Harriet, and Robert Elkin's entry on the scene caused him to take the case.

Travail faced the plate-glass window with a good view of Freedom Lake. He moved his arms back and forth on the elliptical while he watched a man at the end of the long dock on Freedom Lake swing his own arms back and forth, up over one shoulder, down toward the water, and back. As his thoughts swirled around Sue Ellen's role in the turn in his professional life, someone entered the weight room behind him.

"Can I have a word?"

He knew that voice. Becky Trainer. They'd mocked her loyalty to Sue Ellen, but now, her best friend was dead. Travail stopped the machine, asked Becky to take a seat on the couch in the corner and pulled up a metal folding chair. "I'm sorry about Sue Ellen."

Becky fidgeted with her hands and looked out the window. "Is that Yeager out there on the dock?" Her eyes were better than his. He waited for her to say what she'd come to say.

Her voice dropped. "I'd like to apologize."

"No need for that. I should be the one to apologize to you."

She held up her hands, as if to say please hear me out. "I knew what Sue Ellen was up to with the trial. She brought me into her confidence because she had nobody else she could trust." She looked out the window again and spoke without looking at Travail. "I shouldn't have gone along with it. Now Sue Ellen's dead." She teared up.

Travail looked around, found a box of tissues, and handed it to her. She wiped her eyes and found confidence. She still looked like a Number 2 pencil with an eraser for a head, but she appeared sturdier, less breakable now. She'd come to see him for a reason. He waited.

"I used to do forensic work for banks." Another surprise.

Becky took a legal-size manila envelope out of her cotton carry bag and held it tight. "Sue Ellen shared with me some documents the professor had obtained. He was worried about the libel lawsuit against Lori and called in a few favors with his military buddies. I don't know how he got the documents, but they only told part of the story. Sue Ellen asked me to look them over and asked for my help. Give these to Harriet. She will understand what I found."

She looked out the window again, and Travail followed her eyes. The man on the dock still waved his arms back and forth over his shoulder. If it was Yeager, he was having some kind of spastic fit.

"I hope what I've given you helps. Lori is a lovely young woman. She's endured so much."

Travail nodded. "We appreciate your help."

"I would ask you to drop this Meck Dec thing, but I know that won't happen."

She wasn't seeking a response, and Travail didn't provide any. After an awkward twenty seconds, Becky Trainer shook her head, reached in her bag, and pulled out another envelope, this one much smaller than the first.

"Sue Ellen asked me to protect this information with my life. She thought it best that it not be found with her documents, just in case." She pointed to the man on the dock. "Why she ever thought he could do something valuable with the information is beyond me."

The envelope was addressed to Chuck Yeager Alexander and marked "Confidential." She laughed, which released some tension in the air. "Sue Ellen had a dry sense of humor. Marking this 'Confidential' for Yeager means it won't stay secret for long. It has to do with Dispatch 34. I mentioned this at the trial, but Elkin cut me off and you never followed up."

He remembered. He and Harriet had decided against asking any questions about the paper relating to Dispatch 34 because it was too risky. If the answers proved the existence of the Meck Dec, it would have hurt their case. That concern no longer existed. "Why did you mention it?"

"It was the professor's idea. He said you'd be losing the case by then and your team would be dejected. He wanted to offer you a sliver of hope. Kind of a signal, if you will."

Travail couldn't remember feeling any hope at that point in the trial. Confusion, maybe. Not hope. Becky said Yeager had understood.

She was right. That's why he made a scene and was thrown out of the courtroom.

"I'm sure Yeager pestered you about it." She was right about that too. He said Dispatch 34 was the key to solving the Meck Dec mystery, and wasn't happy Travail didn't ask questions about it.

"How important is the information in this envelope?"

Becky Trainer smiled her response as she stood to the full height of her pencil-like figure, held out her hand, and shook Travail's. "God speed, Craig Travail."

On the way back to his cottage, Travail took the long way by Freedom Lake.

"Morning, Craig Travail."

"Is that a fishing pole?"

"It's called a rod. Not a pole." Yeager yanked the leader out of the water and let the line fly backwards over his head to its full extension before pulling it back across his shoulder. "Fly rod, to be exact."

"Is your gun broken?"

"Trying something new. Present from Sue Ellen. It belonged to the professor."

Travail chuckled. Even from the grave, Sue Ellen tried to change Yeager. He took a seat on the wooden bench, where the morning sun felt good on his face and shoulders after his work out. He became drowsy watching the swish of the rod and the soft delicate fly land on the flat water. He made a mental note to sign up for an Indie fly-fishing class. Surely, they had a class for that here. They had a class for everything.

Yeager kicked Travail's foot. "So what do you think?"

"About what?"

"Never mind." Yeager let the line float on the lake as he lay the rod against the rail. He took a seat on the bench across from Travail. "I've been thinking about Dispatch 34."

Travail touched the confidential envelope in his pocket. Before he played mail carrier, he would listen to Yeager's theory.

According to Yeager, during the height of the Meck Dec controversy in 1837, tensions were high between North Carolina and Virginia as the politicians from both states debated the existence of the Meck Dec. North Carolina's governor had published the 1831 report, and it had furthered Mecklenburg's cause. The Virginians were not convinced, however, and there was also the matter of Thomas Jefferson's credibility. "The Virginians worried like hell they might brand old Tom a copycat."

"How did you learn this?"

Yeager said it didn't matter and to listen up. "Like I said, the year was 1837 and everyone was looking for written evidence. They didn't have the Meck Dec, 'cause it burned up, so where do you think they looked?" Yeager became exasperated when Travail sat silent. "Newspapers. They searched them all."

Travail made a guess. "There was a newspaper called *The Dispatch*?"

"Craig Travail, didn't you read the books Lori gave you?" Yeager didn't wait for an answer. "Dispatches were how royal governors kept the British Parliament informed of patriot activities during the uprisings of 1775.

"North Carolina's royal governor was beside himself about Mecklenburg County. That summer, shortly after the meetings on May 19 and May 20, he writes to some earl in London and tells him about the treasonous activities in Mecklenburg and how he needs help, or the colonists are going to kick his butt. He enclosed an article from a newspaper in eastern North Carolina. I don't remember the name of the paper. It doesn't matter. The letter itself was Dispatch 34."

Travail looked at his watch and wondered when Yeager would get to the point. Yeager told him to sit still. "The ending will blow your mind."

Yeager fast-forwarded from the summer of 1775 to 1837. "It turns out, the British don't throw anything away." He explained they kept colonial dispatches in the British Public Records Office. "Kind of like the public library. Anyone could go take a look."

"Let me guess. Someone stole the newspaper article."

Yeager huffed. "Remind me not to tell a joke to a crowd with you in the room."

Travail held up his hands in surrender, and Yeager continued.

"The American ambassador to England was named Stevenson, and he asked another fellow named Turner to remove the document for him in the summer of 1837. On the last page of the letter was a notation in pencil that said the printed paper had been taken out by Mr. Turner for Mr. Stevenson. It was never returned."

"What do you know about Stevenson?"

"Born and raised in Virginia. Lawyer. Elected US congressman from Virginia. Speaker of the House. Slave owner. Elected to a board at University of Virginia. He would have been a fan of Thomas Jefferson. Maybe a close friend. Definitely part of the Virginia club."

Travail was impressed. Yeager had studied the facts. "You think Ambassador Stevenson stole the newspaper because it proved the existence of the Meck Dec?"

"Not just me. Lots of people think that."

"What was his motive?"

"Here's the deal, Craig Travail. Word was the Virginians were hot to trot to find evidence the Meck Dec was a hoax so nobody could accuse Thomas Jefferson of borrowing language from it. They sent their man Stevenson to see what was in the newspaper.

"What happened to the newspaper article in Dispatch 34 after Stevenson stole it?"

"It disappeared, never to be seen again." Yeager stood and paced around the end of the dock. "When Stevenson died twenty years later, they searched his papers, but it wasn't there. I went to the public library the day somebody tried to run me over and searched the microfiche. I found an article in the *New York Herald* in 1875 that mentioned an interview with Senator John Stevenson, son of the ambassador. The case of the missing document had caused a scandal for the Stevenson family. The senator did what all politicians do. He laid blame on someone else."

"How so?"

"He told the journalist that although it was true his father had asked that the newspaper article be removed from the public records office, it was not for his use, but for the use of another person." Yeager laughed. "The reporter wouldn't let up, pressed the senator for a name. You know what he said? 'I have forgotten it.' I bet he did."

"That's interesting. Now, it's my turn." Travail pulled out the envelope Becky Trainer asked him to deliver and handed it to Yeager. "Becky said Sue Ellen would trust you with this information. It has to do with Dispatch 34."

Yeager ripped the envelope open, read what was on the paper inside and gave Travail his biggest smile to date. "As my daddy used to say, we're in the driver's seat now."

"What do you mean?"

But before Yeager could answer, his fly rod hopped, and he jumped to grab it. The rod bent, and Yeager set the hook. "Tug is the drug, Craig Travail."

Travail got up to look over the rail. Sure enough, Yeager had a fish on. And he hadn't fired a single shot.

"Hang tight, Craig Travail. Breakfast is on the way."

CHAPTER 32

A PLAN RUSHES FORWARD

Sunday night dinner at Travail's cottage was a slimmed down affair because Yeager and Tate were missing in action. Lori explained that Yeager was hell-bent on an adventure, and Tate wouldn't let him go alone. "I couldn't go because of the libel trial, and I pleaded with them to speak with the two of you first. Yeager said he'd ask for forgiveness instead of permission, especially since permission was likely to be denied. So they took off for the five-hour drive to Charlottesville."

Travail had been to Charlottesville only once, and it wasn't by choice. It was the city Elkin liked to think of as home and the place he designated the law firm's headquarters when the firm elected him as their managing partner. Travail had to swallow his pride at being bested in the firm's vote when he attended Elkin's mandatory firm-wide partner meeting for his coronation as leader. The firm paid a handsome sum to rent out Monticello for the event and threw a history-infused party, complete with servers dressed in period costume and tours of the grounds.

In Elkin's acceptance speech, he spoke of Virginia's long history of leadership in the country. He ticked off the names of Virginians elected president like he was making a shopping list for the firm's success: George Washington, Thomas Jefferson, James Madison, James

Monroe, William Henry Harrison, John Tyler, Zachary Taylor, and Woodrow Wilson. But the one he fawned over the most, of course, was Thomas Jefferson. A few months later, Elkin overheard three young lawyers in the firm discussing North Carolinians elected president, and he admonished them because Virginia had more presidents than any other state, including North Carolina. The break room incident is where the merger of Cruella de Vil and Robert Elkin took place, the day Robert de Vil was born.

Harriet interrupted Travail's recollections when she placed a bowl of pasta on the table, along with a bowl of meatballs. "Yeager was supposed to supply the beer, so its red or white wine instead."

The consensus was red. Harriet poured, asked Lori to say a blessing, and folded her hands. Lori thanked the Lord for the food before them, for good friends, and for guidance in the days to come. She added a postscript: "Keep Tate safe in Yeager's hands and Yeager safe from himself."

Harriet gave a big "amen" to that sentiment, took a sip of her wine, and directed her question to Lori. "Have they gone to collect the long-lost copy of the Meck Dec?"

"Not quite."

As they ate dinner, Lori brought Travail and Harriet up to speed on what Yeager, Tate, and she learned from the professor's papers and hard drive. "The professor had only made it halfway through the sequel before he died. The information that caused him to become a believer in the Meck Dec came from a woman named Sally Stevenson, a descendent by marriage of Andrew Stevenson."

Travail was intrigued. "A descendent of the ambassador?"

"How did you know?"

"Yeager thinks Ambassador Stevenson was involved in a conspiracy to steal and conceal a newspaper article that was included with Dispatch 34."

"We couldn't confirm Stevenson's role. The professor's manuscript has a table of contents with a chapter about Ambassador Stevenson, but the professor hadn't written the chapter yet. What he had written said that the newspaper article is the evidence that the Meck Dec was real. We also concluded the professor didn't have the article when he died."

"Based on what?"

"Before the professor died, he told Yeager he planned to reveal to him the next day what he'd learned about the Meck Dec. They were going to take a road trip. Yeager was supposed to pack an overnight bag. He didn't know where he was going at the time, but now, we suspect that he was taking Yeager with him to Virginia to collect a copy of the newspaper article from Sally Stevenson. When Yeager showed Tate and me the paper you gave him, the one related to Dispatch 34, it all made sense. Item 1 on the paper was a street address in Charlottesville. Item 2 was Monticello. Since Sally Stevenson didn't live at Monticello, we presumed she must live at the address in Item 1. Yeager decided he had to go. We couldn't hold him back."

Travail wondered if Yeager and Tate would succeed or fall short and whether any danger awaited them. He took out his Jitterbug phone and sent Yeager a quick text: "Be careful."

As talk turned to the libel trial in the morning, Travail's first order of business was to confirm with Lori what she wanted to do about settlement. "Even if we reject Elkin's offer, we can still negotiate, and possibly get a much more favorable resolution."

"Now that I have money, I'm ready to gamble on the congressman's libel claim, even with my stupid headline."

Harriet said the headline was perfect. "What's not to like about 'Congressman Butters His Worth with Taxpayer Money'?"

Travail felt the need to warn Lori about two issues. "You need to know that Elkin will learn about your newfound wealth in the libel trial when he asks you about your net worth. It is a fair question based on the congressman's punitive damages claim. This could substantially increase a verdict against you and tip Elkin off that Sue Ellen worked against him and for you all along. That might put Yeager and Tate at risk. Also, the congressman has a good claim."

Lori wasn't dissuaded. "But you and Harriet have a plan, right? If it works, there may not be a trial."

"It's a risk."

Lori turned to Harriet. "What do you think about the plan?"

"I don't know how our tobacco-chewing judge will react, but the congressman and Robert Elkin are in for a surprise. I think it's worth the gamble."

"That's enough for me."

They finished dinner, said their goodnights, and Travail's thoughts turned to the trial in the morning. Their plan was simple. Put an end to the libel case before it got started, and thwart the government investigation. And then solve a two-hundred-fifty-year-old mystery. What could go wrong?

CHAPTER 33

THE TRUTH ABOUT LIBEL

Blue provided an earlier than necessary wake-up call when he saw some ducks on the lake outside Travail's bedroom window. Travail rolled out of bed and into the shower to ready himself for another day in court. As he let the water beat on his head, he realized he'd been in the courtroom more days in a row while in retirement than he'd been the last six months at the law firm, and it was only getting worse. It was not a habit he wanted to keep.

Travail apologized to Blue for the short walk around the yard. He let Blue do his business, fed him, and said his goodbye for the day. When he picked Harriet up, he measured her confidence level. "Ready?"

"Lawyering isn't that hard. I think I can handle it, as long as you're sure the judge will want to know everything about the case before we pick a jury. Our strategy depends on it."

"No question in my mind. Judge Brady likes to be in charge."

When they picked Lori up, Harriet asked her if she'd heard anything from Tate.

"Tate texted last night and this morning. She said they got to Charlottesville at 1:00 a.m., stayed in a cheap hotel of Yeager's choosing, and were up and out the door at eight o'clock this morning. She said they're in good spirits, excited to be on their scavenger hunt and not to worry. She navigates while Yeager postulates."

That was exactly the way Travail felt about their day. He was about to navigate the courtroom process so Harriet could postulate to the judge. They were scavenging for a quick win, and he wasn't sure how it would go.

When they entered the courthouse, Amanda Rogers with Channel 24 News was nowhere to be seen. A congressman's libel case apparently wasn't the same draw as the case of a ninety-six-year-old author who writes about the Meck Dec, dies on his wedding night, and cuts his loving granddaughter out of his will. Her absence suited Travail fine.

Robert Elkin waited for them in the courtroom. He hadn't unpacked his briefcase and only had one helper, his administrative assistant. Congressman Butterworth was there too, but didn't acknowledge them. Elkin's grin showed he was confident Lori would settle. He had no clue what was about to happen to him and his case.

"Do you have an answer for me?" Elkin was brusque as ever.

Travail tried not to smile, but he couldn't help it. He was fighting a good fight against a side that deserved to lose. He figured his losing streak would have to end sometime, and now was as good a time as any. "Lori rejects your offer."

Elkin didn't take the news well. "You'll be sorry."

Twenty minutes later, the bailiff told the lawyers, "Judge Brady will see you in his chambers."

Lori stood and gave Harriet and Travail hugs. "Good luck. You've got this. I'll be waiting."

The judge was robeless and seated behind his desk, fiddling with a pouch of Red Man when Elkin, Travail, and Harriet entered his office. "Take a seat." He reached into the pouch, pulled out a few inches of dark, stringy tobacco with his thumb and forefinger, and tucked a wad in his mouth behind his right cheek. "Have the parties discussed settlement?"

Elkin had the first word. "We tried, your honor. We made a very reasonable offer."

"Where's your trial team, Mr. Elkin?"

Elkin sat up straight. "I'm handling the case. My client is here and ready to proceed."

Judge Roscoe "Chaw" Brady used the moment to express his opinion. He leaned below the right side of his desk and spit. The sound of saliva hitting something other than the floor made everyone take notice.

Travail knew Judge Brady would not miss an opportunity to assist the parties in settling their case, and though it was highly irregular for a judge to ask about the specifics of the settlement offer in a case he was about to preside over, Chaw Brady did not do regular. "Tell me about the offer."

Elkin spoke to the judge as if Travail and Harriet weren't in the room. "All she has to do is apologize, publish a retraction, and close down We Salute You. It's going to get shut down anyway when the government revokes We Salute You's nonprofit status. I hope this offer eases the pain of her recent loss."

Judge Brady looked at Travail with a quizzical expression. It looked like an invitation not just to respond but to explain.

"My client refuses to apologize for telling the truth."

Judge Brady was old-school. He didn't mind letting the lawyers duke it out in court and dig their own graves if they were stubborn enough to do it. "It looks like you have your answer, Mr. Elkin."

Elkin was agitated, a fact not lost on Chaw Brady. A lawyer who is too eager to settle is a lawyer who is uncomfortable going to trial. Travail tried to remember if Elkin had ever appeared as lead counsel in court, and he couldn't recall a single case. He'd always had other lawyers do the heavy lifting. Maybe he didn't know what he was doing. Maybe he was afraid he'd botch it up. Or maybe—and this was the thought that intrigued Travail the most—the stakes were too high for his client to have a trial if it meant the possibility he might lose. What was Elkin worried about?

Judge Brady also wanted to know. "Tell me about your case, Mr. Elkin."

This question led to a disjointed response by Elkin. He knew the nature of the claim. It was a libel lawsuit. He knew how to say "defamation" and "punitive damages" and how to call the defendant names, but he was short of knowledge of the facts or the law. When he finished, the judge spit again.

"Your turn, Mr. Travail."

"With your permission, I'd like my assistant to summarize our case. She's got an accounting background and is very good with numbers." Elkin's eyes darted at the words "accounting background" and "numbers." He leaned forward and peered around Travail at Harriet.

The judge chewed. "I'm fine with the little lady presenting your case."

Harriet swept into action. She dropped a binder on Judge Brady's desk and handed one to Elkin and Travail. "I'm not a little lady, judge. I'm five feet eight. You'd be just as tall if you didn't stoop your shoulders so much."

Travail's heart beat faster. What was Harriet doing? This part of the plan depended on the judge being on their side, and Trial Practice 101 frowned on judge humiliation.

The judge's face gave away nothing. He had a large plug of Red Man resting inside his right cheek and a wait-and-see demeanor. One thing made Travail's heart rate slow down to a resting position. Judge Roscoe Chaw Brady hadn't spit since before Harriet started talking, and he didn't spit for the next ten minutes.

Harriet started with the role Congressman Butterworth played in arranging defense contracts. He was a highly placed politician with lots of influence. He could make things happen. Get the right contracts for the right companies. He was quite the player in the government contracting business.

Elkin interrupted. "There's nothing wrong with being influential. It doesn't make him a crook."

His bluster did not bother Harriet. "Be patient, Mr. Elkin. We'll get there."

Travail liked Harriet's punch. When he'd moved into the Indie and resigned himself to life in a retirement community, he never thought he'd find such competence among the residents. How naïve he'd been. An ageist idiot.

The first time Harriet said the word "Viribus," Elkin objected, on grounds of relevance. "This case is not about Viribus. None of the libelous articles mention that company."

Judge Brady let go a long stream of tobacco juice he'd been holding in and informed Elkin they didn't do objections in his office. "You can save those for the jury trial."

Elkin turned on Harriet. "Do you have any evidence the congressman illegally funneled money to his campaign accounts with the help of the specific government contractors listed in your client's articles?"

"No."

"There it is, judge. Proof they're going to lose. Libel per se. Defendant accused my client of a crime and has nothing to back it up."

Harriet smiled at Judge Brady. "We have something better."

Elkin complained to the judge, who ignored him as he spit again. He nodded for Harriet to continue.

"To find the crime, we had to match up thousands of Viribus invoices with the same number of purchase orders."

Elkin complained this was an ambush. He and his client needed time to study these documents. Judge Brady spit more tobacco juice in his spittoon and said he'd give Elkin extra time before they picked a jury. "Let her finish."

"It didn't take long to find the pattern, judge. The answer to the riddle was as simple as learning your ABCs. Viribus used three invoices—A, B, and C—for each product shipped, telling the government inspectors they used three Viribus subsidiaries to manufacture the components of each product ordered."

Travail could sense Elkin wanted to object, but Chaw had warned him. He wondered how much Elkin knew about what Harriet had concluded.

Judge Brady had warmed up to Harriet. He wanted to see if he understood by proposing an example. "Let's say Viribus sold a hammer to the federal government for two hundred dollars, which the federal government said was a perfectly appropriate amount to charge. When Viribus bills for the hammer, it sends a cover sheet that shows two hundred dollars is due and attaches three separate invoices with a breakdown. Invoice A might be for a hundred dollars, invoice B for seventy dollars, and invoice C for thirty dollars."

"Exactly." Harriet asked the judge to look closer. "The government then paid each of those invoices to three separate accounts designated by Viribus."

"Which supposedly belong to subsidiaries of Viribus." Judge Brady invited Elkin to jump in. "Would you like to add anything before she goes on?"

Elkin controlled his tone this time. "Your honor, this evidence has nothing to do with Congressman Butterworth, and these legitimate accounting practices have nothing to do with this lawsuit. Lori Collins never mentioned any of this in her libelous articles about Congressman Butterworth."

Everything was going as Travail had hoped. It was true these transactions might pass for legitimate though unusual accounting practices to pay for overpriced hammers, but Becky had broken the codes on the bank account numbers and Harriet did the rest. She put everything together in a format that any jury could easily understand. Now it was time to drop the hammer on Congressman Butterworth.

Harriet slowed her cadence. "The funds the government paid to satisfy the A invoices went to a bank account registered to Viribus, LLC. The funds paid to satisfy the C invoices, however, traveled a circuitous route through eight bank accounts before landing in a personal account owned by Congressman Walter Butterworth." Harriet laid the banking documents in front of Judge Brady like she was laying down a straight flush in a high-stakes poker tournament. "Mr. Elkin was correct. The congressman's campaign did nothing illegal. It did not steal money from the government. Congressman Butterworth did."

She turned to Travail and asked the question like they planned. "What are those claims you said Lori is going to file against the congressman?"

"Malicious prosecution and abuse of process." Travail had the feeling his losing streak with Judge Roscoe "Chaw" Brady was about to come to an end.

Elkin muttered something unintelligible before asking the judge for a few minutes to speak with his client. He returned in less than five minutes to find Judge Brady and Harriet comparing names of old friends they had in common.

"We'll drop the lawsuit if Lori signs a nondisclosure agreement."

After Judge Brady spit in his spittoon again, Travail stepped into the conversation and played his part. "Here's how this is going to work, Robert. Lori Collins will allow your client to dismiss this case with prejudice, immediately. She will not sue your client for the claims I mentioned, nor will she seek attorney's fees and punitive damages, provided Congressman Butterworth calls off the government watchdogs at the IRS who have harassed We Salute You about its nonprofit status. That's it. Take it or leave it." Travail enjoyed that last line.

"What about those documents?" Elkin pointed to the notebook on Judge Brady's desk.

The judge spit again and took it from there. "These documents will be referred to the US Attorney's Office in Congressman Butterworth's home district."

As they rode the courthouse elevator, Travail told Lori how Harriet had impressed the judge. "When we left, he asked Harriet what law school she attended."

"What did you say?"

Harriet laughed. "I told him I went to Indie U. He asked if I meant Indiana, and I said, 'Whatever.'" Lori laughed.

"You really should have gone to law school," Travail said.

"And why would I want to do that? As I said, this really isn't that hard."

Over eggs, bacon, grits, and toast at the Park Road Soda Shoppe, Lori learned how the case was won. But she had a question.

"What about the B invoices? Where did that money go?"

"I have a theory," Harriet said.

Travail used his toast to push his grits and fried eggs together. "I bet you do."

Lori's phone hummed with a text. She took a breath when she read the message. "I need to call Tate." She made the call but got no answer. She showed the text message to Travail and Harriet. "We need to go," Lori said.

Travail took out his Jitterbug and called Yeager. No answer. "I need to make another call, but we can do it while we drive."

His next call was to Crystal Marks. "What's the name of the private investigator in Charlottesville we used on that case a few years ago?"

She gave him the name and contact information and then asked, "Craig, what's going on?"

Travail toyed with whether to bring Crystal Marks into their world of deception and conspiracy. What would she think? Probably that they were all crazy.

"Craig?"

Travail decided he should take a chance on Crystal Marks, provided she didn't tell Robert Elkin. She agreed, and when he was done filling her in, she was confused, and rightly so.

"I don't understand. You spent the entire trial trying to prove the Meck Dec was nothing but a fantasy."

Travail said the world had been spinning faster since the verdict came down. Lots of additional information had surfaced. Pieces were fitting together that made little sense before.

"You're saying the Meck Dec is real, and your friends are in danger because they've gone to find a document that proves it?"

"Yes." He told her about Yeager's near miss with an SUV, Sue

Ellen's death by SUV, and Tate's text about the two SUVs. "I'm concerned they are in danger."

"Should I call the police?"

"I'll call the private investigator first, have him check on them, and tell him to call the police if there are any problems."

As they merged onto the interstate, Travail remembered to make one more call. "Becky, can you feed Blue tonight and tomorrow? The key is under the back porch mat."

CHAPTER 34

THE EVIDENCE ON TAPE

The professor's recorded phone call with Sally Stevenson
Transcribed by Sue Ellen Parker after Matthew Collins died

Q. Please say your name for the recording.
A. Sally Stevenson.

Q. As you know, the purpose of this recorded interview is to discuss
the newspaper article included with Dispatch 34, its location, and
whether it is genuine. Do you promise that what you are about to tell
me is true?
A. I do.

Q. Do you possess *The Cape Fear Mercury* article that was sent by
Governor Martin with his Dispatch 34 to the Earl of Dartmouth in the
summer of 1775?
A. Yes.

Q. How did you come to possess it?
A. It's a long story.

Q. Please.

A. My husband was a descendent of Ambassador Andrew Stevenson. The Stevenson family produced a long line of civic-minded, patriotic men who spent their lives in service to their country. As a family, the Stevenson line never got over the stain on their family name caused by the missing article. Ambassador Stevenson did not steal the document. He was a scapegoat, connected as an ally to Thomas Jefferson and his peers, and seen as the likely culprit when the document went missing, but he was innocent. They set him up.

Q. How was Ambassador Stevenson set up?

A. The Jefferson Venture sent two men from different states to see Ambassador Stevenson in 1837. They pretended to have historical interest in the article. Their credentials appeared valid, and they appealed to his Virginian pride, saying they wanted to put an end to the Meck Dec controversy with their examination of the article. If it was, as they thought, helpful to Virginia, they would reveal the truth that the Meck Dec was a lie. They said it would be better coming from historians from New York and Georgia rather than an ambassador from Virginia.

Q. Is that why the file in the British Public Records Office in London said the paper was "taken out by Mr. Turner for Mr. Stevenson, August 15, 1837"?

A. Yes. Mr. Turner delivered the paper to Stevenson at the embassy, where he waited with the men from New York and Georgia. The men convinced him it was best they examine the document alone in the next room so he would have what we now call plausible deniability should the contents be contrary to his wishes. They examined the document and returned with the good news the paper made no reference to the Meck Dec. They asked to borrow the paper for twenty-four hours to consult with one other expert, and Ambassador Stevenson readily agreed, thinking the paper was about to be disclosed to the world, but the men disappeared with the document.

Q. Was Peter Force involved? The reason I ask is that the newspaper article went missing in August of 1837, and Peter Force became famous one year later for discovering the Mecklenburg Resolves, a discovery he used to conclude, to some notoriety, that the Mecklenburg Resolves constituted the only document created in Mecklenburg in May of 1775.

A. No, he wasn't involved. And if you think about it, he had no incentive to conceal the document if he had it, because he would have been doubly famous for discovering both documents.

Q. What happened next?

A. Ambassador Stevenson made inquiries and searched, but he never found the document. He assumed the two men were spies for North Carolina and had stolen the document to prevent it from becoming public. He went to his grave under the impression the contents were helpful to Virginia's cause, but he had no way to prove it, and given his role in the document's disappearance, he kept quiet about it and its disappearance for the rest of his life. All he could say, when others accused him of absconding with the document, was that it was not taken out for him but for another person, whose name he and later his son, Senator John Stevenson, "had forgotten." This was reported in 1875 in an article in the *New York Herald*.

Q. How did you find out The Jefferson Venture was involved?

A. My husband and I learned about its successor, The Jefferson Experience, when we attended a fundraising event a few years ago at Monticello. On the surface, their work seemed noble. They supported Virginia history and the work of Thomas Jefferson, but two things bothered us after we looked at their brochure and heard their director speak. The brochure said the nonprofit was formed in 1837, the same year *The Cape Fear Mercury* article went missing. That seemed too coincidental. And because the event was held on May 20, someone in the audience from North Carolina asked a question about the Meck Dec, and the director's response was defensive. My husband and I decided to dig deeper. After much investigation, we found a source, a disgruntled ex-spouse of one of their board members, a congressman named Walter Butterworth. She knew the story and was happy to share it, if for no other reason, to get back at her ex-husband.

Q. What else did you learn?
A. The Jefferson Experience kept detailed records of their expenditures dating back to 1837. Their very first expenditure was to hire two men, one from New York and one from Georgia.

Q. To steal *The Cape Fear Mercury* article from Ambassador Stevenson?
A. Exactly.

Q. How did you find the article, and where did you find it?
A. After my husband died, I learned from my source about an annual private event held for The Jefferson Experience's board in the Dome Room at Monticello. Her ex-husband let slip that, for the last fifteen years, the director had led a bizarre ceremony, almost religious, where he removed, displayed, and had board members "lay hands on" an object integral to The Jefferson Experience's mission. Something told me it had to be *The Cape Fear Mercury* article. I volunteered at Monticello, gained access to the Dome Room, and searched for twelve months until I found it tucked behind a false panel in the Cuddy, a small unfinished nook once used by Jefferson's granddaughters as their secret space.

Q. How do you know the document is genuine?
A. I had the paper tested for age, and it fits the time period. Also, an expert in historical newspapers ruled out forgery. But the best evidence is the fact The Jefferson Experience has gone to such great effort for so long to conceal it, and I am sure they are hunting for it as we speak.

CHAPTER 35

YEAGER AND TATE PURSUE THE PRIZE

The address didn't appear on GPS, so Yeager asked Tate to try a nearby address. The directions led them off the paved road and onto a dirt road that ran through thick trees in the Virginia countryside. After a few miles, they came to a mailbox with a nearby address. Two miles further, they passed a dirt path on the left with no mailbox or signage and continued until they came to a mailbox with a higher number. They guessed the unmarked driveway they'd passed a few miles back was their destination. They were right.

The gravel driveway, if one could call it that, needed repair. Yeager's truck bounced through ruts left by heavy rains. It hadn't been dragged, graded, or graveled in years. Whoever lived at the end of the drive didn't come or go very often.

At the end of the track, they got out of the truck and took in the world around them. The driveway ended in a small clearing in a hardwood forest. There was enough room to turn the truck around, but the area could use the attention of a good bushhog operator. They could hear the sound of running water—a river or stream—down the slope to their right.

They faced a single-story wood-sided house with peeling paint, with shades pulled and lights out. An old VW bus was parked under a detached carport. Yeager saw a well-built and well-cared-for barn to the left of the house, up on a ridge. He pointed to the front door of the house and motioned to Tate. She stepped up to the door and knocked. After trying again, she turned the doorknob and shook her head.

Yeager started toward the barn and waved to Tate to follow him.

"Wait," she said, and pointed at the driveway. What he couldn't see through the trees, he could hear. The sound of vehicles. They'd been followed. There was only one way in and no way out.

He motioned to Tate to hurry ahead of him up the hill to the barn. He pulled his pistol and followed her, cursing himself for leaving his rifle in the truck. They climbed thirty yards up a winding path, made level ground, and hid behind the corner of the barn.

Two vehicles pulled into the clearing. Five men got out of the vehicles, and two ran to the front door of the house. Tate tapped out a text to Lori. She showed it to Yeager, he nodded, and she hit send. He whispered. "Now silence your phone." Yeager did the same with his Jitterbug.

Yeager didn't bother to knock. He opened the barn door, pulled Tate inside, and closed the door behind him. The door had three dead bolts. He locked them all. From behind him, he heard a voice.

"Did they follow you?"

Yeager spun around. "Who's that?"

An elderly woman with short white hair sat at an antique desk. The interior of the barn had been fitted out as living quarters. It had a small kitchen in one corner and a bed and dresser in another. There was a bath and commode in a third corner and a living area with a television in the fourth.

She answered Yeager's unspoken question. "My husband retrofitted the barn when the termites moved into the house below." She stood and introduced herself. "I'm Sally Stevenson. We don't have much time."

Sally talked fast. Some of what she said didn't mesh with the story Yeager had built in his head, but he had no time for questions. As she talked, the men who'd followed them banged on the triple dead bolt locked door and shouted, "Open the door."

Sally kept talking even as they yelled and banged.

"Last warning."

Yeager heard the "rat-a-tat-tat" of automatic gunfire.

Tate screamed and Yeager flinched. The woman stayed calm as bullets dented but didn't pierce the door.

She placed what she said was the original *Cape Fear Mercury* article, pressed tight in a thin see-through case, on the desk where they could see. "Read and memorize it."

Yeager heard men running along both sides of the barn. He and Tate moved closer to Sally's desk so they could read the document together. His nerves frayed. Reading was hard enough without men trying to attack them.

Tate gathered herself and continued to read. Yeager only got through the first few sentences before the back door on the uphill side of the barn crashed in and the five men ran toward them.

"Run for the other door," Yeager yelled, offering himself as a shield.

He saw a flash, dropped the newspaper article, and reached for his gun. A fist caught him in the jaw and knocked him on his back. He lost his grip on the gun. Yeager rolled to his knees, reached for his Jitterbug and used it like brass knuckles to punch upward at his attacker's face. He found his footing and threw the mobile device at the man. He'd been a decent shortstop on his high school baseball team, but the throw was wide. The phone sailed out the open back door before someone hit him on the head from the side with something hard. The room went dark.

Yeager awoke with a terrible headache. He was sitting up, his back against a wall. He tried to move his arms, but they were tied behind his back. He looked to his left and right and saw Tate and Sally Stevenson on either side of him. They were in the same situation. The side of Tate's face was bloody, and there was a bruise on Sally's neck.

"How are you two doing?"

Tate winced. "I'm a little banged up, but I'll be fine."

Sally's breathing was shallow. "I have a few bruises, but I'll be okay."

A man came forward and kicked Yeager in the foot. "I could have killed you, old man, but we have our orders. That comes later."

"Untie me, and we'll make it a fair fight this time."

The man ignored him, except to point his gun at Yeager, as if to say, "Don't test me."

Yeager could talk himself out of or into most anything, but talking wouldn't help with these men. The name of the game now was patience, something his mother had tried and failed to teach him.

The men who'd assaulted them were dressed in dark green fatigues. All were white men. Skin heads. Tats on their arms. Well-armed, with knives, small handguns, rifles, and automatic weapons. They looked like they'd treat killing a human no differently than hunting deer.

The drawers in all the desks, dressers, and tables had been tossed, and the books pulled off the bookshelves. The man who'd kicked Yeager held *The Cape Fear Mercury* article in his hand as he made a phone call. He asked Sally Stevenson if she'd made any copies.

"No. But you've figured that out already by tearing up my home." Sally hung her head, as if the defeat was too much to take.

The group leader told two of his men to go move the SUVs. "There's a logging road that leads to the back of the barn. Park them there and hurry back."

They were gone five minutes when Yeager heard the vehicles driven behind the barn. Next, he heard a different vehicle in the driveway below the barn. The leader sent his other two men to check it out. They returned with a man whose hands were tied behind his back. They threw him on the floor. The leader pulled the man's business card from his wallet and admired it as he spoke. "Private eye, huh. Who hired you?"

The man was sullen. "The police are on their way."

The leader laughed. "Sure." He scrolled through the photos on the man's phone and held one up. "This your wife? She's pretty." He spoke to one of the hoodlums playing with his knife. "Would you like to spend a romantic evening with this man's wife?"

The private investigator struggled against his restraints.

"I'm going to ask you again. Who do you work for?" The leader held up the phone with the picture of the man's wife as he spoke. Yeager could sense the man weighing his options. He chose to protect his family.

"His name is Craig Travail."

This fact seemed to tickle the leader. "See. That wasn't so hard. Travail can pay you when he arrives."

Yeager realized he'd screwed up twice. He'd led these men to *The Cape Fear Mercury*, and now he and Tate would serve as the live bait to trap their friends. If Travail was on his way to Virginia to help, he was sure Harriet and Lori were with him.

Two men grabbed the investigator and lifted him. "You need to make a phone call to Craig Travail and tell him you found his friends, they are okay, and they're waiting for him at this address." The men took the investigator outside to make the call, spoiling Yeager's chance to shout during the call. When the men returned, they tossed the investigator on the floor at Yeager's feet.

Minutes turned to hours. The captors allowed bathroom breaks for the women, not the men. It didn't matter. Yeager was full of piss and vinegar and wanted to keep it that way.

As the afternoon wore on, the barn grew colder. Yeager whispered encouragement to the others. "Everything is going to be fine. Craig Travail is sure enough going to bring help." But he had his doubts.

About that time, he heard another vehicle in the driveway below the barn. The leader heard it too. He motioned to all four men, and they vanished out the front and back doors with their guns at the ready.

CHAPTER 36

ELKIN COVERS HIS TRACKS

Robert Elkin returned to the Charlotte office to do damage control. He called the other management committee members to his office and, while he waited, he made some notes. Dunkler and Birdsong arrived in a hurry. They looked every bit as dumpy and thin respectively as on the day they'd witnessed Elkin fire Travail in this very office. Dunkler grumped and Birdsong chirped about rumblings in the law firm. Word had leaked out about the libel trial. Now was the time to set the record straight and have Dunkler and Birdsong deliver it.

The task was to separate Congressman Butterworth from the law firm. Elkin handed Dunkler his handwritten version of a press release. "Clean that up and get it out, immediately." The message was simple: "The law firm has fired its client, Congressman Walter Butterworth. All press inquiries were to be directed to managing partner Everett Birdsong."

Once Dunkler was out the door, Elkin told Birdsong how to handle the press. "They may want you to comment on a potential criminal investigation involving Butterworth. Just say the firm cut ties with the congressman and has no intention of representing him further."

"Won't that suggest he's guilty?"

Elkin marveled at how dense his minions could be in times of crisis. "Of course it will." He added that if the media asked questions about their client, Viribus, he was to say the law firm was engaged to help Viribus recover funds wrongfully stolen from it. He told Birdsong to set up a meeting at five-thirty that evening with all the partners in the law firm. "Attendance is mandatory. Those in Charlotte need to be here in person, and every other partner across the globe needs to be there by video conference."

His next move was to alert Viribus. He spoke with the CEO, who listened and said he'd have the chair of the board call Elkin right away. Elkin answered on the first ring. The Viribus board chair focused first on Butterworth's predicament.

"I understand the congressman got himself into some trouble."

"Greed is not so good after all."

"Will this come back on Viribus?"

"No. We'll say a crooked politician hoodwinked Viribus." Elkin explained how they'd handle the media and asked the chair about the invoice C payments to Butterworth.

"He told us he'd cleared the personal payments with the director."

"Well, he hadn't." Elkin waited for the question he knew was coming.

"What about the invoice B funds? Should we worry about Butterworth or anyone else blowing the whistle?"

This was a point Elkin had considered. He wasn't sure what Travail and Harriet knew about the invoice B funds. Only four people were supposed to know about them. They were Viribus's chair, Congressman Walter Butterworth, Elkin, and the director, all of whom were board members of The Jefferson Experience. The scheme had produced the largest cash influx into The Jefferson Experience since it was founded in 1837. "Butterworth won't talk. Going to prison is safer than the director's wrath."

"Are you sure prison is enough?"

Elkin didn't like where the conversation was headed. Deaths could lead to investigations. He needed no more of that risk. All he wanted to do was make money, live a better life than he'd lived as a child, and show his father he'd amounted to something. It was his father who got him involved in The Jefferson Experience, and it was his father who was going to cause him heartache once again. "I will speak with Butterworth. Can you arrange for his children to receive a lifetime pension?"

"We can make that happen. Off the books, of course."

His next call was to Butterworth, but before he made it, he swiveled in his chair and took in Thomas Jefferson's bust on the pedestal behind him. As a young boy, his father made him study and admire every US president born in Virginia, punished him for getting facts wrong, made him worship Jefferson the most, and forced him to write grade-school book reports about the third president ad nauseam. From the moment Elkin reached the halfway mark in fourth grade, his father had him on a path destined for enrollment at the University of Virginia, the public university founded by Jefferson. At a parent-teacher conference, his father talked in condescending tones to the teacher who'd given his son a B in Virginia history. Things came to a head when his mother said Robert was just a child, called his father "unbalanced," and said she wouldn't stand another day of "historical abuse."

The family breakup and the exile of mother and son to Charlotte did not erase the brainwashing Elkin's father had embedded in Elkin. As much as he despised his father for abandoning him, he revered what his father revered. While he and his mother lived on scraps, he promised himself that, one day, he would be more successful than his father. When he got a scholarship to UVA, he took it. When law school seemed like a profitable route, he became a double Wahoo. Finishing top in his class at a prestigious law school and making all the right political connections brought Elkin and his father back together.

His father called him one day after not speaking with him for fifteen years and asked if he could attend his son's law school graduation. Elkin relented. What followed was a father-son dinner at a local private club, where his father revealed himself as the director of The Jefferson Experience and initiated Elkin into the organization.

In the years that followed, Elkin came to learn his mother was right. His father was unbalanced, and it only got worse as he aged. By the time the director turned eighty, he had become fixated on the dangers the Meck Dec story posed to Jefferson's reputation and by extension his own. He bristled at Charlotte's local ceremonies sponsored by the May 20th Society and demanded his son do something about them. Elkin knew better than to stir up an investigation over harmless ceremonies, and he talked his father down.

Elkin came up with the idea to sponsor Matthew Collins's work. The publication of *An American Hoax* pleased the director and calmed the Meck Dec waters for fifteen years. But when his father learned Matthew Collins had changed his mind and was going to rewrite history, things took a turn. The man's paranoia, combined with his dementia, produced a vicious cocktail Elkin had been unwilling to swallow. It was one thing to ruin people's lives to keep a secret. Another, to use violence to do it.

Elkin phoned Butterworth and kept the conversation brief. "You're going to go to prison, but if you keep your mouth shut, we will take care of your children. And you are lucky to be dealing with me rather than the director." Butterworth was grateful. "Message received. Thank you."

When he ended the call, Elkin thought about *The Cape Fear Mercury* article. Guarding the secret of the Meck Dec had always seemed a folly to him. The Jefferson Experience could do so much more with their war chest than spend it on spies and mercenaries. In his view, which he often expressed to his father, the founders of The Jefferson Experience made a mistake when they tricked Ambassador Stevenson and stole the newspaper article included with Dispatch 34. It stoked the curiosity of those who believed in the Meck Dec, and it created enough of a hint of conspiracy to keep the Meck Dec cause alive and the Meck Dec home fires burning to this day.

The director never listened to Elkin about what to do with the evidence. He told Elkin *The Cape Fear Mercury* article could never come to light, but needed to be preserved. Elkin fired back. "Why keep it? Just burn it like the Meck Dec. End of story."

The director didn't answer, and Elkin knew why. The man was like an art thief with a passion for observing the stolen masterpiece in his own dark dwelling. He loved the feeling of power that came with possessing the evidence nobody else could see. Now that he'd lost the talisman and its power, he might destroy everything they had to get it back.

Elkin's mobile phone rang. If thinking about his father made him call, he'd have to break that habit. "Hello."

"We have *The Cape Fear Mercury* and four prisoners. The other three who know the truth are on their way to Virginia. We'll have them soon." The determination in his father's voice was combined with excitement.

Elkin didn't like the sound of the word "prisoners" and he didn't like the thought of what his father might do with them. "Who is on their way to Virginia?"

"Your lawyer friend, that woman who's been helping him, and Lori Collins." The director sounded self-satisfied. His plan had come together. His laugh was guttural. There was delusion in his voice too. "By later today, it will all be over. The secret will be safe and buried forever, no thanks to you."

Elkin didn't like the word "buried," either.

Robert Elkin stood in the law firm's large conference room on the forty-eighth floor of the America Bank office tower. His back was against a large glass window that looked down on the stadium where the Carolina Panthers played on Sundays. Before him sat the eighty partners who worked in the Charlotte office. A video camera would carry his message to the partners in all thirty offices in the US and to the firm's offices in London, Paris, and Rome. Before long, it would leak out to all associates and staff and everyone would know the "truth," as he told it.

"I want to thank everyone for joining me on such short notice. I have important information to share with you about our largest client, Viribus." The partners would pay close attention at the mention of

Viribus. The company supplied the largest percentage of their shares of the firm's income.

He said they would hear about this on the news, but he wanted to tell them first. It is unfortunate, he said, that we have had to end our attorney-client relationship with Congressman Walter Butterworth. "I trusted him, as did Viribus, but the congressman is facing state and federal criminal charges for embezzling money from Viribus." He assured everyone the law firm did not know of these illicit activities when it agreed to represent the congressman, and he had spoken with the chair of Viribus, who accepted his reassurances. "The chair asked me to thank all of you for what you do, and he looks forward to continuing our relationship." A collective sigh filled the room as the possibility of losing money from a huge client evaporated.

Elkin said he had one more thing to say, and he hated to say it. "One of our former law partners, Craig Travail, along with several accomplices, is suspected of stealing financial records from Viribus. I am putting together a team of lawyers, along with forensic experts, to investigate these crimes and obtain justice for our firm's largest client. If Travail contacts any of you, you must not tip him off the firm is on to him. He is facing disbarment next week. It is our hope this entire affair will be over soon."

Elkin finished by saying he understood how difficult it was to hear that a former client and partner are criminals. "We will get through this. Thank you."

Elkin saw Crystal Marks standing in the back corner of the room and waved her forward. She approached as the other partners left the room.

"I know this is hard for you to hear. Craig was a friend of yours."

"He still is."

"Of course. I need to know where your loyalties lie."

"To the truth. How about you, Robert?"

Elkin didn't like her attitude. He'd have to speak with Dunkler and Birdsong about marginalizing her. She was very popular among the partners, but if she didn't get on board, she'd have to walk the plank.

CHAPTER 37

A LONG WAY TO INDEPENDENCE

The road trip to Charlottesville was long and stressful. Two hours in, Travail pulled off at a gas station and filled the tank. At Harriet's insistence, he changed places with her. In the back seat, he was met by a pile of books she'd bought at Park Road Books while they'd waited on breakfast that morning. He saw books on Monticello, Jefferson, the Meck Dec, and Charlottesville, along with some maps.

As the car rolled down the highway, Travail read that Jefferson died the same day as John Adams, on July 4, 1826, the fiftieth anniversary of the Declaration of Independence. It was fantastically coincidental that two men so important to the founding of the country, sometimes allies and sometimes bitter political rivals, both died on the day America celebrated the fiftieth anniversary of what they helped create. And yet, Adams had accused Jefferson of plagiarizing from the Meck Dec when he wrote the Declaration of Independence. Were they about to find out Adams was right? Or wrong? Or could Adams have been right about the validity of the Meck Dec, but wrong about plagiarism?

Travail received a call from the investigator. Everyone was safe. That was good news, but the situation didn't feel right as they put more miles behind them.

Lori continued to text Tate and call her, but there was no answer. "It's unlike Tate not to respond."

Travail tried Yeager again on the Jitterbug, but he didn't answer either. "Maybe their batteries died." Travail wondered how long a Jitterbug battery lasted anyway, and how far out in the country Tate and Yeager were.

When they passed the state line, they found themselves in the Virginia countryside. Travail had an uneasy feeling as he watched the rural landscape fly by, sprinkled with empty brown fields, abandoned gas stations, and mobile homes. He took in the big grey sky for as far as his eyes could see. It was important to get to Charlottesville as fast as they could.

To take their minds off the safety of their friends, they talked history while Harriet drove. Lori plugged the hard-drive copy of the professor's computer into her laptop and used it as her source. Travail read aloud the following passage from one of the history books.

"Governor Martin fled his palace in New Bern and took up temporary residence at Fort Johnston, near the mouth of the Cape Fear River, thirty miles below Wilmington, where he held a council meeting on June 25, 1775. The minutes of that meeting were included in Dispatch 34."

"What did the minutes say?" Harriet asked.

"The minutes referred to 'seditious combinations' and singled out 'the late most treasonable publication of a Committee in the County of Mecklenburg explicitly renouncing obedience to His Majesty's government of all lawful authority whatsoever.'"

Harriet honked the horn at a slow-moving truck and said, "Sounds like a declaration of independence to me."

"I can't believe it," Lori said.

"Sure you can. It's—"

"No. No. No. I can't believe I missed this document on the professor's computer. It's a transcript of a recorded phone call between the professor and Sally Stevenson. Listen to what it says."

Travail paid close attention as Lori read the document Sue Ellen Parker transcribed of the professor's interview with Sally Stevenson. It answered most of their questions about *The Cape Fear Mercury* article and The Jefferson Experience. The two questions it didn't answer were whether Thomas Jefferson knew about the Meck Dec in 1775, and if he did, whether he copied from it one year later. It also didn't answer the question of what awaited them.

Travail saw a road sign and realized they were close to Charlottesville. He asked Harriet if she could navigate while he drove. She pulled over, everyone stretched, and he took the wheel again. Harriet plugged their destination address into her phone. She had to do a dance with alternative addresses to get close to the address and estimated they were twenty minutes away.

A few minutes later, Harriet's phone rang. She answered, listened, made some notes, and thanked Becky with a smile. She explained the results of Becky's follow-up forensic work.

"The B invoices issued by Viribus led to money traveling through many banks. The money went to an account in a bank in Seattle, then to an account in a bank in Austin, then to an account in a bank in Buffalo, then to an account in a bank in Phoenix, and then to bank accounts in four other states until it arrived at a bank account in Virginia."

"Where in Virginia?"

Harriet pointed to a sign and said, "There." The sign had a green background adorned with the state tree, the buds of a flowering dogwood, and read: "Welcome to Charlottesville."

CHAPTER 38

The
CAPE FEAR MERCURY

Monday June 26, 1775

Charlotte-Town
Mecklenburg's Resolves

The Committee of Mecklenburg met on May 19 and 20, debated the offensive act of uncivil war His Majesty's army ignited in Lexington Mass and well resolved that such reckless, injurious and harmful conduct, together with all the pernicious edicts and decrees to tax the colonies without representation, shall not be abided, and for that reason, put pen to paper and went immediately forth to declare their resolutions well and good and with powerful, excited voice from the Mecklenburg courthouse steps on May 20 that they were now a people free and independent of tyrannical rule. The May 20 actions of the

Mecklenburg Committee, which is supplied on good authority by word of a distinguished signer, is an example of courage to be celebrated, a sentiment not declared so specifically elsewhere but which effusive spirit flourishes throughout the land, as it did this past week with the Committee of Wilmington's resolves that speak defiance to Governor Martin, who has become an enemy of the people and who absconded to Fort Johnston, awaiting reinforcements to cause further harm to the rights of the people, for which His Majesty appears to care very little.

The distinguished signer reports that the Committee of Mecklenburg created two sets of resolves. One set of resolves they created on May 20 declaring the rights of the people in the briefest, most direct and right eloquent, inspiring words, and another set of resolves they created on May 31 which deals with the many details for the governance and defense of Mecklenburg, which we have in writing and publish below in this paper. The Committee secretary was of the opinion, the signer reported, that as Congress funds an army and George Washington prepares to fight and counties form their governments and militias, a wide publication of the May 31 Resolves beyond Mecklenburg will be helpful for those counties who desire a similar course and seek a framework they can borrow from or modify as they deem appropriate in their interests to govern and defend themselves. This news from Mecklenburg and the May 31 resolves published herein no doubt will be rejected by Governor Martin as treasonous and he will proclaim his wrath and report to the government in London, but his and their conduct and that of His Majesty has propelled these responses and should be no surprise.

CHAPTER 39

BURNING THE TRUTH

Travail drove up the narrow path and parked behind two vehicles. One was Yeager's truck. The other must have belonged to the private investigator. Lori was out the door first. She yelled for Tate, but she didn't answer. Harriet found Yeager's truck unlocked, messy as usual but with no clue as to his location.

Travail climbed the three steps to the front door of the small house and tried to open it, but it was locked. He knocked, but there was no answer and no sound inside.

He returned to the rough ground and followed a worn footpath. Harriet and Lori joined him. When they rounded the left side of the house, they saw the barn up the hill. It had perimeter lights that blazed, beacons that beckoned.

When they passed the rear of the house and started up the hill, they heard the demand. "Show us your hands."

Travail turned around to find four men. They held handguns pointed at Travail and his friends. He'd seen guns pointed at people on TV and in the movies, but never expected it would happen to him. He was a civil trial lawyer. The ammunition he carried was words.

The men tied their hands behind them and herded them up the hill.

A few minutes later, they sat with their backs against a wall next to Yeager, Tate, their private investigator, and a woman Travail guessed was Sally Stevenson, the professor's source for *The Cape Fear Mercury* article.

The man in charge made a quick phone call. "Everyone is here." He nodded as he listened. "Yes, sir. See you soon." He stuck the phone in his pocket and told his prisoners to sit tight. "In about thirty minutes, this will all be over."

While they waited for whoever was coming, Lori checked on Tate. She said she was fine, just nervous. Travail asked Yeager how he was doing. "Never better, Craig Travail." The bruises on his face said otherwise.

Harriet introduced herself to the private investigator and glanced down the line to where Tate and the woman sat. "You want to introduce us to your friend?"

"This is Sally Stevenson."

Sally said hello and apologized for the mess and her uninvited guests.

Lori came to her defense. "It's not your fault."

Yeager agreed. "Before these guys broke doors down, Sally showed us the newspaper article stolen from the British Public Records Office."

Travail smiled at Yeager. "Looks like you were right about Dispatch 34."

The sound of a vehicle caught Travail's attention. A few minutes later, a man in scrubs pushed an ancient-looking man in a wheelchair through the splintered back opening. The attendant rolled the old man to within ten feet of his prisoners, set the brake on the chair, and stepped back. Two of the armed men came to stand on each side of the wheelchair-bound man, who's wrinkled face was drawn. His head sprouted strips of grey hair, the sides of his face were pale, and his body was thin. He couldn't have weighed more than ninety-five pounds. Travail was no doctor, but this man looked like he needed to make sure his affairs were in order.

The old man asked the lead ruffian for the newspaper article. Once he held it, the old man flipped the case from one side to the other, admiring what it protected. "Take it out of the case."

The leader popped the edges of the case with his knife, separated the two covers, and handed the newspaper article to the old man. He smiled as he held it up. "Many people have died to protect this secret."

Travail tried to sound friendly, hoping to reason with the man. "You must be with The Jefferson Experience."

"I'm the director. Anthony Elkin." His twisted smile stretched his drawn face and displayed gaps in his mouth where once there had been more teeth. It made him look like a badly carved pumpkin.

Travail made an educated guess. "Are you Robert's father?"

"The boy was a big disappointment." The director coughed and spit in his handkerchief. "Any more questions?"

Yeager's tone was defiant. "You're a psycho."

"That's not a question." Pointing to Sally, the director said, "If it hadn't been for her, none of you would be here. She sealed her fate and yours when she contacted Professor Collins. By now, you know why this newspaper article is so important and why you have to die."

"No one needs to die," Travail said. Why does it matter if people learn the truth about the Meck Dec?"

The director coughed again, and spittle ran down his chin. "The secret is bigger than the Meck Dec itself."

"Is it about what Thomas Jefferson did after he learned about the Meck Dec?" This was another guess, but it had a good chance of landing.

The director whispered in the ear of the leader of the pack, who gave instructions to his men. They checked and tightened the restraints on their prisoners and left by the back opening.

The director pulled himself up to sit as straight as he could. "I am the only person who knows this story, and with your deaths, it will stay that way, so I may as well tell you the truth. My son was supposed to be next in line to know Jefferson's secret, but he doesn't have what it takes to protect it."

The director glared at Travail. "Every nation has secrets, myths, and legends attached to its founders. Some leak out, like the story of Sally Hemmings. They create cracks in the fabric of a nation. We are the guardians of Jefferson's secrets. The last line of defense against those cracks forming."

Nobody said a word. Curiosity had a calming influence, even on Yeager.

"The year was 1776. The committee that included Thomas Jefferson, John Adams, Benjamin Franklin, and others completed their work on the declaration, presented it to the Continental Congress on July 1, and after several days of debate and revision, congress adopted it on July 4, 1776.

"Not all the signers, though, were present, including William Hooper, one of your North Carolina delegates. He didn't sign until August 2, and not until after he confronted Jefferson.

"You see," the director said, "the Meck Dec is not the problem. The problem is what you suspected, counselor. Thomas Jefferson copied a few words from the Meck Dec in drafting the Declaration of Independence." The director emphasized "a few" words, as if to downplay the significance of Jefferson's misconduct.

"Why didn't Hooper tell anyone?"

"Because Jefferson reminded Hooper his reputation would be harmed too. It was Hooper who showed the Meck Dec to Jefferson in the first place, and it was Hooper who had agreed with Jefferson to keep it quiet when Captain Jack delivered it a year earlier."

Travail remembered the history lesson from the trial. The North Carolina delegates told Captain Jack the idea of independence was "premature." He wondered what Jefferson said to Hooper to cause him to keep his plagiarism a secret. Perhaps, as Benjamin Franklin had done in front of the entire assembly, he said, "We can either hang together, or hang separately."

When the director finished the story, not even Yeager said a word. Travail had one other question though, to make the story complete. "How did the founder of The Jefferson Experience find out Jefferson copied from the Meck Dec?"

The director's eyes flared. "Slaves." Jefferson's manservant overheard the conversation between Jefferson and Hooper. He shared the story among his people, and they passed it down, family to family. Sally Hemmings learned the story and, after Jefferson died in 1826 and before she died in 1835, someone with more white blood than Sally overheard her tell the story and took it to our founder. He didn't believe it until 1837, when he saw *The Cape Fear Mercury* article that confirmed the Meck Dec was real.

Yeager finally weighed in. "It seems slavery came back to bite Thomas Jefferson in the rear in more ways than one."

The director glared at Yeager as his men re-entered the barn. "The Jefferson Experience has done its duty since 1837. The only thing my son has ever been right about was the need to destroy the newspaper article." He held it between thumb and forefinger and waved it in the air. "That happens tonight."

Two of the henchmen built a two-foot-high pyre in the middle of the barn, doused it with gasoline, and placed *The Cape Fear Mercury* on top. Two others moved the prisoners into a circle on the floor around the pyre. They next placed combustible material in the four corners of the barn. The plan appeared simple. Burn the newspaper article and everyone who might tell the world about it.

One of the men knelt next to the pyre and struck a match. He looked at the director for his cue to set the blaze.

"It is very fitting, is it not?" The director touched his mouth with his handkerchief as he eyed his prisoners. "In the year 1800, the originals and all copies of the Meck Dec burned in a fire. Tonight, we burn the best remaining evidence."

The director nodded, and the man lit the pyre. Flames jumped from the gasoline-soaked pile until the article on top of the pyre turned at both edges, folded from the heat, caught a lick of flame, and burned. History disintegrated in front of their eyes, and for a moment, the director looked sad, his face drawn even more than before. His totem was gone. As they rolled him away, he said, "It's done." The truth had been extinguished.

One by one, the men lit fires in the four corners of the barn. There were no windows and only two exits. One exit was bolted with three deadbolts and blocked by burning debris. The men piled furniture in front of the other exit, the one with the shattered door. They poured gasoline on the furniture and lit the pile on fire as they backed out of the exit. Two men remained beyond the opening with their guns drawn and pointed at them. If they tried to escape that way, they'd face fire and bullets.

It wasn't long before smoke filled the room, and flames tore at the siding. "Keep down and roll," Travail said to the others.

Yeager added what Travail knew to be fact. "They're still out there."

As they rolled toward the opening guarded by the men with the guns, the men shouted warnings. The sound of gunfire followed. They stayed low to avoid the bullets and rolled toward the fiery opening. The closer they got, the more obvious their predicament. They were trapped.

Another deafening burst of gunfire filled the air, but the bullets didn't fly overhead. It sounded like there were more people outside the barn. More shouts. Different shouts. Travail couldn't see through the exit because of the smoke, and it was hard to breathe. He looked up to see three men knock the burning furniture aside to clear the opening. With the path clear, they sprinted in, and through the haze, Travail counted the prisoners they rescued.

Travail tried to push himself up, using his shoulder. A man bent down behind him and cut away the rope that tied his hands. The man was dressed the same way he was dressed the first day Travail met him. He wore black slacks, a crisp white shirt with red tie, and a well-fitted blue blazer with a soft check pattern, accented by a white rose in the lapel.

What was it he said that day? "This case involves illegal activity. I can smell it." He'd even put his right forefinger to his nose.

∾

The night sky lit up with smoke and flame. Harriet sat stunned with her back against a tree-covered bank on an old logging road one hundred yards away from the fireworks. She watched Travail take off his jacket and put it on the ground for Sally Stevenson to sit on. He helped her get comfortable and said something to her before he stood and looked around, as if searching for something else to do. She saw two of the Godfather's men help Tate and Lori settle next to Sally. She looked at the soot on her pants and felt her cheeks. Her hands had black smudges on them. She must have looked as bad as she felt.

Three Range Rovers were parked a few feet away. Harriet watched as men loaded bodies in the backs of each. She saw the body of the director and felt nausea, but no sympathy for him or the other men who'd tried to kill her and her friends. Travail sat beside Harriet. His presence comforted her.

Maximiliano Esposito knelt and spoke with each person along the line. He started with Sally, then Tate, then Lori. He arrived and knelt in front of Harriet and Travail. Smoke rose behind him, thick in the air. "How are you two doing?"

Harriet looked at Travail to answer, but he deferred to her. She didn't know how to put her feelings into words. What had started in a courtroom ended in a fire that almost ended her life. She wanted to sob, but she was grateful. "Much better, thanks to you." She gave her best effort at a smile.

The Godfather smiled back. "Harriet, you're one of the Indie's toughest, man or woman." He placed his hand on her shoulder. "I'm glad you're going to be okay."

He turned to Travail. "Counselor, I'm guessing this is not your typical day at the office."

Travail's hair was a mess, and he looked dazed. He'd yet to say a word since they exited the barn. "How?" He looked at the Range Rovers. "How did you find us?"

"Let's just say Yeager and I go way back. He gave me this address. Told me if I didn't hear from him by noon today to send help. We got here as fast as we could."

Harriet looked around and felt an anxious shudder. She didn't see Yeager. Had he made it out? The old fool. Where was he? Maximiliano Esposito appeared to read her mind.

"Yeager's okay. He's down in the woods searching for something. Your private investigator and his cousins Lurch and Mad Max are with him. Those two were quite helpful to my boys."

The Godfather looked down the logging road, and Harriet followed his eyes. Yeager was about seventy-five yards away, coming up the rough terrain with his helpers beside him. A loud crash behind Yeager signaled the collapse of what was left of the barn's structure.

Travail asked about the director and his men.

"None survived." The Godfather scratched his head. "They wouldn't put down their guns and kept firing. Even the old man in the wheelchair."

While they waited for Yeager, the Godfather explained they had a van coming to pick them up and drive them to a hotel for the night. "We'll collect your vehicles and bring them to the hotel."

"You're very kind." Harriet got to her knees and gave him a hug.

Lori appeared in their circle before Yeager arrived. She was covered in soot and her hair was wild, but she was strong as ever. Harriet couldn't help but think how proud her grandfather would be of her.

Harriet asked Lori about Sally, the woman who brought them to this place, looking every bit the age of the professor. "How's she doing?"

"She's shaken, like the rest of us, and upset about the newspaper article. She'd hidden copies in the walls of the barn, but they're gone now too."

The wind had blown in the direction downhill from the barn, and the sparks had caught the small house on fire. It burned as they spoke. "She's got nothing left."

Lori had an idea. "I think I can help with that. An empty condo at the Indie."

What Harriet saw next would be hard to erase from her memory.

Yeager stood in the middle of the dirt road, not ten feet away. His pants legs were gone below his kneecaps, and what were left of his pants and shirt were in shreds. His beard spread wide below his chin like an upside-down peacock's feathers. He was covered in ash, so much so that he looked like a black Rumpelstiltskin who'd been through a gauntlet. The only white on his body was his beard and hair, streaked mostly with soot.

"Ladies and gentlemen, and Craig Travail, too."

Harriet laughed at Chuck Yeager Alexander, the man who could perform comedy in hell and make the devil laugh.

"Let me introduce you to the latest in flip-phone technology. It works perfectly for those with poor eyesight, those about to croak, and those who want to solve the mysteries of the world." He flipped open the phone, touched a button, and held it in the air. "Behold, I give you the one and only photograph of the soon-to-be-famous *Cape Fear Mercury* article."

This announcement brought renewed energy to the group. They all, Sally included, were on their feet and at Yeager's side to look at what he'd photographed.

Tate described what had happened in the barn before they were taken prisoner. "Yeager tried to conceal the newspaper article when the director's men charged into the barn, but they came straight for him. I saw the flash of his phone when he took the photo. The next thing I saw was Yeager throwing it at his attacker."

Yeager added his own commentary. "If I had wanted to hit anybody with my Jitterbug, I would have. I pretended the back door was home plate and a runner at third was trying to steal home."

Harriet examined the photograph. It looked fuzzy, but not wanting to dampen hope, she kept her opinion to herself. If the photograph ever was published, she could envision how the Internet would hum with scorn and delight. Was the photo doctored? Some would say yes. Some no. Did it look like the kind of photos taken of Nessie and Bigfoot? Of course it did. Others would see it as proof positive. They'd investigate the photographer, and by the time they were done with Yeager, they'd be ready to commit him to an institution and toss his photo in the trash.

Harriet hugged and congratulated Yeager but whispered a suggestion in his ear he took to heart. He nodded in agreement. They would get an expert to work on the quality of the photo and think carefully about what to do next.

Harriet's next thought was about Robert Elkin's plan to take away Travail's law license. It wasn't time to celebrate yet.

CHAPTER 40

A MAN AND HIS LICENSE

Rain beat against Travail's front windshield, and the wipers worked hard to push the drops away as he drove across town to the local bar center for his disbarment hearing. He'd decided to take the route through uptown. After leaving the Indie, he turned on Central Avenue, crossed Independence, passed Central Piedmont Community College, and slowed as he entered the right turn lane to Fourth Street to observe Captain Jack on his muscled steed. Rain dripped from the captain's tricorn hat, as it must have done on his five-hundred-mile ride. The weather didn't appear to dampen the tavern owner's spirit. Travail tried not to let it dampen his.

Three state bar officials sat at a table at the front of the room when he arrived. A clerk offered Travail the use of a chair and table. Elkin was set up and ready to go at the other table, with three junior associates and an administrative assistant, all of whom looked like this was their first hearing. A court reporter fiddled with her equipment as the woman in the middle of the panel made notes on a stack of papers. A similarly sized stack of papers sat on Travail's table.

Elkin leaned in his direction and pointed at the stack. "Consider yourself served."

The hearing titled *In Re: Craig Travail* opened with a question.

"Mr. Travail, have you had time to read the amended charges against you?"

Travail picked up the charges that looked to be at least one hundred pages. He scanned it and pushed the lies aside, an act that drew a comment from the chair.

"These are serious charges, Mr. Travail."

He didn't respond. The fix was in. The three panelists were beholden to Elkin, who'd recommended each for their position and helped them get elected. They also had a reputation for taking disciplinary action against lawyers on the thinnest of evidence.

Elkin went first with evidence that Travail had shirked his duties to his clients. He presented a letter from the CEO of the largest bank in the southeast who was furious about the outcome of Travail's last case for the firm, the one in which Elkin demanded Travail not settle despite Travail's recommendation to the contrary. It was what Elkin called "willful negligence." Sure, Elkin said, Travail suffered a family tragedy, "but he had a duty to seek professional help for that, and he missed appointments with his therapist." Elkin didn't mention Travail had missed the appointments because Elkin demanded his presence to talk about the case Elkin didn't want him to settle.

The panel paid close attention to Elkin's lies. He said there were more cases Travail lost, all because of his inattention to the clients' needs.

It amused Travail that Elkin thought trial work was like drafting a contract. Trials came with uncertainties. It's why so many litigants settled their cases. One never knew how a jury would rule, except of course, Robert Elkin, who told the panel how the juries in the last three cases Travail handled for the firm would have ruled had he done his job.

"What we have here is a pattern," Elkin said. "Not one case. Not two cases. But three cases in which Craig Travail failed miserably."

All three panelists made notes on their legal pads. They were corporate lawyers too. They would not understand.

Theft was the next topic on Elkin's list. He spoke proudly of "his" law firm's long relationship with Viribus, the country's leading federal government supplier of the tools needed to fight cyber-terrorists. He said Viribus had given permission to discuss these matters because "it wanted to see justice served." He asked the panel to turn to Appendix C, where he'd included banking records with the routing numbers redacted for confidentiality. He explained Travail had stolen the records and used them for an improper purpose. Elkin didn't say the improper purpose was to prove the wrongdoing of Elkin's client. Two of the three panelists narrowed their eyes, tightened their jaws, and pursed their lips at Travail.

Elkin next made up a story about Travail sexually harassing a former paralegal. That was a laugher, but Elkin had an affidavit to prove it, so the panel would believe it was true. Travail had been forced to fire the paralegal because she was continually late for work and failed to complete her assignments in a timely matter. He had given her every chance and asked an associate to help her to improve her performance, but she didn't make the effort. She was bitter when he fired her. She said it wasn't fair. Lying about it was her response.

The list of violations continued. "Look at Appendix D." Then there was Appendix E and Appendix F too. With each new tab, Travail's legal stock sunk lower and lower. When it was at rock bottom, Elkin threw one last punch. He brought up Travail's physical "assault" of Elkin on Travail's last day of work, the best tackle Travail ever made. He'd gladly pay the penalty for that infraction.

As Elkin wrapped up his speech, Travail speculated about what motivated the man to continue to pursue his vendetta against Travail. Was he upset about his father's death? Was this payback for the congressman's libel case? Or was it more personal? Did Elkin feel Travail still wanted his job? He didn't want Elkin's job, and he didn't want to return to the law firm as long as Elkin was a part of it. Maybe he hadn't been clear enough about that to Elkin.

"Mr. Travail. Did you hear me?" The chair's voice was elevated.

Travail looked up at the chair. By the tone of her voice, she must have tried to get his attention more than once. He hadn't realized Elkin had finished his remarks, nor had he realized the panel wanted to hear from him.

"You don't seem to be very engaged today. Are you okay?"

Elkin interjected that this was the behavior that had become the norm. "He gets lost. Can't seem to focus."

One of the panel members asked Travail if he took illegal drugs. Another asked how often he drank alcohol. A third asked if he'd had any further contact with the employee he'd harassed. Travail looked at them in disbelief. He didn't need to defend his honor against hand-picked bureaucrats. He refused to answer their questions with his silence.

The chair whispered with the other two panel members and turned back to look at Travail. "Would you like to say anything before we take away your law license?"

Did he hear correctly? They were going to give him the opportunity to say something *before* they took away his law license. He heard Elkin laugh, a laugh he'd heard before. Part of him wanted to fight. Another part of him was ready to concede, unsure if he wanted to be part of a profession that cozied up to the likes of Robert Elkin. As he thought about whether to respond, he remembered how his friends had urged him not to give up.

Lori had reminded him of his win in the libel case, which was more Harriet's doing than his, but he appreciated the sentiment. Tate added they'd need a lawyer to prepare legal papers for them when they adopted a child and to prepare properly typed and notarized wills, which made him smile, plus they'd need a good lawyer to defend the occasional libel suit, "because I can't talk Lori out of writing more about the Butterworths of the world."

Yeager was Yeager. "Don't let the villains win, Craig Travail. Plus, we may have more mysteries to solve that require the help of a lawyer."

Harriet was furious with him when he admitted he hadn't hired a lawyer for the hearing, saying he had a "fool for a client." She was right, and Yeager echoed her point. "Don't you lie down in there and take a nap like ole Blue."

Travail smiled at the thought of old Blue.

He heard Harriet's voice in his head again. Or had he? The three

289

panelists turned to the closed door. They must have heard her voice too. She was yelling at someone, but not him. The chair went to the door, unlocked it, and Harriet pushed into the room. Yeager followed her. The third person to enter was a frazzled staffer for the local bar. "I told them this was a private hearing, but they wouldn't listen."

The chair told Harriet and Yeager they'd have to leave.

"They don't have to leave." It was the voice of Crystal Marks. She stood in the doorway, holding her briefcase. Two lawyers holding banker boxes accompanied her. "We represent Craig Travail." She handed the chair a piece of paper. "This is the notice exercising the accused's right to have an open hearing."

The chair read it and turned to Mr. Travail. "Is this true?"

Harriet moved into Travail's line of sight and gave him a look that told him he'd better say yes. He was so touched by this show of support he couldn't speak. All he could do was nod in the affirmative.

Elkin went on the attack. He complained about the lack of notice. It was a due process argument, which was laughable given the way he'd arranged this hearing and dropped 90 percent of the charges on Travail at the start of the hearing. Elkin came around the front of the table and strode to where Crystal Marks stood. He was a man used to getting his way, and he liked to invade his opponent's space to make his point. He got up in Crystal's face, and in a loud voice, said, "You're fired."

Crystal Marks glared at Elkin. "The partners relieved you of your managing partner position this morning."

"Ha. You need Dunkler and Birdsong for that, and they answer to me."

"They resigned this morning." She pushed past him, walked to the table where Travail sat, and pulled up a chair next to him. She leaned in and whispered, "I finally found a client who is innocent of all charges. How refreshing."

Marks turned and asked one of the lawyers assisting her for copies of her witness list. Yeager moved to the door and crossed his arms, which caught the attention of the chair. "What are you doing?"

"Ma'am, I don't answer to you." Yeager pointed at the table where

Travail and Marks sat. "They can tell you why I'm here if they think you deserve to be told."

"What?"

Marks thanked Yeager and told the chair they needed Mr. Alexander to help organize the witnesses. "In fact, Mr. Alexander, if you'd be so kind to bring in the first thirty-five witnesses, I'd appreciate it."

Marks handed a witness list to the chair and gave one to Elkin. As the chair glanced at the list, her mouth fell open. Yeager popped out the door and guided the cohort of witnesses into the room.

The first to enter were the five most respected partners in the law firm's Charlotte office. Next came Lori and Tate, followed by Becky Trainer and Sally Stevenson. Three members of the local bar entered next, all of whom had been lead counsel on the other sides of the three cases Elkin said Travail had botched. NASCAR Nelli rolled through the door behind the Skipper and his little buddy. Next came Carrie Roberts and Tommy Do-Little. Dr. Partin and the judges followed. Judge Hernandez was the first judge to enter, followed by Judge Roscoe Brady, who had a nice little chaw tucked in his right cheek. Travail's therapist and pastor entered the room next, followed by Peaches, four Indie staff members, and Maximiliano Esposito, looking dapper as ever.

As the witnesses shuffled for places to stand, the line bunched up in the doorway. Yeager did his job and opened a path for more to enter. Travail saw old high school friends, his college and law school roommates, former clients, members of civic organizations on which he'd served, kids (now adults) he coached in youth sports, and associates he'd trained to become partners at the law firm. His former assistant, Angela, along with his two children and their spouses were the last to enter the room.

Travail felt emotion swirl inside him. When he landed at the Indie, he had lost his way and felt useless. He felt his shoulders shake and couldn't help himself. He let the emotions that had built up since Rachael died flow, and for once in his life, he didn't care who saw him cry.

Crystal Marks put her hand on Travail's shoulder.

Harriet hugged him from behind.

As always, Yeager had the last word. "It looks like we're going to need a bigger room, Craig Travail."

~

The storm had passed and the sun peeked through rolling clouds outside the bar center as Travail took up a position against the trunk of his car. Harriet and Yeager assumed casual poses beside him to create an informal receiving line in the parking lot. The first to wish Travail well were the three panelists. They expressed shame that Elkin had taken them in and wished Travail nothing but the best. The chair thanked Harriet for her presentation on the invoice B funds. She said she planned to start a bar investigation into Elkin's involvement and share their findings with the FBI. One panelist who had become friendly with Yeager during breaks in the hearing debated with Yeager about the best fly-fishing spots in the North Carolina mountains.

Witness after witness offered hugs and congratulations before Crystal Marks brought up the back of the line. She gave Travail a hug, thanked him for all he'd taught her as a young lawyer, and said he could have his position back at the law firm anytime he wanted. He looked at Harriet, then Yeager, and hesitated, but not for long.

"Thanks, but I won't be coming back to Big Law. Didn't you hear? I've got a law office at the Indie with an extremely pushy office manager who has me busier than ever."

Harriet gave him a friendly punch in the arm.

"I even have a sign in my front yard that says so."

Yeager slapped him on the back and said, "That you do, Craig Travail. That you do."

The parking lot emptied, and the sky turned Carolina blue. There was a comfortable silence, the kind close friends feel when together and don't have to express it out loud. Travail had little left to think about until Harriet asked the question. "You ready to go home?"

Travail smiled at the question. Yes. It was time to go home. It was time to live his life with people who didn't see aging as a barrier but as a blessing, people who could do anything they chose to do and chart new paths for themselves no matter their age. This was the first day of the rest of Craig Travail's life, and as Yeager might say, "It's time you started living it, Craig Travail."

EPILOGUE

It was going to be a big day at the Indie. Lots of preparation had gone into the affair, and Travail was up early as a defense mechanism. He wanted to be awake when Yeager pounded on his door and yelled, "Craig Travail, get up." Blue sensed something was different about the morning too. His black and tan coonhound nose was cocked, with his ears flopped, as he waited on breakfast. Today was May 20th. It was Meck Dec Day. It was time for a celebration. Blue barked in agreement.

Travail picked up the newspaper from his front porch and scanned the headlines as he filled Blue's bowl with some dry dog food and sprinkled it with chicken and scrambled eggs, a meal Blue received on his birthday and other special occasions. There was a teaser on the front page for an article about the Mecklenburg Declaration of Independence. He turned to Section B to read the article. By now, he couldn't forget the details if he tried, and there was a mistake in the newspaper's historical sketch. He laughed. Was he going to become one of those people?

A box to the right of the article revealed plans for the day. They included a sunrise fun run at Freedom Park with t-shirts bearing Captain Jack's image for the first one hundred arrivals and a mid-morning bike ride starting at Independence Park near the site of old Memorial Stadium. The ride would take cyclists past the sites on the Liberty Walk and end up at Captain Jack's statue. The Meck Dec reading would take place at noon at Trade and Tryon Street, and like the other events, this was free. The day would culminate with an outdoor presentation at the Queen City History Museum at three, but the public was welcome as early as one-thirty for costumed interpreters, musket firing, dances, tours, and Revolutionary-period food and drink. An anonymous benefactor covered the cost. After the presentation, a surprise guest would speak. Travail smiled at the thought.

After Blue gobbled his breakfast and barked his readiness, Travail and Blue took a jog around Lost Cove Lake. As the morning sky lightened, Travail decided they'd stretch their legs on a trail through the woods. They passed the earthen dam below the lake and came up a slope to an open field, where a work crew was setting up chairs in front of the Rock House, the oldest standing home in Mecklenburg County. It was built in 1774 by Hezekiah Alexander, brother to John McKnitt Alexander, the secretary to the Meck Dec Convention. So much history stared him in the face. The same rock walls that sheltered a family through that chaotic period in American history still stood today. It was a metaphor for something. Independence, perhaps. Or endurance. Or a bit of both. He caught his breath as he rubbed his hand across Blue's head.

Travail and Blue jogged past Hezekiah's statue to Freedom Lake where energetic Indie residents were engaged in morning routines. They passed ten residents who waved while doing power walks around the lake. Next, they passed a group of eight men dressed in nautical clothing placing little motorized boats in the water. The Skipper and his little buddy were among The Yacht Club members. The sailors waved, and Blue barked as they passed.

They rounded the end of the lake for their return to the cottage, where they ran alongside the exercise building and looked through the plate-glass windows. They could see people exercising in the weight room, in a yoga class, and in the swimming pool. And there were a few competitors batting a ball back and forth on the pickleball court.

The participants appeared more enthusiastic than ever today. Had they always been this way? Or had they picked up energy since Travail and his friends had returned from their ordeal in the Virginia countryside?

Something caught Travail's attention, and he and Blue stopped to watch the action. At the end of one pier, a man helped a woman fly-fish. Or was it the other way around? Travail laughed as he and Blue stepped onto the short boardwalk. The anglers turned at their footfall and smiled.

"Morning, Craig Travail. And you, too, Blue. Thought I'd catch us some breakfast."

Blue ran to the pail to sniff but found no fish to harass.

Harriet put down the fly-rod. "I'm about ready to let him hunt fish again with his .22." She walked up to Travail and gave him a hug.

With the trout pail empty, they made plans to meet at the Indie's May 20th brunch buffet. Harriet said she'd call Lori, Tate, Becky, and Sally to join them in the Independence Room. He said his goodbyes and trotted with Blue back to the cottage for a shower and change.

Yeager's photograph of *The Cape Fear Mercury* article had turned out "fuzzy," as Harriet suspected, but they'd hired an expert in electronic photographs and she'd done a fine job bringing the text into better focus. Some edges of the article were missing, which she could do nothing about. That was what she called "operator error."

The real problem had been the flash on Yeager's phone when he took the photograph, something even Harriet admitted Yeager didn't have time to adjust for when the director's men swooped in on him. The flash created a bright spot on the photograph that obscured the words "free and independent of tyrannical rule." Those words, the ones the esteemed signer told *The Cape Fear Mercury* reporter they shouted from the Mecklenburg County courthouse steps, were "lost in a flash," Yeager had said.

To take the sting out of this reality, Travail offered a positive spin. "Sure, those words are missing in the photo, but we now have evidence of two sets of resolves by the Mecklenburg Committee. When historians realize the photo is not fake, they will ask this question. Why would the Mecklenburg Committee create two documents? The answer is simple. One for independence. One for governance. Just like our national declaration and our constitution."

Travail and his breakfast companions filled their bellies at brunch and piled into the front and back seats of Yeager's Hoss for the trip uptown. They made it to the square just in time for the noon reading of the Mecklenburg Declaration of Independence. The reader was dressed in eighteenth-century attire and stood on a block so he could be seen above the heads in the crowd. He read aloud with an impassioned voice for all to hear the news decided that day in May in 1775 and written on the parchment he held in his hand. Resolves 1 and 2 railed against the invasion of "our rights" and "dissolved" the political bands to the mother country. But Resolve 3 stole the show when the patriot actor paused, took a sip from his canteen, and declared "ourselves a free and independent people." The crowd cheered.

When they returned to Yeager's truck in the asphalt-covered parking lot, Yeager gazed toward the minor league ballpark, the professional football stadium, and back at the tall buildings on Tryon Street. He asked Travail if he'd ever heard about gold buried below the city streets. "They say there are still shafts underneath the city. What do you think? Should we look into it?"

Harriet snapped at Yeager to stay focused. "We barely escape one mystery before you dig up another one that may kill us."

Yeager slapped Travail on the back and jumped in the driver's seat. "All aboard that's coming aboard. Next stop, the Indie."

Harriet had Yeager drop her off at her cottage, saying she'd meet everyone at the party. Yeager dropped the rest at Travail's cottage and went to park his truck and get his gear. Travail and Blue entertained the others at their place while they waited on Yeager.

Travail asked Sally how she was adjusting to life at the Indie, and she said, "I love being here." Lori put her arm around Sally and said, "She's fit in well. She's an avid reader, so she helped Becky revitalize the Indie book club. They now have thirty new members."

Travail smiled at Sally while he pointed at Lori. "She can speak to your club when she finishes her colonial romance book," but Lori shook her head. "I asked my publisher to let me write the book about a sixty-five-year-old lawyer who goes to live in a retirement community, meets a group of eccentric residents, and solves the mystery of the Meck Dec." She let Tate offer the punchline.

"They rejected the idea, saying no self-respecting publisher would print it."

Travail agreed and added with a smirk, "Or find anyone to read it."

A knock on the front door set Blue to howling and interrupted their laughter.

Standing at attention in eighteenth-century patriot attire was Chuck Yeager Alexander, ready for a fight but in a playful sort of way. He'd replaced his .22 with a flintlock rifle that hung on a strap on his right shoulder. He took off his hat and bowed to Travail and friends. "May I have the pleasure of escorting this fine group to the afternoon ceremonies?"

When they arrived at the Rock House, hundreds of men, women, and children occupied the normally quiet grounds with eager and happy faces. They had set up a tour line outside the springhouse, the kitchen, and the Rock House. The sound of string instruments came from the barn. Cider flowed. Other men dressed like Yeager formed up for drills and shooting, which reminded Travail how reckless Yeager could be with a gun.

Harriet arrived dressed in what Travail told her was "a beautiful costume."

"It's not a costume. This is my eighteenth-century dress."

Travail stood corrected as Carrie Roberts strolled up, ever the matchmaker. She placed her hand on Travail's shoulder and said loud enough for Harriet to hear. "She looks beautiful, doesn't she?"

Harriet told Carrie, "Mind your own business, and don't ruin a good friendship." Was she talking about her friendship with Carrie Roberts? Or about another friendship she'd developed? Harriet did look beautiful, whether she was wearing a costume, a dress, or the jeans she liked to wear when she played in the dirt. Travail was surprised it took him so long to notice.

At 2:45 p.m., their group found seats together for the presentation. Politicians and civic leaders had turned out in full, along with the boards of the May 20th Society and the history museum.

Harriet looked at the seat behind her and tapped Travail on the shoulder. "Craig, I'd like to introduce you to the local author who wrote the book Lori gave you on the Meck Dec. Craig meet Scott. Scott meet Craig." Scott reached out his hand, and Travail took it.

"Pay attention to what's coming, Scott," Harriet said. "What you learn today may cause you to release a new edition of your book."

The museum president welcomed the crowd and introduced the county commission chair, who introduced Lori. She walked to the podium to polite applause and thanked everyone for coming. Most people in the audience had to know by now that Lori Collins was one of the richest women in the county. Perhaps it explained why so many important Charlotteans were in the audience, curious to hear what kind of presentation she would make.

Lori smiled at the crowd. "Thank you for having me today. I'm honored to be here. Those of you who know me know that my grandfather's death was hard on me, and the last few months have been difficult. I couldn't have gotten through it all without the support of good friends." She looked up from her notes to find Travail, Harriet, Tate, and Yeager and waved at them.

After a few words about the importance of preserving history, she made two gifts. She handed the board chair of the Queen City History Museum a check for five million dollars to fund the museum's work, and though she said it was not required, she said, "I'd love to see a permanent exhibit here dedicated to the Meck Dec." She handed the chair of the May 20th Society a check for the same amount, but not before joking that her grandfather had not always been a fan of their work. "This gift is made in memory of Sue Ellen Parker," an idea Harriet had suggested.

Lori left the podium to generous applause and Travail hugged her as they crossed paths. Harriet had put Travail up to the task of introducing the guest speaker, and though he was reluctant, she insisted he was the best person for the job. From the lectern in front of the Rock House, he could see Freedom Lake. The man he was about to introduce was the first person he met there, on his first day at the Indie. He was reasonably sure that, today, he wouldn't shoot a trout, take his clothes off, and dive in. At least he hoped not.

"Your speaker today is one of the most positive human beings I have ever met. You won't find him on any Who's Who or Top 50 lists, nor did he graduate at the top of his high school class. In fact, he's proud of the fact he finished last in that class. He said it gave him more room for improvement in life." The crowd laughed.

"I met this man at a time when I had decided my career and what I thought of my life were over. Ever since then, he and several other new friends have had my back. They pushed me to see life in a fresh way. It was the jolt I needed.

"I have to warn you that our speaker is full of so much energy and optimism, you may walk away from here feeling a bit lighter. He's become quite the storyteller."

Travail looked to his right. Yeager leaned against the back of a giant oak tree, hidden from most of the crowd. He fired two thumbs up to Travail, which caused Travail to wonder what he was about to unleash on these fine folks. Might as well get on with it.

"Ladies and gentlemen, our speaker today is Chuck Yeager Alexander. He's got a story to tell that some of you will believe and some of you won't, but I promise you this. You're in for a treat."

The crowd applauded for Yeager as Travail left the podium. Yeager intercepted him and gave him a bear hug. "I won't let you down, Craig Travail."

Tommy Do-Little and the Skipper brought an easel forward and placed it beside the podium. Travail knew what it was, but to the audience, it would look like a portrait about to be unveiled.

Travail sat beside Harriet. She took his hand in hers with her eyes forward. She gave him a squeeze, and he squeezed back.

As Yeager readied himself, Travail whispered in Harriet's ear. "Are you sure this is a good idea?"

"It will be fun."

Yeager looked out at the crowd. In a happy, gregarious voice, he started his story with a question.

"How many of you have heard of Dispatch 34?"

THE END

If you enjoyed this novel, please leave a review online. Reviews are a great way to help authors reach more readers.

Get the first ebook in Landis Wade's *Christmas Courtroom Trilogy*
FREE
https://landiswade.com/the-christmas-heist/

AFTERWORD

History – Separating Fact from Fiction

Whenever I finish reading a book or watching a movie with a historical bent, I'm curious about what was true and what wasn't in the telling of the story. Before the days of the internet, I pulled the encyclopedia off the shelf for answers. Today, it's as simple as typing a search query in your favorite online search engine or buying a book from your favorite book store. If you'd like to dig a little deeper on the Mecklenburg Declaration of Independence, I have a section below on my sources and on Charlotte historical organizations. But first, let me tell you what's true and what's not in *Deadly Declarations*.

The letters between John Adams and Thomas Jefferson are historically accurate, though I edited them for brevity. You can see in the 1819 letter at the opening of the novel that John Adams was critical of Thomas Jefferson. Adams says if he had possessed the Mecklenburg Declaration of Independence in its time, he would have "made the hall of Congress echo and reecho with it fifteen months before *your* Declaration of Independence. [emphasis added]" Perhaps John Adams was jealous of the credit Thomas Jefferson received for the Declaration of Independence when he referred to it as "your" Declaration of Independence. The next-to-last line of the letter certainly makes it look that way, when he said, "What a poor, malicious, short-sighted, crapulous mass is Tom Paine's *Common Sense,* in comparison with this paper," as if Jefferson's Declaration of Independence came in third in that group of important writings.

Adams didn't stop there though. In Scott Syfert's extremely detailed and well-written analysis of the Meck Dec in his book *The First American Declaration of Independence? The Disputed History of the Mecklenburg Declaration of May 20, 1775,* Syfert reports that Adams floated the idea of plagiarism in a letter to a friend, when he said, "Either these resolutions are a plagiarism from Mr. Jefferson's Declaration of Independence, or Mr. Jefferson's Declaration of Independence is a plagiarism from those resolutions." But Jefferson denied knowing about the Meck Dec in his letter back to Adams. He called the document "spurious" and went so far as to question whether "the name of McKnitt [the secretary of the Mecklenburg Convention] be real, and not a part of the fabrication." He also said he was "an unbeliever in the apocryphal gospel."

The question whether Thomas Jefferson plagiarized from the Meck Dec did not originate in fiction. In chapters 12 and 13 of his book, Syfert does fine work digging deeper into the accusation. In a letter Adams wrote to a friend, he said of the Meck Dec, "I was struck with so much astonishment on reading this document, that I could not help enclosing it immediately to Mr. Jefferson, *who must have seen it, in the time of it, for he has copied the spirit, the sense, and the expression of it verbatim, in his Declaration of the 4th of July, 1776.*" [Emphasis added.]

Adams was on a quest, it appears, to ruin Jefferson's name, stemming from their long-running political feud. Eventually, Syfert says, Adams backed away from the allegation knowing that his letters might become public one day. In fairness to Jefferson, Syfert offered several explanations other than plagiarism for why the language in the two declarations was so similar. But if any of Syfert's theories about the similar language is what happened, that only resolves the question of plagiarism. It does not resolve the question of whether delegates to the

Continental Congress knew about the Meck Dec in its time and helped conceal it.

Historians don't dispute that Captain James Jack rode five hundred miles at risk to himself and all who signed the paper when he delivered it to the North Carolina delegates in 1775. Jack talked about it in a certificate he signed dated December 17, 1819, included in North Carolina's 1831 report. (Yes, the 1831 report with certificates from witnesses and other accompanying documents are real and survived.) Jack said, "I delivered the Mecklenburg Declaration of Independence of May 1775, to Richard Caswell and William Hooper, the Delegates to Congress from the State of North Carolina." That being the case, what did Richard Caswell and William Hooper do with the document?

Syfert believes it is likely Caswell and Hooper showed the document to the third delegate from North Carolina, Joseph Hughes, to get his opinion on what to do, and he wasn't impressed. In a part of Jefferson's 1819 letter that didn't make the cut in this novel, Jefferson reminded Adams of the reticence to independence of two of the three North Carolina delegates, including Hughes: "Now you remember as well as I do, that we had no greater Tory in Congress than Hooper; that Hughes was very wavering, sometimes firm, sometimes feeble, according as the day was clear or cloudy; that Caswell, indeed, was a good Whig, and kept these gentlemen to the notch, while he was present; but that he left us soon, and their line of conduct became then uncertain until Penn came, who fixed Hughes, and the vote of the State."

In other words, according to Jefferson, the North Carolina delegation was hesitant, a view held by Adams. Syfert picked up on this to suggest that the concealment of the document Captain Jack delivered may not have been committed by Jefferson, but rather by the delegates from North Carolina.

As Syfert and historians concede, we can't prove to whom Caswell and Hooper showed the document any more than we can prove what was in Captain Jack's saddlebags. It is possible that Caswell and Hooper showed the document to nobody. Or just to Hughes. Or, maybe, they showed the document to other delegates, including Jefferson. The enjoyable part of using Syfert's book as the major source for this novel was that he is a lawyer trained to present all sides of an argument, and the possibilities that might flow from those arguments. One of the possibilities he threw out that caught my attention appears early in the book, where he says that William Hooper, one of the North Carolina delegates was "later a member of the committee charged with drafting the National Declaration, and a friend of Jefferson." That was interesting. Might Hooper have shown the Meck Dec to his friend, Thomas Jefferson? Might the document have come up in drafting the Declaration of Independence? Syfert asks, "Was this the original government conspiracy?" He didn't reach that conclusion in his book, but as you know, I did in mine. As a novelist, I had more flexibility than Syfert did as a nonfiction author, because while fiction needs to ring true, fiction is a place where truth and imagination come together.

Taking a side about the authenticity of the Meck Dec depends somewhat on what you want to believe and how you assess the evidence. Scott Syfert said it best in the preface to his book: "The evidence can be read two ways…you be the judge." This gave me the idea to put the Meck Dec on trial, and while that didn't work out for Craig Travail and his friends, it illustrated that a jury of twelve is not perfect, the law is not perfect, and neither is history. The things we do know about the Meck Dec demonstrate that John Adams was right about one thing in his letter when he said that the Meck Dec is "one of the greatest curiosities and one of the deepest mysteries that ever occurred." What better prompt could a novelist hope for than that?

As much as possible, I tried to include undisputed facts in the novel. There were meetings that occurred on May 19 and May 20 at the log courthouse in Charlotte. These were held because of concerns with what happened in Lexington and Concord. Members of Mecklenburg County's local militia showed up and argued what to do. Passions were high. A document was signed. Captain Jack rode his horse to Philadelphia and delivered a document to North Carolina delegates Caswell and Hooper. They thanked him and sent him home to report that the Mecklenburg Committee's action was premature.

Also, the signed document and all copies from the Mecklenburg

Convention were destroyed in a fire in 1800. I didn't deal with what didn't burn in the fire, but Syfert deals with it in his book. John McKnitt Alexander left behind a set of "rough notes" in his hand about what occurred at the convention. There are issues with these notes that would make them difficult to admit in a court of law, including their condition and speculation about whether they were written at the time of the convention, or say, in 1800, after the fire. But they are legible, and as Syfert says, "unmistakably in the penmanship of John McKnitt Alexander." If they were to be accepted as an accurate summary of what occurred, the notes confirm that resolutions were made, among others, that "dissolve/abjure" and speak to being "free and independent" of British rule.

One of the points skeptics raise about the Meck Dec history has to do with what was published and what wasn't published about the events of May 20, 1775, in newspapers of the day. This issue is at the heart of this novel. The part of the novel about Peter Force discovering what became known as the Mecklenburg Resolves in 1838 is true. Those resolutions were published in a Massachusetts paper in July 1775, supposedly written by a committee in Charlotte-Town, Mecklenburg County, on May 31, 1775. Collectively, they became known as the Mecklenburg Resolves. They were treasonous for their vacation of the laws that originated on the British king's authority, but they did not include the word any good declaration of independence must include. They did not declare "independence." This is the primary reason historians were led to conclude that the Meck Dec was a case of mistaken identity. They no longer had to challenge the witnesses. It was easier and much more polite to say the witnesses were confused, a tactic often used by trial lawyers and politicians who don't want the pushback for calling someone a liar.

So what about Dispatch 34 and Ambassador Stevenson's role in the disappearance of *The Cape Fear Mercury* article from the British Public Records Office in 1837? These were the interesting questions I played with in working out the plot for this novel. I knew that having the characters in this book find the long-lost copy of the Meck Dec would be too convenient. What attracted me instead was a part of the historical narrative that was true but ended on a cliffhanger.

Everything in this novel about Dispatch 34 is true up to the point in time where experts from Georgia and New York conspire with Ambassador Stevenson to steal *The Cape Fear Mercury* article. The notation on file that the article was "taken out by Mr. Turner for Mr. Stevenson, August 15, 1837," is true. It also is true that the article disappeared and has been lost forever. And the bit about how Ambassador Stevenson, and later his son, Senator John Stevenson, having forgotten the name of whom the document was borrowed for is true, as is the report about this fact in 1875 in an article in the *New York Herald*. What's not based on fact (as far as we know) is that *The Cape Fear Mercury*, a newspaper active in 1775 in the eastern part of North Carolina, mentioned the Meck Dec or two sets of resolutions in the article enclosed with Dispatch 34. Though some of that newspaper's publications in the summer of 1775 survived and can be accessed in archives, there is no surviving record of the newspaper in question. Like the original and copies of the Meck Dec, it has been lost to time, though not to imagination.

Sources for Deadly Declarations

For an excellent analysis of the history and controversy of the Mecklenburg Declaration of Independence, I recommend Scott Syfert's book *The First American Declaration of Independence? The Disputed History of the Mecklenburg Declaration of May 20, 1775*. Ken Burns, documentary filmmaker, said author Scott Syfert "has rescued and brought vividly to life a little-known story of our Revolutionary past and the urgent need by our ancestors for freedom." I agree. It is well-researched and compelling reading.

Syfert's book was an invaluable source for me in writing this novel. He is a Charlotte attorney and amateur historian who kindly sat for an audio interview on my podcast, *Charlotte Readers Podcast*, and for a video interview we produced with the Charlotte Museum of History, where we had fun discussing the history, including Dispatch 34. Syfert is a co-founder of the May 20th Society, a true-to-life active organization mentioned in the novel. (Yes, although Syfert's book plays the Meck Dec story down the middle, he is a believer, a fact he reveals early in his book.) Given Scott's impact on this novel, I felt it was only appropriate that I let Craig Travail meet him in the book. Those who have read Scott's book likely connected the dots between Lori's gift of the local author's Meck Dec book to Craig Travail and Harriet's introduction of the local author named Scott to Travail in the epilogue. Perhaps if Travail had read Scott Syfert's book more closely and not skimmed it, he may have adjusted his trial strategy and solved the mystery sooner.

Charlotte-Mecklenburg Library and the Mecklenburg Historical Association also offer helpful information about the Meck Dec. For example, among other online postings, including texts of the documents at issue, Charlotte-Mecklenburg Library posted a four-part online series in 2019. They include: "Part I: Is the Mecklenburg Declaration Real or Fake?;" "Part II: The Mecklenburg Declaration of Independence and the Mecklenburg Resolves;" "Part III: The Mecklenburg Declaration of Independence Meets Controversy;" and "Part IV: Celebrating the Mecklenburg Declaration of Independence." The Mecklenburg Historical Association has online links about the Meck Dec history, the Meck Dec text, and the Meck Dec Controversy. Also check out Scott Syfert's post on the Charlotte Museum of History's website entitled "The Evidence Against the Mecklenburg Declaration of Independence."

Charlotte-Mecklenburg Library has available online a 1960 book by V.V. McKnitt, a veteran journalist, entitled *Chain of Error and the Mecklenburg Declarations of Independence, A New Study of Manuscripts: Their Use, Abuse and Neglect.* V.V. McKnitt's foreword leaves no doubt that in his mind there were two resolutions, one set adopted on May 20, 1775, declaring independence from Great Britain, and another set, adopted by the Committee of Safety on May 31, 1775, later referred to as the Mecklenburg Resolves. And yet, as demonstrated below, there were many detractors over the years.

One book published in 1907 caught my attention because it was said to be the book that struck the hardest blow against the authenticity of the Meck Dec. It has a title that says it all: *The Mecklenburg Declaration of Independence: A Study of Evidence Showing that the Alleged Early Declaration of Independence by Mecklenburg County, North Carolina, on May 20, 1775, Is Spurious.* Author William Henry Hoyt pulled no punches with his analysis, coming down on the side of there being only one document signed in 1775, the Mecklenburg Resolves. As a novelist, I perked up at his disgust for the conspiracy theories. He called unfortunate "for the cause of historic truth," the charges of plagiarism against Thomas Jefferson, and the allegation that the disappearance of *The Cape Fear Mercury* article from the British Public Records Office in 1837 seemed "to indicate that Jefferson's defenders destroyed evidence of the Mecklenburg Declaration." It just shows that one author's ridicule is another author's inspiration.

In an earlier draft of this manuscript, the characters in the book discussed Hoyt's theories on their drive to save their friends in Virginia, but it was too tedious and slowed the story. What prompted me to sketch this out was Hoyt's argument that it was unlikely that the missing *Cape Fear Mercury* article mentioned the Meck Dec, and also, his contention that Royal Governor Tryon's summer of 1775 written criticism of what happened in Mecklenburg County was not a criticism of a declaration of independence, even though Governor Tryon called the conduct treasonous. I thought he was simply arguing the case, and as a lawyer, I wanted to take Hoyt on, but my early readers and editors were right to have me trim some of the history from the book. The fact is, like much else about the Meck Dec, neither side can prove for a fact that the other side is wrong. Maybe Hoyt was right. But not according to the characters in this novel.

Hoyt didn't have the last word though. The references in this book to belief in the Meck Dec by the likes of David McCullough, George Will, and Cokie Roberts, among others, are true, as recorded in Scott Syfert's book, as are the actual visits by four sitting US presidents and the Charlotte celebrations in the twentieth century. In her 2009 book entitled *Charlotte, North Carolina: A Brief History*, author Mary Kratt discussed the signing of the Meck Dec and the Mecklenburg Resolves under the heading, "More Hostile to England than Any." And although relations between the state capital of Raleigh and Charlotte have cooled, the legislature hasn't seen fit to change the dates on the North Carolina state flag, one of which is May 20, 1775.

Another source that appears in the book is the walking tour, the Charlotte Liberty Walk. It is sponsored by the May 20th Society, and you can find information and an interactive map at the website for the Liberty Walk (charlottelibertywalk.com). Like the fictional Craig Travail, I navigated the uptown streets of Charlotte for many years as a lawyer without paying much attention to the monuments on the Charlotte Liberty Walk. Charlotte is known for tearing down old buildings, so you won't find any brick-and-mortar colonial history uptown, but you might enjoy the walk. Before completing this book, my wife Janet and I walked back in time, just as the characters did in the book, and we stopped and paid attention to the monuments on Tryon Street and Trade Street. We then drove a few miles to pay homage to the statue of Captain Jack and his mighty horse that carried him and his important papers five hundred miles to Philadelphia. This is where you will find the Trail of History, where you can take a walk through history and meet a diverse group of people who had an influence on the history, growth, and development of Mecklenburg County. The first statue constructed was that of Captain James Jack. Others include Thomas "Kanawha" Spratt, early settler and friend and agent of the Catawba Indians; Chief King Haigler, the greatest leader of the Catawba nation who presided over his tribe in the mid-eighteenth century; Jane Wilkes, volunteer in Confederate camp hospitals and leader in the effort to build Charlotte's first two civilian hospitals; Thaddeus Tate, prominent African-American entrepreneur and philanthropist in the early to mid-twentieth century; William Henry Belk, inventive retailer of the large department store and civic leader; James B. Duke, one of the 20th century's greatest industrialists and philanthropists; Philip Van Avery, engineer of the growth of the Lance snacks enterprise and civic leader; and Julius L. Chambers, prominent lawyer during the Civil Rights era, who won numerous landmark civil rights cases.

The Setting

As a native Charlottean who, after sixty-four years, still has a hard time giving directions in Charlotte (in part, because the street names duplicate themselves or simply change their names while you're driving on them), I wanted to write a book that gave attention to the Queen City. Many places in this novel are real.

The Hezekiah Alexander House, aka the Rock House, is the oldest surviving home in Mecklenburg County, and it is a feature of the Charlotte Museum of History (not my fictitious Queen City History Museum). I came to learn about the good work of the Charlotte Museum of History through my wife Janet, who has served as a docent in the Rock House and the adjacent log cabin kitchen. She is not a Meck Dec believer like me, but she is more knowledgeable about the colonial period, and in particular, who cooked the food in 1775, how they cooked it, and what it tasted like. She also sews her own colonial period dresses, which I made the mistake of once calling—like Craig Travail did in his conversation with Harriet Keaton—"a nice costume." Neither of us will ever do that again.

It so happens that a retirement community by a different name is adjacent to the Hezekiah Alexander House. It is a vibrant community called Aldersgate. I can speak to the quality of their medical attention because their hospice center provided excellent care for my father before he died and was a warm and comforting place for my family during that difficult time. Aldersgate has a lake, but as far as I know, it is not called Lost Cove Lake or Freedom Lake. And while I know that Aldersgate has nice facilities and encourages an active lifestyle, the Independence Retirement Community, aka the Indie, is the product of my imagination. Plus it has two lakes.

I enjoyed taking the characters in the novel to the Mecklenburg County Courthouse, where I spent many years as a trial lawyer; to the Charlotte Liberty Walk uptown; and to Green's Lunch, one of the oldest uptown Charlotte restaurants. It's a great place to get a hot dog or two, and because I had only nice things to say about them, I left their real name in the text. I did not put Elkin's law office in the Bank of America building because they may not have liked me putting him in their building and they have a big legal department. I chose instead the fictitious America Bank building. I gave Elkin membership in the fictitious Mecklenburg Country Club and the fictitious Uptown Queen City Club because real clubs in Charlotte might have frowned at the idea of admitting the likes of Robert Elkin as their member. I mentioned Park Road Books in the novel because it is the oldest independent bookstore in Charlotte, they love books and readers, they are a great place to buy books, and they are gracious to and supportive of authors. Just a few doors up from Park Road Books in the iconic Park Road Shopping Center is the Park Road Soda Shoppe. I knew that would be a place Craig Travail would like to eat, and again, the good guys ate there and had a nice meal, so I used the real name. And since I love the service libraries offer, and in particular, the good work and services of Charlotte-Mecklenburg Library, the library had to be the destination for Yeager to find answers he couldn't find on the computer.

I have a quick word about managing partner Robert Elkin and his Am Law 100 law firm, where Craig Travail worked before he took up residence at the Indie. Though my former Charlotte law firm of McGuireWoods has offices throughout the country and abroad and an office in Charlottesville, Virginia, neither Elkin nor his fictional law firm bear any resemblance to McGuireWoods or its people. The firm was good to me and does great legal work, and I can't imagine Elkin would survive without being found out quickly at a firm like McGuire-Woods. When I retired from the firm to start a career of creativity in my early sixties, I didn't tackle the managing partner, nor did I feel like doing so. I will admit that Travail's comments about the billable hour, the pressure of the law, and the changing face of the law from profession to business are part of my experience in my thirty-five-year career, but these traits are not unique to any particular law firm.

Finally, though I didn't put Olde Mecklenburg Brewery in the book, I did feature one of their tasty beers, and I'm grateful to them (and I should I say, Chuck Yeager Alexander is grateful to them too) for their Captain Jack Pilsner, which they created as a nod to the courage of Captain Jack and the members of the Mecklenburg Convention. I have enjoyed this particular beer for some time, and when I thought about what Yeager would drink, I knew it had to be Captain Jack Pilsner. And when I looked up the tagline, I definitely had to give the beer a shout out in the book. After all, this is the beer where you can enjoy "the unmistakable taste of freedom in every fresh, delicious swig."

Characters

The idea of using the name Craig for one of my protagonists entered my subconscious when I was taking a fiction class with Craig Johnson, the bestselling author of the Longmire series, but the idea stuck after I interviewed Johnson for *Episode 100* of *Charlotte Readers Podcast*. Johnson is such an engaging guy—much more exuberant and talkative than the Craig in this book—but I figured the name might prompt my Craig to find his way. The last name evolved from a suggestion Craig Johnson made to the authors in the class. He says he looks for names for his characters as a way to say something about the characters. That led me to choose the name Craig Travail. I thought the last name "Travail" summed up well the character's cautious, legal-minded personality and his dour outlook on life heading into retirement.

My friends who know me well know that I am a fan of Larry McMurtry's classic tale, *Lonesome Dove*. My companion Gus, who was faithfully on the floor by my side while I wrote this book and who passed away after a long life in the fall of 2021 after he was sure I'd finished the book–he died with his boots on, by the way–was named after Augustus McRae, the protagonist in *Lonesome Dove*. Our younger dog, who passed away in the summer of 2021, who flitted in and out of the room to see if I was still typing or had time to feed her, was named Lori, after one of the independent and spirited women in the *Lonesome Dove* saga. Lori Collins, like McMurtry's Lori, faced difficult challenges. Augustus McRae, played by Robert Duvall in the movie version of *Lonesome Dove*, had a nickname for Lori. He called her Lori Darlin'. Chuck Yeager Alexander did the same when he hugged Lori when he first saw her after the death of her grandfather. And Janet and I did the same when we called to our Lori.

I named Travail's assistant Angela, because my assistant for many years was named Angela and she was just as sharp, proficient, kind, and loyal as the Angela in this book.

The fictitious Meck Dec expert, Lester Partin, was named in memory of two wonderful professors who taught me history at Davidson College. I admired the late Malcolm Lester, who taught me English history, and the late Malcolm Partin, who taught me European history. I'm sorry they're not around to give me a grade on this effort.

I had an aunt named Carrie Mae Roberts who was full of energy and loved to talk. Thus was born the Indie Gossip Queen, Carrie Roberts. Her dog named Sport is in memory of our family's golden retriever by the same name.

If my brother Eddie and my sister Jenny look closely, they will find their names attached to characters in this book—Eddie because he is like the handyman in the book (he can fix anything), and Jenny because she is like the bookkeeper in this story (well organized and attentive to detail).

The name Vance Dagenhart was easy to come by. One of my legal mentors for thirty-five years and one of the most respected corporate lawyers in Charlotte is Larry Dagenhart. He's been a good friend of my family for many years. I am confident that Larry would have handled the representation of Sue Ellen Parker with the same grace as Vance, and he would have been eager to help the good guys.

I wanted three main characters for this novel who I would enjoy visiting with in a second book, and I wanted each character to bring something different to the party. I knew I would have a lawyer in the book because I wanted to put the Meck Dec on trial, and perhaps other things on trial in subsequent books, but the book is not autobiographical. With the one exception of Travail tackling his managing partner early in the book (fiction is fun that way), Travail's personality is that of the gentleman trial lawyer; I was more prone in my thirties and forties to lose my temper if my client was wronged or the other lawyer was a bully. I had a lot of respect for the trial lawyers I met who never got flustered and remained professional at all times. Travail is patterned more after them and after my father, Ham Wade, who practiced law for more than fifty years in Charlotte. Dad was the gentleman lawyer, which is the way I like to think of Travail.

Harriet Keaton was the strong female character I created to put the men in their places. I hope she succeeded. As for Chuck Yeager Alexander, he started out with a bit part, but no matter how hard I tried, he kept demanding space in the manuscript. There were times I felt sorry for Craig Travail for having to put up with Yeager, but both Yeager and Harriet were the salve Travail needed to find the positive in life. I hope the threesome offered the balance needed to tell the story and that you enjoyed spending time with them as much as I did.

The Indie residents were enjoyable to create and name. Sue Ellen Parker had to have three names. There is nothing more Southern than that. Becky Trainer had to train her hair—she was, after all, the Number 2 Pencil with an eraser on her head—train the residents at the behest of Sue Ellen at the HOA meeting, and in the end, train Travail's team on how to break the Viribus case wide open.

As a child of the sixties and early seventies, sitcoms ruled my afternoons after school. That's where I met the Skipper and Gilligan and others whose names I employed with the help of Yeager Alexander. NASCAR Nelli was a nod to local NASCAR culture and the Godfather was a nod to the classic mafia movies I've enjoyed over the years.

One of my favorite names for a minor character was Tommy Do-Little, because he did as little as he could, made more money each year doing it, and was thinking about writing a how-to book. But also, because he served as an example of the mistake trial lawyers make when they try to impeach witnesses for trivial matters. When Elkin tried to make Tommy look bad to the jury for being written up for sleeping on the job, his retort was sweet. Tommy admitted the mark on his record, but then added, "I wasn't sleeping when I heard Sue Ellen say she was gonna take the professor's assets."

John Hart appeared on *Episode 200* of *Charlotte Readers Podcast* to talk about his mystery set in Charlotte, and I asked him what he thought was more important in a novel, plot or characters. He didn't hesitate. He said it was the characters, because if the reader doesn't care about the characters, why should they care about the plot? That was my goal in creating these characters. I hope you found someone to like in this ensemble.

Theme

Most of the time, when authors are asked by potential readers what their book is about, the Pavlovian response is to think of the plot. I sometimes fall into that trap too, saying this book is about a mystery involving the Mecklenburg Declaration of Independence. But that's too narrow a way to think about a novel. The plot is on the surface. The theme is throughout.

I knew I wanted to set this story in a retirement community. I helped my parents move into a retirement community a few years ago and saw their emotional struggle in leaving the home they'd lived in for more than fifty years. I also saw how they eventually settled into their new home and how their fear of change was allayed in their new environment.

Change is never easy, but it is necessary. Aging is one of those topics many people don't like to talk about. When their grandkids arrive, they don't want to think of themselves as grandpa or grandma, so they come up with more clever names to prove they are still young. My father initially balked at moving into a retirement community in his early eighties because he didn't want "to live with the old people." I borrowed that line for my book and laugh about it often. We are always younger than the "old people."

The idea of career transitions also was on my mind as I wrote this book. I decided to retire as a partner from a large law firm at age sixty-one to focus on creativity in my sixties. I joked that I didn't want to die at my desk filling out a time sheet. So instead, I started a literary podcast—something I knew nothing about how to do—and I began writing this book. Unlike Craig Travail, I wasn't kicked out of my firm, but like him, I had to find my path.

317

When I was a child, my mind told me that people in their sixties used walkers and canes, sat in rocking chairs, and took meals from nurses. It's humorous to think about how our perspective changes when our odometer turns over to the sixties. The fact of aging and the fact of making the change from a busy career to something so different as life without a nine-to-five job or living in a retirement community is daunting. Craig Travail didn't know what to do with himself. I wanted to see how he handled the change.

I hope this book helped (at least a little) to smash the stereotype that retirement communities are filled to the brim with people who do nothing but wait for their time to pass. From what I've seen, the decades I'm entering are very active, and activity—if your goal is to live longer—is one way to continue to live.

I have come to think of life the way writers think about novels that have a three-act structure. Act 1 is where we find the inciting incident. We're born kicking and screaming, and we come of age. Act 2 is sometimes called the muddy middle, where authors work hard to make the text less muddy and more interesting. It's where we engage in adventures, meet and overcome setbacks, meet other characters, and figure out how we are going to deal with what life has in mind for us. Act 3 is where things ramp up. We're moving toward the end. In novels, it has to be exciting. Otherwise, readers will put the book down.

That's why, in real life, we need to avoid the temptation to put the book down. We need to keep plugging. Find something challenging and interesting to do. Don't worry about failure. Don't worry about what is going to happen on the next page. Just keep reading. Keep moving. Keep living. There will be a denouement. But let's hope the book is thick before we get there. I hope your story has a happy ending.

READING GROUP GUIDE

Every reading group has their own way of discussing novels. In addition to questions that encourage opinions about the characters, plot, settings, and themes, below are ten areas to consider exploring after your reading group has read *Deadly Declarations*:

1. The Mecklenburg Declaration of Independence is a disputed event in American history, in part because the story lacks written proof–the documentary evidence burned up or was lost–and depends mostly on oral history. What value do you place on oral history? Is it credible? Valuable? Or do you believe written evidence is necessary to prove facts and oral history is flawed?
2. The novel spun a tale about a conspiracy at the highest levels of government. How do you feel about government conspiracy theories? Fake news? Overblown? Real?
3. John Adams implied in his letters that Thomas Jefferson committed plagiarism in drafting the Declaration of Independence. Plagiarism is a serious offense in the academic world. Do you think plagiarism is a problem in

schools, in the workplace, or on social media, and how do you feel about it?

4. The novel opened with Yeager Alexander's optimistic motto for retirement living–"Ain't dead, yet"– but readers soon learned that Craig Travail had a different vision of what it meant to be retired, a feeling that "he was about to be buried alive among people with nothing to do." What are your thoughts about living in retirement and retirement communities?

5. Over the course of the novel, Craig Travail found a way to change his mind about many things–aging, life, his opinions on the Meck Dec, etc.–thanks in large part to the help and encouragement from his new friends. Are you the kind of person that finds it hard to change your opinions? Do you surround yourself with people who think like you or do you like to be around people with different opinions from yours? How valuable is your friend group to you in making life decisions?

6. Sue Ellen Parker was misunderstood by everyone except the professor and her close friend Becky Trainer. The community believed Sue Ellen was too serious, opinionated, and unfriendly, and consequently, incapable of love or being loved. Have you known people who exhibit one face to the public and another in private, who are misunderstood but have positive qualities? Do you think people are too quick to make judgments about others and see them as one dimensional? Is there a way to avoid falling into this trap?

7. Craig Travail said early in the novel that what happened in Charlotte in May of 1775 "was just an interesting bit of disputed local history," and as far as he was concerned, "rather insignificant history in the 21st Century." On the other hand, Robert Elkin and his accomplices sought to keep a lid on the truth for fear of how it might change society's view of Thomas Jefferson. How do you feel about

people seeking to cover up or alter history because of how uncomfortable the truth makes people feel about the past? Is this something you have witnessed? Is there an answer to this problem?

8. Sometimes, history is hiding in plain sight, as it was for Craig Travail and as it might be for Charlotte residents unfamiliar with the Meck Dec. What kind of interesting history have you uncovered that was hiding in plain sight?

9. Craig Travail put the Meck Dec on trial. If you were sitting on that jury, what questions would you want to have answered to make your decision about the validity of the Meck Dec?

10. If you had to vote now, would you be a believer or non-believer in what John Adams called "one of the greatest curiosities and one of the deepest mysteries" that ever occurred to him and what Thomas Jefferson called "the apocryphal gospel?"

ACKNOWLEDGMENTS

Thanks first to Scott Syfert for the fascinating book *The First American Declaration of Independence? The Disputed History of the Mecklenburg Declaration of May 20, 1775*; for your willingness to sit for several interviews; your review and feedback on my manuscript; and your encouragement of this project. A fingerprint expert would have easy work finding your prints on these pages. And to Mary Beth Navarro, thanks for gifting me Scott's book. It unleashed this monster.

When the manuscript was 25,000 words too long, true crime writer Cathy Pickens came to the rescue. You found the villainous words that needed removal, Cathy, and I appreciate your early and steadfast feedback and your good humor when telling me that a whole chapter needed to go. Without your direct but playful approach, the Indie book club of thirty or more kind souls would have met their end too soon. As you suggested, some of the residents needed to survive this book.

Thanks to my early beta readers: my sister, Jenny Cianciola, who read the book many times and provided timely feedback (including, "don't you dare cut anything out about Yeager"); my neighbor and good friend Ellen Patten, who provided detailed notes; my publicist of several years, Hannah Larrew, who made the good suggestion to trim some history near the end of the book; and my wife and eighteenth-century colonial-period expert, Janet Wade, whose steady eye kept me moving forward. Thanks, too, to Mark de Castrique, successful mystery novelist, for input that helped me make some clarifications. Each of you provided excellent feedback. I couldn't have found my early way without your good questions and suggestions.

Every lawyer needs another lawyer to bounce their theories off of before they go to court. The same is true about authors who write a legal plot into their book, even when they have trial experience, as I do. Thanks to attorney Graham McGoogan, one of the best trusts and estates lawyers in Charlotte and my law partner for many years, for your review and feedback of the manuscript. I appreciate your patience with me, a lawyer who, like Craig Travail, had never gone to court to challenge a will. Graham had the inspiration for the pour-over will.

A special thanks to the hundreds of authors I interviewed on *Charlotte Readers Podcast* before publication of this novel. The podcast quest was and continues to be about two things, helping authors give voice to their written words through the medium of podcasting and allowing Landis to learn more about this thing called writing. Reading close to three hundred books in three years in many genres and picking your brains was a wonderful experience. Thank you for helping me become a better writer. And thanks to readers Bud Schill and Dana Hearn for your eagle eyes that led to final corrections.

To my editor, Nora Gaskin, thanks for making me uncomfortable. You've done it for every book. When I receive your track changes, I wince, but then I settle down, read carefully, and think about your questions, comments, and suggestions, and the manuscript gets better. We didn't always agree, but we agreed enough and I'm grateful that you cared to make me work harder. Originally, the novel opened with these words: "Waking up dead is rarely a good thing." We tussled over the language in that first paragraph, and I credit Nora with the suggestion that led to the first line of the book and gave immediate insight into one of the characters: "Yeager Alexander's motto for retirement living was, "Ain't dead, yet."

Books aren't born without the help of people with technical design skills and creative illustrative talent. Jennipher Tripp was responsible for the design of the ebook and print book. You do wonderful work, Jennipher. Kelly Prelipp Lojk handled the copyediting. Thanks Kelly for helping me see commas where none existed, hyphens that needed to go, numbers in prose, and suggested edits that made the words flow better. Tim Barber with Dissect Designs, an award-winning cover designer, created the fantastic cover. Well done, Tim.

Books don't walk into stores or find themselves in readers' hands without promotion. Thanks to Spellbound Public Relations and Hannah Larrew for being the book whisperer to potential readers and making the public relations side of the book world fun. And to the team at Social Grit, thanks for helping get the word out.

Blurbs–an odd name for reviews that appear in books and on their covers–are important and I am grateful to the talented authors who invested their valuable time to read this story and write their blurbs for this book: Clyde Edgerton; Dannye Romine Powell; Cathy Pickens; Frye Gaillard; George Hovis; Heather Bell Adams; Scott Syfert; Tracy Clark; and Webb Hubbell. Your words were kind, encouraging, and much appreciated.

Getting the word out on a new book can be a challenge, but if you are fortunate to have the combined energy and enthusiasm of an advance reader team–as I do for this book–you're on the right track. Thank you advance readers for reading the book before its release, telling your friends about it, and leaving honest reviews. It was fun to engage with you and I appreciate how you jumpstarted the conversation about this book.

Authors are typically connected to a writing community and I am no different. I value the comradery and classes offered by groups like Charlotte Writers' Club, Charlotte Center for Literary Arts, and the North Carolina Writers' Network, where I have been active for several years. You make writing fun.

I am also grateful for you–the reader–for taking a chance on this adventure.

Thanks, again, to my wife, Janet. You've put up with my podcasting and writing and all that other stuff too. None of it would be any fun without you around.

BOOKS BY LANDIS WADE

Learn How to Order Books at www.landiswade.com

<u>The Christmas Courtroom Trilogy</u>

Book 1: The Christmas Heist – Get the eBook Free

Book 2: The Legally Binding Christmas

Book 3: The Christmas Redemption

Get the eBook box set at a discount

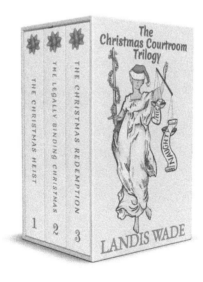

CONNECT WITH LANDIS

Check out Landis's author website
(www.landiswade.com)

Sign up for the newsletters at Landis's website
(www.landiswade.com)

Follow Landis's Facebook Author Page
(www.facebook.com/authorlandiswade)

Follow Landis's Bookbub page
(www.bookbub.com/authors/landis-wade)

Check out Charlotte Readers Podcast's website
(www.charlottereaderspodcast.com)

ABOUT THE AUTHOR

Landis Wade is a recovering trial lawyer, host of *Charlotte Readers Podcast* (where he has conducted more than 300 author interviews), and author of books and stories whose third book—*The Christmas Redemption*—won the Holiday category of the Twelfth Annual National Indie Excellence Awards, and was the 2018 Holiday category Honorable Mention in the Tenth Annual Readers' Favorite Awards. He won the 2016 North Carolina State Bar short story contest for *The Deliberation* and received awards for his nonfiction pieces, *The Cape Fear Debacle* and *First Dance*. His short work has appeared in *Writersdigest.com*, *The Charlotte Observer*, *Flying South*, *Fiction on the Web,* and in more than six anthologies, including by *Daniel Boone Footsteps*.

Author website: www.landiswade.com
Podcast website: www.charlottereaderspodcast.com
Contact: landis@charlottereaderspodcast.com
Contact: landiswrites@gmail.com